PRAISE FOR

field of fire

"With *Field of Fire*, James O. Born comes into his own. This book is chock-full of insider knowledge and experience, but there is so much more than that. There is a story and a character that should put this book as the top of any reader's stack. Alex Duarte is my kind of cop. I hope he sticks around a long, long time."
—Michael Connelly

"*Field of Fire* is a whiz-bang, nonstop thriller, told with the voice of absolute authority. Jim Born never lets the action flag!"
—Tess Gerritsen

"Born . . . keeps to what he knows best—a solid look at Florida, an insider's view of police work, and dialogue that crackles with authenticity . . . while creating an original, energetic story . . . Moves at a breakneck speed, delivering not only an action-packed thriller but also a novel about corruption, greed, and misplaced loyalties . . . awash in chases, a high body count, and tension. Born makes these scenes seem genuine, using the heart-stopping accelerated pace to keep the reader drawn into the action. Born . . . proved with his first novel that he was in the same league as Florida's other top mystery writers. *Field of Fire* illustrates how broad his talent is." —*Fort Lauderdale Sun-Sentinel*

"*Field of Fire* jumps Born into the ranks of the major thriller writers." —W.E.B. Griffin

"Born has talent and momentum; don't be surprised if, soon enough, he has his own [Elmore] Leonard–like breakthrough."
—*Booklist*

"[Born] takes readers beyond his procedural expertise . . . Satisfying edginess." —*The Tampa Tribune*

"Full of violence, dead bodies, and black humor . . . Born is a working cop who knows firsthand how people on the street and in law enforcement think and act . . . He also knows how to build suspense. *Field of Fire* is impossible to put down." —*Mystery Scene*

continued . . .

"BORN IS THE BEST THING TO HAPPEN TO FLORIDA CRIME WRITING SINCE ELMORE LEONARD HIT THE SUNSHINE STATE." —*Chicago Sun-Times*

field of fire

JAMES O. BORN

BERKLEY PRIME CRIME, NEW YORK

THE BERKLEY PUBLISHING GROUP
Published by the Penguin Group
Penguin Group (USA) Inc.
375 Hudson Street, New York, New York 10014, USA
Penguin Group (Canada), 90 Eglinton Avenue East, Suite 700, Toronto, Ontario M4P 2Y3, Canada
(a division of Pearson Penguin Canada Inc.)
Penguin Books Ltd., 80 Strand, London WC2R 0RL, England
Penguin Group Ireland, 25 St. Stephen's Green, Dublin 2, Ireland (a division of Penguin Books Ltd.)
Penguin Group (Australia), 250 Camberwell Road, Camberwell, Victoria 3124, Australia
(a division of Pearson Australia Group Pty. Ltd.)
Penguin Books India Pvt. Ltd., 11 Community Centre, Panchsheel Park, New Delhi—110 017, India
Penguin Group (NZ), 67 Apollo Drive, Rosedale, North Shore 0632, New Zealand
(a division of Pearson New Zealand Ltd.)
Penguin Books (South Africa) (Pty.) Ltd., 24 Sturdee Avenue, Rosebank, Johannesburg 2196,
South Africa

Penguin Books Ltd., Registered Offices: 80 Strand, London WC2R 0RL, England

This is a work of fiction. Names, characters, places, and incidents either are the product of the author's imagination or are used fictitiously, and any resemblance to actual persons, living or dead, business establishments, events, or locales is entirely coincidental. The publisher does not have any control over and does not assume any responsibility for author or third-party websites or their content.

FIELD OF FIRE

A Berkley Prime Crime Book / published by arrangement with the author

PRINTING HISTORY
G. P. Putnam's Sons hardcover edition / February 2007
Berkley Prime Crime mass-market edition / February 2008

Copyright © 2007 by James O. Born.
Excerpt from *Burn Zone* copyright © 2008 by James O. Born.
Cover design by George Cornell.

ISBN: 978-0-425-22183-9

BERKLEY® PRIME CRIME
Berkley Prime Crime Books are published by The Berkley Publishing Group,
a division of Penguin Group (USA) Inc.,
375 Hudson Street, New York, New York 10014.
The name BERKLEY PRIME CRIME and the BERKLEY PRIME CRIME design
are trademarks belonging to Penguin Group (USA) Inc.

PRINTED IN THE UNITED STATES OF AMERICA

10 9 8 7 6 5 4 3 2 1

ACKNOWLEDGMENTS

This is the first book where I had to do some research. As always, I relied on my smart friends.

Tony Mead, Operations Officer for the Palm Beach County Medical Examiner's Office.

Sergeant Paul Laska, Martin County Sheriff's Office (Ret.), Commander of the EOD unit.

Federal Bureau of Alcohol, Tobacco, Firearms and Explosives Special Agent Steve Barborini.

Fred Rea of Vero Beach for bringing a generator after Hurricane Wilma hit us. This allowed me to finish the manuscript.

Al Hazen, retired SAC of the Department of Justice Inspector General.

To all the cops I work with who make casual comments that end up in my books.

1

HE LOOKED OVER THE DASH OF THE NEW FORD TAURUS, already littered with PowerBar wrappers, thanks to his partner. The constantly shifting sea of people spread out over the front of the migrant labor camp for the Bailey Brothers main farm. Even with the good Tasco binoculars he'd been using, he had a hard time telling one man from another. His partner probably had the same problem but would never admit it. That's what you could expect from a guy who was never in the military. He had the "cover your mistakes" mentality.

The big, lumpy man in the passenger seat kept adjusting the binoculars as if they might compensate for the fact that every man between twenty-five and forty in the camp was about five-seven and had dark hair. His partner scanned the large compound on U.S. Highway 27 in extreme western Palm Beach County and said, "Don't see him, Alex. What'd ya say we pack it in for today?"

Alex Duarte looked out over the labor camp silently, then at the afternoon sun. "Only been here three hours. Let's give it a few more."

"A few more *hours*?" His partner, Chuck Stoddard, turned his wide frame. "No way. I gotta pick up the kids at day care by six. It'll take an hour just to get back east."

Duarte shrugged. "I can grab this guy. Go ahead. I'll drop you back at your car."

"Alone? Not a chance. The warrant's for selling guns. We should even have a few more guys with us now."

Duarte let it slide. He'd found it didn't pay to argue about something you weren't going to change. He looked at the warrant again. It was for the arrest of Alberto Salez for violations of criminal statute 18 USC 44§ 922. A federal firearms statute. Duarte knew that it was probably bullshit like a lot of their regulatory cases, but it wasn't up to him. He followed instructions. The whole thing looked simple to him. This guy broke the law, he and his partner were given the warrant and now they had to find him. An informant had told them Salez stayed in one of the trailers at this shithole. He just wished Stoddard wasn't whining about going home already. How could you ever get ahead if you weren't willing to put in a little extra effort? That was the problem with most of the guys he worked with: they didn't want to get ahead. They were satisfied with just being street agents.

After the long silence, Stoddard said, "Okay, we'll wait, but my wife is gonna be pissed." He snatched his cell phone off his hip and started mashing buttons.

Duarte blocked out his partner's pleadings with his wife over the fate of the kids. Instead of being drawn into the call, he concentrated on the information sheet and small, profile mug shot attached to the warrant. He studied the black-and-white photo, trying to figure out something that might single out Salez. Under the section titled "Scars/Marks/Tattoos," Duarte noticed a comment: "Lower left ear missing." It would help up close, but from this distance it didn't seem to apply.

When Stoddard had put away his phone, Duarte said, "We need to get a lot closer. See?" He held up the sheet and tapped a finger on the ear information.

"How do you figure he lost part of his ear?"

Duarte shrugged.

Stoddard said, "But if we go into the camp and he's not there, we'll never get another chance. Once he hears a couple of ATF agents were looking for him, he'll be on the next bus to California." Stoddard took another look through the binoculars. "What if you went down, alone, undercover?"

"What'd you mean 'undercover'? I'd never fit in. They'd pick me out in a second."

Stoddard hesitated. "I mean, ah, they are *your* people."

Duarte was confused. What was his redneck partner talking about?

Stoddard added, "You know what I mean. Spanish."

Duarte turned to him. "I doubt any of those little people

picking fruit are from Spain. And I was born in West Palm
Beach. So I don't know what you mean."

"I know you're a . . . a little taller and dressed nice. I just
meant that they'd pick me right out."

Duarte said, "I can get down there and get a good look without mixing in the crowd. I'll call if I see anything." He opened
the car door and slid out. He wore a loose shirt over a T-shirt that
showed a surfer on a Costa Rican beach. Also under the loose
shirt was a Glock model 22, .40 caliber pistol.

Stoddard started to get out too.

"You wait here. We'll need the car if I see him."

"What'd you mean? Why're you going down there if you
don't think you can mix in?"

Duarte shut the door. He had faith his partner would figure
out what he was doing. He tromped off through the weeds in the
vacant lot next to the car. He could see the labor camp as it sunk
away from the built-up highway, almost making it look like it
was set up in a valley instead of the Florida swamp.

Duarte crossed the highway a quarter of a mile from the entrance to the camp and then turned back, ducking low into the
brush along the perimeter of the flat camp. He felt the stab of a
Florida holly bush in his neck as he dropped down to the ground
and began to crawl through the dirt. His faded jeans were a lot
tighter than fatigues, but he still felt more comfortable doing this
kind of activity than he would have trying to mix with the Central
American laborers. The heat was bearable. It was May, but no one
from the Northeast would consider the temperature "springlike."

The camp itself had a dusty feel. The pathways and the single
road were lime and unpaved. The soil out here in the Glades was
black and rich, but the sun dried the top layer in a matter of days,
which contributed to the haze. In the distance, a cane field fire
added a smell and a soft white dullness to the whole camp.
Duarte didn't mind—in fact, he liked crawling around like this
more than his usual duties at the Federal Bureau of Alcohol, Tobacco and Firearms. At least he wasn't looking at gun store records or typing up a report.

He traveled down one row of brush then crossed over to another that ran closer to the line of trailers where people seemed
to be coming from every few minutes. He found another row of
brush turning right and switched onto it like he was on the 1 and 9
subway in New York. No one noticed his tall, thin frame slide

through the mix of Florida holly, weeds, ficus and areca palms. After a few minutes, he realized there was a system to the brush and figured out it was used as a wind barrier around certain crops. He found a good intersection and then settled in to look for Alberto Salez. From his hiding place, he could clearly see in three directions. It was comfortable in the shade of the brush. He had sat in worse spots in Bosnia, watching Serbian tanks make their short and usually unsuccessful assaults.

He looked down at the scar that ran along his left forearm and thought about that unfortunate low crawl into barbed wire outside Broka. He didn't worry about barbed wire here. Of course he hadn't worried about it in Bosnia either, and now he had a fourteen-inch scar that itched most nights while he lay awake. He reached down and unclipped his Nextel cell phone and carefully turned off all the rings and beeps, placing everything on vibrate. Then he chirped his partner.

In a low whisper, he said, "Chuck, I'm in place, stand by."

"I'm looking with the binoculars. Where are you?"

He kept his voice low even though no one was close and there was a lot of noise from the traffic on the highway and salsa music blaring from one of the trailers. "I'm directly south of the office trailer with the two red flags."

After a minute his phone shook, and he heard Stoddard say, "I don't see you."

"Trust me, I'm there. I'll call if I see him." Duarte had to admit, at least to himself, it was satisfying to have Stoddard unable to see him. He hadn't forgotten all his training from Fort Leonard Wood or Bragg.

He watched the regular late-afternoon movements of the camp and noticed that people knew what to do and seemed to do it without complaint. No one had to yell orders and everyone was busy. After just thirty minutes, Duarte figured he had seen most of the camp's workers.

Then, just as he was contemplating heading back to the car, Duarte heard a female's shout drift across the camp. He turned in the direction of the angry voice and saw the open door to the trailer at the rear of the residential area.

A well-dressed woman in a tan skirt shoved a man outside, emphasizing the act with some sharp phrases in Spanish. He didn't know the exact words, but he caught the meaning well enough.

After the woman had slammed the door, the man looked

around, almost as if he was daring anyone to have noticed the incident at all. In fact, the people in the camp appeared far too busy to worry about a minor argument between two adults. The man, dressed in a colorful polo-type shirt and clean jeans, looked out of place. His clothes didn't belong to a working person. He strutted past some men trudging back from a field. He wasn't working; he was showing off. Duarte had little use for show-offs, especially in front of people like this. He waited as the man came closer. The problem was that as he walked toward the row of old, beat-up parked cars near the highway, his left ear was on the wrong side of Duarte. He wouldn't see it clearly as the man walked past. His right ear was intact, with a giant, round gold hoop earring dangling from it. The single, side view of Salez from the old arrest photo didn't really look like this guy. There was no bushy mustache in the photo, and his skin looked rougher than in the photo that was a few years old.

He waited as the man passed and Duarte could get a good look at him. It was hard to tell from the photo. Then, just as the man passed, Duarte called from the bushes: "Alberto."

The man turned quickly, like someone used to being on guard. He looked down the row of trailers and never even glanced in Duarte's direction. It was enough. Duarte could clearly see the mangled ear. This was their man.

Duarte waited until the man continued his trek toward the cars and then chirped up his partner. "Chuck, he's walking toward the highway near the row of vehicles. Come on down, nice and easy."

"On the way."

Duarte stepped out of the bushes away from Salez. No one even noticed as he stood up and brushed himself off; his army training to always stay neat kicking in, despite his urge to chase after the fugitive. He stepped out to the pathway and started walking casually toward Salez, who was now looking at the rear tires of a beat-up Ford Mustang. Duarte knew to wait for his partner, but what was taking him so long?

Then Salez, still unaware of Duarte as he approached, stood up and turned toward the driver's-side door. Duarte picked up the pace and closed in on the car as Salez lingered at the door. As he broke into a run, Duarte pulled out a badge on a chain from underneath his shirt and let it hang like a necklace down his chest. He looked up but didn't see Stoddard in the Taurus yet.

He surprised Salez while he was still standing next to the car. "Alberto Salez?"

The man's head snapped at the sound of his name. His eyes darted to the badge, and he sprang to the front of the car and paused, his eyes shifting to each side.

Duarte slid to a stop at the rear of the rusty Mustang. He hadn't drawn his Glock, and wasn't the least bit out of breath. He just wanted to give Chuck a chance to roll up and help corral this guy. He said to Salez, "Don't run."

"Why not?"

Duarte thought, that's a good question.

Salez turned toward the road, then saw Chuck Stoddard in the ATF Ford Taurus pulling onto the side of the roadway. The fugitive looked back at Duarte, then toward the rear of the camp, and broke into an all-out sprint away from the highway. He managed to slip past Duarte's lunge by using the trunk of his Mustang to block him, and by keeping a good pace.

Duarte matched his effort, but was a good ways back, and not quite as fast. The gun on his hip threw off his stride, but he preferred it to trying to run with a pistol in his hand. He didn't really like the feel of *any* pistol in his hand.

He watched as Salez tore past all the trailers, attracting the stares of the other residents. Duarte didn't know whether the fugitive was hoping for help or had an escape route. Either way, Salez had company as Duarte chased him past a packing house with a loading dock and then into a crop of tall corn. It wasn't hard to follow the man as he brushed cornstalk after cornstalk. They came out into an open field, and he could see the fugitive start to lose steam. Finally Duarte saw him duck into a long shed with wide double doors. Duarte didn't hesitate to burst into the shed. The biggest problem was that, as he came in from the fading sunlight, he had no night vision in the dark shed.

Duarte still hadn't drawn his gun. He preferred his fists, or even a good explosive, if he had to choose a weapon. He didn't pause by the door, where he was silhouetted by the sunlight. He turned and ducked to the side, then crouched to get what limited view he could of the shed. It was longer than he thought, and there was only one door. He was in here with Salez.

Duarte eased next to a large riding mower and listened. He was breathing a little hard from the run, but this was the kind of stuff he liked. He even smiled slightly for the first time all day.

Then he sensed movement directly in front of him. He felt the swoosh of a shovel as it crashed into the hood of the mower.

Duarte didn't wait for a second swing. He sprang up in the direction the shovel had come from and threw his body into the smaller Salez. The fugitive fell back to the other side of the shed, bouncing off the flexible aluminum walls.

Duarte moved to the right, forcing Salez to move toward the door and into the light. Now Duarte had a clear view of the dark man holding a short shovel like a baseball bat. Duarte feinted toward him, causing Salez to swing full force at him. After the blade of the shovel had passed, Duarte sprang forward and landed an open shuto strike across Salez's face. The hard edge of Duarte's hand made the man drop the shovel and stumble back until he regained his composure again. In a quick, smooth motion, Duarte reached up and stuck his finger through the large hoop earring and yanked as the man passed him. Salez pivoted and screamed in pain, as Duarte delivered a roundhouse kick to his ribs, followed by a left punch on his chin. He dropped straight to the ground without another sound.

Duarte looked at his right hand and saw the hoop earring with a one-inch hunk of flesh dripping from it. He had solved the mystery of the fugitive's other missing ear.

2

ALEX DUARTE OPENED THE DOOR TO THE TWO-BEDROOM apartment over the garage and prayed his brother wasn't home. His car was out front, but that didn't mean he was in the apartment. He stuck his head in and called out: "Frank?"

No answer.

Thank God. Duarte just wasn't up to his brother tonight. It had taken too long to book the fugitive, and he had used up all his patience with the deputies at the Palm Beach County jail explaining that Salez was a federal prisoner but that the marshals had said to bring him to the county jail for the night. Now all he wanted was a shower, food and another night lying on his back and looking at his ceiling. At least it would take the pressure off his knees.

He stretched as he entered his bedroom, his shoes making a hollow sound on the hardwood floors. He carefully threaded his belt out of the hip holster and then placed his Glock and holster on the top shelf of his closet. He always placed it in exactly the same place. He then pulled out his official ATF badge and credential case, keys, nine dollars and a nice BenchMark folding combat knife he had carried since his return from Bosnia in 1998. The only difference was where he lived then. And even that was only a change of about one hundred feet.

As he set the badge on the shelf, it caught the reflection of his closet light. He would often stare at his gold badge. Not one to admit pride, he had to acknowledge the fact that he was pleased to be associated with an agency like the Federal Bureau of Alcohol, Tobacco, Firearms and Explosives, even though everyone referred to them as ATF. The year before he mustered out of the army, as he finished his college degree at Troy State University, he started to ask around about who might appreciate his ability with explosives. There were plenty of options. Local police agencies, construction companies, even the FBI—but everyone seemed to speak with respect of the ATF. The one thing his pop had taught him growing up was that respect was the only thing worth the effort. And it took a lot of effort.

At first, it was a little hard to find information on the relatively small but hardworking federal agency. Unfortunately, many people associated them with the events in Waco, Texas, with the Branch Davidians. But all the ATF had done was make a good criminal case against several of the group's members. Things didn't go as planned, and the rest played out on national TV for months. But if no one ever broke the law, there would be no risk for law enforcement. Sometimes people forgot that.

After the terror attacks in 2001, the various bureaucrats decided that a reorganization of federal agencies was needed. In the shake up, where U.S. Customs and Immigration merged under Homeland Security, the ATF was moved from the Treasury Department to the Department of Justice.

Now, when he spent his time in his office near the other agencies, he was convinced he'd made the right decision.

In his room, as he sat on the edge of his bed, he sighed out his fatigue and glanced at the four books stacked on his night table. He was an avid reader. On his night table, he had a Shelby Foote book on the Civil War he had already read twice, a biography of Robert E. Lee, Jeff Shaara's classic *Gods and Generals,* and *The Plot Against America* by Philip Roth. He figured he'd make another trip to the library if he had more nights like the last one.

After a shower, he changed into shorts and a T-shirt and started to rummage through the refrigerator. Aside from his brother's Slim-Fast and two expired yogurts, he was out of luck. As he considered his options, he heard Frank's heavy footsteps on the outside stairs that led to the apartment.

"Hey, Rocket, when'd you get home?"

"Little while ago."

"Hungry?"

Duarte shrugged.

"Ma's got ropa vieja over rice."

"Really?" Then he caught himself.

"Go ahead. We don't live with them anymore. We can have a meal with our parents."

"Frank, we live over their garage. You eat breakfast and dinner there. It's like we never left home."

"Bullshit. You left in the army, and I went away to school."

"Then we moved back."

"So? No one is forcing you to stay."

Duarte thought about that. On the other hand, he had no reason to leave either. It wasn't like he had his own family, and living here allowed him to sock away some cash.

Frank said, "Go ahead, think of it as a favor to Ma."

Duarte lingered over his second dessert. After the main dish and salad, plantains, soup and bread, he had tried the tiramisu and now the chocolate cake. He didn't want to offend his ma.

His father sipped his coffee, careful to avoid the extravagant desserts his wife made every night. Duarte's father was convinced she was trying to put him in an early grave by offering up the various delicacies and sweets.

His father cut his eyes to Duarte. "You do a good job today?"

"Yes, sir."

The old man nodded. He had a slight accent after forty years of life in this same house off Parker Avenue in West Palm Beach, Florida. It was an elegant accent. He rarely spoke Spanish, and had, since his arrival in Miami from Paraguay in the sixties, taken English class after English class, followed by literature classes. Cesar Duarte was probably the best-read plumber in Palm Beach County.

"I hope your brother works as hard."

"Frank works hard, Pop."

"I guess as hard as lawyers can work."

Duarte shrugged.

His ma came from the kitchen with a plate of food wrapped in plastic. "This is for tonight, Alex, when you get hungry again." She placed it next to him and then leaned down and kissed him on the forehead. "You need to keep up your strength."

"Thanks, Ma." He took the food, cleaned his place and after

repeated good-byes to his ma and a nod to his pop was off to his apartment over the garage.

He was dreaming of fire, as he often did in his short fits of sleep, when his cell phone rang from his nightstand. He was instantly awake and had the small Nextel open. "Duarte."

"Rocket," said his supervisor. "There's been some kind of explosion. We need you to check it out."

"Where?"

"A labor camp off U.S. 27."

Duarte sat up, "The one where we found the fugitive today?"

"Don't know. I was told it's out near Belle Glade. Bailey Brothers farm."

"On the way, boss."

Before Duarte could hang up, his supervisor said, "Hey, Rocket."

"Yeah?"

"Don't know if it means anything to you but I was told from above to put you on this."

"Really?"

"You must be doin' something right for them to even take notice."

"Probably just my background."

"Never know. Do a good job."

"Count on it, boss."

It was after three in the morning when Duarte slowed his Taurus as he approached the sprawling labor camp off the highway. Even from the road, he could see the crime scene tape. The old Mustang that Duarte had chased Salez around that afternoon seemed to be the center of the destruction. The car was turned on its side, with the trunk lid twisted at an odd angle and the driver's-side door missing completely. There were still two fire engines in the lot, a half dozen Palm Beach County Sheriff's vehicles, with their blue lights spinning, and several unmarked cars. Duarte showed the deputy at the front gate his ATF credentials. The uniformed cop just nodded toward a group of seven or eight people listening to a briefing.

Duarte parked and headed toward a large black woman speaking in a loud voice at the center of the group. She clearly had everyone's attention and spoke with authority.

"Looks professional. We figured the two corpses found over there"—she pointed a thick finger toward the mangled row of cars—"detonated the device by opening the Mustang's door. We're trying to determine if one of 'em was the intended target."

Duarte looked over his shoulder at the twisted cars. Then, as he turned back to the briefing, he saw a woman crying, as she leaned against the closest fire engine. Her dark hair sprayed out at odd angles, and her eyes were puffy and red. A beefy fire-fighter stood next to her, holding a box of tissues and looking like he'd rather be sleeping. Duarte knew the feeling, but just the idea of someone from headquarters asking for him personally on a case gave him energy. After a moment, Duarte recognized her as the woman who pushed Salez out of the trailer earlier that day, and that in addition to crying he noted that she wore a long terry cloth robe.

He turned back to the woman addressing the group. The woman looked back at Duarte. "I know you're a cop or the deputy wouldn't have let you in. What's your name?"

"Alex Duarte, ATF."

"Alex, I'm Annette Cutter. I'm the captain of the sheriff's substation here. You an explosives guy or just an agent?"

"Both."

The woman cut through the crowd. "Good, come with me." She was nearly as tall as Duarte, with a few extra pounds on an already-wide frame. She wrapped a meaty arm around Duarte's shoulder. He could tell she had a positive way of dealing with people and got what she wanted. "We got us a mess over here."

"I heard what happened as I walked up."

"We got the two near the car dead, another man who was standing about thirty feet away killed by the blast and a kid who had snuck out of his mama's trailer killed by a freak shrapnel piece about a hundred feet away."

That caused Duarte to freeze. His stomach tightened and he asked, "Where'd he get hit?"

"Head. Dead instantly. A real shame."

Duarte swallowed hard, thinking about his own experiences blowing targets in and around Bosnia. He now understood the sobbing woman at the fire engine.

Duarte recovered slightly and asked, "What type of explosive? Black powder?"

"C-4."

Duarte looked at the woman. "You sure, Captain?"

"That's what my bomb techs tell me. I'm no expert. I'm an administrator now. But they know their business."

"It's just unusual to find something like C-4 . . ." He didn't finish his thought.

"In a shithole like this? I know, my guys said the same thing. We've never seen it either."

Duarte nodded, taking in all the information. He appreciated a boss that admitted she didn't know everything. There were politics and turf wars in police work, but the agents of the Federal Bureau of Alcohol, Tobacco and Firearms weren't usually a part of them. The cops liked it when ATF agents showed up. He didn't want to change that. He just doubted that any local sheriff's bomb tech had more practical experience with C-4 than he did.

Captain Cutter pointed out to the fields surrounding the camp. "A lot of the residents fled into the fields. They don't want to talk to the cops." She yawned. "I'm too old to be out this time of night. I should be in a warm bed with my husband."

Duarte nodded.

"You have someone warm to snuggle up with too?" asked the captain.

"No, ma'am."

"Really? Good-looking boy like you should have women lined up."

Duarte shrugged, then looked up to see the sobbing woman again. He had to look away from her, give her some privacy. He also knew he had to talk to Alberto Salez right away about why someone wanted to blow him up. He didn't need to share this with the local cops. Not yet. This could be his ticket up the ladder.

3

MIKE GARRETTI ALMOST SPIT HIS COFFEE ACROSS THE room when he saw the morning news report. How had four fucking people died at that hour in the labor camp? The whole idea was to make it noticeable and messy, but not like this. Jesus, what could've gone wrong that the bomb detonated that late at night?

One of the reasons he'd been so happy with the job is that no one ever even noticed him around the work camp. His dark hair and olive skin let him blend in with the Hispanics. He was mistaken for Mexican all the time back home. He sometimes wondered about his heritage. His name was Garretti. His brother and sister were pale as sheets and his dad had blue eyes, yet here he was—a castaway Latin. Had his mom been playing around? Maybe that's why his old man had been so rough on him growing up?

The newscaster had no names pending notification of next of kin. He realized he'd be stuck in this fucking Comfort Inn near some run-down mall in West Palm Beach another day or two until he made sure Salez was one of the dead. Then the news mentioned that one of the dead was an eight-year-old boy. Holy shit! A kid! What the hell was a kid doing up in the middle of the night? How could he ever justify hurting a kid? This was the first job he'd had problems on. It was still well paying, and he had his primary job back in Texas, but these little gigs were quickly securing a decent retirement for him.

If it hadn't been for the easy first job a few years ago, he wouldn't have gotten the follow-up assignments, but after his employers hear about this they might decide not to use him again. They wouldn't be happy about the kid either. For different reasons. They'd hate the bad PR. He was upset because he knew that kids didn't bring on their own problems. He was living fucking proof of that. Once they reached twenty-one, they probably had enough sin to pay for, and he didn't sweat too much about the extra noncombatant killed in his jobs. He wasn't happy about them but he could live with it. But a kid? He wasn't happy at all and definitely felt some of it was Alberto Salez's fault. That son of a bitch better be dead.

Since he was already awake and on duty, it was no big deal for Alex Duarte to be at the Palm Beach County jail at six-fifteen in the morning. He knew they got the federal prisoners ready for transport by the marshals early. After a delay at the rear entrance, Duarte finally convinced the sour female jailer that he had to see a prisoner immediately.

It took another fifteen minutes just to have Salez brought from the holding cell to an interview room. These jailers weren't used to dealing with federal prisoners or federal agents, and nobody wanted to get burned over improper procedure. Duarte recognized the attitude from his army days. That's why everything was laid out in procedural manuals. He hated the unnecessary process then, and he hated it now. But he lived with it.

A wide, black jailer with arms as big around as Salez's legs shoved the man into the seat across the metal table from Duarte.

The jailer said, "You got about thirty minutes."

Duarte nodded his thanks and then just stared at Salez until the jailer shut the door tight. He kept his dark eyes on the man, trying to put himself in his position. He noticed the little details of the man's face. A scar around his right eye, the bushy mustache and the fresh, white medical tape wrapped around the lobe of his right ear. Judging by Salez's expression, he didn't appreciate his treatment or the cosmetic adjustments that Duarte had made during the arrest.

After a full minute of mutual staring and silence, Salez said, "We just gonna kill time?"

Duarte said, "You remember me, right?"

"You're the prick that ruined my ear."

"Looks like it happened before."

Salez kept his mouth shut.

"My name is Alex Duarte. You probably remember I'm an agent with the ATF."

"Duarte? I didn't hear that yesterday. My head was ringin'." He leaned back, his hands still secured behind him. "Ahora, podemos hablar nuestro idioma."

Duarte shook his head. "In English."

"Why, you got some of your buddies listening?"

Duarte ignored the paranoid remark. "Look, I don't think you know what kind of trouble you're in."

"The gun beef in Texas. Bullshit. I'll walk on that." He had an accent Duarte wasn't quite familiar with. Maybe it was border Texan.

"I'm talking about the C-4 that detonated in your car and killed four people at the camp last night."

Salez just stared.

Duarte knew his own strengths and weaknesses. Interviewing and reading people was definitely a weakness. But even Duarte could understand this jackass's expression. He was screwed and he knew it.

"The Mustang?"

Duarte nodded.

"The '68? Is it ruined?"

"You don't get it. People are dead."

"No, Mr. Federal Agent, *you* don't get it. I ran from you yesterday because I didn't know you were a cop. I figured someone would be gunnin' for me one day soon."

"Why?"

"That's my business."

"You know what else is your business?"

"What?"

"We may decide you booby-trapped your own car. Between the manslaughter charges and weapons violations, figure on fifteen years state time and ten federal."

Salez was attempting to regain his composure.

"You want to tell me about the C-4 and who wants you that dead?"

Salez kept his eyes on the young ATF agent but remained silent.

Duarte slid back his chair and stood up. He could match anyone's silence. He had an empty address book to prove that. He only needed to put his hand on the doorknob and Salez started to speak.

"It's a long story and I don't know it all, but I know someone who does."

Duarte didn't sit down and didn't speak.

"I didn't want anyone else hurt. I swear to God. Dios mio, I swear."

Duarte turned and looked down at him. "Who knows the whole story?"

"The guy who set the bomb."

"What's his name?"

Salez paused, like he was searching for the right words. "I don't know for sure; calls himself Ed Smith."

Duarte nodded slightly, then turned back to the door.

"Wait. It's Eduardo. He goes by 'Eddie.' "

Duarte turned his head and gave him a look that said it all: *stop lying.*

"Look, I know where he works. I could take you."

"Where?"

Salez hesitated. Duarte turned.

"The big marketplace in Lake Worth. The one with all the booths and produce." He bent his head to wipe the sheen of sweat off on his shirtsleeve. "Look, you spring me and I'll lead you right to him. I swear."

Duarte didn't commit out loud, but he knew what he had to do. Find this "Eddie," solve this case, let that dead boy rest in peace, wait for his next assignment. As a supervisor.

By midafternoon, Duarte sat in his car with Salez in the passenger's seat. And in case Salez caused any problems, Chuck Stoddard was in the backseat. Chuck was a good guy, but he didn't want to run any cases, he only wanted to assist others. That worked out perfectly for Duarte. They drove south on I-95 from the federal courthouse.

Salez said, "Pretty slick how you got me out. You must have some juice."

Duarte kept rolling their plan over in his head. First, have Salez point out Eddie. Then have Forensics link Eddie to the Mustang. Simple. Duarte's real worry was keeping track of Salez. He knew he should have more agents out here, but they all had their own cases. This way Duarte would get plenty of credit for solving this thing. The Assistant U.S. Attorney didn't seem too happy about agreeing to Salez's release since he was a fugitive from another district, but Duarte promised to have him back at the jail by four. That would also keep Chuck happy and quiet.

After a twenty-minute drive, they were across the wide, busy street from the Lake Worth Marketplace, a flea market/produce store/meeting place. It seemed like there were only Hispanics there right now.

Salez asked, "Can we eat first? I'm starving."

Chuck said, "Yeah, there's a Taco Bell a few blocks east."

Duarte ignored them. There was work to do. He looked down at his written description of Eddie. Latin, male, thirty to thirty-five, five-seven, average build. Damn, if that didn't fit most people at this place. Something was wrong with this picture.

Duarte said to Salez. "We're going in with you."

"Bullshit, he'll spot you in a heartbeat. Especially white-bread, in the backseat." He jerked a thumb toward the large, plump Chuck Stoddard.

Duarte considered this.

Salez was ready. "Look, they got one entrance to this place. Right there." He pointed to the double sliding glass door. "You can park right in front and see anyone coming or going."

Duarte silently surveyed the door and the number of people flowing in and out of it.

"C'mon, amigo. You got me out of the can in the first place. I need to do this or I'll be runnin' the rest of my life." Salez looked back to the uninterested Chuck for support.

Duarte tried to gauge the rough, dark man. He seemed sincere and serious. He pulled out of the parking spot and cruised slowly through the lot then past the front door, getting a good view of the inside.

"Hey, man, where are you goin'? We ain't leavin', are we?" Salez became more agitated as they drove away from the door. Then he calmed down as Duarte turned left toward the rear of the large building. They took another left along the rear wall.

Salez said, "See, only one door, and it's marked Fire Exit. No one comes or goes."

Duarte stopped the Taurus. "Chuck."

The pale face popped up from a magazine he was browsing. "Yeah?"

"Get out and keep an eye on the front door while he's inside."

"Where'll you be?"

"I'll go in first and watch from inside where this rear door is. That way, I can keep an eye on him, and he can come to me if he needs to." He gave a hard look at Salez. "No bullshit, now."

"No, sir, I swear."

Five minutes later, as Duarte was about to go in, he turned to Salez. "Remember. For now, I just want you to find him. Point him out to me. Then we're outta here." He grabbed Salez by the elbow. "Try anything funny and I won't be happy."

Salez nodded. "You don't look like you're ever happy. Just give me five minutes to look around and I'll come get you."

Duarte nodded silently as he tried to figure how much of this guy's game was real.

Chuck Stoddard hadn't really paid attention to what was going on in the car. He knew Alex wanted him to make sure the little Mexican guy didn't escape out the front door. He was pretty sure he could do that. After waiting for Alex to chirp him on his Nextel that he was in place by the rear door, he let Salez walk to the front entrance, then Chuck posted himself next to it on the inside. He felt a little out of place as the only white, American-looking guy in the whole building. He'd had worse assignments. One time, the older, hotshot agent in the office named Steve had him follow some guy after a gun show for sixteen hours. This was a piece of cake compared to that. Everyone considered Alex as the young hotshot agent in the office. When Alex's brother told everyone he had been nicknamed "the Rocket" since childhood, the name stuck. It was an appropriate name. He took off fast and—Chuck joked—couldn't change direction once he got going. Chuck didn't care as long as no one asked him to work these complex cases with surveillance and paperwork. He liked to help the other guys. That was his job.

He waited, and bought a hot dog and Coke from a vendor right at the front door. It was a good-looking, dark-haired Mexican girl who smiled and winked at him. He wondered what would happen if he told her he was a federal agent. After ten minutes, Alex chirped him on his phone and said, "Chuck, he's coming out of the bathroom closest to the front door and looks like he's heading your way. I'll follow in a few minutes. Just wait at the car with him."

Chuck pressed the button on the outside of his phone and said,

"10-4." He liked it when things went smoothly. He looked down the aisle and saw the man, Salez, from a hundred feet away, in that god-awful yellow shirt, and with the white tape on his ear.

Salez was tentative as he approached the door, like he was scared. Chuck waved to him, catching his eye, and the man smiled and walked up to him. Salez followed him across the parking lot to the car, and Chuck unlocked it and motioned him into the rear seat.

"Any problems?" asked Chuck.

Salez smiled and shrugged.

"Good, that's the way we like it."

Chuck's phone beeped. Duarte said, "Ask him why he left without talking to me? Did he see the guy?"

Chuck turned in the seat and asked, "Well, was he in there?"

Salez shrugged again.

"What's that mean?"

He just shrugged and kept smiling.

Chuck said into his phone. "I got no idea. He ain't talkin'."

"I'll be right out."

Chuck waited, his stomach full, the AC blasting decent cold air at him. The guy in the back not giving him any shit. It was a pretty good day. He saw Alex "the Rocket" Duarte quick-step across the lot and then race around to the passenger's side of the Ford. He seemed to always be in a hurry.

Before he had the door closed, he was talking to the prisoner. "What about it? Was he in there?"

When the guy didn't answer, Alex looked over his shoulder, and then he shut up too.

"What?" asked Chuck.

Silence. Then Alex said, "What the hell is this?"

Chuck turned and didn't see anything unusual.

"What'd mean?"

Alex reached across and pulled off the tape on his ear.

Chuck said, "His ear healed up fast."

"Chuck, it grew back too. And so did his other ear."

"Are you crazy? He's not a chameleon." Then Chuck froze too. He realized what Alex was trying to tell him

A lex Duarte stared at his partner. God love him, he was big, strong, good in a fight, but he didn't notice that Alberto Salez had given him the slip. And it showed that Salez was smart enough to know the big ATF agent's limitations. He stayed calm. There was nothing else to do.

"Who are you?" he asked their new passenger.

The man smiled. He did look a little like Salez, with his dark hair and bushy mustache.

"¿Habla inglés?"

The man shook his head, leaned forward and said, "¿Habla español?"

Duarte shook his head no, and got the same look his older relatives from Paraguay usually gave him and his brother.

Now he wished he had taken Spanish in school. His father refused to speak Spanish because he said they lived in America. Right now, Duarte wished his father had been a little less rigid through his formative years.

It took a few minutes to find a willing translator, but once they did they found out that Salez gave the man his clothes for free if he walked out and met "the big, stupid-looking white man in the front of the store." He didn't know if he was going to get more stuff if he played along, so he followed Chuck out to the car and waited. Now they had a mess to deal with.

Alberto Salez had walked out of the giant marketplace about thirty seconds behind the ATF man, Duarte. He figured it would take another two to three minutes for them to realize exactly what had happened and scramble to look for him. He had counted on the big white guy's inability to distinguish between the Hispanic men at the market. Not that they all looked alike; he just knew that many people didn't pay attention. Salez was already across the street heading to the library when a pickup truck with day laborers in the bed stopped at the light on Lake Worth Road. A black man in the passenger's seat of the cab said, "Need work?"

Salez smiled and nodded yes.

"Jump in back," said the man, jerking his thumb toward the truck's bed.

He squeezed in between two Mexican gentlemen and nodded to everyone in the bed. He looked over his shoulder once the light changed and watched the marketplace building fade into the background. He had given the ATF the slip, but they were the least of his problems. He had to hightail it out of here and find another place to live. He wished he could have confided in the by-the-book ATF man. Duarte seemed like a real straight shooter. He had seen the type before: military background, raised to believe in a cause. That made him a dangerous man, but he never would've believed Salez's story once he started laying it out. It sounded like science fiction, even to him. No one wanted to believe in conspiracies. He never wanted to either, but now, with one of his buddies dead, and the fact that he hadn't heard from Don Munroe since he moved to Virginia, Salez had to start wondering what he had stumbled into.

He rode in the truck to a farm west of Boynton Beach, then jumped out of the back, headed to a giant convenience store with a check-cashing office and went right to the pay phone. He had to get some help.

4

ALEX DUARTE LOOKED AROUND HIS SUPERVISOR'S SMALL OF-
fice on the fifth floor of an office building that was too nice
to house a federal law enforcement agency but not nice enough
for private businesses. The Bureau of Alcohol, Tobacco and
Firearms, along with the Secret Service and the FBI, had all
scooped up offices at a discount. As a result, anytime someone
from another federal agency visited they were immediately
pissed off the building was nicer than theirs.

Duarte saw the look in the Assistant U.S. Attorney who had
helped draft the order to release Salez for the day. The short,
heavy bald man with round, wire-rimmed glasses acted like he'd
also missed lunch. The combination didn't look good for
Duarte. He silently slipped in and took the chair across from his
generally sympathetic boss. As he sat down, he noticed a woman
who had been standing in the rear of the office looking out at the
biggest perk of the building: a view of the Intra-coastal Waterway and the ocean on the far of the island of Palm Beach. She
was blond and, even in a business suit, had curves that would
catch any man's attention.

His supervisor said, "What happened, Rocket?"

Duarte shrugged. He had purposely left Chuck Stoddard out
of the whole situation. No sense getting that poor guy roasted
over the screwup. His biggest mistake was thinking Chuck could
cover that front door effectively.

The Assistant U.S. Attorney said, "Well, what about it,
Duarte? I told the magistrate you had sufficient protection for
Salez, and that he'd be back inside by six P.M."

Duarte looked at his round, red face. Then he shrugged again. What was there to say? He had screwed up in a big way.

His supervisor said, "Rocket, this is Caren Larson, from the Department of Justice." He turned, stood and shook the blond woman's offered hand.

Duarte finally said, "Am I in that much trouble?"

Caren Larson smiled, and spoke with a clear, midwestern accent. "I'm not here because of the escape. I mean, I was here to talk to Salez, but only because we may have other related bombings in Virginia and Seattle."

Now it was the AUSA's chance to cut in again. "Related or not, we have the problem of an escaped federal prisoner, and you guys let him escape."

He looked at Duarte's calm face.

After a few seconds of silence, the frustrated AUSA said, "Somebody fucking talk to me. What are we going to do?"

"I'll find him," said Duarte.

"How?"

He didn't answer. It wasn't this guy's business.

His supervisor said, "We'll get the whole office on it. Alex will lead it but he has been assigned to work with Ms. Larson too."

The AUSA stood up. "Assigned by who? I thought you assigned what was going on."

The soft-spoken ATF supervisor stayed as calm as Duarte, and said, "Sometimes I do."

Without a word, Duarte stood up and headed back to his office. He already knew his mission was to find Alberto Salez. He didn't need some attorney to tell him what he needed to do. He was almost out the door when he heard Caren Larson say, "Alex, can we talk for a few minutes?"

He was noncommittal to the request, and turned to head down the narrow corridor to his office. The fact that most of the other agents were still at their desks after five gave Duarte a feeling of finding a home. He liked his job, and so did the other agents.

He paused at one office that housed a pair of his mentors. He looked in at the older of the two tall men. "Hey, Steve, what's up?"

The thin agent looked up and said, "Rocket, you didn't admit to anything, did you?"

"Just that I screwed up."

Steve winced slightly. "That's fine. Just don't say anything else."

The other man in the small office, a tall, former Notre Dame linebacker they all called "Meat" said, "Who's the hot babe in Dale's office?"

The blond attorney squeezed around the doorway, and Duarte said, "Caren Larson, Department of Justice."

Both men cringed.

Meat's white Irish face flushed red. Without losing a beat, he looked at Steve and said, "Steve, why would you say something like that?"

Duarte moved on down the hallway, feeling Caren Larson in tow. He heard a loud thump from the office they had just left and could only imagine what it was.

Duarte did his best to ignore her by following his main rule, or at least his father's main rule: mind your own business. But she was persistent. She followed him into the one-person office that housed him and Chuck Stoddard. Since it was almost five, Chuck was already at home with the kids. He squeezed past a pile of old *Shotgun News* magazines and plopped into his desk chair. Caren, showing much more grace, eased into Chuck's misshapen cushioned chair. His girth had squeezed the foam to each side of the vinyl-covered swivel throne.

She scooted up to the desk like it was hers. She leaned forward, with her hands supporting her chin, apparently prepared to stay there for a while. Duarte focused on his notes from his arrest of Salez and on his booking sheet. Somewhere in there was a clue as to where the wily fugitive had gone.

Duarte now doubted every aspect of Salez's story because he realized the gun dealer had probably just told them the first big building with lots of Hispanics that came to mind and then led Duarte right into his trap. It was embarrassing, but what could he do? He admitted his error and now intended to correct it.

He knew Caren Larson was staring at him. He could *feel* it. Her pretty face and deep blue eyes had not escaped his notice. Neither had her petite but shapely body. He figured she was maybe three years older than him, about thirty-two. After a minute concentrating on ignoring her, he got wrapped up in his search for information and really did forget she was there.

After more than ten minutes, she said, "You don't say much, do you?"

He shrugged.

"I noticed you gave the same answer in there." She nodded toward the supervisor's office. "I've never seen anyone shrug himself out of trouble so effectively." She smiled, revealing gleaming, straight teeth. Definitely not a smoker.

"Nothing to do except fix it. I let Salez escape. I didn't mean to. I'll make it right. They weren't going to take me out and shoot me."

"That's the best answer I think I've ever heard."

He started to go back to work, rooting through the information on his desk.

"Are you mad I'm working this?"

Duarte said, "None of my business what you work."

"I thought you'd be interested in similar bombings in totally different regions."

"I would've been until I let Salez escape."

She smiled and said, "That's why they call you 'the Rocket.' You see a target and go right at it no matter what."

"That's what I'm told."

"So you don't care about the other bombings?"

"I do, but I need to find Salez, if possible." He looked into her eyes and said, "Any kids killed in the other blasts?"

"No."

"Where were they again?"

"The last one was in Virginia. The first was in Seattle."

"That's a big distance. You sure they're connected?"

"Positive." She handed him a business card that simply read CAREN BRUEN LARSON, ATTORNEY, DEPT. OF JUSTICE. "Call me when you're ready to work this case. I need to see the migrant labor camp where the bomb went off. I'll have my cell on."

Duarte took the card and glanced at it, then paused.

Caren said, "What's this? Something actually interests you?"

"You're an attorney?"

"Yeah, but I'm acting as an investigator."

"Why isn't the FBI working this?"

"They have their angle. If it turns out to be terrorists, then it's theirs."

"Why use an attorney as an investigator?"

"Why not? If I don't have to make arrests, I'm a good choice.

There's a lot of paper involved and subpoenas. I'm good with both."

"Still, who do you answer to?"

"You'd be surprised."

He shrugged. She'd be surprised how little he cared.

Caren added, "There are possible issues involved that make using an attorney important in the investigation."

"What kind of issues?"

"I'd like to see how long it takes you to figure them out."

He didn't know what that meant, and, again, didn't really care.

She said, "You think your partner"—she looked down at a stack of his business cards at the edge of the cluttered desk—"Charles Stoddard, could show me where the labor camp is?"

"You'd have to ask him." He paused, and added: "That's where we arrested Salez."

"I know."

He didn't even ask how she knew. He had a feeling she didn't miss much.

"Don't worry. I'll keep your secret from the locals."

Duarte just shrugged.

By eight o'clock, he was trudging to the back door of his parents' kitchen. He was so tired he hadn't even gone up to his apartment. Part of it was low energy, and part was that he needed to chat with his father. Avoiding his brother Frank was just a bonus.

"Hi, Ma," he said, leaning down to kiss the only woman in the world he was comfortable with, as she stirred some type of seafood stew on the stove.

"How's my baby?"

"Tired."

"Sit, and I'll make you a big bowl."

Before Duarte could ask where his father was, he heard the fifty-eight-year-old man as he came from the small, immaculate living room.

"Alex, you look beat."

"Yes, sir. I'm tired."

"Did you do good work today?"

For the first time since he was seventeen and had to explain why he had used his karate to break the jaw and the nose of two other bag boys at the Publix supermarket, Alex Duarte had to say, "No, sir, I didn't do such good work today."

"Can you fix it?"

"I'll do my best."

"Alex, everyone does their best. By now, you must realize that is not good enough for you. You will fix it. I have every confidence."

Duarte sat up straighter and said, "Yes, sir, you're right." And now he felt the burning fire in his belly to force him to find Alberto Salez and set the universe back on its normal course.

5

BY TWO O'CLOCK THE NEXT AFTERNOON, ALEX DUARTE had covered every possible address related to Alberto Salez. He had interviewed old roommates, former bosses and landladies. Everything his intelligence analyst could come up with by using the various records indices and even some simple Internet sites like Google or ZabaSearch. He had a criminal record that went back to when he was a teenager in Texas. There were several "loitering and prowling" and two separate "lewd conduct" charges. Both had been dropped. Duarte didn't generally have to deal with guys that had a background with crimes like that, but he knew it was an indicator of a deeper issue. Alberto Salez may have been wanted for selling guns illegally, but he was something worse. At least as far as Duarte could tell.

In this case, if someone was trying to kill him, he was a victim too. That was another reason Duarte was anxious to find him: if whoever set the bomb in his Mustang found him first, he probably wouldn't have much to say when the guy was finished with him.

Records seemed to indicate that Salez had lived in Florida for less than two years, but he had gotten around. He had no current address listed. The closest Duarte had come was a small house in Lake Worth, where Salez had paid the power bill until about eight months ago. The Haitian family that lived there now didn't know anything about Alberto Salez. That was police work.

Now Duarte was on his way out to the Bailey Brothers farm labor camp where he had arrested Salez. This served the extra purpose of showing the Department of Justice attorney, Caren Larson, that he was interested in her case too. He needed more details before he considered it his case.

He sat up straight in his government-issue Ford Taurus as he kept it at sixty-eight on the straight highway west to Belle Glade. He found his mind wandering to Caren Larson's smooth skin and blond hair instead of going over the options for finding Salez. This troubled him because he rarely got distracted by women. Even really good-looking women.

There was still a marked sheriff's cruiser at the front entrance to the labor camp. The bored deputy just waved Duarte in and pointed down the first dirt road. Duarte let his eyes follow the deputy's hand and saw a small gathering of people, none of whom looked like migrant workers. He parked his Ford and walked over the gritty lime road near the bushes he had used as cover while looking for Salez. As he approached the group, he immediately understood the dynamic as three of the four men laughed out loud and the fourth concentrated on the speaker. It was Caren Larson.

Duarte hesitated as he approached. He didn't want to get tied up in chitchat when he had a mission to complete—finding Alberto Salez. Before he could turn toward the twisted form of the old Mustang, he heard Caren call his name.

"Alex, c'mere."

He kept his stride toward the group, knowing it would take more time to avoid her.

She looked around at her audience. "Boys, this is my partner, Alex Duarte." They all nodded a hello, obviously disturbed to find out Caren was attached in any way to another male. "Alex is an ATF agent." No one seemed impressed. "And a former army EOD specialist." That got everyone's attention.

The oldest of the group, a heavy guy about forty-five, said, "No shit. What unit?"

Duarte looked at him and decided to answer. "I was a combat engineer, not EOD."

The man said, "That's cool. Did you have to defuse anything?"

"No, just set it."

A musclehead about Caren's age said, "I was special forces in the first Gulf War." He turned his blue eyes toward Caren to see her reaction.

Duarte asked, "Who do you work for now?"

"Palm Beach S.O. bomb squad."

"Good unit."

"Bet your ass. The best."

Duarte had heard that kind of bullshit all through his three years in the service and now he saw it in certain cops. He never had time for the flash, and he still didn't. He turned toward the office and started to walk.

Caren trotted after him. "Where are you goin'?"

"Talk to the manager about Salez."

"You didn't come out to work this with me?"

He kept walking. She followed like a puppy, trying to get his attention. "I found out a few things you might like to know."

Duarte kept walking, waiting for her to tell him.

Finally she asked, "Aren't you interested?"

"Did I interrupt you? What'd you find out?"

"Salez was here trying to keep the migrants from joining a union."

"Why?"

"Why what?"

"Why would he care if they formed a union?"

"He was probably hired by management. It's very common."

He stopped in front of the main trailer that had two red flags at either end. The hand-painted sign taped to the wall read OF-FICE. He skipped up the three stairs at once and opened the door.

Inside, a young Latin woman in a bright blouse sat blowing on her fingernails. Her dark, oval eyes cut over to Duarte. He could tell that look had attracted quite a few men in the past.

"Who're you?" she asked with a thick Cuban accent.

He reached in his rear pocket and pulled out his black credential case, then flipped it open, saying, "Federal agent. I need to speak to the manager."

"'Bout what?"

"About right now."

She stood up, showing off impossibly tight jeans. "Okay, okay, hang on." She had to waddle in the jeans, taking steps like she had chains on her long legs.

Caren leaned in close and said, "She thinks you're cute."

He ignored her.

A few seconds later, a thick man in his early sixties wearing jeans and a nice western shirt came from the rear office. His face showed multiple attempts to remove skin cancer.

"What do the feds want with me now?" Then he added in a more somber tone, "You ain't Immigration, are you?"

Duarte shook his head. "ATF."

"Yeah, the bombing. Shameful." His eyes ran up and down Caren, and he said, "What can I do for you?"

Duarte showed him the photo of Alberto Salez. "You know anything about him?"

"Berto, naw. He was a tough guy but never caused no problem."

"You hire him to keep out the union?"

"Me? Hell no. I couldn't care less if these people organize or not. I don't know for a fact why he was here. But if he was here to keep 'em from organizing, the owners of the farm hired him. I just run the housing and pay."

"Where'd he live?"

"Not here. Occasionally, he stayed in the big double-wide that houses some of the single males. He'd go out with them sometimes. He was friendly with Maria Tannza too."

"Where's she live?"

"Last trailer. It was her boy got kilt the other night."

Now Duarte remembered her throwing out Salez the day of his arrest. He hadn't thought it was significant and hadn't bothered to ask the fugitive about the incident. That just made one more reason to grab this creep. It took Duarte a few seconds to realize he was feeling emotion about work. That had never happened before. Now he was mad. Salez just seemed to dig himself deeper and deeper into Duarte's doghouse.

After going through some more routine questions, Duarte left the man a business card and turned toward the door, forgetting Caren Larson had been waiting during the entire interview. She followed him out the door as he turned toward Maria Tannza's trailer in the rear of the camp.

She asked, "What do you think? He give you any ideas?"

He shook his head.

"What do you want me to do?"

He shrugged and kept walking. Then he said, "There is one thing."

"What? What's that?"

"How'd you know I was in the army?"

She smiled. "I'm from Washington. I see any records I want. It was listed on your application to ATF."

He didn't look at her again until he was at Maria's front door. This time, he knocked quietly. After a full minute, the door cracked, and he saw the same woman from the other night. Now she was in a clean, simple dress and her hair was combed. She had a scrubbed, wholesome look, and was much younger than he had originally thought. About his age, she looked like a lawyer's wife . . . who did her own housework. She still had that vacant stare. The deep mourning aura. He knew it well. He had seen it often enough in Bosnia. Once, he had even caused it. He knew some people never recovered from it.

She assessed Duarte too. "¿Si? ¿Qué usted desea?"

He held up his ID. "Do you speak English?"

She nodded.

"I know it's a tough time, ma'am, but could I ask you a few questions?"

"About what?" She had a light accent, almost like his father's.

It took Duarte a second to adjust to the woman's clear speech. "About Alberto Salez."

"Alberto? Is he safe?"

"I think so."

"Where?"

"That's what I'm trying to find out."

She opened the door for them to come inside.

As Caren stepped up, she said, "I'm Caren Larson, Alex's partner."

The woman barely acknowledged her. The trailer was immaculate. There were trays of food sitting on the kitchen counter and several bouquets of cut flowers. Probably from somewhere on this same farm. She was obviously popular in the community.

Duarte took the seat she offered on the couch. Caren flopped down next to him.

"How long have you known Salez?" asked Duarte, cutting through any pretext so he could escape this quiet, sad little house.

The woman, Maria, just stared at him with those dark eyes. Then she seemed to come to her senses. "I'd see him from time to time around the camp. Then, as a favor, I let him sleep on the couch a couple of nights because there was no room in the group trailer."

"Did he always stay in the camp?"

"No, he had an apartment in West Palm Beach."

"Why didn't he stay there?"

She shrugged. "He told me he was avoiding someone."

"Who?"

"I don't know. Said it had to do with an old debt."

"He was your boyfriend, then?"

She shook her head. She reached up and pulled a tissue from a box next to her wide cloth chair. She wiped her eyes and blew her small nose. "I'm sorry. It's just been so . . ."

Caren cut in, leaning closer to Maria. "That's all right. Let it out."

Maria seemed to take the advice and let a torrent come out for a full minute. Then, after a few more tissues, she seemed to recover. She added, "He was respectful and very funny. I guess you'd say he was charming. That's why I let him stay. Besides, Hector, my son"—she paused to let out a sob but recovered very quickly this time—"he slept in with me when Alberto stayed. I trusted him but was always careful with Hector." She started to cry, and said, "I guess not careful enough. He slipped out to play after I fell asleep the night of the explosion." Now she was sobbing again.

For the first time, Duarte was glad Caren was with him. He had never been much for dealing with people's emotions. Or, for that matter, dealing with people.

She was the one that subtly asked about photos and Salez's family and contacts in between fits of crying. She asked good questions without seeming to pry. Duarte was impressed.

After the tenth question, Maria said, "I really didn't know him that well. He was just, you know, nice."

Duarte said, "The day he was arrested, you were angry at him, right?"

"How'd you know that?"

"I first saw him as you threw him out."

"He thought we were more than friends. He wanted to leave some personal items in the trailer. I told him no, and he suggested it would be easier for our 'relationship.' "

Caren smiled. "So you explained the nature of your relationship."

Maria nodded, too sad to be proud.

Caren asked, "Did he ever offer to help you with the bills?"

"Here? No, I have none."

"Really? The farm pays for the trailer and electricity?"

Then she nodded. "I see. You think I'm a laborer."

Duarte leaned up. "You're not?"

"No, I'm a teacher. The farm provides for the education of

the kids. I get a little less than I did as a public school teacher, but all my bills are paid, and these people really need me." She paused, looked at a photo of her son and started to sob again. "Now that's even more important to me."

They waited as she quieted down. Once again, Duarte was impressed with Caren's ability to connect with the grief-stricken woman.

Duarte asked about his local haunts and habits.

Maria took some time to consider her answer. "The only place he ever went around here was a sports bar off Highway 80. Across from the Twistee Treat. You know where I mean?"

Duarte nodded. "Near the Taco Bell?"

"Yes. I can't remember the name. It was called a 'club,' or something. He shot pool sometimes."

"Anything else?"

She hesitated. "He usually stayed in West Palm. I had never been to his apartment. I know he had coffee the same place every morning."

"Where?"

She shook her head. "In West Palm somewhere. He'd leave here at six-thirty in the morning to get there by eight." She threw up her hands. "I didn't realize how little I knew about him."

After they had nearly finished, Duarte asked, "What about his charge for dealing guns in Texas? Did he ever talk about it?"

"You mean, a criminal charge?"

Duarte nodded.

"I had no idea." It was clear that was the least of her current concerns.

"Mention anything about Texas?"

She sniffled. "Just that he worked for Powercore."

"The energy company?"

She nodded.

Caren stood up and moved toward the door. "Alex, we've intruded too long." She bumped him with her hip to get him moving. She said a final good-bye to Maria and was outside with Duarte in a matter of seconds.

Caren took a deep breath of the clean, Glades air and said, "What now, partner?"

6

DUARTE WATCHED IN SILENT AMAZEMENT AS CAREN Larson wolfed down her third chicken leg, in addition to potato salad, fried okra, a sweet potato and coleslaw, from Dixie Fried Chicken near the center of Belle Glade. He was hesitantly nibbling on a chicken breast. Not because it wasn't good, but because any food not made by his ma was suspect and usually second-rate. The army had taught him he could eat anything if he was hungry, but it only took a week after he got home to realize there was nothing like his ma's cooking.

Caren had peppered him with questions since they had sat down in the tiny, deserted restaurant. She asked about his childhood, military service, love life—anything and everything that was none of her business. He had dodged it with a series of grunts, shrugs and nods.

Finally Caren said, "Do you have any human contact?"

"I'm not sure my brother counts. He's only an attorney. But, yeah, I talk with my pop almost every night."

"I'm an attorney, and I'll testify that we are just as human as you."

He nodded.

Caren smiled and said, "If you are so uncommunicative, how'd you get by in the service?"

"Great. All anyone cared about was if you did your job."

"So you think I'm nosey?"

"Hadn't thought about it. Don't care, it's your business if you're nosey."

"As good-looking as you are, with a good job, if you had just a hint of social skill you'd be in high demand."

He shrugged.

"You don't care women find you attractive?"

This time he smiled at the idea someone would even care, other than his ma, who was starting to get desperate for grandchildren.

"You're not gay, are you?" She leaned forward like the answer might really impact her.

He shrugged, this time just for fun.

"You're infuriating." She sat back and brushed her blond hair back behind her. "Do you at least have any hobbies?"

"Sure, a bunch."

"Like what?"

"I read a lot of books, I practice karate, I'm a runner."

"You act like a reader."

"How does a reader act?"

"You know. Quiet, detached, introspective."

He just stared at her silently.

Caren smiled. "See what I mean." Then she added, "What kind of stuff do you read?"

"A lot on the Civil War. Good novels. A little of everything."

"You're not one of those Civil War nuts that reenacts battles and stuff, are you?"

"No, I'm not a reenactor, but I can appreciate the effort and knowledge that goes into it."

"Is this part of an assimilation thing?"

"Assimilate to what?"

"U.S. culture."

"I was born in the U.S."

"I know, but with your Hispanic heritage I thought that might spur your interest in something like the Civil War."

"Why not just an interest in history?"

Caren held up her hands and said, "You're right. I didn't mean to infer anything."

Duarte shook his head. "I'm not offended. You were just asking."

She brightened and said, "You want to know anything about me?"

He realized that even though he didn't, he should ask something. It was almost like a test to see if he had any social skills at all.

"Okay," he started slowly, making it seem like he was really thinking about the question. "Your card said your name was Caren Bruen Larson. There's a great Irish writer named Ken Bruen from Galway. Any relation?"

"My family is Irish. But a writer? Nope, I don't recall any drunks in the family."

He just stared at her until she laughed and he realized it was a joke. He smiled to be polite, and he had to admit he didn't mind watching her smile either.

She said, "So tell me the difference between EOD and combat engineer. I thought they were the same."

Finally a question he felt she might need to know the answer to. "EOD stands for 'explosive ordinance disposal.' They find bombs and explosive devices then either defuse them or detonate them. Combat engineers can build things like pontoon bridges or blow things up like bridges or obstructions in a road."

"Did you build or blow?"

A thin smile crept across his face. "I blew things up."

"Like what?"

"A couple of bridges, a building, a gas depot once—that was cool."

"Why would you blow a gas depot?"

"The Serbs were hording gas for a push into Croat-held territory. They stored it near a town so bombers had a hard time getting to it. They sent us in with some Rangers and set a few well-placed charges and, next thing you know, we had separation between the two pissed-off and armed ethnic groups."

She let a broad smile spread across her pretty face. Her cheekbones popped higher, and full lips opened to show her straight teeth.

"What's so funny?"

"That's more words at once than I've heard you speak. Must need the right subject."

He just watched her smile, and realized he even liked the food. He decided to find out more about the mission while he had her relaxed.

"Tell me about the other attacks."

She finished swallowing a big hunk of chicken and said, "The Seattle one was at an apartment. The victim worked for a telephone company that was unionizing. The most recent, last week, was in Virginia near D.C. An amusement park employee shuttle."

"What was the motive at the amusement park? Anyone know?"

"The workers were talking about joining a union."

He thought about that. "Is that why you think they're related?"

"All three used C-4 with military blasting caps."

"Same batch of C-4?"

"Won't know until your ATF lab is done with their analysis."
She wiped her greasy lips with a napkin. "Interested now?"

"Still have to find Salez."

"What if it takes time?"

"I could look into this too."

"Good, because I have two tickets to D.C. for tomorrow evening. I've got to report in, and you can look at the blast site and
talk to the witnesses."

He realized she had him pegged and knew what would happen before he had even shown up at the labor camp. He might be
able to learn something from this attorney after all.

Ever since Mike Garretti had learned that Alberto Salez was not
among the dead at the labor camp, he had been hanging out
near the café where Salez ate breakfast and watching for signs of
life in the little upstairs apartment Salez had near the interstate.
It was a short drive in his clean, little rented Toyota from Tampa,
where he had hidden a stash of explosives. The small trunk had
enough C-4 and blasting caps to destroy this car and any within
fifty feet. He was comfortable enough with the plastic explosive
that he knew it wouldn't detonate without a proper primer.

He had watched the café most of the morning and was now
parked in the lot of a grocery store named PUBLIX. He could see
the front windows to Salez's apartment, but there had been no activity whatsoever. Normally, he considered himself patient, but
he had already been here three days longer than he had intended.
He needed to get home and feed his cat. He felt the grip of the
Ruger .22 caliber pistol in his waistband. Not as showy as an explosion, but he could guarantee no kids would be killed acciden-
tally and Salez would be just as dead. As he scooted out of the
little car, he stopped and popped the trunk. He rummaged around
and pulled out a stick of C-4 and a couple of blasting caps. He
took a timer and homemade release just in case. He slipped
everything into one of the heavy plastic bags he had bought the
day he had arrived.

After making sure no one took notice of him in the rear corner of the big lot, he cut through a low row of ficus hedges and then across the street to the apartment building. One of the so-called Spanish-style houses which long ago had been cut up into individual apartments. This was an older structure with no security measures or surveillance cameras. It was the kind of place where construction workers and old people lived.

He headed to the outdoor stairway and casually trotted up the stairs. He turned to the apartment with confidence, in case anyone noticed him. None of the other three upstairs apartments showed any signs of life either. He knocked on Salez's door and stepped to the side so he wouldn't be able to see him if he looked out the window.

There was no response. Nothing at all. He tried the doorknob and it was locked, probably with a dead bolt as well. He stepped to the jalousie window next to it. The old-style glass slats were cranked out a few inches. He slipped a hand on the lowest one and pulled up. All the slats opened in unison. He looked inside and still saw no one.

"Shit," he said out loud, and made an instant decision to push on the lowest slat. It slipped back and out of the bracket easily. He did it with the next eight windows slats, letting only one actually fall, and it even bounced off a couch on the inside and didn't break. He slipped into the stuffy apartment.

The two-room apartment had some clothes on the bed and a little food in the corner kitchen cupboard. Nothing else to identify the owner. He replaced the window slats and sat on the couch. The place was warm, and had an odd, unclear odor to it. He didn't even know if Salez was coming back. He looked at the locked door and had an idea. That was why he had brought the C-4 in the first place.

He surveyed the door then examined his stick of C-4. The wooden door would splinter easily, throwing out plenty of deadly shards that would shred anyone on the other side of the door. He used a kitchen knife to cut off a few ounces of the explosive. He molded it like clay, then set the plastic explosive right at face level in a big square patch. No time for his usual artistry. His employers wanted a dead man, not a perfectly set pattern that would impress cops when they looked into the explosion. He set a homemade release next to it and tested it by opening the door a couple of times. It worked perfectly. With a little effort, he could set this baby and slip back out. When this asshole did come home, he'd get a nasty surprise.

The whole setup was similar to his job in Seattle, but he had been plenty careful there. The victim didn't live alone. Thank God, he had been able to make use of the victim's wife's vacation. He thought about the big northwestern city and wished he was there at that moment. Cooler, lots of things to do, and at least he had people to visit there. If he was allowed to visit.

Ten minutes later, he was in the rented Toyota and heading back to his hotel for a nap. He'd give it a couple of more days before he tried something else, and admitted to his employers he had fucked up the job.

7

DUARTE HAD DONE HIS BEST TO PART WITH CAREN LARSON as soon as she told him they were flying to Washington, D.C., the next day. If he was leaving, he couldn't put off checking the sports bar that Alberto Salez frequented. Besides, he was in Belle Glade anyway. He didn't think the fugitive would be at the bar, but Duarte might meet someone who knew him. It was something he couldn't ignore and still look at his father and tell him he had done a good job today.

He started to get in his Taurus with Caren at the door to her rental Chevy Lumina.

She called across the hood of her car. "I'll follow you back to West Palm. I'm not sure I know my way around out here."

He sighed and said, "I'm not going back yet."

"Where're you goin'?"

"Business."

"Can I come?" It wasn't as much a question as it sounded. He had already realized this very bright woman made things happen the way she wanted. He was starting to like her style. But now he didn't want her around in case there was trouble. On the other hand, he didn't want her getting lost out here either.

She added, "What kind of business?"

"Gonna check the lead Maria Tannza gave us about the sports bar."

"Shouldn't I come on something like that?"

He didn't answer. This wasn't a TV detective show where he had to join in polite banter. While she had shown she was bright by asking the right questions and was probably a good investigator, she was a lawyer, not a cop. She wasn't paid to get into violent situations.

She leveled her blue eyes at him. "He *is* a part of my case."

"And I let him escape."

She held her stare.

He revisited, knowing the potential risk. He had enough to feel guilty about to last him the rest of his life. Allowing something to happen to this pretty girl wouldn't help his sleep patterns.

She continued to stare.

He looked at her and said, "Okay, get in the car. We'll come back afterward for yours." He waited longer than he had expected or wanted for her to drop off her purse and lock up the new Lumina.

As she popped into his car, she said, "This is exciting."

"What?"

"Real police work."

He was silent at the comment.

"I mean, I've been working on this case, interviewing people and searching records, but not actually going to a bar to look for a dangerous felon."

"'Dangerous felon'?"

"Yeah, Salez is wanted for a felony. He sold guns. Plus, he escaped. You can charge him with that too. That's a five-year minimum."

"That should be the least of his concerns when I find him."

"Oohh. You gonna rough 'im up?" She almost squealed. "I've never gotten to see that. Street justice. Must be satisfying."

The way she said it, like it was a game, made him realize that while he was in the service and seeing the world she was in some Ivy League school drinking beer at parties. She had no experience.

He cruised through the quiet town of Belle Glade looking for the Twistee Treat's signature ice-cream cone roof. She said it was in a plaza across the street. The town didn't have much happening on a weekday night. The main industries were the state prison and the farms. Duarte guessed that working either job didn't leave a lot of energy to get out at night.

Caren said, "How do you know your way around out here?"

"We cover Belle Glade from our office."

"So you're out here on surveillance and arrests."

"Mostly checking gun stores and checking with the Belle Glade PD on things."

"Which do you like more, ATF or the army?"

He shrugged.

"You don't care?"

"It doesn't matter. I'm an ATF agent, not a soldier."

He almost passed the Twistee Treat because it was closed and dark. But the pointy cone roof drew his eye. He turned into the plaza across the deserted main road and saw eight cars parked at one end of the sprawling empty lot. He turned that way. The Belle Glade Sports Club was in the corner of the plaza. Duarte pulled past it but couldn't see inside. He checked the cars but nothing looked familiar. Besides, Salez's Mustang had been blown to bits. To be safe, he parked on the side of the plaza away from any cars. There were two piles of construction materials like boards and bricks. It looked like a renovation rather than an extension to the worn-out shopping center.

"Why didn't we park out front?"

"In case."

"In case of what?"

"In case we need to be parked here." He figured that might keep her thinking about the answer for a while. He opened the door.

"Where's your gun?" asked Caren.

He pointed to the locked glove compartment.

"Don't you wear it?"

"Not all the time."

"Why not?"

"Don't like guns."

She gave him a puzzled look.

"Besides," he added, "if I had a gun, I might not get the chance to hit someone."

She followed him in the bar, this time stayed back a little.

Duarte entered the deceptively large bar slowly, trying not to look like a cop, checking everyone out.

Ten steps inside, Caren said, "You look like a cop, checking everyone out."

He took the comment, and marched on to the bar and found a stool.

Caren pulled a stool closer to him and sat down so she was right against his side.

He looked at her without a word.

"Just trying to make it look like we're a couple."

He kept staring.

"Okay, *and* I'm a little scared."

"I don't see him," said Duarte as he scanned the room again. There were five Hispanic guys playing pool. Three rednecks throwing darts at the far end of the room and a couple watching a basketball game on a big-screen TV.

The bartender scurried around to his new customers. "What can I get you?"

Caren looked up at the bottles on the shelf over the bar. "Mich Ultra."

The bartender looked at Duarte.

"Coke."

"Straight or with a mixer?" cracked the bartender.

"Just a Coke, please."

Caren smiled. "Let me guess. You don't drink on duty."

"No, I don't, but I don't really drink anytime."

"Do you smoke?"

"Never."

"What kind of ATF agent are you if you don't drink, don't smoke and don't like guns?"

He shrugged.

"You're a tough one to figure out."

He had tuned her out when he noticed one man shooting pool, about thirty, who looked familiar. Duarte might have seen the man while watching the camp two days ago. Hispanic, he had a flat, broken nose. The man spoke loudly like he was the leader of the group. Duarte focused on the man and his friends, trying to pick up any clues as to whether they'd be willing to talk to him, or if they might even cause him some trouble. The flat-nosed guy clearly called the most attention to himself. A large man, with a thick, dark mustache, also seemed to garner respect.

Caren continued to jabber, but he didn't bother to try and enter the conversation until she said, "What? What are you looking at?"

"I'm gonna talk to those guys around the pool table. You wanna take the table next to them and we'll see what we can find out?"

Caren didn't answer, but Duarte started to move anyway.

They grabbed their drinks as the bartender set them down.

"That'll be six seventy-five."

Duarte stared at him then dug in his pocket. He flipped through the ten on the outside of his money clip and pulled a five and two ones and left them on the bar.

He grabbed two pool cues and joined her at the empty table next to the group of loud men.

It took about twenty seconds for one of the men to look at Caren and wink, then smile, revealing a rough set of teeth with gaps and cracks like an old moss-covered brick wall.

Another man, the guy with the flat nose, said, "You wanna play with us, baby?" Then he looked at Duarte for a reaction.

Caren shook her head.

Duarte heard the man make a comment in Spanish to his friends and they all laughed.

Duarte focused on racking the balls, but his eyes darted up to the men every few seconds.

Caren broke, sending one ball into a corner pocket. She tried to change positions to shoot from another angle, but a chubby man with long hair refused to move.

Caren said, "Excuse me." And got no reaction. She looked at Duarte.

He shrugged.

Instead of moving, Caren bumped the man so he had to move. This brought a roar of laughter from the group.

The fat guy said, "Your woman got to move men herself?"

Duarte ignored the angry fat man.

"You hear me? What you got to say?"

Duarte looked at the man with a flat stare. "She's not my woman."

That brought laughter too. The fat man said, "She a guy dressed up? He look pretty good if he is."

Duarte shrugged and leaned down to make a shot.

Caren came closer. "You gonna let him talk like that?"

"Apparently."

She stared at him.

Duarte said, "I'm curious. There's five of them and one of me. What would you suggest?"

"I don't know. Something."

"A gesture. Maybe a punch before I'm assailed?"

"Then let's leave."

"Nope."

"Why not?"

"You never give up real estate once it's taken."

"Huh?"

"Army saying. Basically, don't retreat."

"Whatever. I'm going to visit the ladies' room."

Duarte saw all five of the men watch Caren on her march to the restrooms. It appeared to Duarte like she enjoyed the attention and was playing it up. It didn't matter.

The younger, fit man, with the flat nose, called across to Duarte. "Hey, man. Why don't you leave her here with us? We'll get her home safe." They all chuckled.

"Her choice, not mine."

They stared at him as the tone changed. Duarte felt the friendly chatter just die away. The same man said, "What're you doin' in here, man?"

"Looking for a friend of mine."

"You got no friends here, man."

Duarte scanned the five faces that now lined up in front of him.

"Guess I'll look somewhere else."

"You act like you should check La Canberra."

"What's that?"

"Bar, over near Clewiston."

Duarte waited, then asked, "Why?"

"It's a bar for faggots. You'd fit in." They burst into laughter again.

Duarte nodded. He didn't care about gay or straight. He was a graduate of "Don't ask, don't tell," and it seemed to work. These guys had to work on better insults.

The man with the flat nose said, "Whatever you need to do, you need to leave here to do it."

Duarte lined up another shot and wondered what was keeping Caren.

Two of the men stepped forward.

Duarte turned, the pool cue loose in his right hand. He fought to suppress a smile and even tried to look intimidated.

Then the bartender barked, "That's it. You guys have caused enough shit here tonight."

The five men all turned and looked like kids that a parent just yelled at.

"Hit the road before I call the cops."

Two of them headed toward the door, the others hesitated as they focused on Duarte.

The bartender yelled: "Now."

That got them all moving. The way they filed out the door, it looked like they had been through the drill before.

The bartender said, "I'm sorry, mister. Them spics is always causing problems."

Duarte looked up and for the first time tonight felt a stab of insult. He rarely reacted to slurs, but for some reason this one bothered him.

"I'm Latin too."

The bartender looked shocked. "I'm sorry. I didn't mean nothin'. I mean, you look white, is all."

Caren came out of the bathroom and walked across the empty bar.

"Wow, where'd everyone go?"

"I scared them off."

Caren just snickered.

They shot a few more balls and finished their drinks, then headed toward the front door. Duarte looked over his shoulder at the bartender, but the old redneck couldn't meet his stare.

Caren said, "That was a dead end."

Duarte kept quiet as they rounded the corner to the car and saw the five men standing there, one of them with a two-by-four about five feet long. "Maybe not," Duarte said to Caren as he calmly kept on track for the car. Caren hung back as he threaded between the young guy with the flat nose who had insulted him and the older fat guy. He reached in his pocket for the keys. He had parked on the side of the building so maybe he could avoid a confrontation like this. He thought they wouldn't notice a non-local car over here. But now that he had tried to avoid the confrontation, he intended to do whatever was necessary to protect Caren and himself. Besides, he trained most of his life for combat and had few opportunities to use it anymore.

Flat nose said, "Where you think you're goin'?"

"Home."

"What makes you think you'll get past us?"

Now Duarte smiled a little. "Just a hunch."

Flat nose, who was now holding the two-by-four, leaned on

the long plank, resting it on the ground and letting it come up to his eyebrows.

"I think you can leave, but the girl has to stay."

Duarte thought about trying to jump in the car and grab his pistol. But then he figured that would be overkill. These morons had not sized up the enemy well. If he played his cards right and left one or two conscious, he could probably get some info out of them. His concern was Caren's reaction to his methods.

Duarte said, "So *I* can leave?"

Caren called from the edge of the plaza, "Alex, you're not serious."

"We'll see." He looked at the guy with the board. "If you answer a question or two, we might all be better off."

"What question?"

"Do you know Berto Salez?"

They all looked at each other.

"Why?"

"I need to talk to him."

"Yeah, I know him."

"Where is he?"

The guy smiled. "That's enough questions. Now you need to leave. You can pick up your girlfriend at the Motel 6 in the morning."

Duarte stayed even-toned, and said, "Nah, she better come with me." He looked up at Caren. "Let's go."

Caren hesitated.

Flat nose said, "She ain't leavin', and now neither are you." He stood with the board in front of him.

Duarte decided he had given it his best shot to leave without trouble. Now he decided he had to act, and he didn't telegraph a move. He lifted his left leg and delivered a hard side kick to the two-by-four. The force of the kick sent the upper part of the board into the man's face, splattering blood on his partner next to him. He stumbled back, his already-flat nose invisible under all the blood. Then the guy dropped to the ground.

Duarte took advantage of the momentary shock and stepped toward the next-closest man: the fat guy. He faked a low round kick to the man's knee. When the fat man lowered his hands to block it, he recocked his leg and smacked him in the head with another round kick. The fat man bounced off Duarte's Taurus and slid to the ground.

That left three. Duarte had noticed that the next loudest of the group, a thin man about fifty-five, had been tentative and hung back near Caren, away from any harm. He now blocked the man out of his head as he concentrated on the two men advancing on him from the rear of his car. He sidestepped the first man and grabbed him by the shirt. As the man spun back, Duarte launched a devastating elbow square into his face. This took the fight out of him but Duarte held on and used him as shield against the other man. Once he realized he was holding up an unconscious attacker, Duarte dropped him like a bag of coal. He faced the only man who wanted in the fight. With his partner out cold at Duarte's feet, the man hesitated, but Duarte had given all the slack he was going to give. He stepped over the man on the ground, threw a simple punch into the man's chest and, as he attempted to block it, Duarte hooked his left hand and caught the man directly on the chin. Now three men were down and motionless, and the flat-nosed guy with the two-by-four was whimpering in a pool of his own blood. Duarte looked to where the last man had been standing and didn't see him. Instead, he heard him.

"Hey, pendejo," came the man's voice.

Duarte looked toward it and saw the older man with a knife up near Caren Larson's face. He had not intended to put her in any danger. Now his fun had turned serious.

"Don't make me cut her."

Duarte said, "Okay, I agree, don't cut her."

This took the man by surprise.

Caren, to her credit, didn't look panicked, even though Duarte would bet this was the first time she had ever had a knife to her throat.

Duarte said, "Look, what do you want? The fight's over. Get lost."

The man started to ease away from Caren immediately. As he loosened his grip and she stepped away, Caren spun to face the man and threw a hard, low kick directly into his groin. He dropped the knife and vomited even as he hit the hard cement.

Caren let out a half smile, didn't say anything, then rushed to Duarte, who simply guided her toward the car. He turned to find the flat-nosed guy who had started all the shit. He squatted over him and pried his hands away from his shattered nose.

Duarte said, "Can you hear me?" He waited then shouted, "Hey, can you hear me?"

The man nodded. "Yeah, yeah, you broke my nose."

Duarte took the man's two fingers of his right hand and pulled them apart into a sickening angle. The man screamed again.

"Now I broke your fingers too." He got the man to quiet down and look at him. "You understand that I don't care, right?"

The man just kept crying.

"It's not any fun to be bullied, is it?"

The man shook his head furiously.

"You won't do it again, will you?"

"No, nooo," he cried, turning the last no into several syllables in a lilting, musical style.

"Now I need some answers."

The man stopped screaming and looked at Duarte. "To what?"

"Berto Salez. Where is he?"

"I don't know, man."

Duarte took the man's right ring finger in both hands and snapped it like a chicken bone.

The response was surprisingly subdued but obvious as he flinched, then tightened his entire body, waiting for the pain.

"What *do* you know?"

The man gasped and said, "He's scared. He told me he was in deep shit."

"What kind of shit? With the law?"

"No. Something else." He took in some air and let out a cry. "I don't know. I swear to fucking God, I don't know."

"How can I be certain?" He picked up the man's left hand.

"No, please, don't."

Duarte waited. In fact, he had no intention of hurting the man further. He didn't enjoy torture, only combat. He just needed to find out the information. If it taught the man a lesson on bullying people, that was just a bonus.

The man said, "Berto, he, he . . ."

"He what?"

"He eats breakfast at a café every morning. Eight o'clock sharp. Never misses."

"Where's the café?"

"Belvedere, just east of 95."

"Which one?"

"The Sunrise Cafe."

Duarte absently released his fingers

"Good." He looked at the other men as they started to stir. Caren looked like a kid who had just watched the movie *The Ring.* "All right. Now get your friends together. Have that nose looked at, and don't be a bully. Understand?" He gave him a smile to make it seem like this was no big deal.

The man nodded as Duarte helped him to his feet. Duarte helped the others into comfortable sitting positions on the sidewalk of the plaza and then calmly drove off with Caren in the passenger's seat.

She said, "That is way outside the guidelines of the Department of Justice."

"Did DoJ teach you to kick guys in the nuts?"

"I was defending myself; you were interrogating."

"Will anyone ever hear about it?"

She hesitated, and said, "No."

She may be a decent partner after all.

8

DUARTE WAS DRESSED AND AT HIS MOTHER'S BREAKFAST table before seven o'clock. He had a busy day and wanted to make sure she knew he'd be gone for a few days. His bags were in the trunk of his Taurus, and he had managed all this without seeing his brother, Frank.

His father read the *Palm Beach Post* local section and sipped his coffee, just like he had when Duarte was five years old.

"This a big case?" asked Cesar Duarte.

"Could be."

"You fix the problem you told me about?"

"Working on it. It's related to this case."

"Good." The older Duarte went back to his paper, reading local, sports and Accent every day, in that order. He never read the front page. That was what the *NBC Nightly News* at six-thirty every night was for.

Duarte noticed his father looking closely at the cuts on his knuckles from his scuffle in Belle Glade the night before. Those were the only marks on him.

His father looked at his knuckles, then up at Duarte, but didn't say a word. The last time his father had actually asked him about marks on his knuckles was when he was seventeen. He and Frank worked as bag boys at the Publix on Southern Boulevard. Frank had apparently told another bag boy he was going to "sue him" for some derogatory comment.

When Duarte wandered onto the loading dock and found his older brother cornered by the potential defendant and a friend, Duarte took action. He didn't care if Frank had it coming. He didn't care about the odds. Frank was his brother. Duarte put his six years of karate classes to use and then accepted being fired because it was better than having to tell his father that evening. The elder Duarte simply asked his youngest son, "Is that how you earn respect?"

This morning Duarte ate fast, throwing down the ham and eggs and a big glass of orange juice. He had called Chuck Stoddard at his house at six-fifteen and told him he needed help. Duarte had smiled at the thought of Chuck, looking like a big lump in bed, rolling to answer the phone, then having to deal with his irate wife. To his credit, Chuck had agreed to help without complaint.

Duarte stood up and cleared his place. His mother turned.

"Be careful, sweetheart."

Duarte returned her hug. "Yes, Ma."

She squeezed his long, thin body for a full five seconds.

"Ma, it's only a few days. I've been away a lot longer in the army."

"A mother has to worry."

Duarte kissed her on the head, nodded to his pop and headed out the door, relieved as he backed down the driveway that Frank had decided to sleep in a little today.

Forty minutes later, Duarte was briefing Chuck on today's mission. He had to be at the airport by four, so he figured they had some time to let things develop. If they didn't see any sign of Salez by ten, then Duarte planned to go into the café and ask a few questions. And he intended to get some answers. By chance, the Cuban café the mope had told Duarte about the night before was right near the airport in West Palm Beach. Belvedere Road between I-95 and U.S. 1 had about ten little Cuban restaurants of all types: bakeries, cafés and full-service sit-down restaurants. Duarte knew the one the mope had mentioned. The Sunrise Cafe. It catered to an early crowd, with pastries and coffee, and then a light lunch menu. Many of the shadier locals congregated there in the morning. Duarte had followed a couple of gun dealers there over the years and had heard that virtually all forms of gambling, from bets on sports to bolita, went on there.

Chuck drove and Duarte watched as they pulled into a convenience store across busy Belvedere Road. Before he had his binoculars out, Chuck said, "Isn't that bald guy . . ."

Duarte scanned the small crowd. "Yeah, it's my cousin Tony."

"The guy who owns the pawnshop, right?"

Duarte nodded.

"What's he doing here?"

"Same thing he was accused of last time, setting up gun deals."

"You don't say much about him."

"What should I do, brag? He's closer to my pop's age. He came over from Paraguay when he was twenty. About the time I was born."

"I thought pawnshops did well."

"They do, especially if you can sell high-end guns. We'll get him one day."

"You'd arrest your own cousin?"

"If he sold guns, yeah."

They sat in silence as Duarte picked up the binoculars and scanned the crowd. "I don't see Salez."

"You sure of your info? Salez may be on the run."

"Guys like Salez don't run far. He'll look for friends." Duarte thought about his interrogation of Salez's friends. "The guy swore to me he was here every day at eight sharp."

Chuck looked at him.

"What?"

"You saying this is all based on the supposition that you were able to root out the truth from those thugs?"

"What's that mean?"

"Just that, with all your skills, reading people is not top of the list."

"I went to the Reid school of interviewing."

"There's still an instinct to it."

Duarte shrugged. Chuck was right. That was his weakness. But guys that had been beaten that badly didn't usually make up stories. Not this detailed. Threatening someone with physical violence is rarely mentioned at schools like Reid.

Chuck said, "What'd ya think? Wait or go in?"

Duarte considered it. They could be on a wild-goose chase. He looked up at Chuck's round face.

"I can slip in and talk to my cousin. No one'll know."

Chuck grunted. "Yeah, he's so stand-up he'd never say anything."

Duarte ignored him as he opened the door. He crossed at the

light then came up the sidewalk to the dozen or so tables in front of the small café. The umbrellas weren't opened because the sun hadn't cleared the office building across the street yet.

Duarte nodded to the older Latin men at the first few tables. He didn't recognize anyone. These generally wouldn't be his father's friends. His father avoided anyone with a hint of a shady background. He even avoided his cousin Tony, but more because Tony's loud manner annoyed him.

Duarte came up to the table where Tony sat reading the sports page of the *Palm Beach Post.* He sat down before Tony realized he was there.

"Hey, cousin."

A smile crossed the muscular man's face. His gleaming bald head creased with lines as he smiled and said, "Well, well, well, Mr. Straight Arrow, what're you doin' here?"

"Saw you and thought I'd say hello."

"This is the first conversation in English this place has seen since the city health inspector came by."

Duarte stared at him.

"I see you haven't changed. Just like your old man. You should live a little like your brother."

"Tony, I'd love to catch up but I'm looking for someone."

"A crook?"

Duarte nodded.

"And you thought you'd treat me like a snitch, eh?"

"I thought you'd tell me the truth if you knew him."

Tony gave him a long stare, then sighed. "Okay. First of all, who're ya lookin' for?"

"A guy named Alberto Salez."

"Berto? No shit? What'd he do?"

Duarte tried to will his cousin to keep his voice down, then said, "Mainly, he escaped from me the other day. But he's got a beef from Texas on him for guns. No big deal, if I get him soon."

"Why sooner rather than later?"

"There may be someone else looking for him."

"Like a guy with short, neat dark hair."

Duarte eyed his cousin. "Why do you ask that?"

"Because that guy was by two days ago right after Berto had left."

"What'd the guy say?"

"That he needed to find Berto because he owed him some

money. We acted like a bunch of ignorant foreigners, and he left without anything he could use."

"What'd he look like?"

"Average, you know. Thirty-five, buzz cut, trim. Caucasian, but dark complexion. Sorta like you, only with shorter hair."

"I'm as Latin as you are."

"You should act it sometime."

Duarte looked at his cousin and decided he didn't have time for this old argument. "What about Salez? You know where he is?"

Tony shook his head. "He's always here by eight. Stays an hour and then goes about his business."

Duarte looked at his watch. "It's eight-forty. My guess is that he's not coming today."

Tony nodded. "They teach you that in ATF school?"

Duarte ignored him. "Any ideas?"

Tony shifted in his seat. "You're putting me in a bad spot."

Duarte just stared at his cousin.

"Okay, okay. I know he stays out in the Glades some nights at a labor camp. He thinks he can tag some teacher out there."

"Where else?" Duarte didn't think he needed to share what he did and didn't know.

"He's got an apartment off Parker and Southern. Says it's a great location to roam the city or race out to the Glades."

"Can you be more exact?"

"It's on the second floor and he can see the Publix shopping center. Just south of Southern on the west side of Parker. I gave him a ride once. That's all I can think of."

Duarte nodded and started to stand. He knew the building, not far from his parents' house.

Tony said, "Keep this real quiet, cuz."

"Do I speak out of turn?"

"Not that I ever saw."

Duarte was back on Salez's trail.

Mike Garretti first noticed the blue Ford Taurus sitting across the street from the café on Belvedere. He was sitting in a McDonald's, sipping a coffee, and reading a *USA Today* because he didn't give a damn about what was going on in Palm Beach County other than the investigation into the migrant camp bombing, which the local paper had only one story about and that was more about the grieving teacher whose kid had been killed. He really didn't want to read about that. He felt bad enough—then to see that she had voluntarily moved out there to give the little migrant kids a better life and that she was a friend to everyone and that her son was a good student and good kid only made things worse. He had studied the photo and realized she was also a damned fine-looking woman. He snorted, wondering what would happen if he hooked up with her and years later she found out he had set the bomb that killed her son. She'd be all kinds of pissed-off.

Now it was the Ford that held his attention. Occupied by a couple of men he knew had to be the cops. The chances were good that they were looking for the extremely lucky Alberto Salez too. That would make things more complicated. Unless they found him— then it might make things easier. He watched as a tall, lean man about thirty opened the passenger's door and crossed the street. He had a confident gait and appeared to know exactly where he was going. His haircut and manner almost suggested a military background, but he decided a cop might have the same characteristics.

The young man sat down with a bald guy he had seen before when he was looking for Salez. After a few minutes of conversation, the man—who had to be a cop—made strides back to his partner even faster than he had crossing the street initially.

He decided to follow the Ford just in case these cops had stumbled onto something. It only took a few minutes to realize that they had stumbled onto Salez's apartment. They parked on the street right in front of the place. He watched from his car next door as the cops assessed the building and then looked at the community mailboxes.

He realized this could be a worse disaster than the migrant camp bomb. The last thing he needed was heat from a couple of cops getting blown to bits from one of his bombs. He wasn't sure if they'd enter the apartment, but by the way that cop walked and carried himself he doubted a locked door would be much of an impediment to his investigation. He had to do something. Cops were relentless when one of their own was killed. He'd have bet that there was still infighting going on about who was stuck with the migrant bombing investigation, but this would be a different story.

He felt his blood pressure rise as the cops started up the stairs. He had to do something and it had to be fast. He had the pistol, and even thought about sending a shot near them but realized they might return fire or chase him. He took a step toward the apartment complex and considered his limited options. This could be bad.

C aren Larson sat off to the side of the large throng of mourners. Although she had had to deal with the death of her father while she was in law school at Cornell, she realized the loss of a child had to be much more traumatic. Even Caren's mother had started dating within a year after the cancer had finally taken her father. That was almost as traumatic as his death.

She could see Maria Tannza's delicate form in the midst of a group of supportive mourners. The size of the crowd and their manner told Caren that Maria was well loved. Caren had thought, at one point in her life, she would do something that made people love her. The DoJ job had meaning and was satisfying but she still felt alone in Washington much of the time. She dated occasionally and enjoyed flirting like she did with Alex Duarte, but she wondered who would stand by her if something bad happened. Her insecurity about her job had made her make it the most important thing in her life when she knew that it shouldn't be that way. Here she was at thirty-two with no significant other and no prospects. Back in college, she thought she'd be a mother by now.

She admired Maria Tannza not only for working with the migrant children out of conviction but the strength she was showing right now as the funeral for her son came to an end. Caren looked up into the bright blue Florida sky, with the sun blazing, knowing that back in Washington it was a cloudy fifty degrees. This somehow didn't seem like funeral weather. Regardless, she was in a small cemetery in the middle of West Palm Beach feeling more than a little guilty about the boy's death and the fact that he was just an innocent bystander. *Innocent* being the operative word.

She wondered what Alex Duarte was doing at that moment. She hadn't told him she was coming to the funeral. He never would've understood why. She was fairly certain he was spending his last few hours before their flight to Reagan National looking for Alberto Salez. She hoped that didn't put him in too bad of a mood for the flight. Although he wasn't particularly talkative, she definitely found him interesting. It was refreshing to meet a federal agent who wasn't constantly trying to impress you or talk you out of your pants. Maybe that was more an FBI thing. She hadn't worked much with the other Justice Department law enforcers like ATF or the DEA. But if Duarte was any indication of the other agents with the ATF, she intended to start working with them a lot more. When she was told they had found the perfect agent to work the bombing case, it never occurred to her that it might be someone outside the FBI. Now she was thankful for the change.

The crowd started to disperse and Caren walked back to her rental car. She turned her head once and seemed to lock eyes with Maria Tannza. It was enough to make Caren start to cry.

9

ALEX DUARTE PLACED A HAND ON THE FIRST THREE DOORS on the second floor of the old building. The walls had a thick coat of bland, tan paint, covering years of wear and other coats of cheap paint. Chuck Stoddard mashed his ear to the other door. For the effort, neither learned anything about the occupancy of the apartments. No TV vibration, not even a reliable throb of an air conditioner. The mailboxes and information from his cousin led Duarte to believe the apartment closest to the road was Salez's. It was good that no one else was home because he intended to enter the apartment whether someone answered or not.

He looked at Chuck, who shook his head, then brushed back his loose outer shirt that covered the SIG-Sauer 9mm on his hip. Duarte did the same for his Glock, which he almost never took from the holster. He knew it made the other guys feel better to think he'd use his gun if he had to.

They stood on either side of the door to what they hoped was Salez's apartment. Duarte rapped hard with his knuckles. They waited, with no response.

"What'd you think?" asked Chuck.

"I think we need to see if there is anything in there that might point us in the right direction."

"I think we need a warrant for that."

"Based on what, probable cause? We're not even sure this is his place."

"So we should burglarize it?"

Duarte shrugged, as if by not saying it out loud he wasn't committing a felony. He bumped the window next to the door and then jiggled the jalousie window slats. They were loose, and a quick tug opened them. He pushed the bottom one and it slipped backward in its bracket.

Duarte looked up at Chuck and said, "We may not need to break the door." Without waiting for an answer from his partner, he tried pushing the glass harder.

Chuck wrapped his hand around the door handle and shook the door lightly. "I think we could force this open pretty easy."

Duarte stopped pushing the glass and stepped in front of the door and placed both hands on the knob, prepared to give it a tremendous shove.

Alberto Salez was a little stiff as a result of sleeping outside on the grass. It was still safer than being seen. It reminded him of sleeping in the grass with his family when he was a kid. He'd been six when they crossed into Texas and his mama, papa, two older sisters and him had slept on a giant tarp one night on the Mexican side then the next night on the Texan side of the border. It was an adventure then; now it was a big pain in the ass. Or, more accurately, a pain in the back. Although he considered himself in pretty good shape for a man of forty, he had gotten used to beds. Not necessarily comfortable beds, but something between him and the ground.

He missed his family. After his father had been killed in a construction accident, he had lost his hero. It was tough for a ten-year-old to lose his father. Especially with nothing but women around the house. They had all lived in a two-room apartment near Laredo, and by the time Salez was thirteen he had learned to cross the border easily and found that he could make money doing it for the right reason. Sometimes he made more money than his mama brought in by cleaning houses in the border town. He never told her but he always had cash stashed away. By the time he was fifteen, he had had to bash a man's head in with a rock to keep him from taking the cash. That was an important lesson to young Alberto Salez. Not only had killing the man saved his precious five hundred bucks; he had found over a thousand more on the man's body. He had shoved the small man's corpse into a gully on the Mexican side of the border, and never heard another word about the incident. He didn't know if anyone had found the body or if anyone had cared. For all Salez knew, the skeleton was still bleaching under the blazing Mexican sun. But the early lesson was simple: killing solved problems. Over the years, he had found that rule to be one hundred percent accurate.

Now he stood off near the corner pump of the giant gas station off State Road 7 near several of the few remaining farms in eastern Palm Beach County. He straightened his clothes that he had slept in. The guy at the big market who had traded clothes with him had been a size too small so when the sun set, before everyone headed back to the pickup trucks that brought in the extra day laborers, Salez had secured some more comfortable but not as clean clothes. A bloodstain on the back of the shirt near the collar was the only hint as to how he had come by the simple but comfortable clothes. The field where he had left the inattentive and relatively large Guatemalan man had already been cleared, so no one would find the body for a week or two when they started to plow and plant the strawberries. He had fit nicely between two of the mounds and no one seemed to have noticed. If the man had any friends, they would probably assume he had gotten a ride in another truck.

Salez didn't care. The cops wouldn't look into a bludgeoned farmworker, just like they wouldn't look into his death if the wrong person found him before he could do something about it.

Now Salez tried hard not to look like a standard laborer. He needed a ride north. If he was lucky, a trucker might even take him a few states north. If he could get close to Virginia in the next day, he might be able to meet up with his friend before anything happened.

All he had now were the clothes and a long, thin fillet knife he had found behind the Dumpster of this place where it looked like someone scaled fish on a regular basis.

It was near midday, and he decided that if he could manage to steal a car he'd stop at his apartment first and clean up and pack a bag. It'd be a risk, but he had some cash hidden in the small bathroom and wouldn't mind his own clothes.

He thought about going out to the camp and retrieving the envelope he'd left hidden in Maria Tannza's trailer. Then, after reflecting on it, he decided that it was safer there and that he could always get it later. If he was still alive. Besides, someone at the camp might recognize him. Or worse—might blame him for Maria's son's death. That was too bad. He'd liked the kid. He never would've hurt him. Unless he had to. Finally he decided his own apartment was the best choice.

A Honda Element, driven by an attractive woman with long brown hair the same color as the car, pulled up next to the far outside pump. She looked like a thirtysomething Realtor and paid for the gas at the pump with her credit card. Salez wandered closer, since there were no other cars on this side of the store at the moment and the attendants inside didn't have a clear view. He might see a chance here.

He cleared his throat and said "Need a hand?" as he walked up to the boxy vehicle's front bumper.

The woman's head snapped up.

"Sorry, didn't mean to startle you." He made an effort to hide even the light accent he had. He didn't want her to assume he was just a farmworker.

She smiled and continued pumping gas. "Think I've got it."

"Where you headed?"

She looked up, assessing him. She was no idiot. He realized immediately he wasn't going to do this the easy way.

The woman said. "My husband is inside using the restroom."

Salez nodded. He knew she was full of shit. He had seen her drive up. Resting his hand on his hip where the handle of the fillet knife stuck up above his waistline, he stepped closer. "Hope he likes the restrooms. I just cleaned them."

The woman smiled again. "Oh, you work here."

"Yeah, my brother runs the check-cashing store and I handle the maintenance." He edged closer. "The pump should be working well now."

She looked at the dial and said, "Seems fine."

Salez stooped down and picked up a discarded paper towel and tossed it in the large garbage can. He looked at the pump too and nodded. Then he stepped right past the woman to the rear of the car. "Let me know if you need anything or if your husband is unhappy with anything inside."

She smiled and nodded, as the pump clicked off, and she re-hung the nozzle.

He walked around the other side of the Honda and acted like he was cleaning up garbage. Then he said "Uh-oh" as he stooped and looked at her front tire.

"What is it?" She hurried around the rear of the car, no longer wary of him.

Still on his haunches, he said, "Something's hanging down from under the car."

"Where?" She squatted next to him.

Now they were both out of view if someone from inside looked out. He leaned his head toward the cement and said, "Just under the door."

She leaned her head down trying to see the imaginary debris. "Where?" she asked.

He had the knife in his hand and came down in a violent arc before she even expected an answer. The thin, pointed blade entered just behind her ear and traveled up into her unprotected brain in a fraction of a second. She collapsed like someone had turned off the electricity to a light. In a way, that's what he had done. Her jaw was already slack by the time her head traveled the five inches to the ground. There was almost no blood.

He casually opened the passenger door and hefted the deadweight into the seat. Her head lolled to one side, then the other, as he fastened the seat belt around her to hold her in place. Then he just walked around the car and hopped in the driver's seat. In a minute, he was northbound on State Road 7, and would be at his apartment shortly. He wondered about where to drop off the sleepyhead next to him and decided the farther north the better.

He made a quick check of the glove compartment and saw on the vehicle's registration that the owner was Cheryl Kravitz of Palm Beach. He looked over at the corpse. "What's a nice girl like you doing off the island?" He chuckled and cranked up the CD of the Beach Boys, *California Girls,* and started to sing out loud. He knew his passenger wouldn't mind, and it was one of the few songs he knew all the words to. He disagreed with the idea that California cornered the market on pretty women. He thought Florida was better in that department. Texas wasn't bad either. But this girl next to him right now was perfect. Pretty, and definitely the quiet type. At least she was now.

In front of Salez's apartment, Duarte checked for any witnesses. He and his partner, Chuck, crowded in front of the door, gathering their weight to push it open, when he and Chuck heard a voice behind them that made Duarte release the handle and spin quickly. A tall man with short, dark hair and a dark complexion asked, "May I help you?"

Duarte stepped away from the door and automatically

reached for his identification and badge. Chuck stood surveying the man.

Duarte said, "Do you live here?"

"Who wants to know?"

Duarte held up his credential case and said, "ATF. We're looking for a man we think lives here."

The man smiled, stepped forward and said, "I'm Ed Norton, the building manager. Who're you looking for?"

"Alberto Salez."

The man smiled. "I thought so."

"Why did you think so?"

"He was the only resident who's under sixty-five."

Duarte nodded. "He did live here?"

"Right there." The man pointed at the door he was about to push off the hinges. The manager crossed between Duarte and Chuck, standing between them and the door. He smiled, and casually grabbed the lowest window slat, then forced the whole set shut. Turning to face Duarte, he said, "Mr. Salez moved a couple of weeks ago."

"Someone live there now?"

The manager nodded and said, "Yeah, since last week."

Duarte stepped away from the door toward the stairs. There was something familiar about the manager but he couldn't put his finger on it. "Did he leave any kind of forwarding address?"

"Is he in a lot of trouble?"

Duarte shrugged. "We'll see."

The man smiled and shook his head. "No, he left owing me a couple of months' rent."

Duarte nodded. That always seemed to happen with fugitives. He thanked the manager, and went back in the car with Chuck with no clear idea of where to look for the next hour or two before he had to fly to Virginia.

10

MIKE GARRETTI WAITED UNTIL THE ATF AGENTS HAD cleared out, believing his story completely, and then started removing window slats again. He chuckled at the thought that the two ATF agents didn't even recognize the name Ed Norton. They were probably too young for the *Honeymooners*. Really, he was too, but he remembered watching it with his dad in reruns. His old man, drunk enough to think Jackie Gleason was the funniest guy who ever lived. Those two ATF agents would have gone "to the moon," if he hadn't stopped them from forcing that door. He now realized that planting the bomb here was a stupid idea. Either he'd wait the rest of the day for Salez or he'd just move on to another plan. He was inside and had the C-4 packed up in a few minutes. It took a little longer to resecure the window jalousies. He wondered about the other residents of the apartment complex. This was the third time he'd been in front of the apartment and he had yet to see anyone. He risked one more visit to his Toyota to stash the explosive in the trunk with the rest of his C-4.

He opened the windows on the other side of the main room and then cranked open the front jalousies too. He didn't care if Salez might notice—it was hot and stuffy in the apartment, and he needed some fresh air.

He paced for a minute, then checked his pistol and placed it on the small end table near the couch. He sprawled out on the seventies-style couch, with its pattern of red, purple and blue stripes. Immediately his eyes closed lightly. He hadn't realized how tired he was.

* * *

Salez turned off Parker Avenue and drove past the apartment once. Nothing seemed out of place on the quiet block. Most of the residents of his apartment on the corner of the street were elderly. He occasionally saw one old lady at the mailbox. She'd always smile and say something pleasant. Finally, after he barked like a dog, she got the hint that he didn't want to have anything to do with her or any of the other old farts in the dilapidated old building. He turned the Honda Element around, making his passenger slide under her seat belt, her long hair falling across her pretty face. He parked across the street and a building down. The only car close by was a Toyota in front of the building next to his.

He looked at the dead woman and said, "Don't worry, Cheryl, I'll only be a few minutes, honey." He popped out of the Honda and crossed the street quickly, then moved up the stairs, checking his neighbors' doors to ensure no one was snooping.

As he padded toward his door, he noticed the jalousies on his front window open and paused. He never opened those windows; it let in the noise from the street and the Publix parking lot. He considered the implications of the open window and slowly started to back down the stairs. After what happened to his classic Mustang, and knowing who was probably after him, he didn't want to risk opening his door. He'd make do with the cash he'd found on his passenger and stop off I-95 for a shower and change of clothes.

In front of his apartment, he looked back up at his door. He surveyed the street and wondered if the Honda with a dead lady might attract too much heat. He knew he could hot-wire a damn Toyota, and it looked like it was in pretty good shape. He walked past it and glanced in the window. There was a map and some papers on the passenger's seat. He tried the door. Unbelievable—it was unlocked. If he took the car, he'd still have to leave the Honda somewhere else so it couldn't be traced back to him.

He went to the Honda and opened the door. He looked at the body slumped to the side. "Lady, you have any pliers or a screwdriver?" He crawled in and looked in the console. He reached past her and opened the glove compartment. Bingo. A Leatherman Surge, with every conceivable tool packed into one easy-grip, folding pliers. He left the door open, with the keys in the ignition, as he walked the few feet back to the Toyota. If he could get it started, maybe he'd take it anyway, and come back for the

Honda in a few minutes. He just wanted to be away from the apartment.

As he weighed the benefits of walking back from dumping the Honda, the passenger's window next to him in the Toyota splintered and showed a spiderweb of cracks.

He didn't even realize what had happened until he saw fucking Mike Garretti with the black handgun pointed toward him. Then he ducked when he heard the muffled puff of the silenced pistol.

"Motherfucker." he said, yanking the Toyota's door open and springing inside. Before his body had come to a stop, he had the Leatherman pliers open and across the steering column. It wasn't as pretty as most of his work, but he twisted the pliers and felt the small car's engine rattle to life. He didn't dare stick his head up; he just stomped on the gas and felt a thump but didn't look. At the corner, he dared a quick peek to his left, then hit the gas and spun south onto Parker Avenue. After a few blocks, he sat up, and then noticed the blood on his left arm. It took him a panicked moment to find the source. A bullet had passed completely through the top of his left ear.

"Shit," he said out loud. What was it with his ears?

Mike Garretti had stirred from his brief nap and felt like something was wrong. He heard footsteps and sprang up to peek out the window to see Salez as he bopped down the stairs. He watched as he entered a Honda but didn't close the door.

Garretti grabbed his Ruger .22, with the silencer built into the bull barrel, and hustled out the door and down the stairs.

He stopped when he saw Salez was out of the funny-looking Honda and at his Toyota. He didn't hesitate to raise the pistol and fire, but he had overestimated his ability with the small handgun. His real experience with firearms was mainly limited to an M-16. The shot was way off, and it gave Salez time to react and dive into the Toyota. Salez yelled his name, then was out of sight. He fired twice more and paused, thinking he had hit his target, but then, to his shock, the Toyota came to life, and he had to dive out of the way as it lurched down the street. As it was, it still hit him a glancing blow and spun him onto the pavement.

He stood and fired once more as the car turned the corner. He looked around and noticed the Honda with the open door. He limped toward it, the pain in his leg much worse than he thought it should be, and jumped into the waiting vehicle.

Inside, he froze when he realized there was a passenger. He looked at the motionless woman, then nudged her with the barrel of the pistol. No reaction. He set the pistol in his lap and checked the woman's pulse in her neck.

"Bastard," he said out loud. That son of a bitch was a menace.

He slammed the door and hit the gas, following the course Salez had taken. He punched the accelerator and was surprised at the speed of the little sport-utility. He looked over at the dead woman and wondered how Salez had killed her. Up ahead, in the slowing traffic, he caught a glimpse of his Toyota shifting lanes. The Honda had more guts, and maybe that asshole didn't know he was being followed. He swerved around a slow Buick and then back into the lane. Salez was stuck behind a van and a school bus next to it.

He hated the idea of shooting near a school bus with kids. He backed off, hoping Salez hadn't noticed him.

The bus turned, and Salez cut into the lane, although now he wasn't driving as fast.

Garretti, in the Honda, followed Salez as he turned west on a road named Forest Hill, then northbound on I-95. Maybe this could work out. The right shot on the interstate and all his problems could be over. If he could cause a crash, he'd act like he was trying to help, and make sure he recovered all the C-4 he had stashed in the trunk.

He followed the Toyota for a mile, from five or six cars back. He occasionally got a glimpse of Salez moving his hands like he was scratching the side of his head.

Near the airport exit, in lighter traffic, he started to ease the Honda up. He moved to the right so he could shoot from his open window and he'd be on Salez's blind side. In the light traffic, he held his hand inside the Honda so that when he fired no one would be able to tell why Salez crashed. He pulled to within a car's length, then saw Salez look up in the mirror as he started to move into the same lane. Then he looked over his shoulder, and it was clear the asshole had spotted the Honda after him.

Garretti hit the gas in the Honda and closed on Salez, who swung the Toyota to the left away from him. Then Salez sped up and intentionally clipped the front of a minivan.

As the van started to swerve, then sway, Garretti could see

there were kids in the van. He slowed the Honda to give the driver of the van a chance to get the vehicle under control, but it was too late. He watched as it veered hard, then flipped and tumbled right in front of him. He hit the brakes hard, trying to avoid smashing the vehicle, where he could see a little girl being tossed around on the inside. The van continued to tumble until a truck in the far right lane struck it and sent it down the sloping grassy hill off the highway.

Garretti yanked on the wheel of the Honda and brought it to a stop on the shoulder of the road within a hundred feet of the wrecked van. He was out of the Honda and down the embankment before he even thought of Salez. He glanced over his shoulder to see his former Toyota disappear onto an overpass. Garretti turned again, and was still the first person to the crumpled van. He fell to his knees next to the upside-down van.

He couldn't help but breathe a big sigh of relief when he saw the little girl, a younger boy and the mother all crying but apparently not seriously harmed.

He forced open the damaged passenger's door. "It'll be all right. Are you hurt?" he said in a loud voice, like he'd been trained.

The sobbing woman said, "I don't think so."

"Then just relax and I'll get you out." He held his hand out for the little girl with blond hair. Even as she took it, he thought about how to get the dead woman in the Honda out of the area. Salez had really pissed him off now.

11

ALEX DUARTE SAT BY THE WINDOW OF THE DELTA DC-10 on its flight from the West Palm Beach International Airport to Reagan National in Washington, D.C. He had barely made the flight due to an accident on the interstate that had tied up traffic for miles. He had driven past it, and could see a Honda Element to one side but nothing else. Now, sitting next to him, the usually talkative Caren Larson sprawled in the seat, her mouth open and snoring. He thought it might be the result of a small orange pill she had taken just before they boarded the plane. He hadn't asked her what the pill was. It was none of his business. He liked to fly. During his days in the service, he had flown across the Atlantic six times. In a plane, you had to relax. There weren't a lot of options. He knew there was a chance they might fly on to Seattle to the site of the first bombing, which looked related. Now he reviewed report after report of the Virginia bombing, which occurred near Fredericksburg about a month ago. The tram that was used to shuttle workers between an amusement park and an offsite employee parking lot had been destroyed by a pack of C-4 placed under the door to the eight-seat vehicle. The blast had shredded the passenger compartment and instantly killed not only the three workers but the driver as well. It would be a while before the ATF lab could say if it was the same batch of C-4 used in the migrant camp blast. The markers put in by the manufacturers might open up a whole new line of investigation. So far all he knew was that the C-4 used in the Seattle blast was not from the same manufacturer as the C-4 used in the Virginia blast. The manufacturers were different, but both had large contracts with the military.

Duarte studied three photographs, which Caren had provided.

The crime scene photos showed human-sized hunks of flesh that Duarte knew had been people in the open interior of the charred tram. The photos showed the carnage, but it didn't bother him. He had seen worse. Hell, he had *caused* worse. The photos reminded him of Bosnia, and, as always, that brought up memories of his mistake in using too much explosive to keep three Serb tanks from crossing the Drina River on the border of Serbia and Bosnia.

Duarte blinked a couple of times, and then thought of Hector Tannza's smiling face in a photo he had seen at Maria's trailer. He hoped the young woman would recover from the loss of her son but doubted any sane person ever completely recovered from something like that. Family was family. He thought about all that young Hector would miss out on in life.

Caren stirred next to him as her head lolled to the side, striking his shoulder.

The thick file of reports on the Fredericksburg bombing included profiles on the three dead workers. No criminal history, nothing to point to being a victim of violence. They weren't involved in drugs, didn't live in a high-crime area and didn't have occupations that put them in conflict with people. That made the chances of them dying violently remote. A small labor union had just organized in the park, and two of the three dead workers had helped organize it. According to the interviews with others, the unionization had not caused any obvious problem and no protests. Most of the workers joined, but not all. It seemed like a lot of work to scare a small union. Duarte considered the other available info as they started their descent into northern Virginia airspace. This was a new type of investigation for him. If it didn't directly involve a gun or some bush-league explosive device, his experience was limited. He hated to admit that this investigation caused some level of excitement in him. He thought of his potential for advancement, but knew that the look on Maria Tannza's pretty face during his brief meeting also motivated him. Her son, Hector, deserved the effort. Maybe, somewhere in his heart, he thought that by solving this case and bringing the bomber in he might find a way to fall asleep at night and not question his actions in the past.

Mike Garretti pushed the little Honda Element up past eighty-five miles an hour as soon as he crossed the border from

Georgia to South Carolina. He knew where that heartless, brainless son of a bitch was heading. An imbecile would have figured it out.

He said out loud, "He doesn't know about his buddy in Virginia and he's gonna warn him." He looked over at the woman who occupied the Element when he had taken it. At first, he hadn't known where to dump her. Then he worried about the cops looking for the car if they found the body. No one had noticed her at the accident scene near the West Palm Beach airport. He had to scoot before others started calling him a hero, like the lady he had rescued. He drove north on I-95, stopped to make a few phone calls, got some info he might be able to use and kept heading north on the highway. Somewhere around Jacksonville, after he had grown accustomed to her attractive, if graying, face, he realized she was pretty good company. Like a lot of guys in his position, he had gone without female contact many times for long periods. This was nice, even if she wasn't as responsive as he'd like her to be. That fucker Salez had killed her, and he bet the asshole had just met her. He probably didn't know a thing about her.

"I'll find him at the park. You can bet on it." He pushed the whining engine a little harder, and didn't worry that she didn't answer him.

As he made his way through Reagan National, he realized he was following Caren in the same way she had followed him in Florida. She had a clear confidence, as she navigated the crowd to baggage claim, talking over her shoulder like he was a personal assistant.

"First thing in the morning, we'll stop by the office on Pennsylvania Avenue and talk to my boss."

"Why do I need to talk to your boss? Can't you brief him while I head to the site of the bombing and get started on interviewing witnesses?"

"You don't want to meet a deputy attorney general of the United States?"

He shrugged. He didn't want to meet the actual attorney general, if he didn't have to.

"You'd like him. He has a similar background."

"He was in the service?"

She hesitated. "I don't think so."

"He was a cop?"

"No."

"What is similar about our background?"

"He's a first generation Latin American too."

"That's it?"

"I thought it would interest you."

The only things that interested him now were a shower, food—even if it wasn't his ma's cooking—and a chance to lie flat and pretend he would fail into a deep sleep.

Caren's silence indicated he'd make his goal.

He rolled in the crisp bed sheets of room 1701 of a Marriott on the outskirts of Washington. Caren had dropped him off on the way from the airport and said she'd pick him up at eight sharp. That gave him three hours to kill until she arrived. He stretched his long legs in the bed, then rolled onto the carpet and stretched tall, feeling his back crack as he did. With a steady, deep breath, he worked through some more stretches, and held a few balance poses, until a light sheen of perspiration formed across his body. His loose, army-issue shorts gave him plenty of room to move as he settled into a near split. After a few minutes of easy punches and kicks, he dropped for a quick thirty push-ups, then crunches. Then he picked up the intensity. Hard punches and snapping kicks until, nearly an hour later, he felt as if he'd practiced enough for the day. He switched on the TV and caught the opening of the *Today* show, as he finished with a twenty-minute set of stretching. A commercial for a new James Bond film came on and he smiled. He liked the fact that Bond could fight with perfect martial technique and shoot his PPK with super accuracy and never had to practice either. Duarte practiced, and then analyzed his practice, until he knew he could do his best when he had to fight or shoot, even though he preferred not to use a handgun. It was not an easy lifestyle.

At ten minutes to eight, he was in front of the hotel waiting for Caren. Under his light windbreaker, he had his Glock in a leather hip holster. He had an odd feeling about this case he couldn't pinpoint. He often doubted his instincts because he had proven to lack some skill in interviewing and reading people. He was working on overcoming this weakness. He knew some cops

were natural interviewers and could read anyone like a prover-
bial book. This was a skill Duarte had yet to develop. Adding to
his discomfort was his feeling that he was out of his element so
far from South Florida. The brisk breeze and his warm misty
breath was a novelty for him. He had gone through Fort Leonard
Wood in Missouri in the spring and summer and really had never
seen snow until he was deployed to the Balkans. As a combat engineer with a specialized skill, he had never needed to drive himself through the ice and snow. And even though it was too warm
for either, he didn't mind that Caren Larson would be doing
most the driving. He saw her coming down the block in the blue
Department of Justice Ford Taurus, just like his issued car.

"You look eager," she said as he slipped into the clean, class-
less car.

"Ready to get started."

"Well, hotshot, it'll have to wait until we meet with the deputy
AG."

"I thought I could go out to the scene while you briefed him."
He tried the ploy again.

"He thought otherwise. He wants to meet you too. He's very
interested in this case."

Duarte looked out the window without speaking. This was
typical administrative bullshit.

Caren saw the look on his face. "Relax, he's a brilliant man,
you might even learn something."

He considered what his father thought about politicians and
decided not to voice what he believed he could learn.

She said, "We'll be near the ATF headquarters. We can visit,
if you'd like."

"No time. We have work to do. I'll see headquarters soon
enough." He paused, and added, "As a supervisor."

The entrance and security of the main building for the Department of Justice impressed Duarte. Not only was the entrance
awe inspiring; the uniformed security people were thorough,
professional and efficient. His ID was verified in a matter of
moments, and Caren entered with her issued pass. The suite of
offices for the deputy AG on the fourth floor was nearly as impressive. A separate receptionist announced their arrival, flashing Caren a look of superiority while she made them stand there.

The fiftysomething woman looked through wide, thick-rimmed glasses, and gave the impression of years of intimidating young attorneys. Caren stood her ground but clearly wasn't about to buck the system. They were soon motioned on.

As they approached the next set of doors, Duarte heard someone call out, "Alex Duarte. I heard you were coming."

He turned to see a tall man, about thirty-five, in a sharp business suit. His hair looked as if he had placed each strand strategically with a pair of tweezers. His toothy smile showed no flaws.

"Hey, Colgan," was Duarte's only reaction.

"I heard you were on your way, pardner."

"What's with the drawl? Thought you were from Rhode Island?"

"Delaware."

"Whatever. You didn't have that accent when you left Florida."

"You just sort've develop these things around here." He turned to Caren, who was just listening to the encounter. "I knew this hombre when I worked in the FBI office in West Palm Beach. I used to call him Ricky Ricardo." He let out a booming laugh.

Duarte said, "As I recall, you only did it once."

This caught Colgan short, as he rubbed a scar on his chin and seemed to reflect on the incident that had occurred soon after Duarte had arrived in the West Palm Beach ATF office.

Duarte said, "What are you doing over here? I thought the FBI building was a few blocks away?"

"I'm assigned to the AG. I answer directly to Bob."

"Bob?"

Caren cut in, "Deputy Attorney General Roberto Morales."

Duarte nodded. "What do you do for him?"

The taller man smiled. "Whatever is needed."

Duarte shrugged and started to move past the taller FBI agent.

Colgan stepped in front of him. "Sorry, amigo. You gotta give up your phone."

"My what?"

"Your cell phone."

"Why?"

"The man doesn't like to have cell phones in his office."

"But I can be armed?"

Colgan smiled. "He's a Republican. He likes guns."

Duarte looked over to Caren, who was retrieving her phone as well.

Colgan said, "Don't worry, the secretary will have it for you on your way out."

Duarte reached past his gun, enjoying the look on Colgan's face as he reached farther back for his Nextel. "Here you go."

"Gracias, amigo." The FBI man flipped the phone into the air, smiling at the ATF agent.

Duarte just said, "See ya around," then turned and headed toward the next set of doors they needed to enter.

Caren stepped right in with him. "You have a problem with Colgan?"

"Not especially."

"You just sort've walked away."

"I was done talking to him."

"I thought he was a friend of yours."

"Why?"

"Because you worked together in West Palm Beach."

"We never worked together. He's with the Bureau. I was too busy to hang out and gossip. Just like now, we've got too much to do to give him time to try to impress me with whatever bullshit secret job he has."

She smiled at the comment and said, "I see what you mean."

Another assistant, this one a tall, attractive woman, met them in a small conference room outside a door that had a sign reading ROBERTO MORALES, DEPUTY ATTORNEY GENERAL.

She extended an elegant hand with polished nails to match her perfect lips. "Good morning, Agent Duarte, I'm Barbara Gould." She had the handshake of a professional. She gave the slightest of nods to Caren, as she kept her brown eyes on Duarte.

"Nice to meet you." She held his hand, making him a little uncomfortable.

"The deputy attorney general has been delayed. He insists that you wait in his office."

Duarte asked, "How long?"

The woman looked shocked, like no one had ever dared ask about a superior's schedule. She hesitated; then, looking at Duarte's dark, focused eyes, she said, "Maybe ten o'clock."

Duarte turned to Caren. "That's out of line. I have work to do. I'll rent a car and head out to the amusement park."

The assistant said, "That's not a good idea, Mr. Duarte. Mr.

Morales expects you as well. Besides, I'm sure I could make you comfortable."

Caren cleared her throat and said, "We'll be fine, Barbara." She turned to Duarte and said, "If Bob is expecting you, that's as good as a direct order, soldier." She smiled, but it didn't soften his mood.

Alberto Salez had slept in a little motel in southern Virginia the night before. He had not been able to reach his friend by phone, and knew the only other thing for him to do was drive up and meet him near his apartment. More than just warning him about the chance that he could be blown into little chunks, Salez needed an ally, and good old Don would be the perfect one. Big and smart were the first things that came to his mind when he thought about his friend. He may have packed on a few extra pounds since the time they all worked together in Texas, but he could be a handful if he was provoked.

He drove carefully in the Toyota he had stolen on the spur of the moment. It drove fine; he had patched the steering column back together and could start it with either a screwdriver or an extra key, if only he'd go and have it made. The passenger's window had the .22 bullet hole in it, but he kept it rolled down and no one noticed. He had the cash from the nice dead lady in the Honda, so it didn't matter what he was driving. The vehicle switch with Garretti also eliminated the problem of having to dispose of the woman's body. Now Garretti would be stuck doing it, if he ever got away from the cops at the scene of the accident.

His friend's apartment was easy to find, but he got no answer. It was a wide complex, with only two apartments each per tiny building. His next-door neighbor didn't answer either. He had another shot. He'd try the amusement park where Don Munroe worked. At least he'd be safe there. No one would think to look for him at a big amusement park.

12

ALEX DUARTE PACED AND CHECKED HIS WATCH, THEN HE'D look through the bay window, check his watch, then pace some more. He could endure anything—cold, hunger, exhaustion. He had proven this to himself time and again, but waiting and wasting time affected him like a dangerous drug. He felt his stomach rumble, yet if he was on his way to doing something constructive he wouldn't have dreamed of stopping to eat. It was now almost one in the afternoon, and the lovely assistant to the deputy attorney general had told them to sit tight every twenty minutes since ten o'clock, when Duarte started getting really anxious.

Caren took this administrative limbo in stride, and spent the time reviewing some documents. She looked at Duarte and chuckled.

"What's so funny?" asked Duarte.

"You are so clueless sometimes."

"About what?"

"Ms. Barbara Gould."

"What about her?"

"She wouldn't check on me if I was sitting here alone."

"Do you ever give her a reason to check on you?"

"You're saying if I was nice to her, she'd be nice to me?"

"Couldn't hurt. She seems nice."

"She's in here because you are an attractive man. That's the only reason."

He looked at her, then saved his breath.

Caren said, "I mean, really. Where did you learn to deal with women?"

"You make it sound like I had to attend some class."

"No, but we all pick up hints and clues. Experience should have taught you something."

"When do you think I got that experience? When I was seventeen and working at Publix, going to school, studying karate and helping my family? Or would it have been my lovely stay at Fort Leonard Wood? Maybe I should've been able to meet girls while I was deployed in Croatia? Everyone didn't party in college."

Caren held up her hands. "Whoa, I didn't mean to upset you. It just seems like a good-looking guy like you would've learned to be astute about women."

He relaxed as he realized he might be a little sensitive about his lack of experience with women. He kept expecting his love life to pick up, but he was uncomfortable around most women until he got to know them, and that didn't happen when you were uncomfortable around them.

Caren said, "I was just commenting that, in my opinion, Barbara was flirting with you."

"Then it doesn't help our situation. We're still stranded in here, wasting time."

"That's all you think about, work and wasting time?"

"This doesn't bother you?" asked Duarte.

"What?"

"The waiting."

"Part of the job. I thought you federal agent types always say, 'All counts toward retirement.' "

"That's the FBI. We say, 'Let's arrest people.' How can I do that sitting in this dickhead's office?"

"Whoa there, cowboy. Technically, this 'dickhead' outranks us both. I know ATF is new to the Department of Justice, but I bet you still had to follow orders when you were part of the Treasury Department."

Duarte stared at her. He hated when people used logic to make a decent point. It wasn't her fault they were waiting. But he still sensed a personal defense of this deputy to the attorney general. For the first time, he thought he might have felt a pang of jealousy that Caren was interested in another man. He didn't know why. They hardly knew each other, and seemed to just barely tolerate one another. But the idea of her starstruck by

another man bothered him. He had to admit it to himself, but he
knew he'd never admit it to another human being.

M ike Garretti pulled into the service lot for the Classics Land
Park of Fun near Fredericksburg, Virginia. It was a big park
for such a stupid name. He had cruised the nearly empty main
lot and decided that Thursday wasn't a big amusement park day.
He had figured that Salez, knowing he was wanted and not
knowing who else wanted him dead, would avoid airports and
train stations. Garretti guessed he'd still be driving the Toyota
the asshole had stolen from him in Florida. With any luck, he
hadn't discovered the stash of C-4. Not that Garretti couldn't get
more. He just didn't want Salez to try something stupid with it
and hurt innocent people. Garretti couldn't help but think about
the kid who had died by accident in the Florida bomb he had set
to shut up Salez.

If he had analyzed his information correctly, Salez would
drive to this rear lot to look for his buddy. If he had been here already, someone inside would remember and probably tell Garretti, especially if he acted like a cop or some other official. If
you said the right thing with the right attitude, people rarely
asked to see ID. He had been told he'd be safe at the park until
early afternoon. The last thing he needed was to run into cops
working the case. It was already later than he had meant to be at
the park, but he was counting on another hour-or-two window.

He pulled into a spot near the rear of the business lot. The
Honda fit right in with all the other modest, affordable cars fa-
vored by the people who had to man the ticket booths and dole
out the expensive food that tasted like shit—except the damned
smoked turkey legs. Whoever came up with that business ploy
of getting rid of useless turkey legs for five dollars a pop deserved the fucking Nobel business prize, as far as he was concerned.

"I'll leave the air on," he said to his silent female passenger.
He had gotten in the habit of leaving the car running with the air
on for her over the past twenty-five hours. The smell had been
steadily growing, but since he had been next to her the whole
time he hardly noticed. It was like watching kids grow. You don't
notice it day to day, but then all at once they're grown. He liked
his polite and quiet friend, and hoped she wouldn't force him to

dump her soon. He hoped the cool air would keep her fresh a little while longer. Besides, no one would bother the car because it looked like there was someone inside.

He headed toward the office, straightening his clothes so he'd look professional.

The door opened, and the tall, good-looking assistant, Barbara Gould, stood like she was announcing royalty.

Duarte stood up out of habit and lessons taught by his father when Deputy Attorney General Roberto Morales walked through the main office door, in close consultation with three aides. Then the tall, handsome man in the expensive suit with a red ribbon strategically placed on his lapel came into the office, with Tom Colgan on his heels. He greeted Caren with a big smile.

"What has my bulldog found for me?" He had a strong Texas drawl, and his smile felt like a flashlight in Duarte's eyes. Colgan stood to the side, almost like a bodyguard.

Caren blushed at the comment. But before she could answer, Morales turned toward Duarte and said, "This must be ATF Special Agent Alex Duarte." He held out his hand and grasped Duarte's, then pumped it exactly three times. He leaned in closer and said, "You gonna catch this hombre for us, Agent Duarte?"

Duarte kept his eyes steady and nodded. Now he understood one thing at least: Colgan had taken on this guy's accent.

Morales turned back to Caren and said, "I know you're gonna break this thing wide open. Tell me what you've got."

After explaining how she shouldn't get all the credit, she said, "We feel we can connect the bombings to labor organization."

Before Duarte could deny the comment, Colgan said, "I told you that was a good theory."

Morales said, "So you guys will be able to handle it?"

Caren nodded her head hard enough to rattle her teeth.

"Good, good. One less thing for me to worry about." He checked his watch. "Holy frijole, it's after one-thirty, and I have a meeting with the big guy at two-fifteen."

Caren gasped. "The president?"

"The man himself. You'll get a chance to meet him soon. Promise." He walked behind his wide, orderly desk and said, "What'd you got for me?"

Caren stepped up and briefed him on the Florida bombing, Salez at large, without mentioning exactly what happened, and how they planned to look into the amusement park explosion this afternoon. It took less than two minutes. The whole time, Morales studied papers on his desk or searched for something in a drawer. Occasionally, he mumbled "Good" or "Uh-huh."

Then the deputy attorney general looked up at Duarte. "You see, Agent Duarte, having worked in the business world for so long, I have a feel for labor issues—on both sides. That's why I'm so interested. We can't let some dangerous group intimidate people from doing what they think is right. As a fellow Latin, you must feel the same anger I do at the blast in Florida."

Duarte nodded. "Yes, sir. But I'm not in favor of any blast that kills people no matter who the victims are."

"Well said, well said. I've worked as legal counsel to half a dozen corporations in Texas, from a baseball team to a power company, and one thing I've learned is that all labor issues are sensitive. Violence only magnifies the difficulties in dealing with them."

Duarte asked, "Where in Texas are you from, sir?"

Morales chuckled. "Hartford."

Duarte didn't want to admit he had no idea where Hartford, Texas, was. He kept his usual silence.

Morales offered. "Connecticut. My parents were born there too. I just sort've let this drawl seep in in the years I worked there. Besides, nobody gets elected with a northeastern accent anymore, and not many work in this administration without some strong identification to Texas. Being a Hispanic helped, but once the president learned he spoke more Spanish than me I knew I had to lay on the drawl." He laughed, like the story didn't confirm Duarte's perception that he was a dickhead.

Garretti sat at a table under the outdoor cover of one of the two restaurants in the park. Slapping at a horsefly or some other stinging bug, he thought how Virginia would be nicer if it didn't have so many bugs and wasn't so close to Washington, D.C. He sipped his Diet Coke, and got an unobstructed view of every person in the park. Mostly groups of school kids with a chaperone or two. A few teenaged couples holding hands, the boys wishing for much more. He noticed a family with four kids, the father looking haggard and in need of a beer. Maybe his own father hadn't been so bad. He'd taken him and his sisters to a few parks when they were kids. When he was sober, he was an okay guy, but when he'd had a few too many Pabst Blue Ribbons, he was a major ball breaker. Now Garretti believed his dad toughening him up helped. He found that he always worked hard and did his best, he was persistent and, as his visit to this shitty park proved, willing to correct his own mistakes. He thought the army had something to do with that.

After gazing too long at a young mother with two little girls, he let his eyes drift and was shocked to see Alberto Salez staring directly at him from the entrance to the Moby-Dick roller coaster.

"Shit," he said out loud. He had had a strong element of surprise on his side. Now it was lost. How had he been so inattentive to let this greasy asshole get the drop on him?

Salez was motionless as he stared at Garretti. The look on his face said it all.

Garretti smiled and motioned him over to the table, hoping he'd fall for the simple gesture.

Salez moved forward like he would join his pursuer, then hesitated. His dark, clever eyes shifted from side to side, looking for accomplices or traps.

Garretti held up his hands to show he had no weapon. He let a friendly smile cross his lips.

Salez cut through the thin crowd and then eased onto the restaurant's patio. He stopped in front of Garretti, who remained seated on the hard seat bolted to the table.

"Take a break. You look whipped," said Garretti, extending his hand to the empty seat across from him. Then he added, "I won't bite."

Salez sat down, keeping his eyes on the taller man the whole time. Once he was settled, he just said, "How?"

Garretti smiled. "How do you think? I knew you'd come for Don."

"I already heard I'm too late."

"How'd you hear?"

"Janitor. Told him I was an old army pal. He knew all about the explosion. Told me the business office might have some more details. Everyone knew but me."

"You would've too if you read a paper once in a while."

Salez just sunk. "You're still working for them dickheads?"

"Obviously."

"So there's no way to convince you that I'll keep my mouth shut?"

"Only one way to be certain."

"You'd do that to a buddy?"

"Berto, we worked together once; we were never buddies. But to answer your question, yes, I would do it to a buddy. I already did."

"Tserick?"

Garretti just nodded.

"What about the boy?"

"He's fine. Lives with his mom."

Salez stared silently, like he was formulating a plan. Finally he said, "I got a file, you know. If something happens to me, it'll get released."

Garretti read Salez's face. "What kind of file?"

"One with everything. Dates, times, money. Even a few photos I have of all of us together."

Garretti smiled. "You are so full of shit, I don't know why you ever worked with us in the first place."

"You know I'm tellin' the truth. Es verdad, and you are fucked."

Garretti felt a flash of anger at the thought of this selfish bastard keeping records after all the dirty shit he had done trying to stay ahead of the cops and him. "I'll risk it," he said as his hand slipped under his shirt to reach for his Ruger .22.

Salez sprang up, then gripped his own seat bolted to the table and flipped the whole thing over, sending Garretti sprawling onto the ground. He started to run toward the front entrance, and Garretti fired a round from the silenced pistol. No one really noticed except Salez, who had been expecting it. And hearing the puff from the gun and then the bullet ping off a nearby garbage can spooked him in the other direction.

By now, Garretti was up and pursuing his prey at a fast walk, trying not to draw attention to himself. Salez cut left and darted down an access area where there were no customers at all. Then he realized Salez was headed toward the administrative offices. Garretti picked up his pace to an all-out run, once he was clear of the crowds. He pushed himself, feeling his heart pound in his chest as he zeroed in on the door Salez had just shot through. By chance, he had chosen the business office.

Entering the door five seconds later, he immediately noticed the office staff was in a stir. The woman he had spoken to earlier shouted to him: "The man you wanted just ran out the back."

Garretti didn't hesitate; he raced to the rear door and darted into the parking lot in time to see the Honda pulling out of the lot. He saw his passenger and confidante lean from one side to the other as he took the corner quickly. Garretti slowed then stood and stared as the Honda pulled out of the lot toward the main entrance. He realized that Salez had taken the running vehicle and probably hadn't realized who was in the car until it was too late.

He wandered into the office and calmed the staff down, ensuring they wouldn't call the police. He wondered how he would get to a hotel for some needed rest then remembered he had a key to the Toyota if Salez had been kind enough to bring the car to him. He headed out the front gate toward the main parking lot. There were only about five rows of cars to go with the twenty buses. It only took a minute to find the Toyota in the last row. He used his spare key to open the trunk.

"Jackpot," he said as he found his stash of C-4 untouched. He sat in the car a few minutes and looked at his options. Then he checked his watch and realized it was after three o'clock. "Shit," he said and pulled around to the exit, which passed by the main gate. Then he saw how close he had cut it. Standing on the curb was the ATF agent from Florida. They looked at each other briefly, but he knew there was no way the ATF agent would connect where he had seen him. It was too far away and too short a view. Garretti consciously kept from hitting the gas and drove casually out of the park. Now he had to use some help to find this asshole or move on to the next target. Either way, he was gonna be busy for a while.

Caren Larson still felt the tingle at the words of encouragement from her boss, the deputy attorney general. A man who briefed the president. She knew that some of what she was doing was for show, and that the labor issues involved in the case might not be as vital as "Bob" Morales made out to others, but she was a key figure in an obviously well-watched case in the department. She wished that Alex Duarte could gain some enthusiasm for the case. She still wasn't sure if it was his natural reserve or something else that kept him so calm about his work. For God's sake, he had just met one of the big players in government and he hadn't said a word about it the entire time they had been in the car. In fact, the only comments he had made had been questions about certain buildings, and where was the fastest possible place to eat. They had settled on a drive-thru Burger King. His serenity would be her undoing.

She had thought he might be angry at her about her comments earlier concerning his experience with women. Now she realized he was just naturally quiet. She found his apparent lack of experience with women refreshing and cute. He didn't realize his effect on women, and that made him even more attractive.

Since arriving in Washington, Caren had gone out on a number of dates, but every Thursday night when she called her mom she couldn't honestly say she was dating anyone special. Last year, at Thanksgiving, after her sister and nieces, cousins, aunt, uncles and assorted friends had left the house, her mom sat her down and told her that she accepted her and loved her no matter what her sexual preference was. No matter what she said, she couldn't convince her mom she wasn't a lesbian. She was just picky about who she wanted to get serious with. She didn't feel like just marking time with some hotshot DEA agent or a reporter unless she had genuine feelings for him. She liked to flirt but that was just her way of weeding out the guys she wouldn't have a long-term interest in. The problem with her theory was that the only guys she was interested in were the guys who didn't flirt back. That usually meant they weren't interested. That led her back to concentrating on her job and spending less time socializing. And more time trying to convince her mom she was straight.

After twenty or so miles, Duarte said, "Wish we had time to visit Manassas."

"Why?"

"It's a great Civil War battlefield. I got to visit once when I was in the service."

"What's so great about it?"

"Just to see the ground that they fought on, and it helps me visualize the accounts that I read."

"You certainly aren't excited about much but I can tell you love your history."

He nodded like a kid who'd been caught doing something wrong. "It is interesting." He quieted down as the trip progressed.

As they approached the entrance to Classics Land amusement park, he seemed to perk up and take in all of the surroundings.

He asked, "What'd you think when you saw this crime scene?"

"What'd you mean?"

"Did the local cops do a good job containing it? The reports looked good."

"Oh, I see what you mean. I didn't come out."

"Was it before you were on the case?"

"It was the start of the case, even though it was the second bombing. Mr. Morales started getting calls to start an investigation in case it was a serial bomber. He made the connection to labor organization, and assigned me personally."

Duarte nodded, looking out at the vast, nearly empty parking lot.

They parked off to the side, where a security guard sat at a shaded podium. He radioed ahead so they could cut through the park to the administration and business building. Caren liked how Duarte waited for her and opened doors without thinking. He was just polite; there was really no other way to describe it. He even stood in the road, like he would shield her from a car, if necessary, as she came up to the wide sidewalk. He stopped and turned to look at a Toyota pulling out of the lot.

Caren asked, "What is it?"

He didn't turn his head but said, "I dunno. Something about that guy was familiar. Did you see him? Dark hair, dark-skinned, like a Latin maybe."

She shook her head and headed toward the gate. They walked back to the administration building together, and he held the door open once again. She smiled, and thought, I wish he seemed more interested in me. I don't want to go on the offensive here. But he was all business, finding the right person to talk to.

After finding a tall, leggy manager named Lisa Simpson—like the cartoon character only stunningly good-looking, to the point that even Caren admitted to slight feelings of envy—they sat down in her busy, small office.

Lisa said, "Sorry for the confusion; we just had a little incident with the Immigration Service and a fugitive." Her perfect smile and blue eyes were nearly mesmerizing.

Caren asked about the immigration activity, but Duarte seemed anxious to get to the point. He said, "Did you know the people killed in the blast?"

"Oh yes, I handle payroll too, so eventually I meet everyone."

"Can we see their files?"

She stood immediately. "The police have the originals, but I have copies." After a quick search through a standing cabinet, she handed the three files to Caren.

"I thought there were four victims."

The beautiful manager said, "Three employees, and the tram driver who worked here at the park but was employed by McKeague Transportation. On busy days, the employees park in a lot about two miles away. We provide transportation for them."

Alex nodded and took a few notes, so Caren decided to ask a good question as much to impress Duarte as to find the answer. "Were the victims helping to organize the union?"

The manager looked confused, and said, "I don't know. I mean, we didn't care if they had a union or not. I guess they could've been involved."

Duarte said, "That was the only violent incident?"

"I guess. I mean, I didn't think it had anything to do with the union myself. Even the local cops didn't. It was only the papers, and some guy from Washington kept saying it."

Caren knew it was time to wrap this up and move on per instructions from the boss. Duarte seemed willing to move to the crime scene too. As usual, he stood before her and then opened the door as he turned and thanked the manager. Caren saw him look at the beautiful manager and now felt quite satisfied he wasn't gay. Then that brought up the next problem: why didn't he ever give her those kinds of glances?

13

IT HAD BEEN A LONG DAY. THE WASTED TIME AT MORALES'S
office, the ride out to Fredericksburg, interviews and finally
walking the scene. There wasn't much to see except a charred
sidewalk where the flaming tram came to a stop. Sometimes,
when Duarte surveyed the site of some terrible event, he felt like
he could feel the victim's pain and terror. He had never told anyone this. Not even his pop. It was just a faint buzz in his head
that he often felt emotionally. He knew when he first noticed it.
On the side of the Drina River, in Bosnia, as he watched a grown
man cry. Now, even thousands of miles and many years later, he
always thought about that whenever he looked at a blast.

This blast scene was twenty-six days old. He had read the
files of the three dead workers and calculated that there were
now two grieving husbands, one grieving wife, four kids missing
a parent—and that didn't count the driver who was just doing a
simple job and not even paid by the amusement park.

He rubbed his fingers across the black spot on the sidewalk,
as he sat on his haunches and looked toward the park.

Behind him Caren Larson said, "Can you really learn anything by an old smoke stain?"

He shook his head.

"You want to go over to the state police lab and look at any of
the evidence tomorrow?"

He nodded.

Her tone changed. "Hungry?"

He nodded and stood.

An hour later, they sat in the small restaurant of his hotel with
a bowl of hummus and chips in front of them. A nice man with a

slight Italian accent pretending to be the Greek chef had come out to chat with his only customers of the night so far.

"I have great lamb with couscous."

Caren smiled and said, "That sounds perfect."

Even Duarte smiled at the man and had to ask, "What town are you from in Italy?"

The fifty-year-old man paused and smiled. "Is obvious?"

"A little."

"Naples."

"Why not run an Italian restaurant?"

"Too many around. The hotel management wanted Greek. I change a few recipes, make peace with lamb and rice, and got a good job here. Now, what about it? Lamb?"

Duarte nodded his approval as another waiter brought over a bottle of red wine and two glasses.

Duarte held up a hand.

Caren said, "C'mon, live a little. You worked hard today."

He shrugged and allowed the waiter to pour a glass for him. Then Caren had the waiter leave the bottle.

He took a sip of the red liquid and made a face.

Caren laughed. "If you're not used to Merlot, it takes a little while. Keep trying; it'll grow on you."

He took another sip, but it still tasted like fruit juice that had gone bad—only this time the swallow was followed by a warm sensation that washed over him. He'd gotten drunk before, usually on beer, but this was a new sensation. He took another sip.

Caren said, "You haven't given me the slightest hint of what you learned today."

"Because I didn't learn much. So far, it was all in the reports. I started reading the police and lab reports you got me from the Seattle incident and they seem pretty thorough too."

"Should we try to fly there from here?"

He shrugged and nodded. "I was wondering what value the entire trip would have. I mean, so far the only thing I've done up here is waste time."

She smiled. "Some men wouldn't mind wasting time with me."

He took another drink and realized exactly what she meant. "If I didn't have a job to do, believe me you are exceptional company." That was probably the nicest thing he had ever said to anyone he wasn't related to. He took a gulp of wine and then re-filled the glass as the rush of warmth flowed over him.

"You can be charming. In an oddly official and formal sort of way." Caren finished her glass and said, "I still don't know much about Alex Duarte the person. I've seen your army record, your ATF file and your work habits. I've even seen you handle yourself in a fight. But I still don't know much about you."

"Like what?"

She used one finger to twist her hair as she made a show of thinking up a question. "How'd you get that scar?"

"Which one?"

"The long one on your arm?"

"Accident."

"That's not much of an answer."

"It wasn't much of an accident."

"What exactly happened?"

Duarte took a breath and started, "I was in Bosnia, outside Broka, doing some recon before we blew some old buildings. I was low-crawling on a slight rise and didn't notice some razor wire looped through a bush. Before I knew it, I had the wire wrapped around my forearm."

"Ouch."

"Yeah, it hurt. But the stitches at an aid station hurt almost as much." He looked at her as he unconsciously traced his scar with his finger. "Anything else?"

She didn't hesitate. "Why don't you have a girlfriend?"

"Who says I don't?"

"You did when I asked you in Florida."

"Oh. I was right."

They both laughed and drank a sip of wine. And he hoped the question would just die. He hated talking about his personal life. But he should have known that a Department of Justice attorney like Caren wouldn't let it drop.

Finally she said, "I'm waiting for an answer."

He started to shrug, and she said, "Don't shrug me off like you do everything else. I asked you a simple, direct question. Why don't you have a girlfriend?"

He thought about it and said, "You said it yourself. I don't have much experience. I learned that I'm busy, and girlfriends expect a lot."

She stared at him. "You ass, of course they do. We give a lot so we expect a lot."

"Then I need one that doesn't give too much or expect much."

"That's not a bad answer there, Alex. At least it's not the typical bullshit men throw around." She lifted her glass. "I toast your honesty."

He lifted his glass, and they both finished them.

"What about you? You interested in anyone?" He realized it may have been the first personal question he had ever asked a Department of Justice employee.

She let a slow smile cross her pretty face. "If you're asking if I'm dating anyone, I'd have to say no one special."

"What about Tom Colgan? He always had women falling for him."

She stared at Duarte, then said, "You're a little jealous of him, aren't you."

He shook his head.

"C'mon, he's awfully handsome, and very bright. He's going places in the Bureau."

Duarte nodded. He could relate to ambition. He just didn't see the FBI man deserving it based on his performance for the two years he had known him prior to his transfer to Washington. He took a gulp of wine and decided to let the whole thing slip from his mind.

Caren smiled and said, "I had a fairly serious boyfriend in law school."

"What happened?"

"I don't know. I got this job. He had other interests. He's got a little personal-injury practice in Ohio, kinda near where I grew up."

"Where's that?"

"Cincinnati."

"I've never been to the Midwest, other than training at Fort Leonard Wood."

"Where's that?"

"Missouri."

"Did you get to see much of the country?"

"No, I concentrated on training."

"So you were like this from an early age?"

"Like what?"

She took a sip of wine as she figured out what her response would be. "So serious."

"Is that what I am?"

"You're actually beyond serious, but that will do for a start."

He smiled at the comment a little and shrugged.

An hour later, once they had finished what was essentially lamb in marinara sauce and two more bottles of Merlot, Caren said, "I'm not sure I should drive home."

Duarte remained silent.

Caren frowned and said, "This is where you say, 'Why don't you come up to my room.' "

"Then what do *you* say?"

"Okay, but only for a little while until I sober up."

He fought with her over paying the bill, finally allowing her to yank it away from him but secretly relieved he wasn't having to pay for the three thirty-dollar bottles of wine. She locked arms with him on the way to the elevator and rested her head on his shoulder on the ride up. The combination of behavior had caused his heart rate to rise as well as his excitement. He had consumed too much wine to drive, but not enough to inhibit him otherwise. He was not particularly experienced in these situations, but this one appeared to be pretty clear.

At his door, as he paused to retrieve his key, Caren leaned toward him and kissed him on the mouth. He fumbled with the key, and they both popped into the room. They kissed again, and he felt his blood rush through his head and other places. Her firm body pressed against his as their lips met again.

Then Caren said, "Uh-oh."

"What?" was all he got out as she rushed to the bathroom, shoving the door shut behind her. The room spun for him a little too and he sat on the bed. So this is where wine and women get you: alone and awake on your bed. Not much different than any other night for him.

Mike Garretti sat at the pay phone in a Denny's restaurant outside Petersburg in southern Virginia, looking out the small window at his Toyota he had just reclaimed from Alberto Salez. The only problem was that he found he missed his nameless, silent passenger. He sighed, realizing that she wouldn't have been easy to keep around much longer. He had used the Lysol he had purchased in Jacksonville to good effect, but that hadn't been doing the job completely.

He checked his watch. Seven o'clock. He had a ten-minute window to call from a pay phone. He dialed the number, and it rang three times before he heard the familiar voice.

"Yes?"

"I missed him."

"How is that possible?"

Garretti swallowed his comments. "It just is."

"Any leads?"

"That's why I was calling you."

"I have nothing. I'll contact you the usual way if I do. Check tomorrow at noon."

Sensing the call would be coming to an end, Garretti said, "I saw the ATF guy."

"Where?"

"At the park."

"Great. I can't believe we're using you to clean up this mess. You're worse than the others."

Garretti didn't say a word and let the silence speak for him. He knew they needed him. He was tired of this shit anyway.

Then the man said, "Did Duarte recognize you?"

"Negative. He'd never make the connection to meeting me at the apartment in Florida."

"Okay, that's something anyway. Just move on to the next one."

"Oneida?"

"Yeah. Then we'll figure out where Salez is hiding."

"Oneida is in Los Angeles. I have to go home for a few days first."

"Why?"

"Feed my cats, check on my mom."

"Are you serious? We need this taken care of."

"It's been three years. What's the hurry?"

"Don't worry about it, just finish up." There was a pause and he said, "Is there anything else?"

Garretti smiled knowing how this would make him squirm. "Yeah, I spoke to Salez."

"You spoke to him and couldn't shoot him?"

"Long story. Anyway, I spoke to Salez, and he told me he had a file that covered all this shit. He gave me the old 'If anything happens to me' speech."

"You're not serious?"

"I'm just telling you what this asshole said."

"We've got to get that file."

"If it even exists."

"We can't risk it. Catch Salez and make him talk. I'll send you help if you need it."

"Isn't that how we got into this in the first place?"

The line went dead, and Garretti knew he'd have a busy week after few days of R & R.

14

DUARTE TWISTED HIS NECK TO GET THE KINKS OUT. THE floor had been hard on him, but it was the polite thing to do, as Caren was up and down all night on her way to the bathroom. He didn't want to mention it, and now after almost a whole workday she had avoided the entire subject of the night before. She had left the hotel before six, gone home, cleaned up, changed and picked up Duarte before nine. He was impressed.

The Virginia police had not provided any more insight into the bombing. They were efficient and professional but had little to work with other than the device and the theory provided by the Department of Justice. What really amazed him was Caren. With a major hangover, all one hundred and fifteen pounds of Caren Larson had been moving nonstop all day—including lining up airline tickets to Seattle in the morning. They were scheduled to land in Seattle at ten in the morning due to the time change. He had asked her to make an early reservation because he was interested in moving the case along, and now he realized he wanted to move along his growing feelings for the young attorney. This was a new experience for him. Sure, he had dated, but he hadn't felt like this since high school, and back then he hadn't done anything about it. He had just watched the beautiful Joni Livingston from afar. Even when he ran into her at a restaurant last year, he had a hard time talking to her. He knew she was married to a schoolteacher, and she never realized he had a crush on her but he still felt awkward around her. With Caren, it was different. He believed she also felt an attraction to him. But then he thought he could be mistaken.

Finally he said to her, "Can we eat together again tonight?"

She gave a weak smile. "I'd love to but I'm briefing Bob, then I have to pack."

He nodded, understanding the necessities of duty first. That was one of his creeds.

She started to speak, then stopped and finally said, "I'm sorry about last night."

"Nothing to be sorry about."

"I mean, the whole thing. I shouldn't have come on so strong, and I definitely shouldn't have drank so much wine."

"We'll have another chance for dinner, don't sweat it."

She smiled as they left the police building out toward the car. "I appreciate that. I hope I didn't give you the wrong impression."

"My impression is that you're smart, good at your job and good company. Is that the one you want me to have?"

She smiled wider this time and picked up her pace.

Duarte smiled but felt a little regret in his stomach. This reminded him why he worked hard at duty and less at women. Duty never disappointed you.

Alberto Salez used the last of the can of Lysol on his passenger and decided that she had to go—and soon. It had been almost four days since Cheryl Kravitz had died, and the effects were showing no matter how cool he kept the car or how much Lysol he sprayed on her. He had not dumped her body because some smart cop like that ATF prick Duarte might put two and two together and figure out it was him. Besides, having an extra person in the car allowed him to drive in the car-pool lane without a cop stopping him. The tint was dark enough on the Honda to hide her appearance unless someone was right next to the car. He had found himself talking to her more and more, and that was another reason she was still in the seat next to him. It was bizarre and hard to explain. He took another whiff and pointed the air-conditioning ducts directly at her. Thank God, he hadn't been the one who spent most of the time with her.

He was filling up the Honda at the outer pump of a Hess station outside Brunswick, Georgia, and considering how good the gas mileage was on the boxy vehicle. He was on his way back to Maria Tannza's little shithole to recover his file. He originally was going to let it sit there until he needed it but then realized that, in her grief, Maria might decide to move with little notice. Then he'd be in trouble. He just didn't like going back to an area where people knew him and he was wanted. He figured a quick visit, maybe give Maria what she had refused so many times, grab his file and split to someplace entirely new.

He had tried calling his buddy Oneida Lawson in Los Angeles but kept getting an answering machine. It didn't identify the house, but Salez left a message and his name just the same. Oneida had moved shortly after they all had worked together and seemed to have had the most regrets, even though they had been paid well. Oneida wanted to be left alone to coach football. He was crazy for football. Maybe he thought he'd be safe if he moved. Of course, it hadn't done Don Munroe much good to move to Virginia. He knew Janni Tserick had gone to Seattle. He and that lovely wife of his. He'd only seen her once but man would he have liked to indoctrinate her into the Latin culture. At least the bedroom part of it. He'd wait until he was back in Florida to call Oneida again.

Now he took the gas station's squeegee and cleaned the windshield. He looked through the window and saw how bad his passenger looked from that angle. Her flesh was the color of old steak and sagging. He really did have to dump her.

Salez jumped at the sound of a man behind him then turned and let his right hand fall to his hip where he still carried the long, thin fillet knife he had found in Florida.

"What?" asked Salez. He now saw it was a young man, maybe seventeen, in a neat, white Hess shirt.

"I'm sorry, sir, I didn't mean to startle you. I just asked if you needed a hand with anything." He had that soft, pleasant Southern accent, not the harsher Florida Cracker twang.

"No, I'm all set, kid."

The young man smiled and started to walk past Salez, then paused at the pump. "Is she all right?" asked the attendant.

Salez turned to see him staring at the dead woman in the front seat. Now, after being locked in the car, he had grown used to the odor and her slipping skin. The attendant immediately picked up on her melting face. Her eyes drooped like a sad cartoon dog and her lips were nearly black, and patches of her skin looked like marble.

"Yeah, just the flu."

The attendant stepped toward the Honda and stared in through the passenger's window. His eyes wide as he tried to find the words to shout.

"I said she's okay, kid."

"But . . ." Now he had his face to the window, staring at the decaying corpse inside. His brown eyes still opened wide and his surfer's haircut falling across his forehead.

"Dammit," said Salez as he moved toward the boy, gripping the knife and stepping forward.

The young man realized exactly what he had seen and turned to Salez. "But, sir, I think we need to . . ."

Salez never heard the young man's advice because he took his knife and, in an uppercut motion, drove under his sternum directly into his heart. He then wiggled the knife, feeling it cut through the muscle and tissue through the tiny incision the narrow blade made in the boy's chest.

For his part, the young man never made a sound. He stopped midsentence as the shock to his system shut down virtually all other action. His eyes stayed open. They even blinked once. But, in general, they just stared at Salez as he stepped closer to keep the young man from falling. Instead, he wrapped his arm around him and stepped back to the rear passenger's door. With a little effort, he opened the door and slid the boy into the backseat. Since this wasn't a brain injury, and the kid was wearing an essentially white shirt, there was some blood staining the front of it. Salez reached in and set the seat belt across him and was pleased to see the shoulder harness covered some of the bloodstain. Goddamned Jap ingenuity, putting a shoulder seat belt in the rear seat. Maybe he'd look at their products more closely in the future.

Salez checked the lot. He had already paid thirty bucks in cash to fill the tank. He had two-twenty due him but decided it was better to just leave now. He pulled out of the lot at a slow speed and headed west toward I-95 and the trip south to good old Palm Beach County. He looked over his shoulder and said, "I'd introduce you two, but you wouldn't have anything to say." He laughed as he accelerated and wished he had more Lysol.

At the Delta ticket counter, Alex Duarte stood with Caren as they checked in. The burly, dark man behind the counter had already asked them the standard questions when Duarte showed him his credentials.

The man, whose name tag read GARCIA, said, "¿Usted necesita llevar una pistola?"

Duarte said, "Excuse me?"

The man gave him a disappointed look and said, "You need to carry a firearm? The airline makes us ask."

"Yeah, this is official duty."

The man gave Duarte another funny look as he checked through the line.

Finally Duarte said, "What?"

The man shrugged. "My son doesn't speak Spanish either."

Duarte nodded. "It *is* America."

"No penalty to know your heritage."

"I know my heritage."

"Whatever you say, boss."

Duarte didn't pursue it. He took enough flak from his family over the same issues.

With more than an hour until their flight started to board, they found a seat in a sports bar inside the secure zone. Caren ordered a red wine from the waitress while Duarte stuck with Coke.

He responded to a stare from Caren. "I'm on duty and I'm armed."

"I didn't say anything."

He just stared back at her.

After a few more minutes of silence, she said, "So now that you're into this case, what do you hope to accomplish?"

"Find Salez and the bomber."

"I mean, for your career."

"I suppose a good case like this will get me a promotion sooner rather than later."

"Is that what drives you so hard?"

"You have to remember how I was raised. My pop expected us to do better than anyone else. He still wants me to do well. I think it's a good kind of pressure. Most kids today don't have those high expectations."

"My parents didn't push me and I did all right."

"Maybe if they pushed you when you were in school, you would be doing better. You never know."

She seemed to consider the statement as she sipped her wine.

Duarte fell asleep soon after takeoff and the plane ride seemed to be over in a flash. He slept soundly for almost three hours, which was probably the most time he'd spent asleep in a single stretch at any point in the past four years. It was a dreamless sleep, and that explained why he slept so long and had no perspiration on him when he woke up.

The ride into Seattle in the rented Tercel allowed Duarte to take in some of the scenery he normally wouldn't have noticed. Caren, this time the passenger, was quick to point out the Seahawks' stadium and the Space Needle, as well as other local landmarks near their hotel, the Edgewater, which was built over the water. Reading from a travel book she'd bought at the airport, Caren said, "They have an underground here."

"Like alternative-rock clubs?"

"No, the remains of the city when it burned in 1889. They built the new city on top of it."

"Did the bombing occur there?"

"No."

"It'll wait for another time."

They drove on to the hotel in silence. Once inside the hotel, the wooden beams and fireplaces gave the large lobby a rustic feel even with the stream of Beatles tunes being piped in to the room.

At the front desk, Duarte stepped aside so Caren could check in first. The clerk asked, "A single?"

Caren smiled and looked over her shoulder at Duarte, then said, "Yep, just me." Then, after the third Beatles song since they arrived came over the speakers, she asked the clerk, "What's with the music?"

"We always play the Beatles. They stayed here on one of their first American tours."

"Really?" Caren smiled in mock amazement.

"Yes, ma'am. John Lennon fished right from his room."

"That's wild." She had a grin on her face, but the nice young man was not used to East Coast sarcasm.

Duarte asked for directions to the address they had for Tserick's apartment.

Caren said, "We should call first."

"No, we should surprise his wife. If she even still lives there. We might spend the day tracking her down. But we should try immediately; we can always go back later."

"What about the Space Needle?"

"What about it?"

"When are we going to go? We're in Seattle, we should see a little of the town."

"Tell you what. You go now, and I'll interview the widow and check out the crime scene. That way we can leave tomorrow."

"You're no fun."

"So I've heard."

By four o'clock Pacific time, they had the local detective who was investigating the bombing on the phone. The apartment where it had happened had been repaired, but the detective told them he had photos and all the evidence at his office. Duarte could tell the guy was just going through the motions. He knew that when they went to his office and he got a look at Caren, he'd suggest another briefing over dinner.

The detective said, "Someone got into the apartment and placed the charge about face level with the homemade release on the door. When the victim opened the door, the blast nearly took off his head." He paused, and asked Duarte, "You got a female investigator with you?"

"Yes."

"I wouldn't let her see the photos. They ain't pretty. You got a strong stomach?"

"Yeah."

"You'll need it."

Duarte had already checked with the ATF lab and determined the C-4 used in this blast and the one in Virginia was not from the same manufacturer. The manufacturer's fingerprint was one way to compare blasts. Forensic evidence didn't connect the attacks, but the way the bombs were set and the fact that the bomber used only C-4 did link them. Duarte could not imagine two separate killers comfortable working with C-4. It also seemed unlikely that one bomber had two separate supplies of explosive. The other question was: If they were linked, was it because of labor problems? He was starting to have some questions about the theory, but he'd keep it to himself for now.

Once they left their hotel and started looking for the Tserick apartment, Caren asked what he thought about the case.

"Don't know just yet. I think there's a link between Virginia, the labor camp and here. I'd feel better if I could find something about the workers who were killed in Virginia that linked them to Tserick or Salez. I can't believe this is just randomly associated with labor issues. So far, no witnesses at the sites think labor unrest contributed to the killings."

"They may not be in a position to know who's involved with labor. I still think Bob has a really good theory."

"Bob?"

She sighed. "Deputy Attorney General Morales." She looked at him. "He thinks it's actually organized labor trying to scare these independent labor organizations. Think about it. No place we've visited was being organized by one of the big unions. It makes sense."

Duarte, keeping his eyes on the road, said, "How can he make such a wild accusation without looking at the evidence?"

"You met him; he's brilliant."

"He did seem smart and aggressive. I like that, but he'd have to be psychic to jump to this conclusion."

"I thought your main job was investigating the actual bombings. Isn't that what ATF does?"

"It is. But it would help to know the real motive." He looked at her. "Or don't you think so?"

She was frustrated and it showed. She kept quiet and stared out the window at the strange-looking hills and drops and patches of houses stacked together. He thought that maybe he should frustrate her more often. It was more peaceful.

15

MIKE GARRETTI HAD BEEN BETTER PREPARED TO LEAVE HIS home in Texas this time. His mom was fine, and he paid the neighbor kid three bucks a day to watch the cats more closely this time. Last time, an ex-girlfriend dropped by every other day. This time, the kid would visit twice a day, and Garretti wasn't the least bit worried. With a few phone calls, he'd have a small supply of C-4 and a pistol in a locker at a bus terminal not far from Los Angeles International. He didn't know where the C-4 came from and didn't care. The stuff was all commercial quality. None of that "made in a bathtub" shit. He figured it came from a military stockpile somewhere—at least, it wouldn't surprise him. Nothing his employers were able to do surprised him. He'd been told that this time the pistol would be a military surplus Beretta. No .22 to fool with. They didn't say why, but he figured they wanted to make sure he had enough firepower. Especially if Salez had managed to make a phone call to the target.

Garretti stood in front of his seat on the Boeing 727 as the plane eased to the gate. He stretched his long frame and noticed a slight paunch for the first time. He'd have to get back on his workout routine once all this foolishness was over.

An elderly woman in the next row of seats looked at him and asked, "Are you an actor?"

Garretti laughed out loud. "No, ma'am. But I am headed over to Universal Studios."

"For fun?"

He paused. "Not much."

"Well, you should be an actor. You just have one of those faces. You look like you could play a hero. Like a tall Tom Cruise."

"Thank you, ma'am."

"Oh, what nice manners. What do you do?"

"Army. On leave."

"That's where that nice Southern accent and manners come from."

He just smiled.

Once he had recovered the C-4 and pistol, he headed out toward West Covina to see where Oneida lived. He briefly wondered why, if they could get him a gun and some plastique, didn't they use someone out here to do the job? Then he realized that was how this whole mess got started. The fewer people that knew the truth, the better.

On his way out on I-10, he enjoyed seeing the San Gabriels again. He figured he'd use today and tomorrow as recon, then by the end of the week he'd make his move. Ideally, he'd do it at the construction site on Universal Studios to make it look like the others, but he knew the security was rough at the movie studios. If not there, he'd do it at Oneida's house, like he had done to Janni Tserick. That crazy little electrician was too hard to pin down, always traveling around in that phone truck. Once he knew he had the opportunity to do it safely at his apartment, Garretti had set the device. He might use the same tactic again if he could ensure no one else used the house and might set off the bomb. At least no kids. Maybe by then he'd have a line on Salez and be able to wrap this whole thing up for good.

Duarte and Caren knocked and then stood to the side of the reinforced metal door to the Tserick apartment. The door was new, and Duarte understood why. A large chunk of it had been blown out by the blast. About ten feet of the cheap carpet was a slightly different color than the rest. He figured it was better to have unmatched carpet than blood and burn marks.

Duarte stepped to one side of the door, as was his and every other cop's habit. It only took a small shove to move Caren out of the doorway too. The building was not far from the famed underground Seattle that Caren had read about, and the neighborhood wasn't rough, but it wouldn't have been considered ritzy either.

The building was older, with cheap, unmatched indoor/outdoor carpet in the open-air hallways.

Duarte heard someone inside, then the door opened a crack, with the chain still latched.

A woman in her early thirties peeked out. She just said, "Yes?" Her blond hair dripped past her ear, and she leaned down. Then Duarte saw a small child's hand low on the door and realized what she was doing.

Duarte said, "Mrs. Tserick?"

Again the young woman said, "Yes."

Duarte opened his identification case and said, "We were hoping you might talk to us about your husband."

The woman paused and stared at both he and Caren. "Why? Is there something new?"

"No, ma'am. We're still working on the case."

She shut the door and fiddled with the chain. A moment later, the door opened to the cramped living room, with a small but separate kitchen. The child Duarte had glimpsed raced back toward a hallway that must have led to the bedrooms. He was still in a diaper, and had black hair. He'd seen a photo of Tserick—not the one in the crime scene photos—and he was extremely fair-skinned, with light blond hair. The woman was light too. The child was olive-skinned, with dark eyes.

The woman said, "Have a seat," and motioned to the couch with clean laundry stacked at one end. She flopped into a plastic-covered recliner as Caren settled on the couch and Duarte sat next to her.

Duarte said, "Mrs. Tserick, we hate to intrude."

The woman smiled, revealing pretty teeth and clear brown eyes. "Call me Tammy, please," she said in a thick Southern accent.

Duarte cleared his throat, now aware of how attractive this woman—this widow—really was. "Tammy, I know you've talked to the local police, but we have some other questions. Questions about your husband."

"My husband? Why?" She thought about it, and added, "Like what?"

"Like what he did for a living."

"He worked for the phone company."

"As what?"

"As an employee." Tammy looked confused.

"In what capacity?"

"I guess as a phone worker."

Duarte hesitated and Caren stepped in. "What job at the phone company did he do?"

"Oh, I see. He was an electrician. He could get power to anything."

Duarte said, "Was he also involved in the union?"

"What union?"

"Did he help organize labor?"

"What kind of labor? I don't understand."

Caren leaned forward and said, "Did you ever tell the police why you thought someone would kill your husband?"

"What would I tell them? I don't know why he was killed."

Duarte watched the woman closely and noticed that she had started to fidget slightly in her chair.

Caren said, "We're looking into motives."

"Motive for what?"

"To kill your husband."

"Oh, I have no idea. He never caused no trouble here in Seattle."

Duarte caught the comment about Seattle and started to ask about anywhere else that Tserick might have caused trouble when Tammy Tserick started to cry. Then sob.

Caren stepped over and squatted near the recliner, trying to comfort the woman. "It's all right," said Caren softly.

Once again, Duarte was glad he had the DoJ attorney. He would not have had the first clue how to deal with this sort of behavior. He had seen no crying in the army. And only a little in ATF.

Caren obviously wanted to change the subject, and asked, "How long had you been married?"

"A year."

Just then the little boy in diapers came waddling out from the hallway. He fell toward his mother's long sundress and she wrapped her arms around him. She sniffled a little but the boy cheered her. The boy turned and smiled at Caren, who grinned back.

Caren said, "Must be hard to make it as a single mother."

Tammy looked at her and said, "I'm not exactly a single mother." She froze.

"What do you mean?"

"Well, I mean"—she paused again and squeezed the boy—"Michael isn't exactly Janni's son. He knew it. It was no secret. But his daddy lives in Texas."

Duarte didn't think this was any of their business, and even though the boy was young he didn't like talking about the bombing in front of him. Duarte pressed on with questions about Janni Tserick's employment and friends. For a wife, Tammy Tserick didn't seem to know much about her husband or his activities.

After Duarte had exhausted a number of avenues for questioning, Caren asked, "Do you work?"

Tammy shrugged. "Sometimes I do some temp work, as a receptionist or secretary."

"What about when your husband was killed?"

She thought about it, her face twisted in concentration. "No, I didn't then."

"But you weren't home when the bomb detonated?"

"No, I was in Texas, visiting family. The police had to call me from a number they found on the kitchen phone list."

Caren took in the information.

Tammy stood and stretched her lithe frame. "Is there anything else?"

The investigators looked at each other and Duarte said, "No, ma'am, I think we covered it." He got a phone number and info from her in case he needed to call with a follow-up.

He looked down and smiled at young Michael. The shy boy hid his face behind his mother's long dress.

Mike Garretti spent the day as if he were Oneida Lawson. He watched him leave his little run-down house with the dirt front yard in West Covina at about seven in the morning and drive into work along I-10, then onto the 101 until he reached Universal Studios, where he entered through a gate in the rear. He knew Oneida would be working a legitimate job. He and Janni Tserick were decent guys. He never understood how they got involved in this mess. He still felt bad about Tserick. He had used enough C-4 to ensure the man never even realized what had happened to him.

Garretti knew Oneida was a carpenter of some kind, and his source said he had been employed by a contractor for the studio for the past four months. He peered through a chain-link fence near a giant parking garage disguised to look like a forest if viewed from the studio. Garretti saw over a dozen construction types walking around as they worked on some structure that looked like an Egyptian pyramid only much smaller, maybe three stories tall.

This would be the ideal place to get Oneida, and it would be on a work site—just as he'd been instructed. He'd let his employers fill in the rest. But this job had some logistical problems he had not yet encountered. The main one being that the work site, like the entire studio, had good security. Aside from the little construction zone, Garretti couldn't even see the rest of the park. This was one he'd have to work hard on.

He roamed around the area until four o'clock, then parked his rented Dodge down the street from the service entrance. He expected Oneida to leave work closer to five but was shocked when he saw the man's Ford pickup with dented tailgate zip out of the gate and fly past him like he was late for an appointment. Garretti barely had time to bring his car around and follow his next victim.

A couple of quick turns on the congested streets and Garretti almost gave up, then he realized that Oneida wasn't heading back to his home in West Covina. Instead, he drove out north and west toward the 110 into Pasadena. Then, not far from the highway, Garretti saw the old pickup pull up to a high school.

He watched, hoping this was another of Oneida's jobs, so that Garretti could complete his assignment without risking the security and hassles of Universal Studios. He parked way back because he knew Oneida would immediately recognize him, and what his presence in California meant. If Salez hadn't already warned him. Garretti knew Oneida was the toughest of the bunch and probably wouldn't run even if he knew someone was after him.

Over the next hour, Garretti watched the truck; then he saw a group of students running in a formation across a field just off the road and surrounded by a chain-link fence. Then he saw the large frame of Oneida running behind them, shouting encouragement. Garretti smiled, and recalled the man's devotion to football. He was a coach of some kind at this little private high school. He was focusing on the kids and wide-open. But that was the problem: the kids. Garretti was not going to risk killing another child. Especially not one out struggling in the Southern Californian sun trying to make a summer football team. Besides, it didn't fit the profile. He'd have to do it at the studio, whether it was easy or not. He sighed and headed back to Burbank to get another look at the grounds and fence at Universal Studios.

16

CAREN LARSON STARED AT THE FOUR FEDERAL EXPRESS boxes filled with thousands of sheets of paper and a memo from Tom Colgan saying he and "Bob" thought there might be a link in the pages of intelligence investigations and statements from informants regarding the deaths they believed were related to labor difficulties. It would've been nice for one of them to call her and tell her the boxes were on their way instead of having a bellhop deliver them unannounced. She was more than a little offended that Deputy Attorney General Roberto "Bob" Morales or FBI Special Agent Tom Colgan thought she hadn't figured out that the whole labor theory came from inside the department. She just didn't understand why they were pushing it so hard. But it was definitely a priority for Bob Morales and, therefore, a priority for her. She knew that her career depended on her making the crimes fit the theory, but she didn't know if they realized she was bright enough to see that they had other agendas.

But what about Alex Duarte? He was very bright. What would happen if he figured it out? They didn't own his soul like hers. She didn't think the idealistic young ATF man would sell his soul. But she knew her bosses were interested in what his price might be if it came to that. She hoped it wouldn't come to that.

There was a knock on her door. She popped up, knowing who it was but wondering what his reaction would be to the latest task.

As the door opened, Duarte looked at her and immediately said, "What's wrong?"

She stepped to the side to reveal the boxes of records. "The Department of Justice has some ideas for us."

"What's in there?"

"Records. From investigations, intelligence—you name it."

"And?"

"They think we might find a clue into the case by going through them."

He stepped fully into the room and said, "Good, let's get started."

She appreciated his attitude, and couldn't bring herself to tell him that it was a ploy to slow down the investigation for some reason. She wished she knew why, and wished she could share her fears with him. She couldn't do either. She was too embarrassed to consider what he might think of her if she did tell him all she knew.

Alberto Salez was glad to be back in Florida. The weather was hot, but at least it was more predictable than Virginia, and he didn't stick out down here like he did in the white-bread state. If the U.S. was the melting pot of the world, Florida was the melting pot of the U.S. Between Central American workers, neighborhood after neighborhood of Islanders and all the European visitors, no one looked or sounded alike. Salez liked that feature of his adopted state. This time of year, there was also a load of cheap motel rooms he could rent by the week. He couldn't go back to the extra bunk at the labor camp. That place had been great after a night of drinking with those guys—he didn't have to do anything, just sleep in the soft cot and get up a little early in the morning and drive into the Sunrise Cafe. Now it was different. Cut off from the bunkhouse and his own apartment, he felt like fucking Osama bin Laden, unable to sleep in the same bed twice, or use the same phone twice without risk of someone listening.

Now he was considering the best way to get into the labor camp out past Belle Glade and retrieve his file from the lovely but sad Maria Tannza. He hadn't spoken to her in the week since her son was killed. She would probably not be happy to see him, and that meant she'd tell someone he had been there. He didn't necessarily like the idea of killing the young teacher, but it would be easier than dodging that fucking ATF agent, Duarte. That son of a bitch had proven he wasn't the forgiving type. Every time he reached up to his right ear, he thought about what he wouldn't mind doing to the young ATF man. He figured if they both stayed in the area, he might get a chance one day.

He sat low in the seat of his newly acquired Nissan pickup truck he'd bought from a farmhand near Boynton Beach. The nine-year-old truck had some wear and tear, as well as its share of rust, but the mechanical aspect was solid, and no one noticed it rolling down the road. For a three-pound bag of pot he had taken from one of his friend's stashes, the truck was a good deal. What could he do? He needed transportation. He had left the Honda Element in the parking lot of the same gas station where he had met the owner and killed her. He had wiped the odd-looking vehicle clean inside and out. No one would lift a print from that thing. Not even those fags on the CSI show could do it. Salez had even bought a copy of the *Palm Beach Post* to see what the conjecture was about how a rotting corpse and another, fresher body from Georgia ended up at the gas station where her credit card was used the week before. The whole idea made him chuckle when he thought about it. The cops, as usual, weren't talking.

He decided to wait until dark to slip into the camp. Maybe no one would even notice him. Maybe Maria would be out and he wouldn't have to deal with her. Maybe he'd figure out how to get that crazy Garretti off his ass and not have to worry about this shit at all. Maybe, but he doubted it.

It was near eight o'clock when Duarte realized they had been working since early in the morning and he was getting tired. The hotel room at the Edgewater had a spectacular view of the water, and he found himself gazing at some of the passing ships and freighters. He had never seen ships like that pass by from any kind of living room. The cloudy sky gave the image a cinematic quality. He and Caren had shared a pizza in her room that looked out over the Puget Sound and had hardly made a dent in the records. Caren had picked up a six-pack of Budweiser too. He had surprised himself by drinking two. Duarte had to admit that Caren was a hard worker and didn't complain about much. He liked that.

Now he stood and stretched, knowing he'd have to have a hard workout in the morning to get his body back on track. Caren looked up and smiled, her eyes still alert but the exhaustion starting to show in her pretty face. She stood too, stretched her arms, then sat on the edge of the bed.

"Wanna start again tomorrow?"

He nodded.

"You think this is worthwhile?"

He said, "Don't know until we get into them a little bit more."

"You like this kind of work?"

"Not especially, but it needs to be done. We may find the link to the killer in the files."

She stared at him.

He added, "Or maybe not."

"You are just so hard to figure out. Unless I'm asking about explosives or the Civil War, you hardly say a word. I just don't know what to think."

He smiled but didn't answer.

"Why did the South even declare war? They could never win."

Duarte turned to her, his arguments already springing through his mind. "The South didn't lose a battle until Gettysburg. Lee proved that tactics and superior skill could defeat much larger armies in battle. Lee just needed the right ground for a good field of fire and a clear mission, and he stood up to forces twice his size."

He stopped because she was laughing. Laughing at Robert E. Lee. When she didn't stop, he said, "What's so funny?"

"I just proved my point. You need some work on your areas of interests if you want to attract women." She patted the bed next to her.

Duarte suddenly saw how good an attorney she was. He sat down a foot away from her, his hands folded in his lap, realizing she didn't give a crap about the Civil War. He could still smell her subtle perfume, even over the beer on his breath.

Caren said, "What do you want out of this?"

"Out of what?"

"This case, this work, this bullshit."

She had a tone he had not heard from her before. A little caustic and bitter. He shrugged, his natural reaction to almost any inquiry. "Solve it. Move on. Nothing too much to ask."

"Solve it to help get a promotion? Like you claimed last week?"

"Yeah, I guess. It's also the right thing to do. Hector Tannza is only one of the victims. Someone's got to stop this guy, and right now we're the only ones trying."

She nodded. "You make sense. For a cop." Then she shocked him by reaching over, wrapping a hand around his neck and kissing him long and hard on the lips. He responded but was still in a state of shock. When their lips parted, all he could say was: "Wow."

She smiled and said, "I agree." Then she looked into his eyes and asked him, "What really interests you? You can tell me. I really want to know."

Duarte had been raised to be too polite to admit what interested him at that moment.

Mike Garretti had figured the entire plan out while he had watched Oneida Lawson work with the linebackers on getting around the defensive linemen. The answer had been right in front of him all along, but he hadn't noticed it. Then, looking through the chain-link fence, it hit him. He could enter the studio. Anyone could. It was called the Studio Tour. That would give him a recon of the whole studio, security and probably even the construction site. It sounded easy enough, and he had always wanted to take the famous tour.

The ride on the little tourist train reminded him of the tram in Virginia where he had placed the charge under the driver's seat. He was pretty good with simple C-4. Timers and releases—the basic stuff. Considering he'd never really been officially trained, he was confident with it. He considered himself the most proficient explosives expert in the U.S. military who actually worked as a personnel clerk. But like everything else, even the military, people's views are colored by movies, and someone above him had suggested using a bomb that armed after the tram reached a certain speed. He wanted to shout: "When it reaches eight fucking miles an hour?" But he had remained professional. They paid him too much to act otherwise. He nodded without actually saying he would do it that way. Instead, he used a simple radio remote and watched to see who was on the tram. He waited for more than three hours until the fewest number of people were on the bus, then detonated the C-4. He knew it would be a big blast. He wanted to be sure it did the job, but he had hoped the two young women a few rows back and the heavy guy behind the driver would survive. As soon as he saw the intensity of the explosion, he realized that was a futile hope. Just the flash of the blast alone enveloped the whole vehicle. Maybe a whole stick was too much. Those deaths, coupled with the fiasco in Florida, made him more cautious here. This would be a tricky one, but they weren't paying him to just roll up next to Oneida and put a bullet in the back of his brain. There was a bigger picture that he was missing. There was a role for these bombings and he had no clue what they meant. He did, however, know they were paying him cash, to do it their way, and he liked having a good safety net for his retirement.

The tour showed how movies could make things look one way but actually be something totally different. The whole concept made him think about his recent jobs. He had seen the Hitchcock classic *Psycho,* but to see the smaller-scale house and the motel together was a shock. Then to see that the motel was the back of the set of Jim Carrey's *How the Grinch Stole Christmas* made him realize they did manufacture a form of magic here. After listening to the guide drone on about the street with the Munsters' house and Animal House and, across the street, Beaver Cleaver's smart two-story, Garretti noticed the beginning of the construction area. He could see signs for the set for *The Mummy.* Not the classic but the one with Brendan Fraser that he had taken his nephew to.

He looked through the small monocular some people used to view golf shots. He counted nine workers out in the open. Then he saw two men nailing supports into the side of a thin wall. Oneida Lawson was one of them. His solid frame sat to one side of a much older and thinner white man. They both concentrated on their work, and moved about three feet after each series of nails was pounded in by hand. Garretti wondered if that was more efficient than using those pneumatic nail guns.

The tram stopped so people could see Spielberg Street, or some bullshit like that. Garretti took the opportunity to study the construction site. Most of the workers were to one side and the carpenters were on the other. Then he saw Oneida climb off his project and walk to a stack of boards and lumber and get a drink from a big yellow watercooler propped up on the lumber. At the same time, another man from the other crew went to a different area, with canisters and cement, and got a drink there. Then Garretti saw what he needed. The carpenters had their own area. And it was near the fence. This might work out. But he'd have to set it up in the next day or two.

He had a busy day ahead of him.

17

AS HE OPENED HIS EYES, CAREN'S FACE WAS RIGHT IN front of him. So close that his eyes crossed briefly.

She said, "This won't make things weird for us, will it?" Her left breast hung down, brushing his chest.

He didn't know what she was talking about exactly but he shook his head. He sat up and saw it was six-thirty in the morning. He had just slept for more than an hour and a half straight. Not bad.

Caren added, "I had one too many beers, and we've been working so closely together . . ."

Duarte said, "I thought it happened because we liked each other."

She smiled and laid her head on his bare chest. After a few minutes, she said, "So what do you want to do?"

He didn't hesitate. "Go through the records for a while, then talk to Tserick's boss at the phone company, then get back on the records to see what else we can develop."

She remained silent, then slowly inched away from him. Like his other relationships with women, he had no idea what that meant, if anything.

Near noon, Duarte was starting to believe the records were a worthless exercise. He hadn't found anything useful. It mostly had to do with one union, the United Workers of America, and none of the dead would have been involved in that organization. He wasn't sure there was much more to do here in Seattle. He had seen the crime scene, talked to the investigators and spoken to Mrs. Tserick. Then he let his mind sort through all the information so that when they finished with the records they could decide if there were more leads here.

Caren, who had been uncharacteristically quiet most of the morning, said, "We'll finish these up today, if we don't find anything."

Duarte nodded.

"What's our next move?"

He shrugged.

"Phone company?"

Duarte considered it and smiled at her having the same thoughts as him. "Did you learn anything from Tammy Tserick when we spoke to her?"

"Not really. Why?"

Duarte said, "She just didn't seem too upset about her husband."

"Alex, she had a toddler who wasn't even Tserick's kid. It's not what I call a traditional marriage."

"I dunno, but it strikes me as strange."

"She give off any clues that she was lying?"

Duarte hesitated. "I didn't see any, but I have to admit that may not be my area of specialty."

Caren smiled. "I noticed you're more of an action kind of guy."

He smiled for her. It came easier than he had been told.

She returned the smile and said, "I'm hungry. Let's get out for a few minutes."

He didn't mind walking outside and along the waterfront in Seattle with a lovely girl who he realized he wanted to get to know better. After a ten-minute walk, they came to an oyster house. He found himself in a good mood as they climbed the outdoor stairway and caught a whiff of salt air.

After a fine lunch of fried oysters and clam chowder, Duarte and Caren found themselves at the main administrative office for the phone company Janni Tserick had worked for. The office building housed the payroll, personnel and management functions of the second-largest telecommunications company in the Pacific Northwest. In addition to phone service, they had recently expanded into cable television, and security alarms as well. This was the standard speech they had listened to in the office of the company's general counsel. As with many businesses—and now even government offices—more and more contact with the employees was through legal counsel.

Jim Boyette, first-line supervisor for the linemen and technicians in and around the city of Seattle, sat in a seat next to the company's lawyer, an older, gruff man obviously annoyed by such a government inquiry. Alex Duarte was seated on his other side, asking a series of questions that had so far not involved the company and so raised no objection with the attorney.

"How long did you know Mr. Tserick?"

"Don't know, maybe a year. However long he worked for us."

"And he got along with the other workers?"

"I guess. I mean, he didn't see much of anyone else. Just picked up his assignment and got out on the road."

"He talk about himself or his past at all?"

"Nope. I know he was from Texas and worked for the power company there. I guess his references were fine because we hired him."

"You ever know him to try to organize labor or be involved in labor negotiations?"

"Tserick? I never knew him to *talk* to anybody."

Duarte considered this. The only pattern he was seeing was people *not* involved in labor unions. How had someone come up with this labor theory?

Caren stepped up from the corner of the room. "Mr. Boyette," she began, "did you ever meet his wife?"

"Once. The first day. She drove him to the office. She was pregnant, but he never said a word about it—before or after. I saw in the paper that his wife and son were out of town when the explosion happened, so I assumed she had the kid."

Duarte thanked the men for their time and headed out of the office no closer to the truth than before. It happened that way sometimes. He knew things would come together soon.

It was near dark, and Garretti had just eaten at one of the commercial, bland restaurants in the area known as CityWalk next to the studio. The stores specialized in overpriced shirts and hats advertising movies. He hated that kind of stuff, but still bought two hats and a shirt for his nieces and nephew. He thought about buying a tiny *Spider-Man* shirt but wasn't sure how it would be received.

The baby's mother still wasn't happy with the way things had worked out. Things had been tense lately, and he understood why.

He could see the construction site from the outer fence of the studio. He also had noticed a surveillance camera and two patrols. What he needed was a diversion. He knew exactly where to plant the stick of C-4 with nuts and bolts taped around it. He just needed a ten-minute window to get inside and set the device. He already had his entrance set up. The fence was ten feet high, with razor wire over the top. The chain-link was only a small area near the construction. His guess was that it was designed to pull down for big trucks when necessary. Everyone thought about trespassers going over the top, but they rarely prepared for stopping someone coming underneath. He had already cut the bottom strap on three posts, which allowed him to pull up the fence enough to roll under. Then it snapped right back into place. No one would even notice it. Maybe a smart cop would look after the blast, but he'd be back in Texas once he confirmed the death. There was a risk just like in Florida. Unattended blasts tended to go wrong, but his employers knew this, or at least said they knew the risks and told him to do it anyway.

Now he just needed a diversion. He hopped in his rented Dodge and started to cruise around the perimeter of the giant studio complex. He got lost in the rear of the complex and had to pull out a map to get back to where he needed to be. He passed the entrance used by the movie people and actors. It was locked down, with a gate, and two uniformed armed guards inside the shack. That would be a good place for a diversion when the time came.

Alberto Salez drove the battered pickup truck in the front gate and tried not to slow too much so no one would see his face. He kept the window up even though it was hot as hell and this piece of shit truck didn't have an air conditioner. He saw an open space near the front of the camp and realized that was where they had cleared the wreckage of his Mustang and the other two cars that had been damaged. The camp appeared to be functioning normally. A few people wandered around. Some sat on the steps of their trailers and watched the world go by, and some of them used barbecue grills to make their dinner of chicken and vegetables. That was the meal every night, except for the occasional pork and vegetables.

He cruised to the office trailer, which was closed at this time of night, and sat in the truck for a minute just seeing who was around. He recognized most of the faces and knew they'd recognize him. He could just see the front of Maria Tannza's trailer from where he sat. The lights in the main room were on, and her nice Toyota Corolla was parked in front. She was there. Damn.

He pulled the sharp fillet knife that had served him well the past week and realized he didn't like the idea of killing the young teacher. But he had no choice. He'd try to make it pleasant for her first. She may not think it was pleasant, but in the afterlife she'd realize he did her a favor.

He slipped out of the truck and headed behind the office trailer down the maintenance track so he would avoid everyone. About two hundred yards down, he cut through the hedge and found himself directly across from Maria's trailer.

He looked both ways and saw a vehicle driving down the path. He stepped back into the protection of the hedge just as the headlights swept across the area where he was standing.

He would wait to make sure there were no witnesses.

18

AFTER THEY SPOKE TO TSERICK'S EMPLOYERS, ALEX Duarte had spent three hours in the cramped hotel room going through the records with Caren. About six in the evening, they had started to skim them more than search. Even he realized this wasn't a productive task, and he felt they had completed the assignment from Tom Colgan as best they could. By eight, they were finished, and Caren said she needed to clean up but she'd meet him for a late dinner. He made his exit, still unsure what one night of passion meant as far as good-byes. To his relief, she had remained very professional the whole day, and seemed to warm up to him again after lunch.

As he left, she smiled—not expecting a hug or kiss good-bye. That was to his liking. He was relatively new to relationships, if that was what he had with the lovely Department of Justice attorney.

He went to his room and immediately changed into shorts and running shoes. He pulled on a white T-shirt with a Mexican flag across the chest. His pop had brought it back for him from a trip to Acapulco. As soon as he stepped outside in the light T-shirt, he realized that even in May Seattle could be somewhat cold—at least in comparison to his native Florida. He skipped his usual stretches and bounced immediately into a slow jog to warm up. The crowds along the waterway and docks forced him toward the Space Needle, the steep hills a new sensation for his calves and lungs. He marked visually his location from the Needle so he wouldn't get lost in the diminishing light. He knew if he just got back to the water, he could find his unusual hotel.

He picked up the pace, as his back and legs loosened up, and occasionally took a staircase instead of a hill, because the area seemed filled with staircases to use as shortcuts from the street to a park or shop. He circled the Space Needle, catching the attention of a squat uniformed cop near the entrance. Duarte knew the suspicions he felt when there was only one person doing something in an area. Like when one man hung out near a school, or one white guy was in a black neighborhood. Cops were suspicious. They were paid to be suspicious for the general public, and then, more often than not, punished for being suspicious. The look didn't bother Duarte.

As he trotted by the short, heavy cop, Duarte nodded.

The cop said, "What're you doing?"

Duarte slowed and jogged in place. "What do you mean?"

"I mean, I don't see many Mexican runners, and no one over here. What're you doing?"

"Running."

"Why?"

That caught Duarte by surprise. Then he looked at the cop's stomach and realized he didn't understand the concept of physical fitness. Duarte shrugged.

"Got any ID?"

"Not while I'm running."

"You don't have much of an accent."

"I'm from Florida."

"Where originally?"

"West Palm Beach."

The cop looked at him and snorted. "Right. It's time to run on, then, Florida."

Duarte stopped running in place, looked down at his shirt with the Mexican flag and said, "Is there a problem, officer?"

"Just doing my job."

"Do Hispanics commit a lot of crime in this neighborhood?"

"Not really."

"Then why are you hassling me?"

"Because there aren't many Hispanics in this neighborhood."

Then Duarte realized he *did* stand out. Washington State didn't have the diverse population of Florida. Not many states did. He nodded, and started his pace back toward the hotel.

* * *

He stretched inside the room, after throwing a few punches and kicks. He tossed his sweaty clothes into a plastic bag in the small closet and turned the shower on full and hot. Closing the curtain to create a mini steam room, he let the hot water rinse over him. He had been disturbed by the cop's comments, but realized as an experienced cop himself that the officer had simply addressed an issue as he saw it. Duarte had never been considered an issue to police before. In Florida, he was one of many Latins, and just as often mistaken for Italian. He considered himself a Floridian. At least he had been born there, unlike most of the other residents of South Florida.

The steam cleared his pores, and caused a thick haze of white clouds directly over the shower. His dark hair lay flat as the water ran over his scalp. Just as he started to completely relax, he felt an odd burst of cool air. Before he could turn the water off, the plastic curtain parted and he was staring at a naked Caren Larson. She smiled, unashamed. He could see tiny goose bumps on her flat stomach, and her nipples harden as she stepped into the shower with him.

"But, how'd you . . . ?"

"Get in? Easy: a bellhop felt sorry for the cute girl who locked herself out of her room. He unlocked the door." She stepped into the hot water. "Ouch." She turned and adjusted the heat. Then she wrapped her arms around him and said, "No more questions."

After what she had shown him last night, he had a few questions but decided to ask them later. Mainly about where she had learned some of these things, and if they ever hurt.

Mike Garretti sat at a tiny taco stand about three miles from the entrance to Universal Studios. He was considering how to distract security so he could slip inside. He knew exactly what to do after he was inside; but what would be so unusual that it would draw security to one place?

He slowly munched on a good fish taco and sipped his 7UP when a man with a gray beard and a torn T-shirt sat down at the small table across from him.

"Give me the rest of your taco."

"What?"

"No English, vato? Dimme su taco, ahora."

"I understood you, sir, I just refuse to comply."

"Oh, who do we have here? A soldier or convict. Which is it?"

The man's breath carried across the table. His large arms had scars from years of battle. His pockmarked face was red and scabby.

"Look, mister, I'll buy you a taco if you're hungry."

"I don't take charity. I just take what I want and I want that fucking taco." He reached across the table, apparently used to getting his way when he expressed it so clearly.

Garretti slapped his hand like a child and said, "Don't do that again . . ."

"Or what?" The man leaned in close.

Garretti had a brilliant idea at that exact moment. "Look, old-timer, I'm sorry, it must be tough out here."

"Don't you worry what's tough or not. I rule this block and I take what I want." He looked across the narrow street toward two young women sharing an ice-cream cone in front of a Baskin-Robbins. "I think I want them in a minute. Nothing anyone can do about it."

"Really? You think?" He drew his Beretta from his waist and leveled the barrel at the ranting man.

The man saw just enough of the gun over the top of the table to immediately shut up. Then he started to stand and said, "Sorry, wrong person, my mistake."

Garretti used a simple voice. "Keep backing up to that Dodge right there and get in the passenger's side. It's unlocked."

"Why?"

"Because I'll kill you if you don't."

That was all the man needed. He backed away then turned and calmly walked around the car and climbed in the passenger's seat. Garretti was in the car and headed toward Universal Studios a minute later.

"What? What are you gonna do?" asked the man, now with a clear tremble in his voice.

"Just getting you away from those girls. Keep your mouth shut and I'll drop you a few miles away and give you ten bucks to stay away for the night."

"Ten bucks? I woulda walked away for that."

"Thought you didn't take charity."

"That would have been a business transaction. I woulda been reasonable."

"You didn't act like it."

He took a turn quick, slamming his passenger into the door and causing him to fasten his seat belt. Then, six minutes later, he was around the corner from the employee entrance to Universal Studios.

"Get out."

"What about my ten bucks?"

Garretti raised the gun. "Out."

The man climbed out and muttered something.

Garretti leaned toward the open door and said, "The only phone for a few blocks that you could get to for help is around this corner. It's the Universal Studio's security shack."

"So? I don't need to make a call."

"You will."

"Why?"

"To get medical attention." Garretti pulled the pistol's trigger and put a bullet in the man's upper stomach. The sound of the gun was deafening inside the car. "You better hurry."

The man stepped back, clapping his hand over the wound, the blood staining out past his hands. "Don't, mister. Please."

"You'll live, old-timer. Just get to the phone." He had intended the first shot to be dangerous but not debilitating. He couldn't hit the man's legs or he wouldn't be able to run. This way it hurt, but he'd have the steam to get close. Garretti shouted, "Now, run."

The man still stared at him as the blood seeped between his fingers. Garretti fired another shot into the man's shoulder. "Run."

The man finally got the message and started trotting off around the corner.

Garretti climbed out of the low Dodge and walked to the corner and watched the man struggle toward the security shack. As soon as he saw a guard notice the man and start to speak into his radio, Garretti lined up another shot. It was a good distance with a handgun, but he felt pretty confident about his chances. He lined up the sights on the struggling man and squeezed the Beretta's smooth trigger.

This shot echoed in the outdoors and a moment later the man dropped to the ground. The guard stopped and scrambled back to the shack, now screaming so loud into his radio that Garretti could hear him.

He slipped back into the running Dodge and took the first turn, knowing he'd have a good half an hour to slip in the rear of the park. And there would be no witnesses because he knew no one would be brave enough to check the old bum until the cops showed up. But every rented guard in that complex would want to see the dead man and see the cops arrive. That's what they lived for.

Maria Tannza had started teaching again on Monday. Her heart wasn't completely in it, but sitting around her lonely trailer had not been an acceptable alternative and visiting her mother in Orlando was even less of an option. She seemed to get lost in her grief some days, but the visitors had helped. Virtually everyone from the camp had come by with food or kind words. It lifted Maria, but she still thought of Hector almost every second. He would've become a fine man, and she imagined him in the travel industry because of the way he alway had to get out and see things. He never got in trouble. He never bothered people. But he just could not stay indoors. That was what had killed him.

She sniffled at the thought of her boy not seeing the world as he had often dreamed. She was young; she'd eventually meet someone. And not like Hector's father. She would meet a kind and, more important, stable man. Then she'd have another child. She just couldn't see working anywhere but here. The state public schools paid reasonably well, but the wealthy white schools didn't appreciate teachers, and she had found that some of the poorer schools didn't put a high priority on learning. Instead, they focused on discipline. Here, she had eager students whose parents treated her like a celebrity. She even tried to help with other things around the camp like assisting some workers secure visas or driver's licenses. She liked being part of these people's lives, not just the camp teacher.

She sat on the couch with the TV on, but she was not really watching. Things had been quiet in the camp, as some of the workers prepared to move to central Florida for the summer. She was still dressed because she never knew when someone would drop by. As if to make the point, she thought she heard someone outside. A vehicle had passed a minute before, but this sounded like someone waiting by the stairs, hesitant to come in. She got that a lot with the shy Guatemalan workers embarrassed to bother her.

She stood to go to speak to them, thinking she might just talk to them from the door because suddenly she felt tired. She had no apprehension. That was the beauty of this camp. There were no dangerous people here. They were like her family. As she neared the door, she could see a man's shadow from her porch light.

She sighed and started to open the door.

19

ALEX DUARTE STARED UP AT THE CEILING OF HIS HOTEL room listening to the not-so-quiet snoring of Caren Larson snuggled up next to him. It was an odd sensation, sleeping in the same bed with another person. Four years in the army, followed by his stint at the Glynco Federal Law Enforcement Training Center in Georgia, followed by his resumed residence in the garage behind his parents, had not led to an enormous number of opportunities to share his bed. Fort Leonard Wood in Missouri was one of the first places he spent the night away from the bed in which he had grown up. During basic training, it had been quite an adjustment to sleep in a room full of snoring, restless men in a cot less then half as wide as his bed. By the time he had started his training as a combat engineer, he had grown used to the sounds. During his various postings from Fort Bragg to the Balkans, he had shared rooms of all sizes with men of all types, but he took a certain amount of comfort knowing he'd always have a few feet of cot he never had to share with anyone.

One of the issues he had with his brother Frank was his lack of interest in respecting Duarte's privacy. He'd walk into any room without knocking or announcement, despite his father's efforts to teach them manners from an early age. His father attributed it to the natural tendency for a lawyer to be obnoxious no matter how he was raised.

His encounter with the cop at the Space Needle earlier in the day also occupied his mind as he played his nightly game of trying to trick himself into falling asleep. What had attracted the cop's interest? Was it the shirt? Did he really look that much different than the swarm of visitors to the attraction? He had never thought of himself as ethnic. He was a Floridian. No one looked at Floridians as suspicious. Even though he was a cop, he had never looked at someone based solely on their race or national origin. He didn't think others ever looked at him that way. Now he'd have to reconsider how he was viewed. His father always taught him that you get out of life what you put in. Not that you get what they allow or how they see you.

One of Caren's louder snores snapped his train of thought to the case. Supposedly, the biggest case he had ever worked on. He knew there were powerful people pushing the investigation. He had met one in the impressive Roberto "Bob" Morales. This was clearly his ticket up the ladder. He'd solve the case too, but he needed more. The theory that these people were all labor organizers didn't feel right. But he knew they were all connected. The C-4 and the way the bomber had set things up proved that one person was responsible. He'd find the answer whether it was in a box of old records or in a fiber at one of the blast sites.

That made him think of the labor camp and Maria Tannza crying on the step of the fire engine. Her son Hector deserved to have his killer caught. He knew that was the most important thing, but he couldn't deny the value an arrest would have for his career.

He closed his eyes, thinking he might doze off, then Caren shifted in the bed, startling him wide awake.

Maria Tannza was happy to see the friendly, older manager of the labor camp and she enjoyed talking with him. She stood on her front porch because she knew he didn't like to leave his dog, and he knew she would never allow a dog into her immaculate trailer. The man had joked about his wife and her cooking for so long that Maria almost believed it, except for the man's nice round belly. He took vegetables from the farm home most nights, but that was more of a beef belly than a tomato or lettuce belly.

They chatted about how the camp was running and everyone seemed satisfied, but they avoided the subject of her son or the explosion. She liked the man's easy Florida accent, and knew that he treated the workers better than the corporation that ran the farm expected him to.

As the man told another of his famously long stories, Maria

caught a movement across the street. At the same time, a car drove from the maintenance area behind her and the headlights swept across the area. In the moment of light, she clearly saw Alberto Salez's face. He looked over his shoulder directly at her, then slipped into the bushes.

The old manager recognized her distress. "What is it, sweetheart?"

"I thought I saw Berto Salez across the street."

The old man laughed and said, "That old dog is on the run somewhere far from here. Think about it, Maria. Why would he even show up again?"

She had no good answer but knew what she had seen. She didn't want to be alone right now. "Why don't you come in for some coffee?"

"Naw, I couldn't . . ." His eyes drifted to the basset hound in the cab of his truck.

"You can bring Sherman inside."

"I can?"

"If he stays off the furniture." She managed a smile, but her mind raced at what she should do. Then she remembered the good-looking Latin ATF agent had given her his cell phone number. She hoped he could help.

Oneida Lawson tried to keep his tools locked up at the work site most days. But today he had his hammer and measuring tape because he had stopped the evening before and helped the high school maintenance man fix the steps to the ancient concession stand the students used to raise money for the sports teams. They raised five or six hundred dollars a year, and then some rich player's parents would donate fifty thousand and they called it even. Oneida liked it because it taught the kids the value of money and hard work. Now, as he walked the almost quarter mile from the parking lot to the work site, he remembered why he had left his tools there whenever possible.

Even though he built sets, and it sounded glamorous, he realized he was a construction worker. He had made mistakes in his life, and came to terms with the likelihood that he wouldn't ever be anything but a construction worker, but now he could say he was happy. California was a nicer place to live than Texas, and people were focused on other things out here. Like looking good, or their careers. That didn't give them time to be ambitious or try to influence financial markets or do the stupid things that he had gotten involved in.

As he passed the set that had been used on half a dozen movies about oceanside life, he nodded hello to Mel Gibson walking by with one of his kids. The wiry actor was probably the friendliest on the lot and knew most people by name. Oneida had never introduced himself, but appreciated the man's interest in regular workers. He had learned that many actors did not have the same type of personality. He had even seen one man's bodyguard try to chase off a tour guide for having the balls to actually look the actor in the eye. Oneida nodded and smiled at Gibson, and decided he liked the down-to-earth man.

At the work site, he set his tools in place, and thought about his day. As soon as he could cut out of here, he'd head over to the football field. The kids got out of school an hour early today for some reason. He was considering moving to another place closer than West Covina, but they were all pretty expensive. The other reason, the real reason he was thinking of moving, was in case he needed to get lost again. In the past two days, that asshole Alberto Salez had been leaving him messages on his home phone. He had not called the slimy jackass back because at best he wanted to borrow money and at worst he wanted to blackmail him. Either way, Oneida was done with that part of his life. He didn't have contact with any of the guys he worked with in Texas. The only one he knew anything about was Don Munroe, and all he knew was that he lived in Virginia now.

Oneida looked at the plans for the set today as he got ready to work. He saw the other carpenter, Anthony Chapman, come from the direction of the parking lot lugging a box of his tools.

"Why do you take them home every day?" he asked him.

Chapman's New York accent always amused Oneida, having lived here and in Texas. The large man said, "You're too trusting. I leave these babies here and some mope from another set will have new tools. No, sir, where I go, these go."

Oneida smiled. He liked his hardworking partner and didn't care if he grumbled about a few things.

Chapman said, "You fill the thermos yet?"

"Nope, just got here too."

"I'll take care of it."

Oneida nodded as Chapman walked over to the carpenters' section, away from the main site, and tapped the five-gallon jug they filled with ice and water every day. He lifted the thermos and started to unscrew the top.

Even though Oneida had his eyes looking at the plans for the day, the light of the blast seemed to hit him before the sound and the force. Wood and stray nails flew in all directions, as the entire work site seemed to be the center of some giant fireball.

Watching the early news, while Caren took a shower after the night they had experienced, was the only stimuli he could handle right now. Duarte flipped around until he saw live footage of a crime scene in Burbank. He was about to change it when the announcer said, "A bomb on the Universal Studios lot has killed at least one and destroyed the set to the new Steven Spielberg western miniseries." Duarte watched the crowds grow as they were funneled away from the blast site. The announcer continued: "Local police aren't talking about the blast but a source inside the Department of Justice has confirmed that this may be related to a series of labor union bombings across the country."

Duarte sat back on the bed and stared at the TV, even as the next story came on.

Caren stepped out of the bathroom naked, using a towel to dry her blond hair. "What's up?"

"We gotta get to L.A. right now."

They had been lucky to grab a direct flight to Los Angeles from Seattle. Caren put the tickets on her credit card, and was fidgeting because she had not been able to call the office yet to let them know they were on the move. They had packed up the records and shipped them back to Washington, glad to be rid of them, then raced to the airport.

Now in a nice, rented Chevy Tahoe, they were weaving through the thick afternoon traffic of Los Angeles, trying to find their way to Burbank and the famous Universal Studios. Once they were in the area, it wasn't hard to find the scene. Unlike the relatively small crime scene at the labor camp in Florida, where the media hardly took notice, this was a circus, with a manned police line and a street full of news vehicles.

They parked the Tahoe in a lot four blocks away and started the climb up the hill toward the crime scene. At the yellow tape next to a squad car was a uniformed Los Angeles cop with dark hair and eyes. As Duarte came closer, he saw the man's name tag read GARCIA.

Duarte held up his badge. "I need to see the scene supervisor."

"Good luck."

"Where would we find him?"

"You got me, pal. I don't even know who it is."

Caren stepped in front of Duarte. In a soft voice different than Duarte was used to hearing from her, she said, "I'm sure you could use your radio and find out for us, couldn't you?"

The cop just stared at Caren and said, "Does that act work for you often?"

Caren smiled and nodded.

"You're not from L.A., are you?"

Caren said, "No, how can you tell?"

"Because out here, that shit don't cut it. We get it every day of every week from actresses, waitresses that want to be actresses, models, models that want to be actresses and just plain old good-looking girls."

"So you're saying I'm an amateur out here."

"At least you're smart." The cop went back to ignoring them.

Duarte had one more idea to short-circuit the bureaucracy. "My name is Duarte. You know how hard it can be for a Latin working for the government. You got any suggestions?"

Now the cop looked at him and seemed to warm to them. He looked around and then lifted the plastic tape and signaled them inside. He pointed to a trailer near a chain-link fence. "That's the command post. ID yourself there, and someone will figure out what to do with you."

Duarte shook the cop's hand while he shot a quick look at Caren. He was learning something from her after all.

The scene around the blast site was almost breathtaking. Duarte didn't realize there were these kinds of police resources anywhere. Unlike the migrant camp that had one or two TV reporters and a dozen cops, this one had an area designated as a media staging area with more than a dozen cameras already set up and more reporters arriving. Three command trailers had already been deployed. The law enforcement command center had a giant LAPD badge displayed on the side of it, leaving no doubt as to who was in charge.

"This is a circus," said Duarte as he searched for a person or place to start his investigation.

"But circuses can be fun," said Caren, obviously starstruck by the bustle and excitement on the scene.

Lost in all of this were the charred wood scraps and double yellow tape around what was the epicenter of the explosion. Duarte gravitated toward the scene while Caren got swept up in speaking to one of the police commanders and showing her identification.

Duarte barely heard the ring of his cell phone over the sounds of the activity around him. He flipped the Nextel's cover, "Duarte."

"Agent Duarte, can you hear me?"

He didn't recognize the woman's voice. "Yes, who is this?"

"Maria Tannza. I'm sorry to bother you."

"It's no bother, Ms. Tannza."

"Please call me Maria, and I'm embarrassed but I needed to tell someone."

"Tell someone what?"

"Last night, I think I saw Alberto Salez hanging around the camp. It looked like he was trying to visit me, but I had company."

Duarte considered this. "How certain are you?"

There was silence then she said, "Certain. It was him."

"Now, Maria, you have to be honest with me. Did you have more of a relationship with Salez than you told us?"

"No, why?"

"Why would he risk it to come see you?"

"I have no idea."

For some reason, deep inside, Duarte was relieved that the pretty teacher didn't have any kind of romantic relationship with the fugitive. He said, "I'm in California right now. I'll have my partner check on you. Is that okay?"

"It's not necessary. I feel better just telling someone."

"It's no problem. His name is Chuck Stoddard, and he'll call or come by today."

"Thank you, Agent Duarte. Thank you so much."

"Call me Alex."

Ten minutes later, Duarte had his partner Chuck on the phone. His partner immediately started whining about babysitting this paranoid woman.

Duarte said, "Just call her and give her your cell number."

"I'm not giving some crazy lady my cell."

"Then go out and see her."

There was silence. "I'll give her the cell, if you don't think she'll bug me too much."

"It's just until we can find Salez. C'mon, Chuck, I can't because I'm out here."

"Seattle?"

"No, L.A."

"What're you doing there?"

"Touring Universal Studios, what else?"

"Okay, okay, I'll do it." There was a pause, and his partner said, "So what have you found out so far?"

Duarte filled him in on the progress of the investigation.

20

MIKE GARRETTI WAS PISSED OFF. HE KNEW IT WOULD BE easier to shoot these guys, but his fucking employers wanted bombs at work sites. C-4 at that. Now he had missed the mark again. At least this time no kids had been hurt. But by the size of the group around the blast site, he might take more heat over this. The hell of it was, he even liked Oneida Lawson. He was happy the guy got to live. At least for a while longer. He realized that as a professional hit man, he wasn't making the cut. He was two for four, with a number of civilian casualties. He didn't care that this was his first and last assignment. He still had his regular job, although he was running out of leave, and his buddies could cover for him only for so long.

He took in the sights of the carnival unfolding in front of him, hidden in a crowd of more than a hundred people so no one would ever notice him. It was one more sign that Americans didn't have enough to do to keep busy.

His instant message on his cell went off with the code to call in. That didn't happen often, so he immediately walked down the street to a pay phone. He dialed the free number and waited as it rang.

He heard the man himself say, "Hello?"

"It's me."

"Well?"

"No good."

"That's what I heard but I wanted to confirm it. What happened?"

"Can't say yet, but I always tell you bombs are tricky."

"Yes, I know, I know. That's not why I had you call."

"What's up?"

"Keep your eyes open, the ATF man is at the scene in L.A."

"No shit. I'm glad you told me."

"There's more."

"What?"

"Salez is back in Florida."

"You sure?"

"Would I waste my time with this call?"

"Guess not."

"Now, get down to Florida and handle Salez. I don't care how. There'll be supplies waiting for you at the regular place."

"I'll take care of it."

"Don't fuck up this time."

The line went dead.

Duarte watched the people inside the crime scene go about their business. Even eleven hours after the initial explosion, people were still scurrying around. Duarte had read about how in Israel the cops had bombing investigations down to a science and worked hard to get the businesses damaged by a blast up and running in a few hours. It served notice to the suicide bombers that their efforts would not affect commerce. Duarte liked that kind of determination and resilience.

The LAPD bomb guys knew their jobs. He spoke to a couple and realized they were former military guys too. He and Caren were asked a couple of times about their identities and roles in the investigation by the odd captain or detective, but once it was determined they weren't with the media they were left alone. One captain, in charge of special operations, stopped Duarte and Caren as they tried to determine where the witnesses to the explosion were being interviewed.

The fit man in his early forties had close-cropped hair and a uniform shirt that was tailored to show off his hours in the gym working on his biceps.

"Who the hell are you?" He didn't try to hide his authority or short temper.

"I'm Alex Duarte, ATF."

The man relaxed. "You out of the L.A. division?"

"No, sir, Miami division, West Palm Beach field office."

"What're you here for?"

"This may be tied to a case we're working."

"How you get here so fast?"

"I was in Seattle and saw it on the news."

The man smiled and shook his head. "Fuck, we're still wait-ing on the fucking Bureau guys from L.A. to show up. ATF is all right."

Duarte let a slight smile slip across his lips.

Caren cut in, "You need FBI? I can make a call."

"Hell no. Just more people we have to babysit." The sturdy man looked around the scene and said, "They know you guys are here?"

"No, and I have no reason to tell them."

"Don't want them to jump your claim?"

Duarte nodded slightly. "More like I don't want to deal with them. They have a guy in D.C. who is working the case with us. Sort of, anyway."

"On this blast?"

Duarte hesitated, not wanting to give too much away. "Like I said, it may have to do with another blast investigation."

The man looked sideways. "What kind of blast investigation?"

As Duarte was about to answer, by telling him about the bombs, Caren Larson stepped up and said, "Labor intimidation."

Now the man shifted his gaze to Caren. "Since when does the ATF investigate labor problems?"

"Hi, I'm Caren Larson. I'm with the Department of Justice. We investigate labor issues, as well as anything else we want to."

The captain didn't look cowed. "Well, Ms. Larson, you can investigate anything you want, but if you do it in L.A. you do it with the LAPD. Now, fill me in on your case."

"I'm not sure you're in a position that needs to know."

The captain bowed up and said, "Your position is about to be outside this crime scene, baby. ATF here can look into the bomb-ing, but Justice and the FBI can kiss my fucking ass."

Now Duarte stepped up. "Captain, there have been several bombings that the Department of Justice thinks were used to scare off certain labor organizers. If this is related, we'll brief you on everything."

The captain, still hot, regained some composure and looked at Duarte. "Stand by and I'll have my bomb people brief you. That cool?"

"Thank you, sir."

As the captain strutted off, Caren said, "Still pissed about the Rampart division."

"I think the whole DoJ speech was a little strong."

"I *am* with the DoJ. What should I do, lie?"

Duarte didn't want to get into how to handle people. He certainly wasn't an expert in the field. Instead, he started scanning the scene. A tall, muscular black man was sitting alone on a toolbox not far from him. The man looked shaken as he stared straight ahead.

Duarte made his way over to the man and sat next to him. Something about the man's look said he was either a witness to the event or knew the victim. Duarte said, "You okay?"

The man looked up from his hands and nodded.

"I'm Alex Duarte."

"Oneida Lawson," the man mumbled.

Duarte wasn't used to someone who talked less than him.

Duarte started easy, using what little skill he had in interviewing. "You near the blast this morning?"

Oneida nodded. "Saw it."

"What happened?"

Oneida looked up at Duarte and asked, "Who're you?"

"I'm an ATF agent. Just interested in the blast."

Oneida nodded. "I get it." The man's head swiveled on a muscular neck to look toward the blast site. "It looked like he moved our big thermos and the whole area just turned orange."

"What area?"

"The carpenters' area."

Duarte nodded. "How many carpenters are there?"

"Just Anthony and me. Now I guess it's just me."

"Anthony was the victim?" Duarte looked up and saw Caren start to head toward him. He subtly held up a hand to keep her away so he could keep his conversation going.

"Yeah, Anthony Chapman. He was easy to deal with. I'll miss him."

Duarte asked a few more questions about the job and other employees. Nothing seemed vital. He learned that Oneida Lawson coached football at a private high school in Pasadena.

"Yeah, the kids keep me going. Nothing like teaching a teenager the route that accentuates his strengths at wide receiver or how conditioning pays off late in the game. If I could afford it, I'd coach full-time."

Duarte listened, then got the man to open up a little more. "Was Anthony in the union?"

"We all in the union on this job. Man, this is California."

"You don't sound like you're from L.A."

"Naw. I'm from Texas."

"Were you a carpenter there too?"

"Naw. Worked for a big company. Moved equipment for them."

"Oh yeah? What company?"

"Powercore."

"I've heard of them. They're the ones in trouble now for manipulating stock prices?"

"Yeah, that's just the tip of the iceberg."

Duarte nodded, and got back to the victim, Anthony Chapman. "Was Anthony involved in the union more than just being a member?"

Oneida nodded. "Shit yeah. He was the shop steward on this job and vice president of the local chapter. That important?"

Duarte shrugged. "Maybe." He finally took out a notebook to copy down some of Oneida Lawson's personal information, in case he needed to talk to him again.

As he walked back to Caren, he had the distinct feeling that Mr. Lawson knew more than he was telling. Duarte just wasn't confident enough in his interviewing skills to follow his gut feeling.

Alberto Salez didn't know if he was annoyed that his chance to reclaim his property was lost, or if he was mad that Maria Tannza was friendly with the old, redneck manager of the camp. The asshole had bothered him a few times for spending the night on the camp premises and not working in the fields. Salez had snarled and generally hinted that the old man shouldn't bother him if he knew what was good for him. He backed off after that—once he realized that Salez was as bad as anyone around.

Now Salez watched as the old man left his trailer, which was set off on a separate piece of property about three miles from the camp. The double-wide sat back on the property with a big maintenance storage shed on one side and drums of gas, diesel and motor oil under a cement-roofed storage pavilion. A canal ran in front of the wooded property with a twelve-foot wooden bridge that spanned from the dirt road to the property. The owners of the farm believed the bridge discouraged thieves from looting all the machinery and gas stored on the property.

Salez watched from the woods behind the house. Not everyone knew it was there, but he did. He knew the old manager's wife was ill and didn't leave the trailer much. But that didn't keep the old man from stepping out, if that's what he was doing with the lovely Maria.

The simple wooden gate on the trailer side of the canal was down. If the old man wanted to go anywhere, he'd have to stop and lift it himself. He generally left it open all day until he returned at night. Salez knew the manager had to get to the camp soon, and that's when he'd make his move. He worked his way around to the bridge, knowing that if something happened he'd be able to run back to his truck parked off the dirt road around the curve in about five minutes.

As he considered his escape, an old basset hound followed by the manager walked down the three stairs from the trailer to the ground. The dog eased down the few steps from the door with the old man easing after him. Both of them looked like they had arthritis. The manager waddled across the front yard, staying close to the dog, and then headed toward the gate. The dog broke off slightly and veered toward where Salez hid in the bushes near the gate.

Salez pulled his fillet knife. He briefly thought about taking the old man with him and leaving him at the same gas station where he had left the other two bodies. He had only seen one brief newsclip about the discovery of the two bodies, but nothing else.

He heard the man yell for the dog to come closer to him. He continued his slow, gimpy march to the gate, with the dog edging back toward him.

Just as he stepped up to the wooden gate and unlatched the simple metal clasp, then walked the gate back toward the trailer, Salez stepped out of the bushes.

The man looked up in surprise, then his face changed. "What're you doing here?"

"Maria told me to make sure you leave her alone."

The old man didn't hesitate. "You are so full of shit. She saw you skulking around last night. I thought she was imagining things, but now I see you are stupid enough to still be in the area."

"Who're you calling stupid, old man? You spend your life at that stinking labor camp. And you live out here like a hermit."

"Least I'm not wanted. No, sir, it won't be no loss to have you locked up."

Salez stepped up onto the entrance to the small bridge. The old man stepped back, and the dog started to growl.

Salez laughed. "That old hound dog couldn't reach me before I cut your throat." He showed the knife to the man.

"He's a basset hound, you moron, and he's more spry than he looks." As if on cue, the dog growled, and the hair on his back stood up.

Salez feinted to one side, then leaped forward. At the same time, the dog sprang up and snapped his lazy jaws onto Salez's scrotum. The old man took a step back, then slipped on the loose gravel at the side of the bridge. He tumbled backward down the side of the canal and landed with a plop, facedown, in the still, stagnant canal water.

Salez struck the dog with his open hand across his floppy ears and sent it whimpering back toward the trailer. The fugitive checked his pants, unzipping them to ensure the dog hadn't punctured his privates. Satisfied that he was uninjured, Salez stepped to the edge of the bridge and looked down at the body in the water.

With a little luck, the cops will think it was an accident, thought Salez. He strolled out onto the dirt road and whistled on his way back to the old Nissan pickup truck hidden in the woods.

21

PEOPLE FLOWED LIKE WATER IN THE GIANT LAX CON-
course, even at eleven at night. Standing in front of a chicken place
tucked into a cubbyhole in the wall, Alex Duarte felt more like he
was going through a breakup than just returning to Florida to follow up on his investigation. The LAPD had confirmed that C-4
had been the main component of the bomb that killed fifty-five-
year-old Anthony Chapman. Duarte was surprised to hear that
Chapman was, in fact, a serious labor organizer. Maybe the DoJ
attorneys weren't as stupid as he had thought. He was still troubled
by his interview with Oneida Lawson. He still had the impression
that the amateur football coach knew more than he was saying.

Now Duarte's problem was a tired Caren Larson. They had
not slept and were still drained from the flight from Seattle earlier in the day. He had an eleven-thirty flight back to West Palm,
through Atlanta, and she had a direct flight to Washington.

"I'll call you if something develops on the case." He managed a smile and placed his hand on her shoulder.

"Are you a shithead, or what?"

"Excuse me."

"I don't sleep with any old federal agent. In fact, you're the
first one."

He stared at her as he started to get an idea of what was bothering her. "Oh, I see. It's more of a personal issue."

Now she stared at him. "Where did you learn about relationships, Vulcan? Yes, it's a personal issue. I thought we had started
something."

"We did. I mean, we still do. But I'll have to go back sometime."

"One more night in California wouldn't have killed you."

He nodded but knew he had to check on Maria and see if Salez really was in the area. It was Duarte's nature. He couldn't change it, no matter how lonely it made him.

"Or you could have come back through D.C."

"What would I do in D.C.?"

"Bob might need a briefing."

"I'm sure you could brief your boss better than me. Besides, he likes listening to you more than me."

"You are a tough one to figure out."

"Glad I never tried to do it."

Caren's face softened slightly, then she smiled a little and reached out and hugged him. "At least I know you're not throwing me over for another woman."

He relaxed in her embrace, and realized what his army friends had felt when they would ship out and hug wives and girlfriends as they left. He had only had his ma at a couple of his departures. It was nice, but not the same thing.

He was surprised how he thought of Caren his entire walk to the gate. Once on the plane, he pulled out his notebook and started sorting through the information he'd gathered to see if there were any connections between the people he had talked to so far. By the time the plane's wheels were up, he had only one thought on his mind: who was doing these bombings?

Caren Larson dozed on the Delta flight back to Reagan National. As she slipped in and out of consciousness, she continued to think about the odd man she was starting to have strong feelings for. Alex Duarte had proven to be near the opposite of any federal agent she had ever met. He was quiet and introspective, to the point of being antisocial. But it all added up to a pleasant package, and that didn't even count how he looked.

Despite her comments to Alex about his lack of experience with women, the fact of the matter was that she had only had three serious boyfriends. Her first boyfriend, Vince Weiner, was a freshmen at the local junior college when she was a senior in high school. He had sweated out meeting her father, waited through five months of celibacy until she was ready to lose her virginity and done all the right things after. He was a great first boyfriend, but he wanted to live in the Florida Keys, and live a life devoted to boating and drinking. They parted on good terms, but she felt like the love she had shown him was wasted when he wouldn't buckle down at school and try to do better for himself.

Her second boyfriend lasted through most of her time at Cornell Law School. She thought he was The One until she realized he had lower expectations than she did.

Her last boyfriend was an investment banker who had a house in Alexandria. He was tall and handsome and had ambition to spare. The problem was that that was all he cared about. Investments and making money. They traveled a little, and she met a wide range of nice and wealthy people. And she was lonely. She had dated him for nearly two years, finally breaking it off about eight months ago, but she knew it was the right thing to do when she realized she wasn't the least bit upset she was single again. His saving grace was that he had talked about his desire to have kids, but she could never pin him down.

She felt like Goldilocks, because she could never find the guy who was "just right." She took responsibility for her pickiness and didn't regret it. At least, not most nights. She had cried to her mother on the phone more than once—one time, for so long that her mother had felt compelled to fly to D.C. to visit her picky daughter for the weekend. Despite her job and apartment, and all the things that went along with them, she still felt like a displaced Midwestern girl. She couldn't say she was happy with her life.

Now, riding home, she had to make a decision on where she intended to take this case. Should she voice her concerns that the theory of the bombings could actually be slowing down the case or just go along with the suggestions made by the boss? Where did her legal ethics leave her? She wasn't charging anyone maliciously. She was just investigating a case. In her limited investigative experience, she had never had to ask herself these questions before.

The whole situation, the complexity and stress of her life, made her think about her college days. She had been happy. Especially at Cornell, where she had spent most of her time knowing she was one of the brightest in the class. This feeling was reinforced by hour after hour of tutoring her boyfriend, Barry. He was cute and charming, but she had learned early on that those kinds of attributes didn't add up to any kind of academic success. She didn't mind Sunday afternoons going over simple concepts with her cute boyfriend. She dozed off again, thinking of the simple times in her life, and her simple, middle boyfriend, Barry Eisler.

Duarte arrived in West Palm Beach about nine in the morning and decided he'd never get any sleep at his apartment, so he retrieved his government Taurus and headed back to the office. His boss, Dale, was probably the coolest supervisor in the ATF. He never got frazzled or sweated the small stuff. He only asked if Duarte had been successful on his trip, and didn't require a detailed briefing. That only left Chuck Stoddard to deal with.

"I'm telling you, she's fine," said the big man after Duarte's inquiry.

"You're certain?"

"She didn't want to leave the trailer and appreciated the concern. Left her my cell and she hasn't called." Chuck leaned back and looked across the tiny, cluttered office. "What are you so worried about? Why on earth would Salez go back there anyway? She just got spooked."

Duarte nodded slowly, barely listening to his partner. He'd ride out there later to see her, but he knew who he had to see first.

His mother hugged him like he had been gone for a yearlong deployment in the Persian Gulf. She made him a lunch of chicken fricassee with black beans and rice as she told him how his father had been working on a big plumbing job in a Palm Beach mansion and his brother was in trial on a lady who had fallen off a toilet in Wendy's. All in all, he felt glad that he had missed nearly a week with his family.

The labor camp looked quiet and orderly as he slowly drove through to Maria's trailer at about three o'clock in the afternoon. He noticed several nice cars parked at the manager's trailer, and the pretty young secretary smoking a cigarette on the front steps and looking upset. He wondered if someone had come to fire her.

When Maria answered her door with tears in her eyes, he knew something worse had happened.

She surprised him by hugging him at the door, then inviting him inside.

"Is something wrong?"

She explained how the manager of the camp had been found in the canal by his trailer. He had slipped and died while opening the gate. The whole camp was in mourning for the popular manager.

Duarte had spoken to the manager when he investigated the blast. He seemed like a decent guy. Duarte didn't know what to say so he followed Maria into the trailer silently and wished Caren was here with him. She usually knew what to say. And he had to admit that he missed her company.

Maria sat on the couch, and Duarte slipped into the overstuffed chair across from her.

She blew her nose, and said, "What a hard few weeks. I never thought I'd have to deal with anything like this."

"I'm sorry you've had to."

She bowed her pretty face and lowered her dark eyes. "Thank you."

He waited a moment, and asked about her seeing Salez.

"It was just a glimpse, really. He was across the road near the bushes. If a car's headlights hadn't hit him, I never would've seen his face."

"Did anyone else see him?"

"Just . . ." She started to cry. "The manager was visiting."

"He saw Salez too?"

"No. In fact, he told me it couldn't be Salez. He'd be too busy running from you."

"He's running, but I'm not sure if he's running from me."

She looked up. "What do you mean?"

"He's wanted, and an escaped fugitive—but someone serious is trying to kill him. That's what he's afraid of. I think of him as almost a victim. There's no evidence he's hurt anyone. Aside from giving me and my partner the slip, his only charges are in Texas." Duarte paused. It felt as if he had met a lot of people from Texas lately. He couldn't recall everyone, but it seemed like the Lone Star State was well represented in transplants.

Maria said, "I don't want to ever see him again. That's why I was shocked to see him, or least think I saw him. He has no more business here. We weren't dating or anything."

"Did he know that?"

"Of course. How do you not know if you're dating or not?"

"Some guys don't understand. At least, that's what I hear."

She let a small smile creep across her face for the first time since he had met her. "Do you have a lot of experience with dating?"

He shrugged.

"I didn't think so. You seem far too nice to be a womanizer."

He didn't know what to say, so he shrugged again.

"Where's your partner, Miss Larson?"

"Washington. If I find something, I'll let her know, and she'll do the same."

She nodded. "She seemed like a very nice person, and pretty too."

He shrugged again, then remembered the purpose of his visit. "Do you feel safe if Salez is around?"

"I suppose so." She stood and picked up an empty glass.

"You can call me if there is a problem. My cell is always on."

"I wouldn't want to disturb you late if you are asleep."

"Don't worry, not much chance of that."

She stopped on her way to the kitchen and looked at him. "That's sweet, thank you." Then she leaned down and kissed him gently on the cheek. "I'll be fine."

22

BY SEVEN-FIFTEEN IN THE MORNING, CAREN LARSON WAS at her desk and writing up a memo detailing the progress she and Alex Duarte had made on the case so far. The day's rest after their trip west had been much needed and changed her outlook drastically. She was quite encouraged that the latest victim, Anthony Chapman, had been a labor organizer. Maybe her suspicions about the labor theory being a diversion were incorrect. Maybe the concerns that had weighed her down during the flight had been overblown.

There were a number of reasons why she liked to be in the office early. For one, the traffic from her Alexandria apartment was light at this time of the morning. Another reason was that the office was quiet, and her phone silent for a change. She also intended to have the memo on Roberto Morales's desk when he arrived at his customary ten o'clock—usually after he had briefed the attorney general on whatever was going on at the moment. Some people in the office took advantage of the boss's usually late arrival. It was rare to see Tom Colgan in the office before nine forty-five.

As she hammered away on her computer's keyboard, she constantly thought about Alex Duarte and what he might be doing at that moment. She knew he lived in an apartment behind his parents and thought it was sweet, adding to the ATF agent's considerable charm. He had proven to be gentle and conscientious, if not overly romantic. She couldn't help but regret the way she had come on so strong, and the way in which they had developed the personal relationship. It didn't feel professional somehow. But, on the other hand, she had been lonely, and he definitely filled a void in her. Now she found that she missed him.

As that thought passed through her mind, her desk phone rang.

"Caren Larson." It was her usual greeting.

"I'm impressed you're in so early. Something told me you would be."

She smiled at the sound of Alex Duarte's voice.

"And you're starting early too."

"Now that I'm keeping regular hours again, I find myself getting up early."

She didn't want to admit that she had a serious case of jet lag. "What gets you to call so early?"

"I visited Maria Tannza last night."

"Oh yeah?" For some reason, Caren felt apprehensive hearing that. "Did she really see Salez?"

"I think so. She was upset because the manager of the camp had died in an accidental fall."

"The man we spoke to?"

"Yeah."

"That's too bad." She leaned back in her chair, and then looked behind her to make sure she was still alone in her tiny office. "What's our next move on the case?"

"I'm going to hit the streets hard for Salez. What about you?"

"I'll brief Bob and see if there's anything new. I'll call if there is."

There was silence. Then Duarte said, "I don't know, Caren. There's something about this case. I just can't get it out of my head."

She sighed, and blurted, "I was hoping you might say that about me."

"Say what?" Then he added, "Of course I'm thinking about you too."

"Save it, Kojak. You are what you are. I'd rather you were honest with me."

There was no response.

She said, "That might become my pet name for you."

"What?"

" 'Kojak.' At least it will make you nervous when I call you it. I know you. You're already worried that I'm stuck on you."

"No, I'm not."

"All right, Kojak."

"Don't call me that."

She couldn't help smiling as she said, "I'll call you after I speak to Bob."

Duarte felt comfortable in the passenger's seat of Chuck's government-issued Ford Expedition as they cruised down Olive Avenue in West Palm Beach. After all the travel, it was nice to be in a place where he knew every alley and shortcut. The big man insisted on driving his brand-new sports-utility behemoth to Duarte's cousin Tony's pawnshop in the north end of the city. If his cousin had seen or heard about Alberto Salez, he'd share it with Duarte. Especially if they talked to him in the privacy of his pawnshop.

Chuck said, "It was awful quiet without you here."

"Steve and Meat didn't keep you busy?"

"Nope, I avoided them. Those two make me nervous working so late."

"It's called 'working hard.' "

"They don't tell me anything. I don't think they like me."

"Chuck, they're just busy. You should try it. It's fun." Duarte even smiled at his own comment.

"I thought I missed you." He let out a laugh, and repeated, "It really was quiet without you around."

"Appreciate you checking on Maria."

"No problem. I doubt she saw that shithead anyway."

"I don't know, she seems pretty certain."

Chuck nodded, then said, "What about the other bombings? They related?"

"Yeah."

"You getting NRT involved?"

"Caren says that DoJ doesn't want to use them yet. I'm not sure I'd keep the case if the National Response Team was called in."

"Why not? I mean, this is what they do."

"DoJ wants it lower profile for now."

"At least tell me they're using our lab and not the FBI."

"Yeah, everything is with us."

"So everything is entered in BATS."

"Yeah, I don't think they could keep it out of the tracking system."

"Then what do ya got on the case?"

Duarte spent a few minutes filling him in on what the DoJ's theory was and what he and Caren had found so far. Then he added his own commentary. "I tell ya, Chuck, there's something about this case I can't get past. Something doesn't feel right about it."

"You get that feeling from interviews?"

"Very funny. No, just the idea that there is some conspiracy to screw up labor organization. It doesn't make much sense."

"What does?"

"I don't know. I have no alternative—that's why it's stuck in my head. I think I did pick up one thing in an interview that you'd be proud of."

"Really, you? What'd you learn that someone didn't say out loud?" He smiled.

"I talked to a witness to the Universal Studios blast, a carpenter named Oneida Lawson."

"And what did a man named after a China manufacturer tell you?"

"He didn't say much. Saw the blast, lost his buddy—that sort of thing—but there's something about him that's eating at me. He knew something more but didn't tell me. The more I think about it, the more sure I am of it."

"I'd like to see the look on Dale's face if you asked to fly to L.A. just to talk to this guy again."

"I'd sure like another shot at him. It's true what they say: you have to take your chance while you have it."

"I agree. Look what that philosophy has done for my career."

Even Alex Duarte had to chuckle at the big man.

Chuck nodded, keeping his eyes on the crowded street in front of them. The farther north they traveled, past Good Samaritan Hospital and the medical offices that followed, the worse the neighborhood looked. As they turned west onto Broadway, there were more people on the street.

Chuck finally said, "What about the cute DoJ chick, Caren?"

"When did you meet her?"

"I saw her around the office one afternoon."

"What about her?"

"You do her?"

Duarte had never been able to answer yes to a question like that before from a coworker. Not even in the army. All of his encounters with the opposite sex had occurred off base and away from curious eyes. He still didn't answer honestly. "We just worked the case together."

"C'mon, you can tell me. She's hot."

Duarte pointed to a small stand-alone building and said, "Pull in to the side so he can't see us coming." It was enough to keep his large partner off the topic of his personal relationships.

His cousin kept a calm expression on his face as he buzzed the two ATF agents in to his pawnshop. Tony D's Pawn and Gun had been a staple of the north-end business district for fifteen years. His cousin Tony was proud of the fact that he had only been arrested three times for trafficking in stolen goods and twice for illegal firearms sales, and that all charges had been resolved prior to him getting a record. Duarte wasn't sure what that meant, but his cousin was able to retain his federal firearms license, and seemed to make a ton of cash through the store. Legally or otherwise. There were, however, consistent rumors that Tony had a good, exotic firearm connection and distributed nontraditional firearms for the right price. If Duarte could ever prove that allegation, his blood ties to Tony wouldn't change a thing.

The short, bald man stayed behind the glass counter with dozens of cheap handguns and one nice nickel-plated Luger. "What have I done now?"

Duarte said, "I can't just visit?"

"Have you ever before?"

"I suppose not."

"I got nothing to hide anymore. Even your self-righteous old man can't look down on me as a crook."

Duarte stared at him. "Don't talk about my pop like that."

"Jesus, sorry. What? Did Frank get all the sense of humor for you two?"

"No, but I'm on duty. I don't have time for laughs."

"On duty. For Alcohol, Tobacco and Firearms? That should be a convenience store, not a government agency."

Chuck grinned at Tony's quip.

Duarte got to the point. "Look, Tony, this is important or I wouldn't bother you. I need to find Alberto Salez."

"Still? I thought you were looking for him last week."

"I was."

"Maybe he's not around anymore."

"I think he's here."

"What he do that's so bad?"

"He escaped from me, but the real reason is that he knows who's been setting some bombs, and he knows why. I also believe he might be a victim if I don't find him soon."

His cousin smiled. "So you're just looking out for him, right?"

Duarte shrugged.

"Most cops say something like that and I think they're full of shit. You say it and I know you mean it. It's sad you wasted your life as a cop. You'd have made a fine priest."

Chuck leaned in on the conservation. "His sex life wouldn't be much different."

Tony looked at him and laughed. "Always this one has been too serious to chase girls. He's missing one of the great pastimes God ever created."

Duarte said, "I hate to break this up, but do you know anything about Alberto Salez?"

The small man sighed. Then he had to mash a button to let in a tall, very thin black man with a lawn mower and chain saw balanced on top of it.

The man said, "What can you give me for this fine mower and matching chain saw?" His smile revealed a mouth of gold bridgework and filling.

Tony looked at Duarte, then the man, and said, "Twenty bucks, if you start the mower outside and show me how it works."

"Twenty bucks," the man said loudly. "How 'bout forty?"

"Forty is too much. I said twenty. But if they're in good shape, I'll go twenty-five."

The man shot him a harsh look. "You crazy or just a crook? This here is a three-hundred-dollar mower, and the chain saw is worth two bills, easy."

Then Tony cut his eyes to Duarte and Chuck. "How 'bout I introduce you to these policemen here? Maybe they'll give you a better price."

"No, twenty is good." The man started to back out of the store. "I'll come back for the cash when you're not so busy." He slipped out the door and was headed down the street before anyone said a word.

Tony said, "Maybe you do have some use."

"Maybe you do too. If you can get a line on Salez for me."

"What's in it for me?"

Duarte shook his head. He didn't want to turn his own cousin into a paid informant. "What do you want?"

"One of your inspection guys is after me for some tax issues on some Tokarev pistols I had brought in. Can you clear that up?"

Duarte hesitated, and said, "I can look into it if you can find Salez for me."

"Make it go away."

"I can't make that promise and you know it."

Tony nodded. "All right, you're no welcher. If I come through, I know you'll do your best."

"You have my cell. Call me if you hear anything at all."

"I promise you'll be getting a call if I ever hear anything about Salez."

Mike Garretti was supremely annoyed at his situation. He had done exactly as he had been instructed and it didn't work out, so now he was forced to wait here in Los Angeles until they decided what to do. The initial call was to wait a week or two, then stage a simple accident where Oneida Lawson was killed. Garretti didn't mind that option because he could go home and come out here on a weekend and not miss any more of his day job. Now he was in limbo. He had a buddy covering for him, so no one even knew he was off the base right now. Working in personnel made it easy to disappear, and if he bought a few rounds of drinks and a couple dinners everyone was more than happy to look out for him.

He had checked into the Hilton, right next to the CityWalk. Since all his expenses were covered, he didn't mind running up the tab. He'd rarely gotten to live so comfortably. Besides, he could keep better tabs on Oneida from here in L.A. He had spent the day conducting checks on Oneida's activities. The big carpenter had come back to work, and everything looked like it was running as usual at the Universal Studios. The tour Garretti took that day made no mention of the blast several days before. Workers were back at the same set like nothing had happened. He had followed Oneida to the high school where he coached football and then back to his dreary house without incident. The big man knew what had happened and what it meant. He had to; he was no idiot. He just didn't seem to care. At least he hadn't run right to the cops. Garretti would've gotten a call about that. He just went about his business.

The newspaper had covered the blast, and had even included a line about a labor dispute. The LAPD wasn't saying anything. They maintained that it could've been an accident and that they were investigating. Garretti thought it was funny that no one on any TV channel or in the newspaper made any mention of the bum who had been shot in front of the studio the night before the blast. One paper covered the shooting, calling it a "drive-by," and suggesting it had to do with drugs. He wondered if the cops had put it together.

He took the bus nearest his hotel to Rodeo Drive and Beverly Hills. He never knew L.A. had such an efficient mass transit system. He intended to make the most of his time out here, even if he'd rather be home in Texas.

Caren Larson felt like she was about to be interrogated. Roberto "Bob" Morales sat behind his desk, and FBI agent Tom Colgan was to one side, leaning on a library table and cleaning his manicured fingernails with a small nail clipper.

Caren had just summarized the interviews and progress she and Alex Duarte had made on the case during her trip to the West Coast.

Morales looked across his clean desk and said, "So you decided to traipse down the coast from Seattle to L.A.?"

"It seemed to be the smart move."

"You couldn't call us first?"

"I'm sorry, sir. It just sort of happened."

"Did Agent Duarte learn anything of value?"

"Not that he discussed with me. The last victim being involved in labor issues seemed to strengthen our hypothesis. He felt that he had to see if Salez was still in Florida." She considered asking about the origin of the labor theory, but the setting didn't seem right. Especially with Bob Morales staring her down from across his wide desk.

Colgan laughed out loud. "He wanted some of that woman's snatch down there."

Caren turned. "Excuse me?"

Morales added, "Tom, I don't believe there is any reason to speak like that."

Colgan cleared his throat. "Sorry, sir. I just mean, I saw a photo of the teacher from the migrant camp. If I had the chance, I'd hotfoot it down there too."

Caren felt her face flush and hoped no one else noticed. "If you mean Maria Tannza, I think you're off base. She's grieving the loss of her son, and Alex, I mean Agent Duarte, doesn't think that way."

"You mean he's gay? I knew it. That son of a bitch was just too neat all the time." Colgan slapped his own hand.

"That's not what I mean. And before I forget: Tom, you're a pig."

Morales brought the conversation back around to the case. "Caren, dear, are you certain the ATF man is with us on our theory for the bombings?"

\"I think so."

"Will he keep you in the loop on his search for Salez?"

"Yes." She paused and added. "On anything he finds."

"What do you mean? I thought he was only looking for Salez."

"He's on the case. He doesn't strike me as someone who gives up too easily. For instance, he spoke to a witness in L.A.—another carpenter who saw the blast—and he's convinced the guy knows something. He can't let it go. He'll follow up at some point."

Morales nodded his head like he knew others with the same habits. "I see. Very industrious." He stood behind his desk. "Good job, Caren. You understand that we may need you to go down there at some point and help Agent Duarte."

"Any time, sir."

"Good. Good attitude. I'll let you know." As she left, she got the feeling they were waiting for her to close the door before they were going to speak.

23

ALEX DUARTE SAT AT THE DINNER TABLE WITH HIS MA, pop and brother, and felt the exhaustion building in him. The table was set like a birthday celebration, with courses of food and two cakes. Even though his ma claimed that it was nothing special, she was obviously thrilled to have her youngest son home again after his trip. Duarte ate as if he had not been fed for a week, and felt some of his strength returning. His father sat impassively as his brother explained the complexities of a recent case.

Frank said, "No, Ma, it's not whether the lady was really hurt at the Wendy's; it's if they were doing the right thing to prevent the injury."

Duarte's father said, "If she wasn't hurt, there was no injury."

"But Wendy's doesn't know that. Besides, it's only some franchisee, not a corporate store. If it was the corporation, I would have had to back off because they can outspend me in court. They'd have worn me down."

"It's a simple question," started the elder Duarte. "Was she hurt in the fall?"

"It's not that simple."

Cesar Duarte threw up his hands and let his head sag. "Dios mio, who has taken my son's place?"

"C'mon, Pop, welcome to the twenty-first century. I'm an attorney; this is what I do."

Cesar Duarte shook it off and looked at Alex. "You don't look so good. Too tired. Too thin. What's wrong?"

"Nothing, Pop. Just a little jet-lagged."

"You solve that case?"

"Not yet."

"I think maybe you work too hard."

Frank looked up and said, "You never say that to me."

"When you work hard someone has to pay. Alex, he works because it's his duty."

Frank shook his head. "So I'm no good because I charge for my time. Alex coulda gone to law school too. He could be something other than a government sap."

Duarte didn't acknowledge his brother's dig. He never did. Since they were kids he learned that by ignoring Frank or any other loudmouth he got his own dig in.

Then he saw where he had learned it, as his father looked back at Alex, not answering his oldest son's comment. "What's got you traveling so long and working so late? The same problem you talked about last week?"

"Yes, sir. I haven't fixed it yet."

Cesar Duarte smiled and sat back. "Good man. You'll go far."

The dinner proceeded smoothly with Duarte's mother graciously accepting compliments on the carne asada, plantains and other assorted dishes she had labored over all afternoon. The fifty-five-year-old woman had found her calling in raising a family and helping her husband find a place in the community. Only twenty-one when she came to America with her husband of only one year, she had found a balance between her heritage and the demands of her new country. Only now could Duarte fully understand how well she had integrated into the culture. She had been to every PTA and Cub Scout meeting that Duarte could remember. She helped at the church with everything from bookkeeping to feeding the homeless. By every standard Duarte could think of, his ma was a smashing success, but he knew that some people might look at her as nothing more than a housewife or a nice "Spanish" lady. After his little encounter with the Seattle cop, he now wondered a little more about how people might view him too.

As they each sat picking at pieces of cake and sipping coffee, Duarte looked at his father and realized he knew little of what the owner of a small plumbing company did at work besides answer the calls of desperate homeowners with various issues involving their pipes.

"Hey, Pop," he started, searching for the right way to ask the question. "You ever join a union?"

"For work?"

Frank laughed and said, "No, Pop, for credit." He laughed at his lame joke, but the other Duartes ignored him.

Alex continued. "Yeah, as a plumber."

"When I started out as an apprentice, I had to join briefly. Since I always worked in Florida, and it's a right-to-work state, I didn't join. I attended meetings as an apprentice and it seemed like the men there were not as interested in good work as ways to cause mischief. I decided it was better to mind my own business and just concentrate on work and feeding you two."

Duarte considered this. He had always worked for the government in one way or another and never felt the need to be an active member of a union. The loose union that covered his current position as a special agent with the ATF was really an association, and had no power to demand or strike or even interfere in the day-to-day decisions of management. He could see where ordinary carpenters or plumbers could be taken advantage of if they didn't band together. His pop was very smart and strong-willed. He probably wouldn't have been bullied by an employer, but what about others? Duarte was starting to understand some of the reasons for a union and what might cause violence around one.

His father said, "This case you've been working, it has to do with a union?"

"Maybe."

"How so?"

"Well, the last man killed, in California, was an organizer for the union out there. The attorneys with the Department of Justice think that all the bombings in the case revolve around labor issues."

"To scare off organizers?"

"Not exactly. They think that one organization is discouraging other labor groups from organizing so that they can swoop in and gain more members themselves. At least that's how the theory goes."

His father considered these facts and seemed to withdraw as he contemplated the information. Duarte, looking at his father, realized just how much he had learned from him. He wondered if people saw the same thing when he withdrew to mull over problems.

Finally Cesar Duarte looked at his son and said, "What purpose would killing a carpenter serve?"

"That's what I'm trying to figure out."

"But what have you asked yourself? Does it discourage others from organizing?"

Duarte hadn't considered the motives of the attack like that.

"Does it create a position for someone else to fill?"

"I don't think so."

"Or does it distract you from the real reason for the bombing?"

Alex Duarte stared at this father. His plumber father, who had just hit on an idea that no one on the case, including himself, seemed to have considered. Distraction. Was the labor issue a sham used to throw him and Caren Larson off the track of the real reason for the bombings? If it was true, what was the link he needed? The victims? The locations? The companies? He had everything at his office. Files, interviews, even maps, if he needed them. Tomorrow would be a long day.

Alberto Salez walked into the Belle Glade Sports Club as if he had never left. The thin bartender nodded to him, obviously not realizing he was a fugitive and the target of the bomb that had ripped the labor camp to hell a few weeks back. He let his eyes search the open space of the bar and billiard room and saw a group of his old friends.

Walking over, he noticed one had his arm in a cast, one had his hands bandaged, and Raul, his closest friend in the group, had his nose taped and fingers splinted. His nose had been flat before, but now the way it just folded into his face was really creepy.

"Raul, what happened to you?" he said, walking up on the group.

Two of the men flinched at the sight of Salez and backed away.

"What's wrong with you guys?"

Raul looked at Salez. "You're wanted, man. You made a lot of bad shit happen around here."

"What're you talking about?"

"The bomb in your car killed the teacher's son, then a cop came around here looking for you."

"What cop?"

"The tall one, with a good-looking white girl. He made us tell him where you had been living."

"He made you? All of you? How?"

"Look at us, bro. He was like a kung fu hurricane, man."

Salez lifted a hand to his ear and recalled how quick the ATF man, Duarte, was. Maybe he was meaner than he looked after Salez had escaped. He said, "One man did all that to you guys?"

They all nodded.

"What he do? Pick you off one by one? Isolate you?"

No one spoke.

"You mean, all of you together couldn't take this cabron? Tell me that's not what happened. I thought you guys were tough."

Again, no one answered.

Salez sat down among the wounded men. This was a group he could control if they were beaten down like this. He raised his hand to catch the eye of the young Hispanic waitress who had apparently started since the last time he was here. She was thin, with a graceful neck, and moved smoothly like a dancer over to him.

Salez smiled and said, "¿Hola, cómo se llama?"

"Elenia, and I've already heard every possible comment from your friends here."

"These aren't my friends. My friends are a little tougher than this group. No, these are just peons that work down the road." He held out his hand. "We haven't met yet. My name is Berto."

"Hello, Berto. Now, what would you like to drink?" She smiled with the question, and it was so brilliant it took Salez by surprise.

"Why on earth is a beautiful girl like you working in this dump?"

"It's a long story, but my mama lives in South Bay and she's sick, so this was the best I could do and still be close to her."

"Now, that's nice. An old-fashioned girl. And beautiful too." Now he cut loose with his best smile. He knew he was a step up from the lowlifes that usually wandered into this place.

The pretty waitress returned his smile, and seemed sorry to leave once she had his order for a beer.

Salez looked around the group of men. "You guys don't want to let this pendejo cop get away with this, do you?"

They all shook their heads, but not with much conviction.

"Then leave it to me. He might come out here again, and this time we'll be ready for him."

Raul asked, "You know this cop?"

"I do."

"And he's a real cop, not something else?"

"Why would you ask that?"

"Because he didn't act like no cop we ever saw. He was tough, man. He broke my finger just to hear me scream."

Salez sat back and considered this information. That didn't sound like the quiet, professional ATF agent he had met. Then again, you could never predict what someone might do when their back was against the wall. He smiled as the lovely Elenia came back with his beer. This time, she sat next to him, after he gave her a ten-dollar bill and told her to keep the change.

24

IT WASN'T EVEN SEVEN O'CLOCK, AND ALEX DUARTE HAD stacks of files laid out across his office floor. He'd made notes on each of them as he did his best to find a link between the victims, not involving the Department of Justice's prevailing hypothesis about labor issues.

He had a small place-mat map of the United States by Chuck's desk with pins where the explosions had occurred. He looked at it and saw nothing remarkable. He wasn't sure what he had expected to see: maybe the design of a flower, or a name spelled out in the pins, but he thought it was worthwhile to look at it. Two on the West Coast and two on the East Coast. Nothing in the middle of the country. He briefly contemplated searching the airline records for flights before each blast, but he didn't have enough information. He needed a name or at least a firm time frame. And how was this guy transporting C-4 across the country? How was he getting it in the first place? Duarte seemed to have plenty of questions, but not many answers. That's what bothered him so much. He was used to answers. Action and answers. This type of investigation was entirely new to him. He decided to focus on the victims for a while.

The target of the Belle Glade labor camp was easy, as far as he could see: Alberto Salez. And no one except some suit in Washington could say he was involved in labor organization.

Janni Tserick was the apparent target of the Seattle bombing. He wasn't an organizer either. Anthony Chapman in L.A. was a target and an organizer. That left the bombing in Virginia, the second in the series. None of the three amusement park employees had appeared to be labor organizers. Their backgrounds had been void of anything that would point to an event that would lead to this. All three had been born in Virginia and had worked steadily in legitimate jobs since they graduated high school. He didn't see any link there either.

He stared at the notes and printouts on the victims and tried to imagine the ride on the small tram away from the park on the afternoon of the blast. No one would have had a clue until it was far too late. The driver wouldn't have even known a bomb caused the problem. At most, he would have heard the blast as he felt the jolt, then the metal from the tram torn up by the blast would've cut through him.

Duarte froze. His mind whirring in his head. The driver. There was no printout of the driver. He was as much a victim as anyone else on the small bus. He had been a nameless, faceless accessory to the tram itself. Not a human who had been deprived of life like the other three on board. Duarte started to pore through the reports from Caren Larson and found only the man's name in an attached local police report of the incident. Donald Munroe, age thirty-eight. He lived alone in a suburb of Fredericksburg. Duarte started to set down the report when his eye caught one more fact. He had moved from Texas less than a year before.

Alberto Salez returned from the bathroom next to Elenia's bedroom wearing one of her mother's robes. He didn't want the sickly old lady to catch him wandering around her shitty little house with no clothes on. Elenia had said not to worry, that her mom was so wiped out by the chemo that she rarely ventured out of her room. Elenia didn't check on her until after nine in the morning most days.

As he came back into the small room with the single mattress, the young waitress tittered at the sight of Salez.

"What's so funny?"

"You, in Mamma's robe." She leaned up from the bed, naked, and pinched his stomach. "With your little belly popping through the front."

He let the robe slip off his shoulders. "Don't laugh," he said flatly.

She continued to snicker and stare at his hairy stomach. "And look"—she reached up again and cupped his penis with her hand—"your belly makes your pee-pee look really small."

He shoved away her hand. Did this bitch know who she was talking to? He crossed the room to his clothes, which were piled in a heap in the corner.

"Don't be mad," she cooed, but still smiling at her previous wit.

He slipped on his jeans and T-shirt, suddenly conscious of his forty-year-old body. The fifteen years between he and Elenia looked like a century right now. He flinched at her next spurt of giggles and instinctively reached for his fillet knife. It wasn't there. He had left it in his truck when they had pulled up the night before.

"Berto, c'mon back to bed," she said, flipping back the single sheet to show off her tight, muscular body with a ring piercing her navel.

By now, his anger had seeped into his soul. How could anyone look down on him like that and tease him about his appearance? Without thinking, he squatted next to her and acted like he was caressing her face with one hand, then used the other to run his fingers through her dark, silky hair.

She smiled and purred slightly as she lifted her face to him.

Then he gripped both hands tightly on opposite sides of her head and twisted as hard as he could. The force snapped her head far to the right just like he had seen assassins do in the movies to break someone's neck.

When he spun her head all the way, she squawked like a bird. Then he released his hand, expecting her to drop like a sack of lifeless beans. To his shock, she looked back at him.

"What are you, fucking crazy?" She held her hands up to massage her long neck. "That fucking hurt, you asshole."

"Jesus," he said out loud, shocked at the limited effect his attack had on the girl. He improvised, and picked up a small metal jewelry box and, without warning, slammed it hard against her temple. The blow silenced her, and dropped her onto the messy, small bed. He leaned down and realized she was still breathing. A little line of blood started to drip from her temple.

"Shit," he said and pulled her up to a sitting position. He put his hands around her head again and this time twisted really hard. Her head snapped and she fell onto the bed. He leaned down and discovered she was still breathing.

"Fuck me," he murmured and pulled her up again. This time, he snapped her head to the left, and held it twisted all the way to the side for a full minute. When he let go and she fell to the bed, he checked her again. Finally this woman seemed dead.

Then he had another thought. A number of witnesses had seen her leave with him the night before. He couldn't just leave her body lying here. He'd have to do something.

Duarte had all the piles of information stacked in one corner of his office. After almost a full day of work, he had whittled down the necessary facts to a file folder with some reports and printouts. He had run the tram driver, Don Munroe, through the computer a couple of different ways and discovered that he had no criminal record, but he had worked near Austin for several years. The more Duarte thought about it, the more he believed that Munroe had been the target of the bomb. That also meant that maybe Anthony Chapman had not been the target of the bomb at Universal Studios. He had a lot to consider and check out. As he stared at the file folder, he was startled by his cell phone ringing.

"Alex Duarte."

"Kojak, what are you doing?"

He smiled at Caren Larson's cheerful voice. "I'm reviewing our files. What about you?"

"It's always work work work with you, isn't it?"

"It is at three o'clock in the afternoon."

"Anything new?"

"I have a few ideas."

"Like?"

"Have you ever considered that the target in the tram bombing was the driver?"

"No, I'm not sure I even know who the driver was."

"A fella named Don Munroe. From Texas."

There was silence on the line, and then Caren said, "What led you to that conclusion?"

He hesitated, both because he didn't know the exact path that had led him to the idea, and also because he suddenly realized that Caren had been on this case longer than him and that she was very smart. Had she come to the same conclusion and not said anything? He thought back to his father's comments about a distraction. Was Caren a distraction? If she was, why even involve him in the case to begin with?

From the phone, he heard her say, "Well, what *did* give you that idea?"

"What idea?"

"That the driver was the intended victim."

"Oh, I don't know. Just an idea. One of a bunch I need to check out over the next week or so."

"Need a hand?"

"I think I can handle it."

"Does that mean you don't want me coming down at all?"

He hesitated. Yesterday, besides solving the case, he had wanted to see Caren Larson probably more than anything. Now he wasn't so sure. "No, I'd love to see you, but it's just gonna be crazy for a few days."

"I see. Well, I'll check again later in the week, Kojak."

He could sense the colder tone, and understood. That was an improvement, because he rarely understood things like that before. It didn't make him feel any better, as they said their good-byes and the line went dead.

He looked down at his cluttered desk and noticed one name he had scrawled across a legal pad. Oneida Lawson. He knew he needed to speak with Mr. Lawson again, and soon.

25

IT WAS EARLY IN THE MORNING. TO DUARTE, NIGHTTIME often had no meaning. It was a time when things were quiet and he was awake. Sometimes he made use of it, reading more books than most people his age, even occasionally working out or hitting the heavy bag behind his apartment. But he usually saved the bag for the daytime so his brother wouldn't complain. He found it ironic that he should have problems sleeping, and his brother, the attorney, slept like a baby every night, as if he had no cares at all.

Last night, though, Duarte had really made use of the time. It was just after five in the morning, and he had driven all the way down to the Miami airport to snatch up a direct flight to Los Angeles. He put it on his own credit card, and was leaving his pistol behind because he still wasn't certain he wanted this trip to be on the department's official radar. He wasn't so worried about ATF or any of its agents; it was the rest of the Department of Justice he was starting to have his doubts about.

The ticket, on such short notice, was shockingly expensive. Something that went against Duarte's frugal nature.

The flight was scheduled to depart at seven A.M. and arrive in Los Angeles around ten o'clock Pacific time. He'd rent a car, find Mr. Oneida Lawson and get down to business. He had no luggage, and knew that would attract attention, so at the desk he explained that he was returning to California on business and he showed his ATF identification. The ticket clerk's only concern was that he would be flying unarmed, which, of course, he was.

Just before the flight boarded, he used his cell phone to call

Chuck at home. He hated to bother the guy, but he wanted someone to know where he was in case there was trouble.

He heard the rough voice of Chuck say, "Hello?"

"Sorry, partner. It's Alex."

"What now? We need to follow someone else to Salez?"

"No, I just wanted to let you know I am flying to Los Angeles."

"When?"

"Right now."

Chuck sounded more awake now. "Why? When did you get approval?"

"Listen, Chuck, I'm flying on my own. I'm just telling you in case I have a problem. Don't tell anyone."

"You want me to lie?"

"No, just don't offer the truth."

"What if Dale asks where you are?"

"Tell him I'm working on the case. That's the truth."

"When will you be back?"

"Don't know. Maybe tomorrow, if all goes well."

"What exactly are you going to do?"

"Talk to this guy Lawson again. And talk to him my way, if necessary."

"Be careful, Alex."

"I will."

"Call me with an update this evening."

"Later." Duarte shut off his phone and prepared to board the jet for what was turning into one odd investigation.

It was early on the West Coast, and Mike Garretti had been stuck in L.A. long enough to adapt to the time change. The sun hadn't risen yet, and he was sound asleep when the phone rang. The cell phone was spewing a salsa beat when he fumbled for it on the nightstand next to his comfortable king-sized bed.

"What?" was all he said.

"Use the emergency process to contact us."

"When?"

"Now."

"Bullshit."

"Excuse me?"

"You heard me. That's bullshit. You better give me an idea of what is going on right now or don't expect a call for a few more hours."

There was silence on the phone, then the guy with the New England accent said, "Do it today."

"Do what?"

"Your fucking job, asshole."

"It might take a little while to set up." He knew enough not to be specific when he was talking about killing someone.

"We don't care how it's done, but it needs to be today, and as early as possible."

Garretti smiled and said, "Was that so hard? Explaining things without the effort of having to call you back. You could learn a little about doing things the easy way." Before he could continue, the line went dead. "Asshole," he mumbled, and decided since he could get a few more hours sleep he didn't care what that jerk-off wanted.

Alberto Salez still had the problem of retrieving the file from Maria Tannza's trailer. Since he was in the area, and she obviously hadn't moved, he wasn't all that worried about it. It was as safe there as anywhere else. He was also getting his posse—the boys from the sports club—to help him if Mike Garretti showed up to finish things up. He had one other problem, which he looked across the small cab of his truck to confront: the body of the pretty waitress from the sports club. When he realized that too many people saw him leave with her, he knew he couldn't just leave her at her mother's. Besides, with the old lady going through chemotherapy he didn't want to cause her any extra stress. He remembered how tired his own mother got in her losing battle with breast cancer.

"Where would you like to be put to rest?" he asked the corpse out loud. He had already started talking to her like he had the body of the lady from the gas station. He wondered if that was a common occurrence. He had been surprised to find the dead lady still in the Honda Element when he had run from Garretti in Virginia, and only briefly wondered why the guy had kept her around for so long. Now, as he looked at the dark-haired girl with the funny-looking neck in a simple sweatshirt and baggy jeans, he realized that dead people were pretty good company. If he had thought about keeping her any longer, he would have put nicer clothes on her, but, as it was, he had a hard time pulling up the jeans over her limp but shapely legs.

He took a minute to decide where he could hole up for a few days without any hassles. He knew a cheap hotel on the south edge of Belle Glade that wouldn't ask questions, and he had enough cash—especially with what he had stolen from Elenia's house—to grab a room for a week or so. By then, he'd know what to do about the file and where he'd head to next. New Orleans sounded like a decent stop.

He looked at the corpse and said, "You wanna stay in a hotel for a day or two before I find a nice place for you?" He smiled, knowing it was okay with her.

26

ALEX DUARTE RENTED A FORD TAURUS JUST LIKE THE ONE he drove at work. He knew the vehicle, and it was the cheapest available car at Hertz. This one didn't have a blue light with a magnetic bottom under the seat, or an ASP expandable baton stuck under the console, but it was clean and ran well. It took some maneuvering to find Universal Studios. His flight had arrived late, and by the time he had grabbed a sandwich and found his way he wasn't sure he could catch the big carpenter at work.

He found the street where the news crews had been the previous week, and parked in the only spot available for several blocks. He wandered up the slight incline of the street to the spot in the fence where there were still stray evidence markers and police tape. He could see some of the construction crew inside the fence. He waited, hoping to avoid having to identify himself at the front and be escorted back to the site. Just in case it got back to the LAPD captain who had spoken with him the other day.

After a few minutes, Duarte called to one of the nearest workers, a Latin man who was working with a cement mixer but hadn't yet turned on the generally loud machine.

"What do you want?" asked the man warily.

Duarte held up his badge. "I'm not a reporter. I'm looking for Oneida Lawson."

"Never heard of him," said the man calmly.

Duarte wondered if the big carpenter had quit the job. "He's not in any trouble. I spoke to him the day of the explosion and had a few more questions. That's all."

The man looked at him carefully.

"¿Es verdad?"

Duarte just smiled and nodded.

"Hang on, I'll get him."

A few minutes later, the man and Lawson came walking up to the fence. Duarte heard Lawson say, "It's cool, Jose. Thanks." Then, as he came to the fence, he said, "What can I do for you, Mr. ATF?"

Duarte smiled. "Good memory. I bet you talked to a lot of people that day."

"Yeah, but you seemed to be looking for something else. That's why I remember. You seemed smart."

"I'm smart enough to figure out that you might have been the target of that bomb."

The big man looked at him, silent.

"Maybe you even knew some victims of other bombs across the country."

"Like who?"

"Janni Tserick in Seattle."

His eyes shifted, giving away the truth. All he said was, "Who else?"

"Don Munroe in Virginia."

"Shit, I didn't know Don had bought the farm." The big man stepped away for a few moments.

Although Duarte was sorry he had to deliver bad news, he also felt some level of satisfaction he had never known. He had actually figured out at least part of some conspiracy, and now he had a witness to prove it. When Lawson stepped back to him, Duarte said, "Will you lay out what the hell is going on? Because I don't have the full picture."

The carpenter took a moment to compose himself, then seemed to feel the defiance glow inside him. He looked around and said, "Yeah, I'll talk to you. It ain't gonna hurt now."

"Great, you want me to meet you out front?"

"How about after football practice. I'll give you good directions. That way I'll have plenty of time to explain this whole fucked-up mess."

Duarte nodded, and then copied down some detailed directions to a school in Pasadena.

As he walked away from the fence, Duarte said, "I'll see you around six."

Lawson just nodded.

* * *

Mike Garretti drove past the work site at Universal Studios around one o'clock and could see men on the site. He silently cursed himself for being so rebellious on the phone earlier. If he had jumped right to it, he could have caught Oneida Lawson at his house in West Covina and been done with the job by now. Instead, he had to show them he wasn't just a puppet, and lost a good chance to finish early.

He stopped for a fish taco at Baja Fresh and then checked out of the hotel. Whether it was at the football field or at Lawson's house tonight, he was gonna end this thing today and be on a plane back to Texas tonight, and he didn't care what time he had to catch it.

Even with the directions, it still took Duarte almost an hour to find the private high school in the upscale suburb of Los Angeles.

He pulled along the side of the street that bordered the fenced-in football field. He could see a group of young men working on pass routes, and there to one side was Lawson in his long carpenter's pants and T-shirt, smiling and shouting encouragement to the sweating boys.

Duarte decided to wait in the car until after practice. He didn't want to interrupt something so natural as boys learning football routes in the heat of a summer afternoon. He knew how having a stranger around could distract you.

Caren Larson sat at her desk in the quiet office, contemplating what was important to her. She had badgered poor Alex Duarte about what was important to him. He had told her a promotion, and that made her feel closer to him. Too many people denied their desire to climb the ladder. Whether it is a corporation or a government agency, it's imperative to find the right people to advance. Although she had not been raised to be competitive, there was something inside her now. Something that caught on at Cornell that made her want to move up. More than want, she felt a drive to advance. At first, that's what she thought she saw in Alex. Then she saw he was interested in doing the right thing as well as advancing his career. That didn't disappoint her; at least she wasn't disappointed in him. Now, at eight o'clock in the evening, thirteen hours after she had started her day, she sat alone. And, worse still, lonely, in her little office in the main building to the Department of Justice, just one of dozens of attorneys assigned to one of a dozen assistant attorneys general. Is this all there was? Had she overlooked things just to be stuck in this shitty office?

She snatched up her phone and dialed a number she now knew by heart.

"Duarte," came the distant voice on the second ring.

A smile creased her face and she felt better already.

"Kojak, what are you doing this evening?"

"Watching some kids play football."

"This late?"

"It's not that late." Then he paused. "They're almost done. Where are you? The office?"

"How'd you know?"

"Because you're a worker. Good for you. Don't be ashamed of it."

She had enough to be ashamed of that staying late at the office didn't even make her notice.

Duarte said, "Caren, can I call you tomorrow?"

"Sure, anytime."

"See ya."

"Bye."

She hung up, wondering if he had a personal matter pressing at this time of the evening.

As she started to lock up her desk, a shadow crossed her door, then backtracked. She looked up and was surprised to see Deputy Attorney General Roberto Morales at her door.

He flashed that perfect smile and said, "I like dedication, but this is too late even for you."

"I was just tying up some loose ends on the bombing case."

"You guys have done a great job on that. Anything new from your partner?"

"Nope, nothing to speak of."

Morales stared at her and nodded. "Well, I can't have you burn yourself out on this thing."

"I'm fine."

"No, you've been hitting it too hard lately. I want—scratch

that—I'm *ordering* you to take Thursday and Friday off to have a good long weekend. Maybe visit your mom."

"I couldn't. I have so much to do."

"You can, and you will. It's an order."

She looked at his face, and for the first time saw that he was dead serious.

Mike Garretti sat in his SUV across the street from the field where Oneida Lawson was coaching football. He had the pistol that had been supplied to him, some C-4, a good knife he had bought at a camping store and, if necessary, his bare hands to get this fucking job done now. He didn't want to wait, but he didn't want to risk hitting any of the kids either. In fact, he had hoped he could do it away from them altogether, so they didn't even get psychological scars of seeing their coach killed.

The street was fairly empty, with a few cars parked on either side. Oneida Lawson's truck was directly in front of him about five spaces. The big man would cross directly in front of Garretti if he wanted to avoid that long walk back to West Covina. A cop had rolled down the street a few minutes before, but he didn't look interested in anything in particular. Just routine patrol work.

Garretti could clearly see Oneida Lawson's big frame as he yelled encouragement to the sweating, panting high school boys.

Garretti had thought about planting the C-4 at his house, but so far planted bombs had not worked out so well. If it hadn't been for his luck in heading off the ATF agent in West Palm Beach, he would have had to explain that fiasco too. No, his days of planting bombs were definitely over. In fact, after he finished up Lawson and Salez, his days of killing were over. If he didn't have a personal interest in keeping those two quiet, he'd walk away right now. Instead, he was going to kill a guy he liked and admired. This was a shitty job.

27

ALEX DUARTE WATCHED THE FOOTBALL PRACTICE SILENTLY, and tried to see if he could guess what Oneida Lawson was going to tell him. Try as he might—even allowing his imagination to run wild—he had no clue what was going on other than that the victims knew each other, and that the bombings had nothing whatsoever to do with labor organizations. Duarte had been surprised by the phone call from Caren Larson. He felt a little guilty for not telling her he was in California, and that it was only five o'clock instead of eight, but he still wasn't sure if he should tell her, or anyone in DoJ, everything he knew. It would be better to talk to Lawson first, and find out what wild tale he had to tell.

Duarte saw Lawson giving his full attention to those kids, and suddenly realized what he might be doing. Duarte had done it himself. Lawson was seeking atonement. He had done something that he felt guilty about, and he was trying to make it right. It was one of the oldest human gestures. Everyone did it to some degree, but most people didn't have as much to atone for as Duarte. He remembered the first time he saw Milla Bronz and her newborn son in their modest home near the town of Tuzla in Bosnia. The young woman's eyes were red, and she held a baby so tiny he looked like a toy. At first, he brought food to them. Then found himself keeping watch on the house as more and more people came to pay their respects. It was about three months later, after a man named Radu Zandronic, who was not the baby's father, arrived to help her that Duarte felt comfortable enough to relax his vigil. About a month later, they asked if he could help them emigrate to the U.S. Looking back on it, that was his initiation into circumventing the rules. He had found a way to get them into Hungary via an army supply truck, then arranged visas by claiming them as distant relatives. His youthful face and sincere manner had carried the ploy, and his pop, without any questions, had helped the young family arrive in Florida and settle in, of all places, Mississippi.

Once he realized some people didn't live by any rules, he found it easier to break some himself. He knew that Department of Justice procedures explicitly forbid threat of physical harm as a method to obtain information. Yet he had found that, occasionally, it worked quite well. He found, however, that he could only use it when the person being interviewed deserved it. Criminals that preyed on other people; crack dealers and bullies were good examples. Oddly, Duarte found that simple, unlawful gun dealers didn't warrant rough treatment, even though that was his main area to enforce laws. The gun dealers just didn't seem to deserve it personally.

Duarte's eyes blinked as he started to doze off, and his thoughts about his past receded in his head. He did think he should call the Zandronics soon. They had not spoken in several months. Now, as he leaned back in the Taurus's front seat, Duarte realized how tired he was. His customary two hours of sleep a night was usually plenty to carry him, but the added travel and stress had conspired to make him feel the exhaustion sweep over him. He closed his eyes for a moment and suddenly it was cold. At least in the dream about Bosnia.

Mike Garretti saw that practice had broken up. He knew Oneida Lawson's truck was five spaces in front of him, so at some point the man had to come out to his ride. There were a few cars nearby, but no pedestrians. This might be a good time to handle it. His heart rate climbed as he pulled out his Beretta. He pulled the slide back slightly to ensure the .40 caliber bullet was seated properly in the chamber. He was still playing this by ear, but figured that Lawson would walk across the field through the chainlink gate near his truck, cross the street, and enter the truck that was parked with the driver's-side door facing the road. It would be a simple matter for Garretti to roll up slowly and calmly—the key to any combat situation—and put three rounds into Lawson as he got in the truck. By the time the cops got there, he'd be at LAX, looking for a one-way ticket to Austin. The sixty-mile drive to Fort Hood was the roughest part of the trip. The open road, and his level of exhaustion, might make it tough to stay on the road.

After a few minutes of the empty field, he started to get a little concerned. Maybe Oneida was giving the boys a pep talk. Maybe he took a shower here instead of at the little house he owned in West Covina. Garretti gave it a few more minutes and was rewarded to see the big man come out of the gate at the far end of the field about a hundred yards in front of Garretti. It would take a minute to walk it, but Lawson would end up at his truck just the same.

Then, as he came off the sidewalk, he started to walk up the street in the wrong direction, along some of the parked cars. Garretti saw that he was going to talk to someone in a Taurus instead of going straight to his truck. He couldn't tell who Lawson was going to speak with, but Garretti had waited long enough for this. He had five thousand pounds of weapon sitting right under him, and it was time to use it. He threw the big SUV into gear and pulled away from the curb. Slowly at first. He liked the idea of a hit-and-run. Sort've like a giant bullet traveling at a much slower speed.

Duarte snapped awake as soon as he heard the rap on his windshield. He was shocked to see the big carpenter standing in the street. Duarte was also embarrassed that he had been able to sneak up on him without even trying.

Lawson smiled and said, "Don't sweat it. I know traveling can take it out of you."

Duarte smiled. "I was watching practice then was out cold."

Oneida eyed him and said, "You don't know what any of this is about, do you?"

Duarte shrugged. "Hoping you could tell me."

"You may not believe me."

"No harm in trying. You're not wanted. I can just walk away if I don't believe it."

"Maybe you can, maybe you can't. Seems like someone is going to a lot of trouble to keep this story from getting out."

"You mean, like a conspiracy?" Duarte tried to suppress a smile at the crazy ideas he had come up with.

"Call it what you want, but I know there's at least five of us to kill. Unless one of the five is doing it."

"For what? What did you guys see?"

"Look, I'm not proud of it. It is the plain truth: what we did to that boy wasn't right." Oneida looked up and around, then said, "You wanna talk over dinner somewhere? This could take awhile."

Duarte hesitated.

"You'll need something to eat. I got a lot to say."

"Sure, jump in." Duarte wiped his eyes, still ashamed he had fallen asleep on duty. He noticed a green Ford Expedition pull away from the curb down the street and head toward them. At first, he paid no attention, but then the vehicle picked up speed and seemed to list over to their side of the roadway. Before Duarte could say anything, he heard Oneida say "Shit" and spring to the rear of the car.

As the Expedition swung in close to Duarte's rental car, he looked up and saw the driver clearly. A dark man with close-cropped hair. Something seemed immediately familiar about him. The driver even looked over at Duarte and seemed surprised himself.

Somehow the Expedition missed the rental Taurus altogether, and Duarte could see Oneida Lawson running like a deer down the sidewalk, then darting into a residential neighborhood. The Expedition made the same turn, its tires squealing as he took the corner.

Duarte threw the car into gear and pulled away from the curb, then made a quick U-turn to get into the chase as well.

Mike Garretti saw Oneida stop to speak with someone in a parked Ford Taurus. His wide body leaned out into the street like he was wearing a sign that said HIT ME. It was perfect. After all the problems Garretti had experienced with this job, it was nice to see everything line up nicely. He needed an easy one. And it would be just a simple hit-and-run when it was reported. The parent or teacher he was chatting with wouldn't be able to give any kind of description, or even a decent account of what happened.

The key was to hit him hard and cleanly. He didn't want to assume the man was dead. The best bet for that would be to have the body dragged under the wheels after he struck him. To accomplish this, Garretti drifted to his left and picked up speed. He intended to almost scrape the car Oneida was leaning against.

When he was only a couple of car lengths away, Oneida looked up. In an instant, the big man had jumped behind the parked car and, without hesitation, he was in a full, all-out sprint down the street that would have been inspiration to his players.

Garretti looked over at the parked car and was shocked to see the ATF agent from Florida behind the wheel. Man, did that guy get around. He hoped the agent didn't recognize him. Right now, it didn't matter. He had to find Oneida or he might not have another chance.

Oneida Lawson had played fullback at a community college in Texas for two years. If it hadn't been for an incident where he beat up a mall security guard, and the fact that he smoked a lot of pot, he probably could've gone to Texas A & M and been an Aggie. But he liked pot, he pleaded guilty to a battery charge and he had a tendency to fumble the football on a regular basis. A record that still stood at his alma mater. Nine fumbles in one game.

Running was never the issue, even though he was a little big. He could run fast, though he hadn't had a reason to for years. Now he found that his feet weren't failing him, as he turned on the jets and sped down the street away from what, at best, was a really bad driver but more likely was someone from his past who intended to kill him before he could tell anyone his story. His one question was whether the ATF agent, Duarte, was part of the trap, or just as surprised as he was at the appearance of the speeding SUV.

Oneida didn't care about how many people wanted him dead right now. One was too many. He realized as soon as he took the first turn that if he stayed on the sidewalk or the street, the Expedition would catch up quickly. He took a hard right, away from the school, between rows of small houses. He didn't want to risk the kids by taking the easier route back into the school. He didn't know what the driver was prepared to do.

Behind him, he heard the Expedition speed past, then slam on the brakes. Oneida kept up his pace, then felt it all catch up as his lungs started to ache and his breath came out in short huffs. He had to slow down, then finally, after cutting through an open fence gate, he leaned back against a metal toolshed and put his hands on his knees to breathe. He thought he had run far enough into the neighborhood that he had given his pursuer the slip.

The rear door of the house in front of him opened, and a head that looked like it had a hat of white cotton candy popped out.

"What're you doing?" came a shaky female voice.

"Restin', ma'am."

"Rest somewhere else or I'll call the cops."

"Call 'em." He gulped some air. "Please, call the cops."

The head slipped back into the house, and Oneida started to feel some hope that he might survive the day.

Garretti had lost the swift son of a bitch somewhere in the middle of the neighborhood. He knew he didn't have much time because the cops would be coming soon. If a big black guy running behind the houses didn't trigger a call, Oneida might try to get them. Having someone trying to kill you could do crazy things to a vow of silence.

Now Garretti was out of his rented Expedition and ducking around houses, hoping to see Oneida. He looked down a long, grassy area but didn't see anything unusual, then he heard a voice. Low and hushed.

"Hey, officer. Over here."

Garretti saw an older man at the window of the house across from where he stood. Garretti looked up and said, in his best official tone, "Yes, sir?"

"You looking for a big black fella?"

"Yes, sir. Where'd he go?"

"He's in the backyard of the next house. He's leaning against a toolshed, catching his breath."

"Thank you, sir. Now go back inside."

"Want me to call 911?"

"No, sir. They're on the way." Garretti scooted off to the house and pulled his Beretta from under his loose shirt. He liked being thought of as a cop. He suddenly felt naked without a badge. He slowed at the corner of the next yard and peered around a hedge. An old lady with white hair stood at the back door, talking to someone in the backyard.

Garretti didn't hesitate. He bolted around the hedge, gun in front of him, looking toward the rear of the yard, but was surprised to feel movement right next to him.

Strong arms wrapped around his outstretched wrists with the pistol in his hand. Oneida Lawson twisted and tossed him ten feet into the yard, the Beretta flying off toward the house. Oneida stepped in to deliver a kick to Garretti's midsection as Garretti scurried to one side and deflected the kick. He scrambled to his feet and squared off against the big man. He glanced to each side to try to locate the fallen pistol.

Garretti said, "Now, relax, Oneida. We can just part ways and it's over."

"I did that and you came looking for me."

Garretti stepped to the side, and Oneida took a counterstep so that they remained a few feet apart. The old lady came out of the back door.

Oneida said, "Lady, get back inside."

Garretti added, "Yeah, get inside."

The old lady said, "What kind of L.A. cop are you? Kick his ass."

Then Oneida flew into him and grabbed his shoulders, as they both went down hard on the grass. With a couple of moves, Oneida had a decent choke hold around Garretti as they settled into a steady position.

Garretti felt his oxygen start to go and his vision get blurry.

Duarte felt hopelessly lost in the maze of streets with houses that looked identical to one another. No unusually big trees, no cars up on blocks like Florida, to help distinguish one block from another. He punched the gas of the Taurus and sailed down one street to the next.

He craned his neck and still everything looked the same. Bosnia had not been as confusing as this little subdivision, and there were no signs in English there. Fleetingly, he realized that the attempted hit-and-run on Lawson verified his belief that a conspiracy surrounded the bombings, but his military training taught him to put it out of his mind and deal with the situation at hand. He had to find Oneida Lawson and get him to safety.

Slowing the car, Duarte cruised down the street so that if Lawson saw him he could cut out from behind the houses and jump in the car. If the carpenter didn't think Duarte had been a setup to kill him. He felt frustration boil in him as he wished, possibly for the first time as an ATF agent, that he had a gun with him.

He lowered the window to see if he could hear anything, then he heard a gunshot. Clear, and fairly close. It rang between the houses, and he stepped on the gas to find the source.

Garretti started to black out from the pressure of Oneida Lawson's choke when he heard a loud noise. His ears were so muffled by the lack of oxygen he couldn't tell where the noise came from or what it was, but Oneida instantly loosened his grip. Then the big man toppled to one side, and Garretti scooted back to gulp some air.

A few feet away, the old lady stood staring at the bloody head of Oneida Lawson with Garretti's Beretta still in her tiny hands.

She said, "Damn, this kicks more than my son's Glock 9."

Garretti stood up, and then eased the gun from the old woman's hands. "You did a good thing. The mayor will give you an award."

"Really?" asked the lady.

"Yes, ma'am. Now, just let me go get help and I'll be right back." He looked down at the motionless body to make certain he was dead. The hole in the rear, left side of Oneida's head was a pretty good indication that he was done. The blood and brain matter on the grass was another tip-off.

Garretti backed out of the yard and said, "I'll be right back."

He was to his Expedition and headed down the road less than a minute later.

Duarte saw the Expedition speed away. Since he had a good lead, and Duarte had no gun or anything else to use for an arrest, he pulled over where the Expedition had been parked and ran back behind the houses. He looked down the long, grassy lane and saw two older people in a backyard two houses away. He raced over to see them looking at a body on the ground. It only took a second for him to recognize who was on the ground, and that he was most definitely dead.

The elderly woman said, "Where's your partner?"

Duarte looked up. "Excuse me?"

"The other cop. Where'd he go?"

Duarte realized their mistake. He wasn't sure he wanted to identify himself at this moment. "Are you okay?"

She nodded, and the man next to her said, "She saved your man's ass."

"How's that?"

"The big black guy was choking him, so she used his pistol to cap his ass."

Duarte looked at the man, who was in his sixties. "To what?"

Exasperated, the man said, "Shoot the perp."

"Where's the gun now?"

"The cop took it back."

The old lady said, "He's coming back, isn't he? I want him to tell the story. It'll sound better."

Duarte thought it over, and said, "I'll go get him." He trotted off toward his rental car. He knew the killer, or at least the reason he wanted to kill Oneida. If he tried to explain to the cops, it could get confusing and slow things down. He had a lot of good reasons for keeping his mouth shut right now. He wasn't even supposed to be in California. If he were caught, he'd be off the case. Even if he could explain, he'd be tied up in interviews out here while the killer got farther and farther away. The most troubling reason was that he knew something odd was going on and he didn't know who to trust. He wouldn't be able to help the investigating detectives. They already had witnesses. As he threw the car into drive and was turning toward the 101, he saw the first patrol car with its lights on racing past him.

He was avoiding the police. What was this case doing to him?

Maxine Harrington and Buck Buchanan tried to explain to the responding officers that two cops had already been there, and that Maxine had used one of their guns to save him. There was no doubt about a body being in Ms. Harrington's backyard, or the cause of death. The rest of the story was confusing, and caused the detectives called to the scene more than a little wasted time as they looked into the death of West Covina resident Oneida Lawson.

28

ALEX DUARTE LEANED BACK IN HIS LA-Z-BOY IN FRONT OF the twenty-seven-inch TV he shared with his brother. They only had basic cable now because he had been forced to yell at Frank for buying an illegal satellite TV receiver that received every channel for a onetime fee to the local computer geek who hacked the cards. It was one of the many instances where he felt like he might need to strike his brother to bring him back to reality. Even though his father would never admit it, he often felt the same way.

Frank had been proud the day he walked in with the receiver under his arm. Duarte knew something was up when he offered to pay half the monthly fee and his brother told him not to worry about it. Now Frank paid the price by having only fifty-nine channels instead of a potential three hundred, including porn channels.

It had been a truly exhausting two days. He caught the red-eye back from Los Angeles and made a brief appearance at the office before finally conceding that he was too tired and deciding to go home early. It was so nice to be in the little apartment without his loud brother either talking incessantly or on his cell phone.

Duarte had weighed the advantages of staying in Los Angeles and telling the cops what he knew, but he didn't think it would be of benefit to anyone. It was part of his case, and he'd solve it. If not, if for some incredible reason he couldn't, he'd tell the cops everything he saw. The problem was that he wasn't sure whom he had seen. He knew the face, and remembered talking to him at Salez's apartment. He now also recalled his face from the amusement park in Virginia. He was on the same trail as Duarte. It was way beyond happenstance. The ATF agent could even give a description of the guy, but that still didn't identify him. It was no coincidence that the killer was so close and struck at the same time Duarte intended to talk to Oneida Lawson. The odds of the killer being in that spot, at that time, were astronomical. It was planned, which meant that Salez wasn't idly worried when he said someone was trying to kill him. Duarte believed the fugitive, and knew what the killer looked like. He just had no idea how to place a name and history with the killer. And he didn't want to go through the Department of Justice because he still wasn't sure what was going on with them. He was starting to feel isolated and alone. Throw in the exhaustion he felt and he knew he had to take some time to recharge.

He flipped on ESPN to get lost in one of the reruns of an old NCAA football game, this one between the Florida Gators and the Tennessee Volunteers. He didn't know how it would come out, so it was like watching a live game. He mainly wanted to lose himself in something other than this case for a few hours, and maybe doze off for a while. And he got his wish, as he drifted off between Tennessee drives, until something started to knock around inside his head. Like an engineering problem with explosives when he was at Fort Leonard Wood, back in the days when he slept eight hours a night. Back before anything bad had ever happened to him.

He came wide awake in the chair like someone had shouted his name. He knew exactly why he was awake, and knew he'd never get back to sleep until he tried out his theory.

He knew how to identify the killer. And with his heart rate thumping ahead of its usual calm beat, he got up from the comfortable chair, stretched and changed into some clothes for work. He had his Glock from his closet on his hip and was ready to go four minutes after he woke up from his short nap. It was funny, but now he wasn't the least bit tired.

Alberto Salez felt like he was safe in an old-time fugitive hideout. He'd paid the old hag who managed the twenty-room motel a hundred dollars up front and promised to pay another hundred a week each Friday. It was off-season, and the place was an absolute shithole, with one small room, and a simple bathroom attached. The other tenants seemed like the usual fare. Mostly prostitutes, a few crack dealers and the odd tourists from Finland who didn't realize what they were getting into when they booked the room over the Internet.

His Nissan pickup was parked in the alley out back, so an enterprising cop wouldn't see it from the main road. He still had his knife, and he now wanted a handgun. He could buy one off the street, or at one of the pawnshops that didn't adhere to the local ordinances having to do with waiting periods and positive identification.

He had brought the body of the pretty waitress, Elenia, with him for the first night, but she had started to stink really bad almost as soon as he had her inside the small room. He found a roll of black, thick garbage bags along the outside wall of the motel and wrapped her in two of them. One over her head and the other from her feet to her waist. He used duct tape to seal them up, and then laid her out in the back of his truck. It looked like yard debris. A quick, fake fishing trip to a canal west of Lake Worth, and the use of two concrete cinder blocks, and she was secure at the bottom of the canal for a good long time. He thought about their night together, and realized he might have been too harsh on the young woman. He missed her now. But at least he knew never to try the head twist like they do in the movies.

Now, as he sat in his dreary room, he was a little pissed he hadn't been able to get ahold of Oneida Lawson. He didn't know if that meant the big man was dead, or if he just didn't want to talk to him. He also knew for a fact that good old Don Munroe was killed in Virginia. So it made sense that Lawson was dead too. Garretti had told him that Janni Tserick was dead. The little electrician wouldn't have been any help trying to stop Garretti anyway. He couldn't even keep the asshole away from his wife.

Garretti had been the one who planned their little mission and run the operation. It made sense he'd be the one to make sure everyone was shut up permanently. At first, Salez thought that Garretti was some kind of psychic, the way he had found him so easily, then he realized it had a lot more to do with his contacts than anything else. It meant that Salez couldn't talk his way out of things. But maybe, under the right circumstances, he could use the file hidden at Maria Tannza's house to walk away from this thing and then be left alone.

One thing he *could* do was find out what the ATF agent, Duarte, knew. If he could find a way to trick the guy into being at the right place at the right time so he and his buddies could get the drop on him, things might work out. He owed the son of a bitch for his ear, and for his status as a fugitive. On the other hand, the ATF agent had saved Salez from being blown into a million pieces by preventing him from using his Mustang the night it exploded.

He felt satisfied that his next move should involve squeezing Duarte.

Duarte stood in front of the old apartment building where he had been told that Alberto Salez had lived—the same building where he had seen Oneida Lawson's killer before. The so-called apartment manager he had seen in Virginia too, but he still didn't know anything about him. Now his brain had zeroed in on the man's face. The dark skin, sharp features. A man who stayed fit and sharp.

Duarte knocked on the first door downstairs and waited. Finally the door opened and an elderly man, with no shirt, sagging hairy breasts and droopy eyes, said, "Yes, what do you want?"

Duarte held up his badge, then let the wallet fall open to reveal his ATF identification. "Sir, my name is Alex Duarte. I'm looking for the manager of the building."

"I guess that'd be me. The owner gives me a hundred dollars off the rent a month to handle a few things. What do you need?"

"How long you been managing the building?"

He shrugged his stooped shoulders and said, "Dunno, maybe five, six years."

"Anyone else ever fill in when you're not here?"

"Nope."

Duarte twitched at that. "Who's the owner?"

"A lady named Berg, from Boca. You need to talk to her?"

"No, just making sure who is who."

"Okay, young fella. What else do you need?"

"Who lives upstairs in the apartment closest to the street?"

"Now? No one. Been vacant a couple of weeks."

"Who lived there?"

"Spanish guy. Young for this building. Don't remember his name."

"Alberto Salez?"

"Think so. Not a friendly guy. Just sort of up and left toward the end of last month. Never came back to pay the rent or nothing."

"Is the place empty now?"

"Pretty near. Got a couple boxes of his stuff. I'm waiting to hire someone to clean the place and throw out his shit."

"When's the last time you saw him?"

"Long time. Maybe more than a month. Why? He wanted?"

"Yes, sir." Duarte looked up the stairs and said, "You have a problem with me looking around up there?"

"Hell no. Go ahead."

"You got the key?"

"Don't need it. The place is unlocked. I don't care if someone sneaks in and steals shit. I was going to throw it away anyway."

"I need to take a window jalousie too. That a problem?"

"Just one? Go ahead. I got a stack of them in the storage locker."

Duarte thanked the older man and trotted up the stairs. He looked at the closed windows and thought he had a pretty good chance of getting a print off the window that the other "manager" had touched when he closed the window. It was the bottom slat. He could stand there and visualize the man reaching down to force the windows shut.

Duarte opened the door and was struck by the heat and musty smell in the unair-conditioned apartment. He took a quick look through a set of drawers in the kitchen, and then two more in an old desk set against the wall. All were empty, and he figured they were dumped into the five storage boxes sitting by the front door. It didn't look like anyone had organized the stuff inside the boxes. Just dumped it inside. He poked through the boxes, and a large plastic bag with some clothes in it. Nothing seemed useful in building a case or finding the fugitive.

Then, in the bottom of the third box, he found a ripped four-by-six photograph. It had no frame or enhancement, just a standard photo, with a little less than half ripped off. In the photo, Salez sat at a bar with a young, dark-haired man with thick curly locks in his face. Both men were smiling, and there was someone else's arm around the young man's shoulder. Duarte studied it, looking for some hint as to the identity of the third man, or the location of the bar. There was a beer tap behind them with a plaque. He held the photo up to the light from the open front door, hoping to read the writing on the plaque more clearly. It said SECOND STREET something. He strained his eyes and shifted his feet, hoping to catch the light: SECOND STREET RETAIL DISTRICT.

Now he had something, but he had no idea what it was. Where was the Second Street Retail District? What town? What state? Was it even important? He had no idea. He then tucked the photo in his rear pocket, as he wondered why it was ripped and who else was in the photo. He knew he wouldn't let it go. He never did.

Then he went to his immediate objective. The glass jalousie. He found that the metal frame had little flanges that had been bent back. Duarte pried them back and carefully slid out the jalousie that he hoped had the man's prints. Holding the window by the edges, he knew just where to take it.

The Palm Beach County Sheriff's Office main building was an impressive structure with good security. The modern building housed one of the most effective police agencies in the state of Florida. The entire complex included the county jail, first-appearance court, the medical examiner's office, as well as the main patrol division and detective divisions. Duarte had been inside a few times while working joint investigations or retrieving reports he had used to charge armed felons with federal firearms violations.

He identified himself, and was on his way to the second floor with his pane of glass held carefully by the edges. The county crime lab was tucked off to one side, but he knew the catacombs of fingerprint technicians, DNA scientists and forensic specialists were busy behind the simple counter that greeted the cops delivering evidence.

A young woman with light brown hair and a bright smile said, "Hi, can I help you?," as Duarte stopped at the counter.

He set the glass on the counter and said, "My name is Alex Duarte. I'm with—"

She cut him off. "Oh my God, you're Rocket, aren't you?"

He looked at her to see if he recognized her in any way. "That's a nickname." He paused, and said, "Do I know you?"

"Almost, I'm Alice."

"I don't understand." He looked more closely at her fresh face and clear eyes. She didn't seem remotely familiar.

"I went out with Frank a few times. He told me all about you."

"Frank, my brother?"

"Of course, silly. He told me about how they named you the Rocket in high school because you got so focused and went full speed. He said that he made sure the guys in the army and at ATF knew your nickname too."

"Yeah, he did that." Duarte managed a smile. The one he had practiced for Caren Larson.

"I know all about how he helps you on some of the big cases and advises you on current legal issues."

"Yeah, he's a huge help." He looked at her and said, "What do you do here?"

"I'm a forensic scientist, but right now I'm filling in while the secretary is at lunch."

She seemed awfully smart to have dated his brother. "Do you still see Frank?"

"No, he was a little unreliable."

"Tell me about it."

"He used to say you were in your own world and had no idea what he was doing."

Duarte nodded and said, "He gets confused when he's not the center of attention. I like him confused."

She gave him a good giggle and then looked at the jalousie. "What have you got there?"

"I was hoping you guys might try to lift some prints from this."

"I thought ATF had a lab?"

"I was hoping to keep this local."

"For Frank Duarte's brother. No problem." She added, "But it'll cost you a drink sometime."

"Done," was all he could manage.

Duarte plopped into his chair at the office about three o'clock, satisfied that he had done all he could for the case today. He had the jalousie, and it was at the lab. It was odd to him that a young lady as smart and interesting as Alice at the crime lab would have dated his brother Frank. Not that Frank didn't date; he just wondered what a young woman like that saw in his brother. A lawyer.

His partner, Chuck Stoddard, wandered into the small office, and reminded Duarte of a hippo looking for a soft spot to lounge. He backed into his chair and flopped into it. Duarte smiled at his image of the big man, and how he had lived up to Duarte's characterization.

Duarte was going to bring him up to date on his case when the big man said, "What do you have for me, Rocket?"

"What'd mean?"

"On the case. What'd you find in L.A.? What's next for us?"

Duarte had known Chuck for his full four years at ATF and liked the man, but he wasn't exactly known for his enthusiasm or work ethic. What had made him so interested now? It made him consider how the bomber had known his moves and how he had anticipated everything Duarte had done on the case.

Without thinking, Duarte said, "The trip was a bust. Didn't even talk to the witness."

"Short trip too."

Duarte shrugged. "Anyone ask where I was?"

"Nope, not a soul."

Duarte nodded.

Chuck said, "Let me know what you need. Any place, any time."

Duarte nodded again. Thinking how un-Chuck-like that sounded. Then his desk phone rang.

"Alex Duarte."

"Rocket, you holding up okay?"

Duarte recognized the Miami Division's special agent in charge, or SAC. His voice was familiar, as was his habit of assuming everyone knew who he was when he called. It had led to several embarrassing situations, but he kept doing it nonetheless.

"I'm fine, sir."

"Heard you're doing a great job on the DoJ case."

"Thank you, sir."

"So good, in fact, that I was just informed that there is a GS-14 job as a supervisor waiting for you to say yes."

Duarte sat silently stunned. "A supervisor's job?"

"Yep, in D.C."

"When?"

"I was told it was as soon as you could travel. You get a house-hunting trip, and we'll give you any time you need to get your shit together. So to speak."

Duarte listened as the SAC let loose with one of his custom belly laughs.

Duarte almost said, "I'm ready now." Instead, from some-where deep inside him, he asked a question: "Could I wait until I'm finished with this case?"

"Don't think that's what they had in mind. Just hand it off to that dim-witted partner of yours."

"Chuck Stoddard?"

"He can see it through."

Duarte thought about Chuck and Caren Larson and Maria Tannza and the face of the man he knew set the bombs. "Can I let you know about this, sir?"

"Let me know? I thought this is what you wanted?"

"It's exactly what I wanted. But I have to look at a few things."

There was a hesitation, then his boss said, "Get back to me soon. I want to give HQ a definite answer. And I want to tell them yes."

"So do I, sir. So do I."

Duarte picked at his fine dinner of pot roast. His ma had spent the majority of the dinnertime filling in the family on the wedding plans of one of his cousins who lived in Miami. Frank kept asking about the maids of honor, and how he was hoping the bride had a lot of hot friends. He was already planning his weekend around the distant event. Finally Cesar Duarte asked Alex what was bothering him.

Duarte hesitated. He didn't want to trouble his family. On the other hand, he was interested in his pop's opinion.

His father asked again, adding, "It's all right, Alex. Maybe we can help."

Duarte nodded, and finally said, "Well, Pop, I got a job offer today."

Frank cut in, "From who?"

"ATF. A supervisor's slot."

His mother clapped her hands to her mouth; a proud smile spread across her face.

"How much?" asked Frank.

His father glared at his crass son and asked the right question, "So why are you worried?"

"It's in Washington, D.C."

His mother's smile changed to a look of horror. "So far?"

Duarte nodded.

His father said, "But that's not what's bothering you, is it?"

"No, sir. I'd have to give up this case I'm on."

"The bomber and the fugitive?"

"Yes, sir."

"But weren't you on the case to get a promotion?" asked his brother.

"At first, but now . . ."

Cesar Duarte leaned in toward his son. "I see your concerns. About setting things right, about finishing the job. Sometimes, you have to make a hard choice that's good for you in the long run. I have every confidence you'll make the right decision."

Frank said, "Go for the cash."

Duarte looked around the table and still felt like he had a weight on his shoulders.

29

BY EIGHT O'CLOCK, DUARTE HAD ARRIVED AT THE little café where his cousin ate breakfast. He seated himself at the table before the short, muscular bald man could even see him. When he did look up, it wasn't with an air of family loyalty.

Cousin Tony squawked, "Jesus, what the hell do you want now?"

Duarte just said, "Did you hear anything about Salez?"

"Don't you think I'd call you if I did?"

"Not really, that's why I'm here."

"You don't even try to hide your feelings or care about anyone else's, do you?"

Duarte just stared at him.

His cousin Tony said, "No, the answer is no, I haven't heard a thing."

"Keep trying."

"What, you order me around now. Keep trying or what?"

"I'll start to eat with you every morning."

This caught the pawnbroker by surprise. His eyes shifted from side to side to see if anyone was listening.

"You wouldn't," was all Tony could say.

Duarte smiled. "I would, and"—he paused for emphasis—"I'd even pick up the tab every morning."

"But people will think that I'm telling you things."

"Exactly."

"Look, I'm completely legit now."

"Then it doesn't matter if I'm seen with you, does it?"

"You're an asshole, and I don't like this treatment. I should report you."

"To whom?"

"The ATF."

"For what?"

"Harassment."

"By offering to buy you breakfast? I doubt that would fly."

"Now you get a sense of humor? You know what you're doing to me?"

"This is my job, Tony. Sorry we're on opposite sides of it, but it's my job. If you want me gone, find Alberto Salez for me."

Tony gave him a vicious glare.

Then Duarte pulled out the photo he had found at Salez's apartment. "You recognize the guy with Salez?"

Tony looked, then reluctantly took the photo to hold it up in the light. "Looks like an Arab to me."

"You know him?"

"Never saw him before." Tony looked around the other tables. "Is that all the snitch work you got for me today? Can I go back to my newspaper?"

Duarte was up and out of the chair before his cousin could make another comment. He headed to his car, and was westbound on Southern Boulevard in a matter of minutes.

The labor camp still looked subdued. Between the bombing and the manager's death, the residents had really shut themselves off. He pulled his Taurus into the slot in front of Maria Tannza's trailer. As he stepped out of the car, he saw a man with his hand in a cast and immediately recognized him as one of the men from the fight at the Belle Glade Sports Club. The man made no threatening move, didn't even give him a harsh look. Instead, he pivoted and hobbled away toward a long trailer at the end of the camp.

Maria met him at the door with a covered dish in her hands.

"Oh, Agent Duarte, you surprised me."

"Please, call me Alex."

"I'm sorry, I forgot. How are you? How is the case coming?"

"Everything is fine. I just wanted to check on you to see if there had been any more Salez sightings."

"No, none."

Duarte looked at the covered casserole dish and said, "I'm sorry, am I keeping you?"

"No, I was going to drop this off at the manager's trailer down the road. His wife doesn't get around that well. I thought a little chicken might help."

Duarte stepped back down the little steps to give her a free exit.

She said, "Why don't you come with me? It's not far, and it'll give you a different view of the Glades."

It didn't take much to convince Duarte. He offered his car, and five minutes later he was bumping down a country dirt road lined with the thick trees and brush. Maria had him turn onto a small wooden bridge over a canal and onto the property that used to house the now-deceased manager of the labor camp.

Duarte looked the property over and asked, "He own this or does the company that owns the farm?"

Maria shook her head. "I guess the farm because of what they store out here. I know there's gas in those drums." She pointed to a set of six fifty-five-gallon drums. "And there's all kinds of stuff in the sheds."

Duarte parked, and tried to scurry around the car to open the door for the pretty teacher, but she would have none of it.

They climbed the set of stairs and waited after knocking. An elderly woman, who used a walker, came to the door and let them in. Maria seemed right at home, the way she bustled in and got to work straightening the kitchen and storing the meal she had made.

Over her shoulder, in the kitchen, Maria said, "Clare, this is Alex Duarte."

The old woman smiled and looked at Duarte. "Boyfriend?" she asked in a loud tone.

Maria came out of the kitchen and said, "No, he's an ATF agent."

"A what?"

"He's one of the policemen looking into the blast that killed Hector."

"I see," said the old woman. Then asked Duarte, "You married?"

"No, ma'am."

"Good manners. What do you plan to do when you're done with police work?"

Duarte flinched at the question as he tried to figure out her meaning. "I intend to stay a policeman."

"I guess that's not too bad. Where are you from?"

"West Palm Beach."

"I mean, where are your people from?"

"Paraguay."

"Now, that's a new one. I meet lovely people from Guatemala, Mexico, and Maria here from Venezuela, but never anyone from Paraguay, or Uruguay. Why is that, Mr. Duarte?"

"I don't know, ma'am. Maybe because they are relatively small and stable countries. My father came here in the sixties."

"That's when my husband and I came too. We've lived in this same spot, different trailers, but same spot since 1980. Not bad, eh?"

"No, ma'am."

"Then my husband had to slip on the damned bridge. The same one he'd been crossing for over twenty-five years."

"I'm sorry, ma'am."

The lady settled back into a chair, and set her water to the side. "You're not real comfortable with people, are you, Mr. Duarte?"

He smiled a little. "I guess not."

"Nothing wrong with that. Means you'd be a lousy liar."

Maria walked into the living room and sat on the short couch next to Duarte.

The older woman said, "She's a lovely girl, isn't she?"

Duarte didn't know what to say, but that didn't stop his host. She raised her voice. "I said, she's a lovely girl, isn't she?"

"Yes, ma'am."

The woman smiled and said, "He's smart too."

The short ride back to Maria's trailer through the woods reminded Duarte of one of his postings outside Camp McGovern in Bosnia. It was wooded, and he had practiced war games several times with coalition forces. He and his unit would retreat into the heavy woods and then lay booby traps to slow the advance. Of course, they were just nonfragmentary smoke grenades, but he saw their effectiveness. Once, he had actually lured a British company to a clearing then set off bombs all around it to signify that he could have blown the clearing. The umpire for the scenario had given Duarte credit for the destruction of the company until the British major lodged an objection saying that they had not been told about the possibility of a trap and demanded the exercise be repeated. Duarte didn't care, and next time set the exact same trap much earlier in the exercise and caught the same company in it. That time, the British just pulled out without complaint, and the only comment was from Duarte's commanding officer, who simply said, "Good job, Rocket." Duarte smiled at the recollection.

In the car next to him now, Maria said, "You have a nice smile. You don't use it much."

He looked at her. "I was just thinking about something that happened a long time ago in another patch of woods." He looked out over the brush. "Is that lady going to be okay alone?"

"I worry about Clare out there, but she's going to her daughter's house in Lantana in a day or two. Then she'll decide where she wants to stay."

"She looks like she's handling her husband's death reasonably well."

"It's amazing what you can do to get past a tragedy. I'm going to a counselor who says as long as I keep thinking about Hector, I'm going to be all right. I'm starting to see what she means." Maria turned in the seat to face Duarte as he pulled the Taurus to a stop at the entrance to U.S. 27. "You won't give up on Hector, will you?"

He looked back into her dark eyes and knew what his answer was. "I promise I'll find out the truth about the bombing."

"I believe you." She leaned over and kissed his cheek.

Alberto Salez risked visiting his old café for two reasons: he was hoping to find someone else to face down the ATF agent, and he missed the excellent coffee the owner made. He had the promise of the group from the labor camp who said they'd help, but by the looks of them they had not fared well in their last encounter with Alex Duarte. They swore that he had surprised them with a baseball bat, knocking them down one at a time, but Salez was skeptical of the story, which changed each time someone told it. He wasn't sure who he could get to help, but he knew the majority of the men who gathered here most mornings were not fond of any policeman.

He greeted the owner, picked up a guava pastry and cup of coffee and found one of the small round tables on the sidewalk.

He settled into the straight-back metal chair as best he could, nodding hello to a couple of the regulars he had not seen since he had been on the run. He had his fillet knife tucked into his belt and had his little pickup truck parked down the street, so if he had to run for any reason he could pull away from the curb and be on his way in the right direction without much maneuvering.

After a few minutes, a small, sturdy bald man he knew as "Tony" started to walk past him, then did a double take and stopped to say hello, and started speaking Spanish to Salez. Salez missed his native language, and was happy to offer the man a seat.

Tony said, "Haven't seen you around for a while."

"Been traveling." Then Salez remembered the man owned a pawnshop, and he had bought a pistol from him without any paperwork a while back. "You got any good pistols at your store?"

"A few."

"Can I get another one without papers?"

The man shrugged and said, "No, I'm watched too closely now. I had forgotten you bought a revolver from me last year."

"Know where I can get one?"

"What do you need it for? Or should I not ask?"

"Don't ask."

"Where are you staying now? Still over by Southern Boulevard?"

"No, I'm in a motel in . . ." Salez looked closely at the man. He knew where Salez had lived. Salez had gotten a ride home with him once when his Mustang had broken down. Had he told someone else where he lived? Was this man a snitch? Salez kept calm, and said, "I live in North Palm now." He hoped the man believed he lived in a little town at the opposite end of the county.

Salez knew he had to get this man away from the café to find out if he had told anyone where he lived. If he had, there was a price to exact.

Salez said, "I have some jewelry to pawn, can I show it to you?"

"Yeah, bring it by the shop."

"It's in my truck. Take a look at it now."

"No, that's all right, bring it by the shop this afternoon."

"There are five diamonds, all over a carat. I'll let 'em go to you right now, cheap."

The man hesitated, and Salez could see his greed working

over the profit margin in his head. Finally the man said, "Yeah, okay. I'll take a quick look, to make sure they're real."

"They're real. C'mon." Salez stood up casually and led the smaller man around the back to his truck parked for a fast getaway. He opened the passenger's door and said, "Get in." He hurried around the front and slipped behind the wheel. He had his hand on the handle of his knife before the man even said, "Where are the diamonds?"

Salez had never used the knife as a questioning tool, but found he was almost as excited by the possibility as he had been by using it to eliminate witnesses.

30

DUARTE GREETED HIS PARTNER, CHUCK, AS THE BIG man tore through another Krispy Kreme doughnut. He checked his mailbox, and then sat down at his desk just as the phone rang. The voice on the other end said simply, "HQ says you have to give up all cases for the promotion. What's your answer?"

Duarte knew the SAC, and his style, so he kept it short too. "I have to decline, sir."

"Really? Why? I thought you wanted a promotion since you got here."

"I did. I mean, I do, sir. But if I have to give up this case, I can't take the promotion right now."

"Alex, there are a million cases out there. This is just one."

"One that's important to a few people."

"Like a promotion is important to you."

"Yes, sir. Exactly."

"You still don't want it?"

"I'm sorry, sir, no."

The line went dead.

Duarte shrugged to himself and turned to his computer screen. There wasn't much he could do about the call now. He also knew he couldn't just abandon this case. He had plenty of logical reasons to move on, but logic said he should sleep most nights and he couldn't. He needed this case.

He could give the photo he had found to an analyst and see what they found out from the plaque reading SECOND STREET RETAIL DISTRICT, but he decided to stick with it himself. He ran the phrase through Google and found several compelling hits. The best was a redevelopment project in Austin. Everyone else in the case was from Texas. The theory on the bar made sense.

After reading a few pages, he learned that the bar could very well be part of the Austin nightlife. Now he considered how to confirm his theory.

As he contemplated how he could find out more about the photo, his cell phone rang, with his cousin Tony saying, "Hello."

Duarte asked, "What's up?"

"I can get Salez to my store tomorrow afternoon if you want me to."

"Do it."

"You coming alone?"

"Probably. Why?"

"Because I don't want a scene. Just want you to take him and go."

"Why's he coming by?"

"To sell some diamonds."

"What time?"

There was a pause, then his cousin said, "Tomorrow, three o'clock."

"Good job, Tony."

"Thanks," was all he said as the line went dead.

This had been a busy morning already. Duarte thought about the conversation with his SAC. If he caught Salez and wrapped up the case by tomorrow, would it be too late to ask for the job again?

He looked up at Chuck, but the big man showed no sign he had listened to either call. Duarte decided he'd go to his cousin's pawnshop alone.

Tony shut the cover to his tiny cell phone as Salez removed the knife from his throat.

"Satisfied?" Tony asked. There was still a considerable tremor in his voice.

"If you believe what'll happen to you if you double-cross me, then I'm satisfied."

"You just want to talk to him?"

"Alone, yes. I won't hurt him."

"He may be a cop, but he's my cousin's boy. I can't let him get hurt."

"You made the right move; otherwise, you'd be on the sidewalk trying to keep your Adam's apple in your throat with your hand."

Salez sheathed the knife and said, "I'll see you about three. And don't fuck this up."

"I promise I won't," said Tony, backing out of the small truck.

Mike Garretti was sitting at his desk on the base, all his paperwork up to date and no one the wiser he had been gone, on and off, for three weeks. It paid to have friends. Especially friends who would cover for you for the cost of five good lunches, which Garretti intended to deliver this week.

He also pondered some personal trips. He needed to visit Seattle sometime, and maybe his brother in Atlanta. For now, Fort Hood provided most of his needs.

His cell phone rang, and he knew who it was.

"Yep," was all he said.

"Call on a pay phone." Then the line went dead.

Garretti took a few minutes to drive off the giant base and toward the first gas station on Route 190. He dialed the number by heart, and it was answered on the first ring.

"Salez is in Florida again."

"You're sure?"

"Absolutely."

"I need a day or two."

"He may not last past tomorrow afternoon."

"What time?"

"Three."

"I'll check flights. Any backup plan?"

"Just get down there, and we'll see what needs to be done. If he's in custody, we should be able to arrange for him to get out. At least long enough for you to find him."

"Equipment?"

"In the same locker as last time. Get a rental car and handle it."

"This will end it all?"

"Absolutely."

"I'm on my way."

* * *

Duarte sat with his father, and felt the tension he had built up over the hard week start to release. He considered it likely that he would sleep tonight and did not need to set an alarm for the morning. If he could just keep his brother quiet as he prepared for work in the morning, he might start the day refreshed. He knew his cousin Tony was unreliable, and recognized that his scheduled meeting with Alberto Salez might not occur, but at least he had made some headway. He knew the fugitive was in the area, and, more important, alive. Duarte would be open to stories of conspiracy involving a hit man now. He had seen the guy in action firsthand. His problem now was deciding who to tell.

Cesar Duarte said, "You look better tonight. Something happen on your case?"

"Yes, sir. I think I might catch the fugitive who has troubled me for the past few weeks."

"Excellent. You'll be careful, yes?"

"Yes, sir." Duarte hesitated, but then realized his father was trustworthy. "In fact, Cousin Tony helped me out. He set up the meeting at his pawnshop."

Cesar Duarte grunted. "Figures, Tony would know a crook. If you were looking for a doctor or a priest, Tony wouldn't have had a clue. But a criminal, and my cousin will know exactly where he is." Then the older Duarte looked at his son. "You'll be able to keep him safe though, right?"

"Oh yes, sir."

"He may be shady, but he's family."

"Yes, sir, I understand."

Cesar Duarte then asked, "Anything else new at work?"

Duarte thought about it and told him what he had learned from the photo, and how he needed to confirm the location of the photo.

His father asked, "Is vital to your case?"

"I don't know. I just have so little, anything seems important."

"It's good to be curious. If your heart tells you the photo is important, you should investigate it more thoroughly."

"I'm trying to figure it out now."

"You can't easily fly to Austin to show the photo around."

Duarte agreed.

"What would you do if you wanted a policeman in Texas to look for a fugitive?"

"E-mail him the information and a photo."

"Why not for a bar? See if an Austin policeman recognizes it."

Duarte smiled. "Thanks, Pop. That's a great idea."

After an hour of news and talk, Duarte kissed his ma and nodded to his pop, then headed out the back door and up the stairs outside the two-story garage. He was relieved to see that his older brother was out, and took the opportunity to shower and grab a book from his growing pile. This one, different from his usual Civil War books, was *The Plot Against America* by Philip Roth. It was engaging to him not only because it dealt with an alternative history but, more important, the story of a family. Sometimes he felt like that was all he had, his large friendly family, and usually he realized that was all he needed. He stretched out to start the book and glanced out at the last few rays of the May sun through his jalousie window.

Caren Larson, with her packed suitcase and tickets for a six A.M. flight to West Palm Beach in her purse, was on her way out of the office when Roberto Morales caught her.

"You're all set for the trip?"

"Yes, sir."

"I know you have a good rapport with Agent Duarte. Make sure he stays on track."

"No problem, sir. He's a good worker. He'll get to the bottom of the bombings."

Morales paused, then said, "Yes, of course he will."

"Sir," started Caren slowly. "Why don't we call in the ATF National Response Team for these bombings?"

Morales looked at her closely. "I don't think the NRT is necessary at this time. I'd like to get a better idea of who's behind this first. I think you and Duarte will handle it nicely. If you get stuck, I could send Tom Colgan to help. I think he worked in West Palm Beach, so he'd know his way around."

"I'll brief you by tomorrow night at the latest."

"Excellent. I'll let Tom know to be ready to go if necessary."

Caren smiled but didn't say anything. If she had, it would have been a foul word.

Alberto Salez had moved quickly to get the whole gang together. He had already paid for dinner at the sports club and now was springing for a couple of pitchers of beer. He didn't want to go overboard and give these guys hangovers tomorrow, so he intended to cut them off soon.

"So you'll meet me tomorrow at the Days Inn off Forty-Fifth Street about two-thirty, right?"

The toughest of the men, Raul, who still had a bandage on his nose from his last encounter with the ATF agent, said, "We'll be there and we'll be ready. This time, I'm bringing a switchblade I got. A big blade. That fucking guy will shit in his pants when I whip out that thing."

"Yeah, yeah, you guys can scare him, but no one cuts him or seriously injures him till I talk to him. We'll take him somewhere from there. That little store owner won't say boo. If he does, you guys can do him, and we'll clean that place out before we go."

Raul smiled and nodded. He looked like a man ready to set fate right. Salez hoped he was up to it this time.

31

DUARTE ROLLED OUT OF BED, DISAPPOINTED HE HAD not slept like he hoped he would. He had grabbed a few hours early, then the nightmares set in and he was awake by three, and finished his Philip Roth novel before the sun was up. He sat at his kitchen table with a bowl of fruit as his brother padded across the living room in his gym shorts and T-shirt. He plopped in the chair across from Duarte.

"Rough night?" asked Duarte.

"Aren't they all?" replied Frank.

"Yeah, I guess so."

"You got anything interesting going on today?"

"Gonna see Cousin Tony about three."

His brother looked up. "Really, why? I thought you two didn't get along."

"We get along fine. We *are* family. He's helping me out with something."

Frank nodded. "I heard you ran into Alice at the PBSO lab."

Duarte nodded.

"She called me. She must miss me terribly."

"I'm sure."

"She said to tell you she got a print, and to go by to see her today."

Duarte nodded. "That was quick. I like that girl already."

"She doesn't want to hook up with me again, so she ain't that smart."

Duarte didn't answer but couldn't help smiling.

* * *

By eight-fifteen, he was at the counter to the crime lab at the Palm Beach County Sheriff's Office. Alice Brainard smiled at Duarte as she handed the glass back to him.

"I already ran the prints through AFIS and the FBI. Nothing yet, no wants, no record. I'm gonna try Department of Defense and some public works databases too, just in case the guy held any kind of government job."

Duarte was impressed. "Thank you very much."

She smiled and said, "I can't believe I called Frank."

"Thought you guys were still friends."

"We are. I mean, I can't believe I asked him if you had a girlfriend. That was just so crass. I'm sorry."

Duarte felt his face flush and managed a smile. Somehow, his brother had forgotten to mention that. "It's fine. Don't worry about it."

She smiled back. "Well, do you?"

"Do I what?"

"Have a girlfriend?"

Duarte thought about Caren Larson and their odd semiromantic relationship. "That's a question I've been asking myself." He left it at that, because it was the truth, and it seemed to confuse Alice long enough for him to leave with the evidence.

Caren Larson could see the surprise in his face when he walked into his office to find her sitting at his desk. In fact, she had just arrived, and the secretary had let her in. She had hoped he might register something other than surprise. It was all she could do not to jump up into his arms.

Instead, she said, "Hey there, Kojak." The smile was mischievous.

He stood, and seemed to contemplate how to treat her.

She understood his confusion. They had slept together, should he hug her? But they were in a federal law enforcement office. She knew he would never be so impetuous as to kiss her in any form of professional setting. Even if no one else was around at the moment.

Duarte finally regained enough focus to say, "Wow, I didn't expect you."

"Ever?"

"No, I meant today. I would've picked you up at the airport."

"Had an early flight and I didn't want to bother you. Bob sent me to stay closer to the case and see if you had found anything new."

He hesitated, then just shook his head.

"What about Maria? How is she doing?"

"She's fine."

"And you. You look a little tired."

"I am, but nothing out of the ordinary."

Caren looked past Duarte to the supervisor of the office, a younger guy named Dale, striding with a purpose toward the tiny office they were in.

"Alex, the boss just told me you turned down a promotion. Is that right?" Then as Duarte moved, he noticed Caren and said, "I'm sorry, I didn't know you were busy." He gave Caren a professional nod and looked at Duarte, still waiting for an answer.

Duarte mumbled, "Not the right time."

"Not the right time? You been waiting for this for years. Are you crazy? You should jump on it."

Duarte shrugged, and then skillfully waited his supervisor out in silence. That impressed even Caren.

Once Dale had disappeared back down the hall, Duarte plopped into his partner's empty chair. He was clearly torn by his decision.

Caren said softly, "You wanna talk about it?"

"Not really."

"You told me you wanted to be a supervisor."

"I did. I mean, I do. It's just . . ."

"What?"

"I'd have to give up this case, and it doesn't seem right somehow. Maria and Hector Tannza deserve justice."

Caren cringed at that simple truth. Could she help? Did the information she had locked in her head really mean anything? What would he think of her if she confessed her fears and how they affected the case? She realized then how much this tough, intelligent ATF agent meant to her. She wanted his approval. She didn't want to hurt him. She wanted her damned dignity back.

Alex Duarte used the time that Caren was in another office on the phone to call the detective bureau of the Austin Police Department. He had found the number on the PD's Internet home page. After speaking to a secretary, he stayed on hold for three minutes until he heard a man's voice say, "Carl Shedlock. May I help you?"

"Detective Shedlock, my name is Alex Duarte. I'm an ATF agent here in Florida."

The detective seemed friendly, saying, "That's where I want to live. I grew up in upstate New York, but I can't handle the cold anymore." He paused, and apparently realized Duarte wasn't going to chat. The detective said, "What can I do for you?"

Duarte explained about the photo and what he suspected. He had scanned the photo and e-mailed it while they were talking on the phone.

After a minute, Detective Shedlock said, "Yeah, this looks like the sports bar in the new area. It's kind of a yuppie place."

Duarte noted the detective's disdain for yuppies. "I'm trying to ID the younger guy in the photo. The other man is Alberto Salez. Ring a bell?"

"Nope, not at all. Neither one looks familiar. Let me show it around the Bureau and see if anyone can tell me more about the bar. Maybe I could even run the photo past the manager, if it's important."

"I can't tell you how important it is because I just don't know. But if you have a chance, I'd appreciate anything you could find out." Duarte gave the helpful detective his cell phone.

Duarte had a nice lunch with Caren, and had purposely invited Chuck Stoddard along so she didn't consider it another date, if that was what she was thinking. He recognized that he had no clue what this beautiful attorney was thinking. But, he also had to admit, he liked her being around.

He had felt guilty earlier when he had lied about having anything new on the case. The possible capture of Alberto Salez was new. It could bust the whole thing wide open. He just thought it was prudent to wait until the wily Mr. Salez was actually in custody before he made any comment. That rationalization made him feel better until he lied to her about what he was doing that afternoon. Instead of informing her about the possible meeting with Salez, he said he had to see his cousin at his Northwood pawnshop. Technically not a lie, but by no ethical standards the truth either. He hadn't told Chuck about the meeting or Salez.

Another ethical lapse if he was wrong about a leak somewhere in the case. He wanted to face Salez alone. Especially if he had to go outside the official guidelines on questioning. He wanted answers and he wanted them now. He wanted to know about Oneida Lawson, the killer and why everyone and his brother was from Texas. He was tired, and ready for some direct information for a change.

At about two-fifteen, he left the office with a promise to Caren to return shortly and then headed the few miles north to his cousin's little pawnshop on Dixie Highway in the Northwood section of the city. He parked his Taurus behind the shop on a residential street so no one coming to the store would notice it. It took him a couple minutes to walk around the building to the front and then wait until his cousin buzzed him inside.

Tony looked up from the counter and said, "Where's your partner?"

"The office."

"Shouldn't he come too?"

"Don't worry so much. I can handle Salez. I have before. Won't even bust up the store." He looked his cousin in the eye and added, "Unless I have to." He even gave Tony a sly smile.

"It ain't three yet. Call him over for backup." Then the little bald man offered his desk phone to Duarte.

"Tony, what's bothering you? Relax." Duarte looked around the store crammed with pawned merchandise. It felt funny to think that most of it at one time had been someone else's personal property. Whether they pawned it or stole it first, it still seemed to belong in someone else's house. Personal stereos lined shelves on one wall, racks or tools and yard equipment cluttered another aisle.

Tony said, "You never know. This asshole could have friends with him."

"Has he called or anything?"

"No. Nothing since I seen him at the café."

"You seem awfully jumpy. I thought you were half-assed criminal. Don't you meet up with crooks all the time?"

"That ain't funny, Alex. I gotta make a living."

"Thought loans and sales from this place made a living for you."

"It does now. Now that you guys cracked down on me, it's all I got to feed the family."

"Tony, your kids are out of the house. Jimmy is in Hawaii. Your wife has got a good job at the hospital. What family do you have to feed?"

"Stop breaking my balls. I done what you asked. I found Salez. Now I just want you to be careful in case he don't want to surrender."

"Tony, are you trying to tell me . . ."

But Duarte was interrupted by the sight of Salez at the front door and Tony hitting the buzzer instantly.

32

MIKE GARRETTI ARRIVED IN THE NICE LITTLE AIRPORT AT west Palm Beach, Florida, rented a Dodge Intrepid, then drove to a public storage warehouse a few miles west. He checked his note for the unit number and combination. He trudged up the outside stairway to the closet-sized storage unit that was tucked into the hallway on the second floor. It never failed to amaze him how, despite all the money his employers obviously had at their disposal, they cut costs at every opportunity. This little unit wasn't good for much, but a slightly larger one on the first floor could be used to hide all kinds of things. He let it go.

Once he had the door open, he found several boxes stacked in the corner, and a smaller one with his name on the lid sitting on top of the others. Next to it was a sleek Browning 9mm. The single-action auto pistol was perfectly balanced and felt good in his hand. They had left two clips of ammo in addition to the one in the gun. He had one single brick of C-4. Plenty, if Salez was his only target. By now, it didn't matter how he died—just that he did. That would put an end to this whole mess. He wouldn't even have to use the C-4 unless he had to set a booby trap. And that seemed unlikely now.

He had followed the directions given him and now realized that they were right on the money. His heart rate climbed as he knew everything would be resolved, and very soon.

Mike Garretti watched as Alberto Salez entered a pawnshop around three o'clock, just like he had been told would happen. The only question was, when to do it. He'd definitely wait until the shithead had left the little pawnshop. He had parked a beat-up Nissan pickup in the small lot in front of the store. As Garretti scanned it with his little binoculars, he didn't notice any corpses in the passenger's seat this time. That was a nice change.

Then, almost as soon as Salez entered the store, Garretti noticed another vehicle. An older Ford Bronco, with a bunch of Latin guys crammed inside. The car made one pass, then lingered in the street in front of the next building, out of sight of the pawnshop.

What the hell was going on?

Salez said "Surprise" as he walked inside. "I guess it wasn't a surprise, because your cousin told you I'd be here."

Duarte turned his head toward Tony.

"I had no choice. He woulda killed me."

Salez smiled and said, "You can't pick your family." He just had a Band-Aid over the end of the ear Duarte had ripped off during their first meeting.

Duarte looked at him and said, "At least you were smart enough to show up. I was getting tired of chasing you."

"I wasn't running from the law, bro. Now I need to know who I *am* running from."

Duarte sensed that this wasn't a simple surrender, and scanned the crowded little store for any potential weapons Salez might use. He hoped the rows of pistols in the glass cases weren't loaded. He needed to make sure Salez wasn't armed now.

"Before we go any farther," started Duarte, "put your hands on the counter and spread your legs."

"No problem, Agent Duarte." He reached to his hip and said, "Let me dispose of this first." He tossed a long fillet knife, in a dirty leather scabbard that didn't fit it well, onto the counter. "I'm clean."

Duarte edged closer and ran the palms of his hands over the fugitive's waistline and then along the lower legs of his jeans. Then he stepped back, picking up the knife as he backed away.

Duarte said, "Now, what are you babbling about?"

"Who sent you after me?"

"My boss. You had a warrant."

"That's not what I meant. Who else do you work for?"

"Look, I know someone is trying to kill you. I've seen him."

"What'd he look like?"

"Dark, short hair, thirty-five, lean."

"And cold as ice. He blew the shit out of my sweet Mustang."

Duarte wanted to strike the heartless fugitive. Instead, he said, "Not to mention Hector Tannza, and the others who were killed."

"That's what I said, he's a killer."

"Why is he after you?"

Salez said, "That's all the questions I'm gonna answer, but you're gonna have to come with me."

"Why?"

"I gotta make sure you really don't know anything."

"And if I don't?"

"I'll find a use for you, and, at the very least, you can find out how much it hurts to lose an ear."

Now Cousin Tony cut in. "You said you wasn't gonna hurt him."

Duarte said, "Don't worry, Tony. I've dealt with this mope before. It's no big deal."

Then the front door rattled. Salez motioned the man in but the door was still locked. He rattled the door harder, making a huge racket. Tony backed away from the counter to show he wasn't going to use the buzzer to unlock the door.

Then a second, larger man ran from the side and put his weight into the door and forced it to pop open, sending a couple of pieces of metal jingling onto the floor. The men rushed into the pawnshop, followed by three more. One of them with a shotgun already aimed at Duarte.

Duarte shook his head. "You guys. Didn't we already have this dance?"

The man with the flat nose, now with a bandage over it, said, "This time, we're ready." He nodded toward the man with the shotgun. "And we got some firepower."

Duarte looked around the motley group. "How're the fingers?" he asked flat-nose, his right hand still bandaged from Duarte breaking his fingers during their last encounter.

"You better worry about your own fingers, pendejo." He pulled out a switchblade with his left hand and popped the five-inch blade open.

Salez eased toward Duarte, then said, "Put your gun on the counter. Slowly, or my man Ralph here will ventilate you good."

Duarte reached to his right hip under his loose outer shirt and carefully drew his Glock. He set it on the glass counter next to him.

"Now slide it to me."

He pushed it just hard enough for it to slide almost to Salez. He cut his eyes to his cousin and instantly realized the little man was too terrified to help. Duarte stayed calm, and when Salez reached for the Glock Duarte threw out his right hand and grabbed the fugitive's arm, then tugged him hard. Salez flew right to Duarte, like a female dance partner in a tango, as the big man with the shotgun tried to aim around his friend. Immediately Duarte wrapped his arm around Salez's neck and moved out of the line of fire into a row of used sporting goods.

He heard some shouts in Spanish, and saw through the racks and shelves two men start down the row next to him.

Duarte tightened his grip around Salez's neck. "Tell 'em to back off—now."

Salez tried to gurgle out a command for his comrades to stop, but it was barely audible.

Duarte dropped Salez and his deadweight, then immediately plucked a metal tennis racket out of a bin. He had just enough time to swing it on an angle and have the frame catch the first man in the head, sending him yelping back. Duarte stepped around the shelf to the tool aisle, where the second man, flat-nose, looked confused as to what to do next with his extended switchblade. Duarte was not confused and grabbed a ball-peen hammer hanging on the rack and drove the rounded head into the man's clavicle, shattering his shoulder and knocking him down in the process.

There were three left, but the only one he wanted to focus on was the one with the shotgun. As he bounded around the next shelf, ready to throw the hammer if necessary, he froze. This was something he had not counted on.

Caren Larson laughed at one of Chuck Stoddard's corny jokes. This big, friendly man was the polar opposite of Alex Duarte. He seemed to care about people, and genuinely liked to laugh. It was the type of personality she had always been attracted to.

She wondered how much her father played in her choice of men. He had been jovial and friendly, except to boys coming to pick her up. Then he'd grunt and nod instead of speaking, and once even poked a boy in the chest as he interrogated him about why they were home at five after eleven instead of eleven on the nose. That incident had made her a night owl in college determined to stay out late. But then she realized her father's concerns as she met more and more men. Many of them really didn't have any respect for a woman. That was a big factor in her attraction to Duarte. His respect for people. Not just women, but the workers out at the labor camp. He didn't discount anyone. That was also just like her father. But her father had a new joke for every day of her life. He'd wake her with a kiss and a joke.

How, then, had she fallen for a sullen, determined guy like Alex Duarte? She didn't know, but, as her mother would say, these things just happen and we shouldn't fight them.

Now Caren looked at Chuck's massive head and said, "You don't know where Alex went either?"

"Haven't seen him. We tend to keep different hours. He's an early riser, and I like to go home early, so if he's not in the office between ten and two it's his loss." He laughed at his own joke, and that made Caren smile too.

She said, "He said something about his cousin."

"Tony? He has a pawnshop in the north end of the city."

"Is Alex close with his cousin?"

"Alex and Tony?" He just laughed.

"Why would he go see him, then?"

"Tony was trying to find Salez for us. Maybe he had something on that."

"Can we go meet him?"

"At Tony's?"

"Yeah. I'm just worried about him. It gets you out of the office for a few minutes."

Chuck shrugged and said, "Yeah, sure. It's not far."

33

DUARTE FROZE AT THE SIGHT OF THE BIG MAN WITH the shotgun to his cousin Tony's bald head. His cousin was shaking uncontrollably, and sweat glistened on his crown under the fluorescent light hanging from the ceiling.

The big man, standing to the side, said, "What you gonna do with that hammer, Mr. Policeman? Less you want this man's brains all over the wall."

Duarte let the hammer fall harmlessly to the ground as Salez came up from the back of the shop, massaging his throat. "Yo, my man here is some kinda half-assed Bruce Lee. He's quick." Salez also had the Glock in his hand now. "Tell ya what, ATF. We're goin' for a little ride and have us a talk." He turned to the man with the shotgun. "Ralph, you come with us."

"What about us?" asked one of the others.

"Help Raul, and wait here with Cousin Tony till I get back." He looked at his friend on the ground uselessly clutching his misshapen shoulder.

"We don't even got guns."

Salez leveled a stare at the man and said, "Look at the counter, bro. Take one of them." He shook his head and waved Duarte toward the door.

Duarte turned and decided to wait until they were outside before he tried anything. He didn't want his cousin to get hurt.

As if reading his mind, Salez said, "If this cabron gets away, we'll kill Cousin Tony here."

Duarte stepped through the door first, with Salez and Ralph behind him, both with their guns pointed down in an attempt to hide them from any cars rolling down Dixie Highway.

Salez said, "Around the corner. The Nissan."

Duarte walked slowly, hoping to think of something, then turned the side of the building right into a familiar face.

Mike Garretti had the nice Browning in his hand, as he heard them tromping around the side of the building. He had wanted to cap Salez right away, but knew he needed to find out about the file and its location.

The ATF man was first; Garretti waved him down out of the way. When he dropped quickly, it was so fast it took both Garretti and Salez by surprise. But now, Garretti had his former partner plainly in his sights. The big man behind him was also caught by surprise and couldn't move.

Garretti said in a calm voice, "Keep coming, gentlemen. And drop the guns."

The shotgun and Glock both clunked to the ground with the litter that was strewn across the small parking lot.

"All right, Agent Duarte. You come too."

Duarte stood up, brushed a little dirt from his pants and fell in next to Salez and Ralph. "I appreciate the help."

Garretti let out a smile. "And everyone says you don't have a sense of humor. I think that's funny."

"I didn't catch your name."

"Which is the only reason you're still alive."

Salez said, "I'll introduce you two."

"You might find that uncomfortable." He stepped over to Salez, well away from Duarte, and handed him a small package. "Put this in your front pocket."

Salez just stared at him.

Garretti raised the pistol to his forehead and Salez complied without hesitation. Then he asked, "What is it?"

Garretti held up a palm-sized electrical device and said, "A small compliance measure. You act up and I hit this switch. Then your legs and dick get blown off. Got it?"

Salez went pale.

Garretti looked at Duarte and said, "Any prepared federal agent has cuffs."

Duarte nodded.

"Cuff him."

Duarte turned and pulled Salez's arms roughly down, then

behind him. He clicked the arm of the cuffs into place, securing Salez's hands behind him. Duarte looked up at Garretti and said, "Anything else?"

"You know you could thank me."

"For what?"

"For saving you now, to start with. Then the other times I coulda killed you. I don't want to kill a cop. You don't deserve it." He paused, and said, "Especially you. I read your recommendation for award. The Form 638 in your jacket. You should've gotten that Silver Star. That bridge you blew on the Drina River was heads-up play." He watched Duarte as he stared at him. Garretti wasn't sure if he was surprised he had access to his army records or that he thought the ATF agent should've received a commendation. Garretti finally added, "You did some good work in Bosnia."

Duarte muttered, "About as good as yours."

"And I feel just as shitty." He looked at Salez and said, "Get in the car, asshole. Front seat." He backed around to the driver's door and said, "We still have issues, but I'll work them out later." He paused, and pointed the pistol at Duarte. "If it'll make you feel better, I'll order you at gunpoint to knock that big son of a bitch out."

Duarte didn't hesitate; he spun, using his hips, shoulders and arms, to propel a perfect right cross directly onto Ralph's big chin. The big man stumbled back against the wall and then crumpled to the ground.

Garretti smiled and said, "Glad I never tried to tangle with you. Good luck." He slipped behind the wheel, looked at his terrified passenger, threw the car into reverse and was away from the sharp ATF man in a matter of seconds.

Duarte recovered his Glock and Ralph's shotgun as he decided on the best way to get back into the pawnshop. He had to rescue his cousin, even if it was only to kill him himself. He paused at the corner of the building, then froze as he saw Chuck Stoddard pull up in his new SUV with Caren Larson in the front seat. How in the hell did they know to come here? He leaned away from the wall and waved, immediately catching Chuck's eye. They pulled past the shop and into the lot in the back, away from any window where they could be spotted from inside.

Chuck eased out of the Expedition and said, "What are you doing out here? Where'd the shotgun come from? Why . . ." He noticed the unmoving body on the ground.

"Hang on, Chuck. We gotta get my cousin out of there."

"What's going on?" He pointed at the large, unconscious man. "Is he dead?"

Duarte turned and looked at the unconscious Ralph. "Him? No. I just popped him on the chin." He looked up at the corner of the store. "Some of Salez's buddies are inside with Tony."

Caren cut in. "Did Salez show too?"

"He showed, but he's gone now."

Chuck got back to the tactical situation. "Are the guys inside armed?"

"They probably are now. But we have surprise on our side. The door has a buzzer, but they broke it in earlier. I think we could force it again."

Caren said, "What if I act like a customer and they buzz me in?"

He looked up at her, impressed with the lawyer's courage. "It won't work. They know you. It's the crowd from the sports club in Belle Glade." He looked at his partner. "Might work for you, Chuck. If it doesn't, you could knock it open like they did."

"You gonna explain exactly what's happening?"

"First, we get Tony. Then we need to talk." Duarte froze as he noticed something he had not before. There was a door in the rear of the pawnshop and Tony's little Nissan sports car was parked next to it. "We may have an alternative." Duarte raced to the door, tried the handle and was surprised to find it open. It opened out. He peeked inside to see a second interior door that opened into the shop.

Duarte turned to his big partner and said, "Give me a minute and then try the front door." He looked at Ralph, still on the ground. "Secure him too."

Chuck just nodded and stood up to go back to Caren.

Duarte added, "And make sure she stays in the car."

Garretti didn't like distractions when he was dealing with someone like Salez. The target of his frustration was cuffed and sitting at an angle in the front seat next to him as they headed west on Blue Heron Boulevard. He had driven due north, away from the pawnshop, in case Duarte had been able to follow them. The ATF man had proven to be very determined. Maybe he had learned that in Operation Determined Effort in Bosnia. Garretti smiled at the name of the operation. There was always some cute name attached to those kind of things. Determined Effort, Just Cause, Desert Shield and the other Bosnian one: Operation Joint Endeavor. He had been deployed to Desert Shield as a new sergeant. It wasn't as if a clerk in personnel saw a lot of action. He was first housed in a comfortable base in Israel, then a big-ass tent in Saudi Arabia, helping the flow of men and women find their place in the building conflict. It didn't really matter what he did because when he got home he was still a Gulf War veteran. It still got him laid, and eventually, through chance and a lot of beer prompting a lot of boasting, it got him the first gig outside the army. It was a lot of money. Fifty grand. Then all the work since. But he was relieved it would end here. Now that he had Salez, the last one. Once he found out where the file was, he'd do what he had to do.

Now he juggled driving, keeping an eye on Salez and trying his cell phone. Finally he got through to one of his contacts, who told him to use a pay phone in five minutes.

It took a little longer because, as he drove out on the main highway, even past the Riviera Beach City Hall and police department, he realized that this place was a dive. There was no place he wanted to stop. He didn't want to have to shoot someone here and have people looking for him. So he kept driving until he crossed under I-95 and found a phone near a gas station just past a bunch of cheap hotels like the Knight's Inn and Motel 6.

He parked so he could see Salez clearly and shoot him in the head if he had to, but still have a private conversation on the phone.

He stepped out of the small car and then leaned back and said, "No bullshit." He held up the electric button he had shown Salez at the pawnshop. "Remember, boom, and then no dick."

Salez just nodded as he looked at the pocket the device was in.

Garretti turned his attention back to his call. The phone rang once, and he heard, "Go ahead."

"I have the principal."

"Good. Any problems?"

"The ATF man saw me."

"We'll work it out. Find out about the file."

"That's my plan."

"Your backup just arrived. One of them will find you soon."

"Don't need backup."

"Everyone needs backup. Good work."

The line went dead.

Garretti got back in the car, and Salez said, "Mike, we could drive off right now and go our separate ways."

"No can do, amigo. I got a job to do. Besides, I let you go you might kill another woman, like the one in the Honda."

Salez leaned back. "I didn't kill her, bro. She was in the car when I took it."

"Oh, please. After all we been through, don't even try that bull-shit."

Salez didn't try, instead he said, "What makes you think they'll let *you* walk away from all this any more than they let the rest of us?"

Garretti didn't answer, but did think about his backup coming down to meet him.

34

ALEX DUARTE'S BLOOD WAS UP. THAT'S WHAT HIS COM-manding officer used to say when they were about to do something to the advancing Serbs. They'd plant booby traps, occasionally take potshots, but whatever they did there was a real emotional charge surrounding it. Duarte had fed off it during his stint in Bosnia. He loved the excitement, and missed it here in civilian life. Occasionally something happened, an arrest or chase, but not very often. Now, in this one odd situation, his blood was definitely up as he prepared to rescue his lowlife cousin from these lowlife idiots.

Duarte turned the knob to the newly discovered rear door and slipped in through a back storeroom. The next-door room was empty, and then he saw the inward-opening door. *That* was the one with the giant bolt and crossbar you could see from inside the store.

He tried the door and it didn't budge.

"Shit," he said quietly to himself.

He put his ear to it, but it was so thick he didn't hear a sound. He was about to back out and race to meet up with Chuck as the big man assaulted the front door when he saw something else that might work.

Chuck Stoddard had been a cop in Tampa for three years before joining the ATF. He had been a dynamo for a few years, jumping in on any case that came along, then, with the birth of his son, and two years later his daughter, he started to realize that there was more to life than work. He wasn't lazy, as many thought, he just had other priorities. He worked hard, just not hard for long.

But on something like this—a chance at some action—he had never lost his enthusiasm. He secured the big, unconscious guy by sitting him up then cuffing him behind his back to a light pole. By then, the guy was coming around. The large Hispanic man vomited once, which was common for someone who had just been unconscious, then offered no resistance as Chuck hooked him up.

Caren said, "What's our next move?"

"My next move is through the front door."

"I'm going with you."

"Sorry, baby. You gotta sit this one out."

Caren surprised him with a forceful, "Bullshit. I'm coming."

Chuck settled the matter by using his backup cuffs to secure her to the big Ford's armrest. He didn't have time to argue.

He waited a minute after cuffing the DoJ attorney, then took up a good position by the door. He figured that if Alex hadn't returned to the front of the pawnshop, he must be ready to get in through the back. That was something he was quite sure of; no matter what he did, or how he did it, his partner, Alex Duarte, would not let you down.

Chuck stepped up and tried the door as he looked in through it. It was locked but loose. Inside, a small Latin man, not Tony, said, "We closed. Come back later."

Chuck didn't hesitate and burst through the shaky door, pulling much of the frame with him. Immediately he saw Tony in a chair against the back wall and three men near the counter. Chuck brought up his Glock, as he noticed the back door was still bolted. Just as he thought he was in this alone he heard a crash and the ceiling panels seemed to vaporize. Duarte dropped through the ceiling onto the man closest to his cousin Tony. He dropped straight down, knocking the man unconscious on impact.

Chuck swung his gun onto the remaining two men, who were completely frozen by the shock of Duarte's entrance.

Tony said, "My ceiling. You ruined my ceiling."

Chuck resisted the urge to point the gun at the ungrateful store owner. He didn't know the whole story yet. Then, behind him, he heard, "Thank God." He turned to see Caren Larson, with a handcuff on her left hand and the armrest to his Expedition stuck in the other cuff.

35

MIKE GARRETTI HAD ALBERTO SALEZ SECURELY TIED TO the lone chair in his cheap motel room. Salez wasn't going anywhere, and Garretti needed a few minutes to figure out what he was going to do next. He had his stuff together if he needed to leave. He was parked directly in front of the room, so in the evening, if he needed to dispose of Salez, it would be easy to just walk him outside and drop him in the waiting car. There were so many canals in Florida that getting rid of him wouldn't be an issue. By the time the body was found, Garretti would be back at Fort Hood and his life would be back to normal. He'd never come back in Florida. Too many bad memories. The chances of Duarte seeing him again and identifying him were nil. A rough drawing—that's all he'd be able to come up with. His employers would also help hide his identity. And he didn't have to live with the death of a federal agent on his hands. Now, looking at his prisoner and thinking of how he had resolved so many of the recent complications, Garretti started to relax. This might work out after all.

For his part, Salez had been suitably sniveling since Garretti had brought him to the room.

Garretti finally said, "What'll shut you up?"

"Get this bomb out of my pocket, for one thing."

Garretti picked up the electronic detonator and put his thumb over the red button. "This would get rid of it."

Salez squirmed in the wooden chair. "Quit it."

Garretti smiled and couldn't resist mashing the bright red button.

Salez cringed and cried out, "No!" His eyes squeezed shut as he waited for the blast that was supposed to rip him in half. Then, when nothing happened, he opened his eyes and looked up at Garretti, shouting, "What the fuck? If that thing worked, it woulda killed me."

Garretti stepped over to the bound man and dug into his pocket, retrieving the little device he had given Salez earlier. He held it up. "Why does a garage door opener in my hand and a circuit board from a radio with a light glued on it make you so nervous?"

Salez just stared at his captor.

It was a ploy that worked. It being hilarious was just a perk. Garretti chuckled at Salez.

The phone in the motel room rang.

"Hello."

A male's voice with a slight New England accent said, "I'm your backup. Where can we meet?"

Garretti didn't want the guy here at the motel, and he didn't want to lug Salez with him to go out. He said into the phone, "Hang on a sec." Then drew his Glock and whacked the seated Salez in the head.

"Ow! Fuck, what was that for?"

"Sorry. It works in the movies," said Garretti, hoping the blow would have knocked his captive unconscious. Into the phone he said, "Meet me in the parking lot of my motel." He proceeded to give the man directions. Sometimes you had to compromise.

Alex Duarte had the three men from inside the pawnshop and the still-groggy Ralph lined up on stools in the back storeroom of his cousin's shop. Tony had already clearly expressed how he didn't want to press charges and he wanted the whole situation to just disappear. He was also sorry he had set up his own cousin.

With his doubts about the motives of his partners, Duarte no longer cared what was or was not within the boundaries of the Department of Justice. He paced back and forth in front of the four men.

"I won our first fight. Now I've done it again. What will keep you from bothering me again?"

Ralph shook his head. "It wasn't us; it was Salez."

"Where was he staying?"

"Don't know. He met us at the sports club."

"What did he want with me?"

"He say you ruined his ear and might know something that would help him."

"Like what?"

They all shrugged and shook their heads.

Duarte looked over at Caren. "What do you think? They telling the truth?"

Caren looked shaken. He didn't know if it was the current situation or something more. He started to think of ways to figure out who was on the level and who had another agenda. He thought of how the killer had appeared at the same place as him when Lawson was killed. What about Chuck? He had called him from the airport. He shook his head, realizing how it couldn't have been a coincidence. Who had he told other than Caren or Chuck? But he never told Caren he was going back to Los Angeles.

He had to focus. Right now, his main problem was that he had to make sure he was done with these guys forever.

He looked up at Chuck and said, "I think we should kill them so we never have to deal with an ambush like this again."

Chuck said, "If that's what you think." He racked Ralph's shotgun to emphasize the point.

All four men started jabbering in a combination of English and Spanish. The gist was that they didn't like that plan.

"I tell you what." He looked up and down the line of captives. "I let you go, you have to promise never to bother me again."

They all nodded vigorously.

"And if I give you my cell, you'll call me if you see Salez again."

More nods.

"Do I have to break any fingers to emphasize this deal?"

He didn't bother to look at their nods. Now came the harder task: who could he trust?

36

ALEX DUARTE SAT ALONE WITH HIS COUSIN TONY IN the quiet store as they waited for a repairman to come fix his shattered door. Everyone had left. The five mopes crammed back into the old Bronco and headed back to the labor camp. Chuck had taken the still-shaken Caren back to her hotel. And now Duarte had the odd feeling of sitting with his cousin, who had just allowed him to be set up by a wanted fugitive, and still felt like he could trust Tony more than his partners.

Duarte had helped sweep up the broken ceiling tiles and straightened up some of the merchandise he had knocked down during the encounter. Tony mumbled behind the counter as he looked through the phone book for someone to fix his ceiling.

Duarte said, "What're you pissy about? I'm the one you tricked into coming here."

"I'm not pissy; I'm annoyed. This is bad for business."

"A fight in the store?"

"No, people finding out I'm related to an ATF agent."

Duarte nodded. He could imagine the shame.

Then his cousin looked up from the Yellow Pages and said, "Look, Alex, that nut Salez held a knife to my throat and swore to me he wouldn't hurt you. I shoulda known better. I shoulda warned you."

Duarte didn't answer.

"We're family, and even though you're an officious prick with no sense of humor I love you. Forgive me."

Duarte looked up and felt the real emotion behind his cousin's comment. He could tell by looking at him that he was telling the truth. Duarte realized he had been reading a lot of people correctly recently. Maybe he should start trusting his instincts when he talked to people.

Mike Garretti had the smooth frame of the Browning tucked into the front of his pants, with the tail of his polo shirt hiding the butt of the gun. He stood directly in front of the door to his room at the little motel where Alberto Salez was securely tied to a chair with handcuffs still holding his hands behind his back. Garretti was sorry he had told the creep about the fake explosive device he had stuck in his pocket. It might have helped to control him. But the look on his face when he realized he had been tricked was worth it.

Now Garretti was worried about meeting his backup for the first time. What kept the backup from killing him just like Garretti had killed everyone else involved in their little adventure three years earlier? If Garretti tried to duck the backup, they'd end up finding him eventually, so at least this way he got a look at them. But he still hoped that there wasn't anything to fear in the first place.

He leaned on his rented Dodge as a Ford Expedition slid into the lot and parked sideways. There were three men inside, but only one got out. A tall guy, with short, almost military hair and a cockiness that often came with Special Forces training.

The tall man said, "Hey, Mike. We've spoken on the phone before."

Garretti eyed the man and Ford without offering his hand.

The tall man said, "You got Salez?"

Garretti nodded, letting his hand rest near the butt of the pistol. It was just getting dark and cooling down, but he could feel himself start to sweat slightly. Finally he asked the man, "Why are you guys here?"

"To tie up any possible loose ends."

"Like me?"

The man looked shocked. "No, not at all. In fact, we're here to ensure your safety."

"Besides Salez, what loose ends are there?"

"You don't need to know."

Garretti shrugged, knowing he'd have to change hotels as soon as these guys left. But the guy seemed like he was telling the truth. The fact that he hadn't given his name or tried to introduce him to the others was another indication that he didn't intend to silence Garretti.

The man said, "Where's Salez?"

"Locked down."

"Get that file before you do him."

"Thanks, I figured out the order of the agenda by myself." Then Garretti realized they couldn't do anything until the file was secured. This might affect how he proceeded.

The man handed him a cell phone. "It's safe to call me on this." He handed him a slip of paper with a local phone number. "Any time, day or night."

Garretti examined the phone and pocketed the small Nextel. "I'll let you know if anything develops."

Duarte sat at the little kitchen table he shared with his brother. He was picking at a bowl of black beans and rice, as he thought about his day, when his cell phone rang.

"Duarte."

"Hey, it's Carl Shedlock from the Austin PD."

"Any luck with the photo ID?"

"Luck? More like the lotto."

Duarte sat up. "What'd you find out?"

"The manager didn't know the name of the young Middle Eastern guy, but he remembered the face from a bad bar fight they had there a few years ago. I remember reading about it but wasn't involved in the case."

"You guys open cases on bar fights?"

"We do if they're homicides."

"He killed someone?"

"Nope, he was the victim. I checked with our crimes-persons detectives and it's still open. They have it as a hate crime. You know, post nine-eleven. They started calling him names, and then took it out into the street."

"Do you have his name?"

"Wahlid al-Samir."

"You know anything about him?"

"He was the son of a big-shot Saudi oil guy. The Saudis sent their own security people to follow up the investigation. We ended up with nothing."

"No suspects?"

"He was friendly with some guys that night at the bar, but no one could identify them or ever saw them again. Someone said they thought they were the ones that beat him."

Duarte offered, "The other guy, Salez, is a fugitive."

"Will you question him about the incident if you lay your hands on him?"

"I promise I will."

Shedlock said, "They beat this kid bad. Ruptured spleen, lacerated liver, even left a shoeprint in his head. No need to be gentle if you find him."

Duarte smiled a little and said, "I think I can accommodate you."

It wasn't quite dusk, and Duarte was enjoying the quiet of his apartment. He couldn't believe how little time he spent in the place. He liked it, appreciating being alone after years spent in group housing and bustling offices. He liked using the privacy to contemplate things.

After his conversation with the Austin detective, he tried to fit the pieces into place without success. He had only been involved in one bar fight and he was still embarrassed by it. It was back when he was in the service, on leave in Italy. In a bar in Pordenone, near the Aviano air base, Duarte had sat brooding about what he had just done near the Drina River on the Bosnian and Serbian border. He wasn't drunk, but the four beers had affected him. He hadn't wanted to go on leave, but his commanding officer had ordered it. He wanted Duarte away from the area to get his head on straight. He had tagged along with six men and the captain from his combat engineer's unit.

The small bar with six tables was empty on a Wednesday afternoon except for the silent Duarte and a surly, middle-aged woman with a spare tire that would've fit a tractor trailer. Two U.S. Air Force sergeants wandered in around four. It obviously wasn't their first stop at a drinking establishment that day. They sat at the table with Duarte despite all the others being vacant. Immediately they started in on him. He looked too young to be in the army. Why the army? Too stupid to get into the air force? The standard bar trash talk.

Duarte ignored them. Then one of the sergeants, a burly man about thirty, flicked his ear and said, "This boy hasn't seen any action."

Duarte looked at him and said, "Don't touch me again."

The other sergeant, leaner but taller than the first, chuckled and said, "What's your name, boy?"

Without thinking he said, "Duarte, Alex." Like he had been trained.

The burly sergeant smiled. "Duarte. That's Mexican, ain't it?"

Duarte glared at him.

"I thought the Mexicans were a friendly bunch. You ain't friendly at all." He reached over and clamped his big hand on Duarte's shoulder.

Duarte didn't hesitate now. He let out all the anger that had been building in him since the incident on the Drina River. Aided by the alcohol in his system, he slapped his hand on top of the sergeant's hand on his shoulder and pivoted in his chair, pulling the sergeant off balance. Then Duarte sprang to his feet, pulled the sergeant's hand off his shoulder and, while it was still extended, brought his other elbow down on it. He felt the bones snap under the force.

The other sergeant stood and swung at Duarte's head. He ducked the clumsy punch easily and delivered a front kick to the man's exposed ribs, sending him crashing onto the table, then in a heap on the floor.

Duarte turned to the bully with the broken arm and snatched him up by his shirt. Before the man could speak, Duarte pivoted and, using his hip, flipped him onto his friend.

As Duarte considered what he would do next, the front door to the bar opened and his captain appeared like magic. It took a few shouts of his name for Duarte to look up and come out of his focus on the fight.

The captain looked at the gigantic, screaming barmaid and the two battered airmen, then said, "C'mon, Rocket, we gotta split." The captain tossed two twenty-dollar bills in American money on the bar and shoved Duarte out of the building.

Duarte didn't get a scratch in the fight, and now rarely had a beer. At least, not in little bars when he was feeling sorry for himself.

The call from the Austin detective had given him more information. But was it useful? Now he tried reasoning out his own situation. How did the bomber know where he would be? That was what tortured him. Then meeting the guy really threw him for a loop. The bomber was right; he could've killed Duarte at almost any time, but he had not. Why? Duarte also didn't feel he could tell anyone about the weird shit that had been happening because he didn't know who to trust. If Chuck or Caren Larson were the leak, then someone would hear about the encounter with Salez and his buddies. If they weren't, Duarte figured he had a few days to find out the truth and try to bring the bomber to justice. At least now he knew what the man looked like. Then he remembered the print he had left with the sheriff's lab.

He reached for the phone on his kitchen wall, then rifled his wallet for the number Alice Brainard had given him. He knew it was a little late, but maybe someone would answer.

To his surprise, he heard "Hello" after the third ring.

"Alice?"

"Yes."

"Hey, this is Alex Duarte."

"Hello, Alex, I was wondering if you'd ever call me."

Then he realized this was her cell phone. She expected business calls through the sheriff's office, not at this number. Man, he was slow to catch on to women's cues, but at least he was beginning to get with the program. He recovered from his shock and said, "Sorry, things have been crazy."

"You still working on the case with that print you gave me?"

She brought it up so he moved ahead. "Yeah."

"I was going to call you tomorrow."

"Oh yeah?"

"The check came back as a hit in the Department of Defense. I have a contact in Washington that I sent the reference number to. He should be able to give me a name tomorrow."

"Alice, that is really good work, thanks." He felt himself relax as he realized that everyone couldn't be in on the conspiracy. This young woman had just done some good police work to help him, and it was all outside the reach of the Department of Justice.

Then she added, "I also sent the print through the Department of Justice again. I have a lab guy with the FBI who's really good and knows everyone up there. He might find something too."

Duarte tensed again.

Alice paused and said, "So what are you doing tonight?"

"I, ummm, I have a few things at work to clear up."

"You tryin' to duck out on our drink?"

"No, not at all." Caren Larson's face flashed through his head, then Maria Tannza's. Something like that had never happened when he was speaking to a woman. "I'll be freed up in a few days, if you're still able."

Alice said, "It's not usually this hard to get a man to go out with me."

He didn't know how to reply. "It's just . . ."

"I know, Frank said you're really dedicated. I know cops like you. I'll wait. Just not forever."

After a quick good-bye, Duarte sat back and stared at the phone for a minute. He wasn't used to a full-sized receiver after using his cell phone so much.

His brother, Frank, burst through the door shattering his concentration. "Yo, brother man. Not used to seeing you at home."

Duarte fought to keep his focus on the phone. He had an idea. "Frank, you got your cell on?"

His brother held up a slim cell phone. "Right here."

"Who's it registered to?"

"You mean, who pays the bill? The firm. Why?"

Duarte didn't answer. Instead, he said, "Hang on while I call you."

"What the hell you talking about? I'm right here."

"Look, it's hard to explain, maybe crazy to explain, but I just need to call you. Just go along, and say 'Okay' when I call."

Frank shrugged as his younger brother dialed his number. He answered it on the third ring after Duarte motioned him to pick up. "Hello."

Duarte nodded his approval, and said into his cell phone, "Hey, it's Alex Duarte."

"Hey, Alex." His brother looked at him from across the room still confused.

"I got the evidence Lawson gave me in Los Angeles. Meet me tomorrow at eight at the Sunrise Cafe on Belvedere."

Then Frank smiled a little. "That dive?"

Duarte shot him a harsh glance.

Frank said, "I'll be there at eight."

Duarte said, "Good." Then he closed his phone.

Frank looked up at his brother and said, "Now, tell me what that was all about."

Duarte came closer and sat on their small couch. "You gotta keep it between us."

"Not even Dad?"

"No, he may not like how I handle this."

"Okay, so spill it."

And Duarte did.

Mike Garretti lay on top of the sheets in his Dockers and polo shirt just in case he had to jump up in the middle of the night. Handcuffed and tied to a chair in the corner of the hotel room, Alberto Salez dozed from his upright position. They had concluded most of their business, but Garretti had to admit that he didn't have the stomach to torture someone, even someone as low as Salez. Luckily, all he had had to do was threaten the ruddy-faced creep and Salez had told him the file was hidden at Maria Tannza's trailer. Garretti believed him, but just in case it wasn't there he had to keep this slime around. If they went out there and bothered that poor, grieving woman and the file wasn't in the trailer, then Garretti would give up any regrets about torture and guarantee that Salez would tell him anything he needed to know. Then he'd report it to his employer and even let his backup team look into it. Just as long as he could be on his way home when this whole thing was over.

The cell phone his backup had given him rang on the nightstand. He twisted and glanced at the clock as he reached for the phone. It was five fifty-five in the morning.

In the corner, Salez stirred but didn't wake up.

Garretti flipped open the phone and said, "Yes?"

A man's voice said, "Call on a pay."

"Why? They said I could use this phone."

"Not to call me." The line went dead.

He hated this cloak-and-dagger stuff, but figured he had time to slip to the corner and use the phone. He'd almost be in view of the hotel, and Salez was in a deep sleep now. It had been a long day for the asshole. And he figured Salez was tied securely enough that he'd have a hard time escaping in the time Garretti was on the phone.

He pulled on his Top-Siders and slipped his Browning into his belt, then pulled the end of the shirt over it. He opened the door and slipped out quietly into the humid and dark South Florida morning. There was no traffic on the road, and no one on the street. Once on the sidewalk, he could see the lone pay phone in the corner of the strip mall parking lot. He quickly stepped over to it, glancing over his shoulder at his room door. He could see the door until he crossed the street.

He dialed the number he knew by heart, and, after someone picked it up, he said, "It's me and this better be good."

"It is. Duarte has evidence from Lawson."

"No way."

"We have no reason to doubt him."

"What kind of evidence?"

"That's what's so troubling. We don't know. It seems this quiet operation has gotten out of control."

"Not my problem. I have Salez. I'll get his file later today. That will end it, as far as I'm concerned."

"We would like you to intercept Duarte at the Sunrise Cafe at eight this morning."

Garretti looked up the street. He had spent many hours conducting surveillance on the little café. It was just a few blocks west.

"What happens to Duarte?"

"Same as Salez."

Garretti thought about it. "Can't. I have Salez in hand."

"We have other options but would prefer to keep it all with you. We'll pay."

Garretti thought about the nice pay package his employers offered.

Then the voice said, "Double."

That surprised Garretti. He thought about it but knew what his final answer would be. "No, no thanks. It ends with Salez. Then I'm clean."

"But," started the voice, but Garretti hung up. He headed back to the room at a slower stroll. He could just make out the first ray of sunlight rising from the east. He had made the right decision no matter what they offered. This whole business seemed more interesting and glamorous before he actually had to kill people. He had enough to be remorseful for with just the kid out at the camp. No way he wanted to add an ATF agent who was just doing his job. It wasn't right. He was tired of soldiers and cops doing the dirty work for the country and then getting the shaft. He thought about the subject as he approached his motel room. But when he opened the door and saw the smashed remains of the empty chair and loose ropes on the ground, it popped out of his mind.

He drew his pistol and ducked into the bathroom to make sure Salez wasn't planning a later ambush, then raced out the door to look up and down the street in front of the motel. There was no sign of Salez.

37

DUARTE PARKED THE TAURUS IN PLAIN SIGHT ON THE SIDE
street next to the Sunrise Cafe and waited to see if he noticed any
movement. He checked his watch. Seven-fifty. A little early, but
if someone had tapped his cell phone, as he suspected, and they
wanted any evidence in this case, they would be here early too.

He slowly opened the door and then climbed out onto the
sidewalk. He had his usual loose shirt over a T-shirt to conceal
his Glock model 22, with the full fifteen .40 caliber rounds in it.
As little as he liked to use handguns, he wanted it with him this
morning. As weird as things were getting, he knew it might
come in handy.

Before he had made it to the corner to the café, a figure turned
the corner in front of him and then stopped.

Duarte froze, then relaxed slightly.

"Well, well, Señor Duarte." FBI agent Tom Colgan let a broad
smile cross his face.

"What are you doing here, Tom?"

"I'm down to meet with you and Caren. I'm staying up the
street at the Crowne Plaza, so I came for coffee here. It's only a
few blocks away. This is where we used to eat breakfast when I
was assigned here."

"I didn't know you were coming."

Colgan chuckled. "Hey, amigo, the FBI doesn't report to you.
I answer to the deputy attorney general. And he wants this shit
wrapped up."

"I wouldn't mind it being over either."

"Make an arrest, hombre. Make an arrest."

Before Duarte could reply, another man stepped around the corner with a pistol in his hand.

"Don't move."

Duarte leaned around Colgan, "It's okay, Frank."

Colgan said, "And who the hell is this?"

Duarte didn't answer directly. "I've got some trust issues. He's my backup."

Colgan looked from Duarte to his brother Frank. "What are you talking about, vato?"

But Duarte had his eyes on a Ford Excursion turning onto the street from Belvedere Road. Something about the deliberate speed, and the way it swung on the street right next to the three men, made him realize, even before the window rolled down to reveal a man with the barrel of an MP-5 pointing at Duarte, that this vehicle was trouble.

A short, dark man with sharp eyes looked calmly over the front sight of the short submachine gun. "The first man to move gets everyone killed. Understood?"

Duarte nodded. Colgan froze. Behind Colgan, Frank Duarte dropped his pistol to the sidewalk. Duarte looked down at his backup Glock model 28 he had given his brother for the assignment.

Frank's shaky voice said, "Just . . . just don't shoot."

The man in the Excursion's passenger's seat said, "Now, Agent Duarte, you have something from Mr. Lawson we need."

Duarte stayed cool, and said, "And if I don't?"

"I will shoot these men."

Duarte looked up at the man in the Excursion. He was a professional who would carry out a threat like that. Duarte couldn't see the driver clearly, but knew even if he managed to take out the immediate threat that the driver was armed too. And there was someone in the backseat.

The man with the MP-5 said, "What's it going to be, Agent Duarte? Do you have what we need, or do I spray these two and take you with us?"

Then another man popped up on the other side of the truck and slapped something on the windshield.

The men in the big SUV's front seats both jumped when they saw the pistol pointed at the driver's head and what was on the windshield.

Duarte recognized the man immediately. It was the bomber who had taken Salez yesterday.

"You," was all Duarte could say.

The man smiled like he had run into an old friend. "I know, I know, I get around pretty good." He motioned for the driver to lower the window. When it was down, the man said, "I guess you know what's on the windshield?" He smiled at their silence. "It's a decent-sized chunk of C-4. The way I wedged it on the windshield and the edge of the hood, it will make a great fragmentation device that'll cut you two so bad you'll look like a piece of paper cut by an epileptic with scissors."

Duarte had to ask, "What are you doing?"

"In case you couldn't figure it out, I'm saving you."

"Why?"

"Does it matter?"

Duarte shrugged. "What now?"

"Walk away. I'll let these dopes go on their way. Without the element of surprise, they'll leave us alone for now."

Duarte said, "Frank, pick up the pistol and come with me." He looked at Tom Colgan. "C'mon, Tom. We'll stick together."

Colgan could barely move. "What the fuck is going on?"

"Wish I knew. And until I'm sure about your role in this whole thing, I'm not confiding in you."

The bomber said, "That's a good plan because I don't even know who all is involved, but I know they have a hard on for you. I'd watch my back, ATF man." He held the gun up to the driver, then used his other hand to retrieve the C-4. "Drive, asshole. Drive, and don't let me see you again."

The driver turned and said, "Same here."

Duarte watched the Excursion ease down the street as the bomber backed away quickly to the parking lot across the street. Duarte didn't have it in him to chase the man right now. Besides, he had Colgan, and he had a lot of questions.

Frank, sweating profusely, said, "What are we gonna do?"

"*We* aren't doing anything to do anything." He kept the gun on Colgan, reached in the tall FBI agent's coat and retrieved his small revolver. "I have to find out who's involved and on which side." He looked over at his older brother and said, "You did well. I appreciate it."

"We're family. I couldn't leave you hanging."

"It might get worse."

"Now that I'm used to it, I might not pee in my pants next time."

Duarte looked over and was shocked to see he wasn't kidding. His jeans were stained dark around his crotch.

Duarte said, "Happens to everyone."

"But as my brother, I know you'll never tell anyone."

Every muscle in Alberto Salez's shoulders felt like fire. Aside from having his hands locked behind him for hours by Garretti, he had strained them when he managed to jump up and down with enough force to shatter the chair he was tied to. Then fumbling with the motel door and running had aggravated his injury. Now, after a good twenty-minute run, then hiding in the bushes for he didn't know how long, he found himself in another extraordinarily awkward position. He was in a small detached garage in an older section of West Palm Beach that he had heard people refer to as El Cid. He knew it was home to the up-and-coming, as well as some older residents. The neighborhood was a favorite of attorneys, doctors and investment types. The big Spanish-style houses sat on curving streets that ended at the wide Intracoastal Waterway.

He had picked this garage by chance. The side door was poorly secured, so it gave way easily when Salez shoved with his shoulder. He had stumbled inside, then spent some time regaining his composure. As the sun rose, he began to get a better impression of the dank one-car garage. It was crammed full of all sorts of junk: unused lawn equipment, a workbench, lawn mower, mountain bike, and tools were scattered everywhere.

While Salez sat and caught his breath, his eyes wandered endlessly over the amazing chaos of the building. Did these people even know they had a garage? After standing and stretching his legs, he tried forcing the cuffs from the rear to the front by stepping through them, but he couldn't bend his leg nearly enough. Instead, he found himself momentarily stranded on the floor of the messy garage with his right foot caught uncomfortably in the cuffs. Finally he had managed to untangle his foot, and found himself still handcuffed behind his back inside a smelly, moldy garage. Except now he realized he was hungry too.

Then he saw something that might help. Shoved in the corner, between the end of the old, shaky workbench and the dinged wall, were a pair of bolt cutters. A medium-sized pair, with two-foot handles. Maybe it wouldn't cut a padlock, but it would do fine on the links of the handcuffs. He scurried across the room and used his foot to wrestle the bolt cutters to the floor, then kicked them into the open. That turned out to be the easy part.

He fumbled with the clumsy implement, as he sat next to the cutters and tried to use his cuffed hands to move them. How would he ever be able to open them and then apply enough pressure to cut the handcuffs? He tried the obvious maneuvers without much success. Then he found a way to open them with his feet. He placed one handle flat on the ground against the leg of the workbench. He carefully lined up the pincers with the cuffs, then twisted his body so he could kick the bolt cutters. He kicked the handle hard, and felt it close in a quick, smooth motion, only to realize the sharp pincers had come off the handcuffs and closed with stunning speed on his left pinky.

He let out a sharp yelp, and he felt the bolt cutters close just below his middle knuckle. When he twisted around to get a look, he knocked his severed little finger across the floor. He felt sick to his stomach but knew now he had to act quickly if he was going to survive. He hoped his short scream hadn't been heard by anyone in the house.

Salez took a deep breath and tried to focus on maneuvering the bolt cutter into place a second time. As he was about to try another kick to the bolt cutters, he closed his hands into fists to avoid another amputation. He twisted his foot to kick, and then saw the door to the garage swing in and someone step inside. He knew he couldn't wait any longer and swung his foot again.

Caren Larson let the water from the massaging jets of the shower run over her. The hotel near downtown West Palm Beach was the nicest she had stayed in during any trip she'd made in connection to the bombing investigation. She had been feeling run-down, not to mention a little lonely, when Alex Duarte hadn't even called to check on her last night. She had gone to bed early, slept well and then made good use of the hotel's gym. She was later than usual in starting her workday, but after the month she had been through an hour here or there didn't amount to much.

She was tired of running the case, and the other, nonlegal elements of it, through her head. She may have been naïve at first, then perhaps purposely obtuse, but now she knew something was very wrong with the investigation. The problem was, she didn't know exactly what was wrong, or who she could turn to for help in fixing it.

She felt an odd sensation like a chill, then thought she saw a flash of light from the bedroom under the bathroom door. She shut off the water, pulled a towel off the rack and wrapped it around her as she slowly and quietly stepped to the bathroom door. It was opened a crack, and she could see that someone was sitting in the large cushioned chair in the corner. It looked like a man, and he had his legs crossed casually like he was just waiting to greet her.

She felt her heart start to beat faster, and then glanced around the bathroom for a weapon of some kind. Anything. She picked up a brush with a pointed, solid handgrip and gripped the bristles like a handle. She looked out of the cracked door again and tried to estimate if she could make it out the front door. If the intruder had locked it with the bolt, she'd never get out before he was on her.

She took a breath, clenched the brush, then burst out of the bathroom to confront the intruder.

Mike Garretti snickered as he watched the SUV pull away from the corner with all three men inside. He knew the guys inside were fuming, but he didn't care. This shit had gone too far. Killing a cop? Please.

He nodded to Duarte as the ATF agent and the other two men left the area. Garretti didn't know the tall guy but noticed that Duarte didn't trust him too much. He liked Duarte's style.

Garretti intended to retrieve the file that Salez claimed was hidden in the trailer out at the work camp. He intended to scoot out there right away. He'd come up with some story for Maria Tannza that wouldn't upset her too much. God knows the poor woman had been through enough, and Garretti realized it was his fucking fault. Maybe that was why he had felt he needed to rescue the ATF guy. He had seen Duarte's army jacket, and read the report about his action in Bosnia. The guy could relate.

After the SUV was out of sight, Garretti, who had simply walked across the street to his own rental, headed back to his hotel to clear everything out. He'd be on alert because he knew the three men that just drove off were not happy with him at the moment. He also realized his long-term employment prospects were in the shitter as well. If he could retrieve the file and claim to have it as well as other evidence, he might be able to negotiate some form of a life. All he wanted now was to be left alone. If not, then maybe he could come up with a few tricks of his own.

38

SALEZ FELT HIS FOOT MAKE CONTACT WITH THE HAN-
dle and then the handle close solidly on his cuffs. His hands
burst free, with matching stainless steel bracelets on his wrists.
His left hand was streaked with blood, and he had to blink at the
open space where his pinky should have been. Then he looked
up at the man who had entered the garage.

"What the hell are you doing?" shouted the man. He was
younger than Salez, maybe thirty-five, and very clean-cut. He
was wearing a nice suit without the coat. Definitely a lawyer.

Salez was dizzy from the pain in his left hand. He hadn't lost
as much blood as he thought, but it still hurt. "I'm sorry, sir. I
just wanted to stay dry and sleep."

"Another fucking homeless bum. Why here? There are more
houses along the highway."

"Just found it. I'll leave and never come back, I swear."

The man sighed and visibly relaxed slightly. Then he saw the
blood on the floor. "What'd you do? Are you alone?"

Salez nodded. "I cut my finger bad. I just want to leave."

"Hang on, I'm not so sure."

Salez stood up and tried to hunch over so he looked more fee-
ble. Blood still poured from his severed finger. "Sir, I'm sorry,
I'll leave."

The younger man put his hand on Salez's chest and said,
"You're not leaving until I say so, buster."

Salez had had enough of this pompous ass. He swung both his
arms up so the handcuff bracelets struck the man simultaneously
in the temples on either side of his head. The man shuddered, and

Salez brought a knee up to his groin. The impact even hurt Salez's left hand with the missing digit.

Once the man was on the ground and holding his crotch, Salez kneeled down and said, "Where are your car keys?"

The man gulped air and tried to look at Salez. "Kitchen," was all he could wheeze out.

"Is anyone else home?"

The man shook his head. "No, my wife is at work. Just take the car and go."

"Wallet?"

"With the keys. Now, just leave."

Salez stood up, satisfied the man had told him the truth. He needed to bandage his hand, then get the hell out of here.

He looked down at the man and said, "Close your eyes and count to fifty while I leave. Don't open them until you reach fifty and by then I'll be gone. Okay?"

The man nodded furiously. "Okay, okay."

Salez glanced around quickly and saw the handle of some garden tool within reach. He looked down at the man and said, "Close those eyes, now."

The man squeezed his eyes shut and started to count. "One, two, three . . ."

"Slower."

". . . four . . ."

Salez reached over and grasped the handle with his right hand. It was heavy enough to make him step closer and pull up. Once it was clear of the debris on the floor, he saw it was a sledgehammer. A heavy one too.

". . . five . . ."

He hefted it, then lifted it above his head and swung down hard just as the man was about to say "six." His skull cracked and twisted like an eggshell, as blood and a clear fluid poured onto the ground. The pain in Salez's left hand was so intense he dropped the hammer right where he had been standing. He took two steps, leaned down and picked up his mangled finger off the floor near the workbench, then turned quickly toward the house to get a bandage and something to eat.

Caren Larson froze as she came through the door and then almost felt like she would faint with relief.

Alex Duarte said calmly, "That's some entrance."

"How'd you get in?"

"I may not be a cute girl, but sometimes a badge works well too."

"You scared the shit out of me." She felt her heart slow down. As she stepped closer, she noticed for the first time that Duarte looked concerned. Not his usual somber but something else. "What's wrong?"

"More than I can tell you, but I was hoping you might tell me."

"What are you talking about?"

He just stared at her.

Caren grabbed some clothes and said, "Let me change. I'll be right back." She slipped back into the bathroom to change, but really she was buying some time. What should she tell him? What did she know? She took her time dressing and brushing out her hair with the brush full of crushed bristles. She was almost as reluctant to go out in the room and face Duarte as she had been when she didn't know who was there. She almost would have preferred fighting her way out. She took a breath and stepped back into the large bedroom.

She plopped onto the bed closest to Duarte and returned his gaze for a few moments. She did have feelings for this man. Strong feelings. She knew what was right, and slowly started to feel some shame for her efforts to impress her bosses and move up the chain at the Department of Justice.

Duarte said, "I'm not letting this go."

"I've seen you in action. I believe you."

"Someone just threatened me with a machine gun."

"What did they want?"

"Evidence from Oneida Lawson."

"What evidence?"

"Doesn't matter. They didn't get it."

"I'm just glad you weren't hurt. How'd you get away?"

"I had some help."

"From who?"

"The bomber. Looks like there's some friction inside the group. Why don't you fill me in."

"Fill you in on what?"

"Tom Colgan just happened to show up at the same time."

"What's he doing here?"

He looked at her with those intense, dark eyes. "I'm out of patience, Caren. What the hell is going on?"

She just stared at him, still a little surprised Tom Colgan had come to Florida. What should she do? What should she say? Was it already too late?

Duarte still kept his eyes on her.

She felt sick to her stomach but knew what had to be done. Finally, realizing that she'd never wait him out in a silence contest, she started to speak. "I'll tell you everything I suspect. But I never thought they'd use violence."

"What do you call the bombings?"

"I just thought they wanted to use them as a tool. I didn't think they caused them."

Duarte eased back into the chair and said, "Just start from the beginning."

Caren found herself relaxing, and then start to talk.

Alberto Salez was in the nice Cadillac Seville he had taken from the house where he'd cut off his finger. He had also found a little over two hundred dollars in cash, enough Percocets to keep him pain-free until he died, a good first-aid kit and a ready-made breakfast of eggs and toast. Not bad for a random place to stop. He had gone back into the garage and used a thin screwdriver to work the mechanisms on the handcuffs and slip them off his wrists. He also had his severed pinky in a baggie with ice. It was just in case. He figured it was probably lost for good.

He wasted no time, and started down Southern Boulevard, heading straight to Maria Tannza's trailer to get that file with the photos and his notes. He needed something to negotiate his life. He had to be careful because Garretti might have the same plan. But he couldn't waste time either, so he pressed the big car a little harder as he headed toward Royal Palm Beach and then out west of Belle Glade near Lake Okeechobee.

He hoped Maria was in a good mood. Otherwise, she'd be having a very bad afternoon.

For all Alex Duarte's trouble reading people in the past, he was confident he was hearing the truth now as Caren Larson started to lay out what she knew.

"Bob Morales asked me to take this case a month or so ago. He said it would help my career and give me valuable experience. He offered suggestions and I listened."

"This was after the first bombing in Seattle?"

"Exactly. He told me to focus on the motive because we'd have cops looking at the actual attack and deaths. He wanted me to prove that this was all a plot from the United Workers of America to dissuade other unions from organizing outside of their influence." She stopped talking and looked at Duarte.

"What?" asked the ATF man.

"I did more than just believe the theory."

"What do you mean?"

"I helped plant the idea in some heads."

"Besides mine?"

"At the labor camp in Belle Glade. The older manager even believed it, or at least thought about it. I think there are political reasons for the theory, but there's more."

"What?"

She swallowed and added, "I left out things too."

"Like what?"

"When I heard Salez worked for Powercore, I didn't let it register with me."

Duarte considered this news carefully. This might be the first solid information he had gotten on the case. "Why the United Workers of America? There are unions bigger and with higher profiles than the UWA. Why does the fact that Salez worked for Powercore even matter?"

"Bob Morales worked for Powercore too."

"What are the political reasons for blaming the union?"

"I think it goes back to his days in private industry. Aside from the fact that the UWA lobbies hard for Democrats, there's also a personal element. Bob had to put up with some kind of shit from them when he was the legal counsel for Powercore."

"In Texas?" His mind started to race.

"Where else?"

"You think that's related to Salez and Morales working together at Powercore?"

"I don't know. It was a huge company."

Then Duarte felt his mind click into place on a number of details. "Oneida Lawson worked there too."

Now she stopped talking and looked at him.

Duarte continued, "Janni Tserick worked for an electric company in Texas. That's what his boss said. You think that company could have been Powercore?"

Now she looked interested. "Maybe."

"The tram driver, Munroe, was from Texas. Just through statistics, that seems unlikely. How many people move from Texas every year? Everyone on this case is from Texas, including the deputy attorney general who's running the investigation."

Caren kept her blue eyes glued to him.

He gazed into her beautiful face. No way she was lying to him. He could read her now. She was just as shocked as him.

Finally Caren said, "You think Bob Morales is directing the bombings?"

"He sure seems to have worked with everyone involved." He dug into his pocket for the photo he had taken from Salez's old apartment and carried with him ever since. He held up the image of Salez with his arm around a smiling Wahlid al-Samir, with his dark, curly hair. "You know this guy?"

She studied the torn photo. "No, no idea. Where'd you get it?"

"Salez's apartment." He looked at the photo again. "This kid was the victim of a homicide in Austin."

"You gonna try to blame Bob for that too?"

"More like Salez. But now I think Roberto Morales was connected with him."

"So?"

"So, I don't know, but I have a feeling this is part of this case."

Caren looked like she was considering all this information, then said, "It comes back to the question of the union. Why throw that whole theory in the mix?"

"Who knows? Maybe slow us down. Maybe he wanted to screw with the union." Duarte looked up into her eyes and nodded.

"What is it?"

"My father had it right. It's a distraction. The union issue pulls everyone's eyes away from the real motive."

"Which is?"

"The bomber has a list. My guess is, this is to eliminate witnesses. A cover-up."

"Why didn't Bob use the FBI, or just leave me on the case alone?"

"He needed outside corroboration in case something went

wrong. He needed to say an ATF agent found this or that, not 'My staff backed up my stupid theory.' "

Caren remained silent while she seemed to contemplate this load of conjecture. "How'd I get picked for this?"

He took some time to consider the question then to phrase the answer so as not to insult her. "He must figure he can control you."

"Why were you assigned?"

He shrugged. "That could have been chance."

Then her eyes brightened. "I know why you were picked. It's obvious now."

"I'm listening."

"You're the Rocket. You get so focused, you lose sight of everything else. Everyone knows it. They wanted someone who'd run with the union theory. They didn't realize you were a smart bomb in disguise, and could change course. They had to handpick who'd worked the case,"

"That's why Morales wouldn't let us use our National Response Team."

"Where did he get the bomber?"

"The bomber said he'd seen my army jacket. My guess is he's connected with the government, not a private business."

"Anything to hide in your army file?"

He thought about it, and said, "Yeah, the bomber and I have something in common."

39

THE CADILLAC DROVE EASILY, BUT SALEZ'S HAND THROBBED
even with the three Percocets he had taken to deaden the pain.
He couldn't keep his eyes off the blood-soaked bandage wrapped
around the nub of his little finger. Then that guy giving him shit
about staying in his fucking garage. Salez had done the right
thing cracking him in the head. He was a jerk-off.

Driving west on Southern Boulevard, he had a hard time focusing on the road, or on what he was going to do after he recovered his file from the lovely Maria Tannza's trailer in that
shitty labor camp. He didn't know if it was the pain, loss of
blood or the Percocets, but he started to drift first to one side,
then to the other side, of the busy road. He blinked, but his vision started to blur. Finally he pulled to the side of the road at
the entrance to Lion Country Safari. The big car had good air
and comfortable seats. He eased back and just shut his eyes for a
moment, and that was all it took. Inside of a minute, he was
dreaming narcotic-enhanced dreams.

In the parking lot of Caren's hotel, standing next to Duarte's
Taurus, they considered their options and who they could trust.

Caren said, "Chuck?"

"I think so. What about in DoJ?"

She shrugged.

Then Duarte snapped his fingers. "I almost forgot." He
quick-stepped to the rear of the car and used his keys to pop the
trunk.

From her position near the hood, Caren heard a male voice,

then was shocked to see Tom Colgan climb out of the cramped trunk.

Colgan brushed himself off, and said in a remarkably calm voice, "Y'all gonna explain that to me?"

Duarte didn't look inclined to explain anything to the tired-looking FBI agent.

Caren said, "What're you doing here, Tom?"

"Bob sent me to see where you were on the case."

Duarte said, "And you just happened to be at the Sunrise Cafe at eight o'clock when I got there?"

"That *is* breakfast time."

"And that's why you ride in the trunk until we clear up a few things."

Caren looked at the two men she had worked so closely with. They were polar opposites. Colgan loud, brash, charming and useless as a cop, and Alex quiet, intense and the best cop she knew. It was no wonder she had fallen for the ATF man. Now she needed to know what Colgan knew.

"Tom," she started slowly, "what do you know about this case?"

"Only that you guys haven't made any progress."

"Why'd you send me those intelligence forms in Seattle?"

He cocked his head like a puppy.

"The reports on the union activity."

"Bob told me to."

She started to see the value in some of Duarte's interrogation tactics. She looked at the ATF man. "What's our next move?"

He didn't hesitate. "We have to make sure Maria is safe. For some reason, she seems to be a focal point. If Salez is still here because of her, we need to find out why."

Caren said, "I'm ready. Let's go."

Duarte looked at Tom Colgan and popped the trunk again.

Colgan said, "No, no way."

One look from Duarte sent the FBI man scurrying for the open trunk.

Salez awoke with a start. How long had he been out? He wasn't sure but could tell by the sun it hadn't been too long. He wiped his face with his left hand, then flinched at the pain. Now he remembered all that had happened. He had hoped it was just a dream. He patted his pocket and felt the end of his pinky in the baggie. The whole idea made him a little queasy. Then he figured out why he had fallen asleep in the first place. He patted his waist to feel the comforting handle of his fillet knife.

Now he could think a little more clearly. He could consider what he'd do with the file on the Powercore job once he had it back in his possession. Blackmail wouldn't work except to bargain for his life, and if Garretti was the negotiator he was screwed. For a guy who killed people with bombs, he was way too judgmental. During their long questioning sessions, Salez had admitted to killing the woman at the gas station because he needed her car. Garretti seemed to find this repulsive. Salez had kept his mouth shut about the farmworker from whom he had stolen the clothes, Elenia the barmaid, the farm manager and the Hess station attendant in Georgia. And he didn't know he was going to kill another guy after he escaped. He felt confident Garretti would not have approved of that one either. Prick.

He'd killed a number of people recently, but did it really matter? He was in Florida, where they executed killers whether you killed one person or fifty. You still had to pay the price. He planned on leaving the Sunshine State before it became an issue. But if he didn't resolve this mess, he wouldn't be able to live anywhere without looking over his shoulder.

He slowed down as he cut through Belle Glade on his way to the camp. The local cops were not lenient on speeders, and one check of this car would lead to a world of hurt for Salez. He passed the Belle Glade Sports Club and a series of fast-food joints as he followed the road to its union with U.S. Highway 27. He knew his pals from the sports club would be pissed that things hadn't worked out at the pawnshop. He knew that with Duarte loose when Garretti kidnapped him, his buddies didn't stand much of a chance. He had tried to call Raul on his cell phone, but once his friend figured out who was calling he hung up. Salez was on his own now.

Salez took a right onto U.S. Highway 27 and found the camp a few miles later. It was relatively quiet, so he didn't hesitate to drive through the front gate and directly to Maria's trailer. The big Caddy never would've fit in the small slot in front of her trailer, so he just left the land yacht on the street. It didn't really matter if he was seen now. He would be in and out quick.

He scooted out of the car, felt for his knife out of habit and then realized he had an erection to go with it. As he approached the door, he wasn't sure if the idea of a naked Maria excited him as much as the idea of a dead Maria. He could always do both, but with the big car, and all the other issues, he thought the time factor might limit his choices.

He hesitated at the front door, smoothing out his hair and running his hand over his rough face.

He didn't bother knocking, knowing that a surprise would be his best asset in this quick reunion.

He pulled the door open and froze.

Sitting in the recliner in front of the door was Mike Garretti with an automatic pistol pointing right at his face.

The sly man simply asked, "Where's the file?"

In the small, unpaved parking lot of the empty office trailer, Alex Duarte opened his trunk again so the tall, and now very angry, Tom Colgan could stretch his legs.

"How long you plan on keeping me in there?" asked the FBI man.

Duarte shrugged. "Until I know what's going on and if you can be trusted."

"Or until I suffocate."

"Whichever."

Caren walked back to join them at the trunk. "Should we just walk in and tell her she has to get out?"

Before Duarte could answer, his cell phone rang. He turned and barked, "Duarte."

"Hey, Alex, it's Alice Brainard from the lab."

He smiled, but suddenly felt uncomfortable taking the call in front of Caren. He mumbled, "Hey, how are you?"

"I got a hit on your print."

"Really? What'd you find?"

"It's from the army. A guy named Mike Garretti."

Duarte nodded to himself, not really surprised. "Hey, that's great, I appreciate it."

"Want me to do the follow-up to find out exactly who and where he is?"

"Could you? You're great."

"Did I earn that drink?"

He looked up into Caren's face and froze. Then he said, "Yeah, sure." He looked around and said, "It's sort've a bad time right now. Can I call you back?"

"Sure, anytime."

Duarte closed his phone and looked down the road toward Maria's trailer. "There's a strange car there. A Cadillac."

Caren said, "Should we call for help?"

"Call who? Besides, my phone is tapped." He looked hard at Colgan.

"Hey, I don't tap phones. You're probably imagining it anyway."

"We'll see." He waved to an older man shuffling by, and said, "Excuse me, sir."

The man said, "No English," and smiled. Duarte stuttered through a few words of Spanish without success, then let the man go. As he turned, he found Caren looking at him.

"All right, I admit it. I should speak Spanish, but I don't." He looked down the road and said, "Let's just knock on the door."

As he said it, he noticed a woman walking from between the two closest trailers. She looked at the trio and smiled, turning toward them.

It was Maria Tannza.

40

MIKE GARRETTI SETTLED INTO THE COMFORTABLE RE-
cliner with his Browning Hi-Power 9mm pointed at the distraught
Alberto Salez. He wrestled with his feelings of relief, satisfaction
and anger. His long second job was finished, although his employers might be pissed off after what he had done to blow their
shot at the ATF man. Following Salez's directions, he had just
retrieved the file from a ceiling tile in the bathroom, and managed to get Maria Tannza out of the trailer without her being too
upset or finding out what role he had played in her son's death.
She wouldn't care how upset he was by the incident, she'd still
want to kill him. And he couldn't blame her.

"What now?" grunted Salez from the rigid kitchen chair
where he had been ordered to sit. He held his left hand up in the
air to keep the bleeding down. A blood-soaked white gauze bandage was still draped around his missing pinky.

Garretti glanced at the photographs in the file and the single
page of notes. "I thought I tore up this photo of me, you and al-
Samir?" he said, holding up the four-by-six-inch photo.

Salez smirked. "Double prints. I had the other one, where
you tore off the side with you in it."

Garretti nodded, looking at another photo of the whole
group: himself, the young Saudi prince, Oneida Lawson, Don
Munroe, Janni Tserick and Salez. That was the night they did the
job. Poor kid had no clue. Never understood what was happening, or why. When had Garretti lost his ability to judge right
from wrong?

Salez stared at his hand. "When's Maria coming back with
that first-aid kit? This shit is killing me."

"She said the office was closed. It might take a while."

"And she believed you were a cop. She's sharper than that."

"It's the haircut. I look official."

"I like how you hustled her out so we could get the file and talk. But, mainly, I like how she has no idea you killed her kid."

Garretti leveled his eyes and gun at him. "And if she finds out, you're dead on the spot."

"I'm dead anyway."

Garretti shrugged. He looked through the file again. "Anything else?"

Salez shook his head.

"I'm gonna verify this, if I have to. You won't like my verification process." Garretti stood and casually strolled into the small kitchen, with its linoleum floor. He kept the gun up at his side, pointing at Salez's head. "Is this all the dirt you have on us?"

"I told you *yes.*" He threw an emphatic huff at the end of the sentence.

Garretti leaned down slightly and, without telegraphing his intention, grasped Salez's bandaged fingers and squeezed. Salez leaned back, his eyes wide, and gasped. Garretti in a steady tone said, "I'll let go when you tell me what else you have about this incident."

Salez looked like he might faint. He panted like a dog as Garretti kept a firm grip, and added the barrel of the gun to the mix by putting it to his forehead. "What else?"

"Nothing. Nothing at all, I swear to God."

"Let me ask a control question to see if you're telling the truth." He released the bloody hand and stood up. "You killed the woman in the Honda Element?"

The injured fugitive nodded his head without hesitation.

"Now we're getting somewhere. You kill anyone else since?" He almost laughed at the question; just wanted to see his reaction and denial.

Instead, Salez nodded his head.

"You did?" Now Garretti was confused. "Who?"

"Kid in Georgia. Attendant at a Hess station."

Garretti stepped back. "You're an asshole." He wanted to put a bullet in him right there but didn't want to explain it to Maria. "Stand up."

A shaky Salez rose to his feet, still a few inches shorter than his captor. "Why? What're you gonna do?"

"Turn out your pockets."

Salez used his good hand to reach across and pull his left pocket first. It was empty. Then he pulled the baggie holding his severed little finger out of his right pocket. He held up the baggie. "That's it. That's all I have."

Garretti stared at the bloody baggie with the flesh-colored piece in it. "Really? You saved your finger?" Garretti had already heard the story of how he lost it.

Salez nodded.

"Let me have it."

"What?"

"C'mon, toss it."

"Why?"

"Because I'll shoot you in the dick if you don't." He pointed the pistol at Salez's crotch.

Salez tossed the small bag the few feet to Garretti, who caught it in his left hand but never let the gun drop off the target area.

"Now sit back down, asshole." Garretti had to admit he was enjoying this a little. Salez had caused a lot of suffering. Killing that poor woman, and now admitting to killing another person. He was a remorseless ass-wipe. Garretti looked forward to capping him near a canal and just letting him rot in the water where he landed. Maybe a gator would get to him.

Garretti backed to the sink. "Now, Berto, you're sure there's nothing else linking me or you to al-Samir?"

The broken Salez shook his head slowly.

Garretti started the garbage disposal by flicking the switch with the barrel of the pistol. He opened the seal on the baggie.

Salez perked up and snapped his head forward at the jarring sound. "What are you gonna do?"

Garretti dangled the baggie over the whirring disposal.

Salez jumped up and screamed: "No, don't."

Garretti couldn't help but smile as he dumped the bag's contents into the running disposal. The blades grinded and stuttered as they ground up the severed finger.

Salez dropped back into the chair and looked as if he might vomit.

Garretti dropped the baggie into the empty sink and shut off the disposal. "They wouldn't be able to save it anyway." He moved back to the recliner. "Now you know a little suffering yourself."

"You have no idea how I've suffered."

"And you have no idea how those people you killed suffered. I live with what I've done, but I still am bothered by it."

"What if I am too?"

"Then you won't be much longer."

Salez slumped back in the hard chair and said, "There is no God."

Garretti leaned up. "Yes there is, and He doesn't put up with assholes like you."

Salez was silent.

"I'd start asking for forgiveness right now. Admit your mistakes and mean it and maybe you and He can work something out."

Salez looked up. "You're serious?"

"You think after all I've done I don't worry about what God thinks of me? I'm hanging my hat on all the Christians telling me He can forgive anything. You and me got a lot to forgive."

Salez just shook his head. He seemed to try to gather his strength. Garretti could feel it like the asshole was going to make one last attempt to escape. As much as he didn't want to shoot him in the trailer, he felt like that might be his only choice as Salez started to stand.

Garretti aimed the Browning pistol, then heard Maria on the outer steps.

Salez heard her too.

"Sit down and I may go easy on you. She's coming."

Salez looked beaten as he eased back into the chair. Maybe he didn't want to upset her either. Maybe he realized he had no chance of rushing his captor. Garretti didn't care which, he was just glad he sat back down.

"Smart move," said Garretti, tucking the pistol back into his waistband and yanking his polo shirt over it.

The door opened, and he was prepared to greet his lovely host, but instead was shocked to see a pistol pointed at him and ATF agent Alex Duarte behind it.

He said, "Hello, Mr. Garretti. I'm glad we have this chance to talk."

Alex Duarte wasn't sure which emotion was bubbling in him more intensely: relief for having all the principals of the investigation together, fear for not knowing who to trust or excitement for believing he might, finally, hear the entire story. He had the dazed and whining Alberto Salez at one end of the couch and the bomber, Mike Garretti, at the other. Duarte leaned against the small table, which held the TV. He held his Glock in his right hand but not aiming at anyone. These two knew what he was prepared to do. They wouldn't cause any trouble.

Salez had already told him about his missing digit, and accused Garretti of trying to kill him if Duarte hadn't arrived. Surprisingly, the more the fugitive ran his mouth, the less Duarte cared whether he was killed or not.

He glanced to the front door, which was opened a crack, so he could see Caren Larson as she chatted with Maria Tannza, who was out of his line of sight. Caren had Garretti's nice Browning 9mm, and also had an eye on Tom Colgan, because no one knew if he could be trusted, although it was starting to look like the FBI man was on the level. Stupid but on the level.

Duarte didn't dare call for help yet. There was too much he needed to know, and at this point it wasn't necessarily for a court case. His inquisitive nature didn't allow him to leave things alone. His training in the military, and the things he had witnessed, gave him the will to do what was needed to uncover information. And his newfound skill in interviewing gave him the ability to discern bullshit. But it was his willingness to ignore the rules of police interrogation guidelines that concerned these two at the moment.

He had so many questions, he started with the most pressing. "Mr. Garretti?"

The man looked unruffled, which was disconcerting. Did he know he would walk away from this?

Garretti asked his own question. "How'd you find my name? I'm just curious."

Duarte hesitated, but figured if he handled things correctly Garretti wouldn't have a chance to make the same mistakes twice. "You left a print at Salez's apartment. After our encounter in Los Angeles, I remembered where I had seen you."

"Very sharp. Very sharp indeed. I'd expect no less from a combat engineer."

Duarte cocked his eyebrow and said, "Is it my turn yet?"

Garretti calmly looked up, smiled slightly and said, "What would you like to know?"

"It's that easy?"

"Why not? We'll either be dead in a few hours or I have some payback I'd like to deliver, for my treatment in this matter. You may be able to help me with my payback efforts."

"That just brings up more questions."

Garretti nodded and said, "That is the nature of life complicated by conspiracy. I have found that humans tend to fuck things up."

Duarte had to agree with some of that philosophy. "Why were you trying to kill this moron?" He turned his gaze to the silent and pouting Alberto Salez.

Garretti said, "You still think he's my victim, don't you?"

"You *did* try to kill him."

"Do you have any idea what this guy has done?"

"Why don't you tell me."

"He confessed, just a few minutes ago, that he's murdered two people in the last few weeks. And that's just what he admitted to."

Salez cut in: "Because he was torturing me. He squeezed my fingers." He held up his freshly soaked bandaged left hand for emphasis.

Duarte said, "Did you kill someone?"

"Like you could use it against me. I'm under arrest. Believe me, I got as much to trade as him." He nodded toward the still-calm Garretti.

Duarte said, "This is for me. Did you kill anyone?" He stared at Salez, and noticed his Adam's apple bob and a slight jerk of his head.

"I have not killed anyone."

Duarte leaned over and reached like he would grab Salez's fingers. The fugitive flinched and gasped, "You wouldn't."

"I will if you lie to me." He stood to get closer to Salez. "Did you kill anyone?"

"That's how we got in this mess together." He pointed at Garretti. "We killed a guy in Texas."

"You mean Wahlid al-Samir."

That caught both Garretti and Salez by surprise.

Garretti said, "I figured you were on the ball. How'd you come up with that name from the past?"

"Just lucky." He still focused on Salez. "Who is he talking about you killing recently?"

Salez hesitated, and finally said, "This murdering nut thinks I killed a woman and took her car. I didn't, I swear to God."

Duarte nodded. "I already fell for that. The day you swore you were on the level and wouldn't escape."

"I had to escape. I didn't know who to trust. You probably realize that now."

"I do believe you are the target of some kind of conspiracy, but I can't figure out who'd want to go to the trouble of killing a lowlife like you."

Garretti smiled and said, "I know the answer to that."

41

CAREN LARSON FELT RELIEF THAT SHE HAD TOLD ALEX
Duarte the truth about what she knew. Now she wanted to make
amends. She wasn't sure if Alex had asked her to keep an eye on
Maria and Colgan outside because he needed the help or because he didn't want her to hear what Garretti would say. Either
way, she knew not to argue with the intense ATF man. He was
operating on his own set of ethics now, and she thought that violence wasn't prohibited in his code of conduct like it was in the
Department of Justice's.

Colgan asked from across the car hood, "When do you think
Alex will give me back my gun?"

"When he drops you at the FBI office. Till then, it's locked in
his glove compartment."

"What are they talking about?" He pointed toward the air-
conditioned trailer.

"Wish I knew."

Maria cut in. "So the man with the dark hair is not a policeman, is he?"

Caren shook her head, not sure if she should upset Maria
with his true identity.

Maria leaned in closer. "And this man out here with us is a
FBI agent?"

Caren nodded.

"I am completely confused as to what's going on," said the
young teacher.

Caren smiled and said, "Join the club. All I know is, Salez hid
evidence in your trailer and that's why everyone is here. I think
things can return to normal for you very soon."

Maria looked down silently.

Caren immediately said, "I'm so sorry, I know they'll never be like they were. I just meant no one will be bothering you."

Maria nodded and wiped a tear from her eye. "That's okay."

Looking down the road, Colgan said, "Caren, dear, I think we got problems."

Caren turned to see the tall FBI agent watching a vehicle slowly turn down the dirt road toward the trailer.

Colgan said, "That looks like the guys that tried to grab Duarte this morning. We better do something."

Then the driver saw them and gunned the engine as the passenger's-side window lowered. While the big SUV was still a hundred and fifty feet away, a man leaned out of the passenger's window with an MP-5 machine gun and opened fire in fully auto mode.

Caren shoved Maria's head down below the Taurus's hood and shielded the teacher as rounds bounced off the car and trailer behind her. She had a pistol in her hand but was not familiar with the Browning.

She peeked around the front of the car and aimed the 9mm, squeezing the trigger like so many federal agents had taught her to do over the years, but nothing happened. She did like she had always been shown, and used her left hand to rack the slide back in case there was no bullet in the chamber. A stupid way to carry a pistol, but she did as she had been taught. A live round ejected, then she remembered Duarte's instruction that it was a single-action automatic. The hammer had to be pulled back. The action of her racking the pistol locked back the hammer, and she leaned around the car again and this time squeezed off three rounds.

The SUV skidded to a stop and all three men slipped out of the vehicle.

She peeked around the car and felt like she could only see down a narrow space directly in front of her. She didn't even notice Maria next to her. Was this the combat tunnel vision she had heard so much about? Then she felt a shove, as Tom Colgan piled into her and Maria huddling behind Alex Duarte's Taurus.

If this was the action she had heard so much about, she didn't see what the attraction was. She ducked as more rounds pinged into the trailer.

* * *

Mike Garretti was almost glad he was going to tell this story to someone now. He hoped the ATF agent had enough juice to get the story investigated. He hoped Duarte even believed him. In a real way, he felt this was his chance to make up for his incredible stupidity for getting involved in this in the first place. He now realized that retirement on a master sergeant's pay with free medical for life was not such a bad thing. He wished he would've seen things this clearly a few years ago.

"I can tell you who told us to kill al-Samir and why, and about the bombings."

Duarte said flatly, "In return for what?"

"I know I'm screwed, but this is big enough I think someone will cut me some slack, and you can tell everyone how I saved your ass this morning."

"I know I could do that. The rest isn't up to me."

"I expected an honest answer from you. Good man."

Salez fidgeted in his seat.

Garretti looked at the Latin fugitive and said, "This asshole sort of started it. He knew all of us. Me, Tserick, Munroe, Oneida Lawson and, most important—" He stopped himself. Once he continued, he knew there was no turning back. He looked up at the attentive Alex Duarte and wished he had a life like his. Doing good work for good pay. No temptation to do anything as illegal as murder.

Duarte prompted him. "Who else did Salez know besides you four?"

Salez squirmed openly in his seat now. "I don't know if this is the right time to talk about this subject."

Duarte said, "It's the right time. You missed your chance to talk. Now Mr. Garretti has the floor." He looked at Garretti. "Who else was involved?"

"Bob Morales."

As Duarte was about to speak, they all heard a shout from outside, then the lamp next to Duarte shattered and all three men instinctively ducked then fell to the floor of the trailer.

Duarte had his pistol up as he crawled to the door. Before he reached the slightly opened door, he heard more gunfire, this time coming from directly in front of the trailer. More automatic gunfire struck the trailer high, as he reached the door and saw

Maria, Caren and Colgan wedged behind the Taurus. He sprang out the door and fired at the SUV he saw, recognizing it from this morning. As he raced across the dirt road hoping to draw fire away from the trailer, he could see all three men from his earlier encounter in position near their SUV. They looked as if they were planning an assault. He stole a look across the road and saw Caren and the others still pinned behind the Taurus. He found cover behind a twisted banyan tree trunk that looked like a hurricane had ripped up from its roots.

Then he noticed something flying through the air above the men from the SUV. It smashed the big vehicle's windshield. Then he saw something else as it bounced off the SUV's roof. Then more objects from all directions started to fall near the surprised men.

Duarte stared, not immediately realizing what was happening.

It was the residents of the camp. Duarte saw one small Guatemalan man step into the open and heave a piece of cement up in an arc so that it landed within five feet of the gunmen. It caused the men to leap out of the way, but, more important, it kept them from shooting.

The residents of the camp were coming to the aid of their beloved teacher. The pace of the attack picked up, as rocks, trash and even some fruit started to fall from the sky like rain.

The men moved as a group back toward the SUV like a well-trained military unit. Duarte thought he could disable the vehicle with his Glock, but right now he wanted these guys out of here. He didn't know who they were, or if there were more of them, but he knew this was not the place to fight. Too many people could get hurt. But, right now, the people looked like they were doing all right on their own.

He watched as they piled into the Excursion and backed up, bumping a trailer, then spun dirt up as they tore onto the road and down the street. More rocks followed them as they took the corner at high speed.

Duarte started to relax, until he looked across the street and saw Salez backing away from the others with a fillet knife to Maria Tannza's bare throat.

Caren watched helplessly as Salez backed away from her. She knew she couldn't accurately shoot Salez without risking

Maria, but she had the handgun up anyway. Garretti had stepped out of the trailer and said calmly, "Give me the pistol and I'll cap that son of a bitch."

Caren didn't know if she should point the weapon at him or at Salez. Then Duarte came running back from across the street with his pistol up.

He pointed the Glock at Garretti and said, "On the ground—now."

Garretti dropped.

Duarte said to Caren, in a steady voice, "Keep him covered. I'll deal with this."

He stood where he was, as Salez shouted, "Come any closer and I'll open her throat." He pressed the long, thin blade tighter against Maria's neck, causing a thin line of blood to dribble down.

The sight of the blood, and the potential for more violence, made Caren's stomach flip-flop, but she kept her focus. She had been told to watch Garretti, and she didn't intend to let Alex Duarte down again.

Duarte stopped his advance and concentrated on Salez over the sight of his Glock.

From the ground, Garretti said, "What's your plan, hotshot? You need to kill him, soldier, and need to do it now."

Duarte seemed to hear the command and pulled up the slack in the trigger.

Then Caren saw movement next to Salez, and Maria fell to the ground. Salez slammed against the end of the trailer, and she saw Tom Colgan pop up from behind him with the fugitive's arm twisted at a sickening angle behind him.

Colgan looked down as Maria scurried toward the car, and called, "You all right, ma'am?"

Duarte lowered the pistol and looked at Garretti, saying, "I got a plan, and a new partner."

42

DUARTE FELT LIKE HE PRETTY MUCH HAD THINGS UN-
der control, considering he was responsible for two prisoners,
a civilian, a non-sworn DoJ attorney and an FBI agent who
was beginning to prove he wasn't as useless as he appeared.
Maybe.

He had given Tom Colgan back his little Smith & Wesson revolver and assigned him a job as lookout as they got ready to
move as a group. He still didn't know where they were going,
but they couldn't stay here. His parents' house briefly flashed
through his head, but he dismissed it. He'd be replacing one set
of Latins in danger with another.

There was no one to call. At least, not yet. He had taken the
C-4 Garretti had in his rental, but they had only three handguns
between them. But there was a lot of C-4, and the bad guys
weren't expecting it. That was his biggest advantage, but now he
found himself in the same position as Robert E. Lee at Gettysburg. The fight had started and he wasn't on the right ground. He
had to seize the high ground to give himself a clear field of fire.
Then an idea started to work its way into his head. They were
near the Everglades. The place was nothing but fields. He just
had to find the right one.

Now he waited as Maria composed herself in the master bath
and Caren hung out by the bedroom door, still looking shaky
from her baptism of fire.

Duarte looked over at Garretti, sitting comfortably on the
couch, untied. Duarte felt he owed him that much. Salez was on
the ground, handcuffed behind his back, and whimpering about
his aching hand and the arm Colgan had twisted.

"You okay?" Duarte asked Garretti as he peeked out the window.

Garretti nodded and said, "Now do you believe me about this douche bag?" He pointed toward Salez.

Duarte's eyes dropped to Salez and then he nodded. "Tell us about Morales. That's the story that sounds slim."

"Look, I met the guy once with Salez, and he's been my contact ever since. I guess he liked my military background and figured I was trustworthy. I woulda been too, if they hadn't kept asking for more and more. Do you know how hard it is to set a bomb to kill the right person? You did it in Bosnia on a battlefield and still fucked up. Just like I did."

Duarte flinched, and stole a quick glance at Caren to see if she had caught all that. Of course she had. She was as sharp as they came.

"Let's start with al-Samir. Why'd you guys kill him?"

"Far as I can tell—and it makes sense—he was the son of some big-shit Saudi oil prince. Right after nine-eleven, with their image shattered, and the U.S. getting bowed up to kick some ass, they approached officials at Powercore about some deal to deliver more oil, outside of OPEC, directly to the U.S. at discounted prices."

"Yeah? I don't see the problem."

"Because you're a stand-up guy, not like these cocksuckers." Garretti gathered his thoughts, and Duarte took the moment to scan first the bound Salez on the floor, then Caren, then out the window to ensure Tom Colgan remained vigilant.

Garretti continued. "The government was apparently in favor of it. It was a personal thing from this raghead directly, not the Saudi government. But once it started, it would have been hard to stop. Powercore—or, more precisely, from what I've found out, Bob Morales—predicted a horrendous effect on Powercore stock and their oil exploration efforts if cheap oil flowed into the country. When the kid flew out here to finalize some aspects of the deal, under the protection of the U.S. government, Morales had us take him out to a bar in Austin after we'd spent the evening drinking. The five of us, each had a role. I hung back to make sure witnesses were either confused or clobbered. Tserick drove the car, and Salez, Munroe and Lawson beat his ass outside the bar. The whole time, they shouted shit like 'Remember the Twin Towers' and 'Fuck you, Osama.'"

Now Caren cut in. "Say I believe that load of crap, which I don't. Why did he have you kill everyone involved? They were the killers too. It was in their interest to keep their mouths shut."

"My guess is that as he moved up politically he got nervous and decided to hide the whole thing."

Duarte said, "Why bombs? It's neater and lower profile to use a gun. They never woulda connected four shootings in four different states."

"I think it was a couple of things. First, to make my services more attractive I may have overstated my ability and experience with C-4. They liked that kind of shit. A lot more sexy than a drive-by."

Garretti nodded, thinking.

"The second reason, as I figure it, was economics. He needed the labor bullshit for his own political agenda, and instead of hiring someone to stir that shit he killed two birds with one stone."

Caren said, "He told you to make it look like union unrest?"

"He told me to use the C-4 at work sites. He was very specific. The only one I couldn't do that with was Janni Tserick, because he was always on the move checking lines."

Now Salez chimed in. "You didn't mind doing Janni."

Garretti kicked at him.

Duarte asked, "What's he mean?"

Salez pushed on. "Garretti here knew Tammy Tserick a little too well. She popped out his baby instead of Janni's. Garretti had to do him, if he ever wanted a life with his kid."

"That's not true. I mean, I did him for the same reason as everyone else."

Duarte wondered why it was important to Garretti for people to know he killed someone for business rather than personal reasons.

Garretti looked up at Duarte. "You got a plan yet? I don't think the bad guys are done with us."

Duarte smiled. He couldn't help it. "I got news for you. I'm not done with them either."

43

ALEX DUARTE FELT NEITHER HURRIED NOR STRESSED. HE
had learned in the army that stress only screws things up. In the
history of the world, panic had never helped any situation. Aside
from those compelling arguments, he had no reason to be stressed.
He had what he thought was an excellent plan, and he was
preparing to execute it at a location of his choosing. He had read
books on the Civil War his entire life. He knew personally what
combat was. He had his plan and he would stick to it. If only Lee
had followed his plan.

Maria was his main concern, because she had no idea what
was going on, and the events which had just taken place had
scared her. Not car accident scared. More like "everything I've
ever believed in has been shattered" kind of scared. She knew bits
and pieces, but understood that someone in the U.S. government
had tried to kill her, or at least people around her. He had made
certain Maria didn't know the role Mike Garretti played in her
son's death. It might complicate his plan. Duarte didn't want her
to be a casualty of this plan, either physically or mentally. He
knew she was plenty tough and would get through this as long as
he projected calm and competence.

Maria had been calm enough to suggest this location when
she heard Duarte mutter about needing an isolated place that he
could defend. He had come out to the old deceased manager's
trailer a few miles from the camp once before. It wasn't too hard
to find. This time, he studied the landscape as they drove in his
Taurus. Five people in the passenger compartment and Salez in
the trunk. Maria informed him that the manager's widow had
gone to stay with her daughter for an extended period. She had

asked Maria to keep an eye on the old homestead. Duarte felt as if it were divine intervention. This place was perfect, with the small bridge and the wide field leading to a trailer. He thought the trailer could provide some measure of cover if they stacked the furniture forward. He hoped even that wasn't needed.

Now he had Tom Colgan holding both Salez in cuffs and Garretti at gunpoint, at the far end of the room.

Caren sat on a couch with Maria. Both of the women had demonstrated that they were no cowards. Duarte had been particularly impressed with Caren's confession of her more in-depth knowledge about the case. It was tough to step up and do the right thing after you'd already made a bad choice. She had done it.

Duarte stooped down and said, "Maria, you're certain no one is supposed to come to this trailer?"

"Not for three more weeks." Her brown eyes looked into his. "Who's coming to help us?"

Duarte gave her a small smile. It wasn't hard; this was what he had lived for. "You need to ask who is coming to help the men who come after us."

Colgan called out: "Alex, Caren."

When they looked up, he jerked his head to motion them closer. When they were next to the tall FBI man, he started to speak quietly, so the prisoners couldn't hear him.

Colgan said, "I been thinking about this bullshit about Bob."

Duarte said, "What about it?"

"I don't think it is all bullshit."

"Why?"

"Couple of things." His Texas drawl was starting to fade. "You remember when you were in D.C.?"

"Yeah."

"Bob told me to make sure you didn't get out of the office that day until after one in the afternoon at the earliest."

Duarte thought about that, and said, "That's the day we went to the amusement park." Duarte snapped his fingers and added, "He was keeping us from seeing Garretti when he tried to kill Salez at the park. He had a time frame."

Colgan nodded and said, "I thought maybe it fit in with his story. And then there's the box of leads I FedExed to you in Seattle. Bob told me to load up the box with anything I could find on the union. He wanted to slow you down on the case."

Duarte said, "It worked." He looked at the FBI man. "And you helped."

"I did. I followed orders."

"So did the Nazis."

"I didn't know what was going on."

Duarte said, "Now we all know." He stood and nodded to Tom. "I'll be back in a while. Check the window, in case we're surprised." Duarte ducked out the front door, then waved to his audience through a wide bay widow with the curtain pulled back.

Alberto Salez had been in tough situations before. Maybe not like this, but at least now he had seen several possible escape routes. He knew the area, for one thing. He had caused the old manager to slip off that bridge just a week ago. He could cut through the woods to his car at the camp in about twenty minutes, if he had to.

The other thing in his favor was that everyone thought he was hurt much worse than he was. Sure, his hand ached, and he was missing his pinky. But it wasn't bothering him to the extent that he had been whining. He kept acting like he was drifting off now and then from the pain, hoping to lull everyone into a false sense of security.

He knew it wouldn't be easy. The ATF man, Duarte, had proven himself to be smart and tough. He'd be tough to slip. The woman, Caren Larson, was also alert and intelligent, her blue eyes scanning him every few minutes. Even his fellow prisoner, Garretti, was a problem. That self-righteous ass would be the first to stop him, if he ran. Maybe if the gunmen came back, he'd have a chance to slip away in the confusion. He was prepared to wait it out. He could see a knife on the counter in the kitchen. A thick, heavy butcher knife. Not his fillet knife, but it would do. He knew it was sharp, because he had seen the ATF man use it to strip some wires and to cut bricks of Garretti's C-4. That boy had a party he was setting up. That might be enough to escape right there.

Salez leaned his head down on Garretti like he was passing out again.

Garretti scooted away, allowing Salez to fall on his side.

Garretti said, "Hey, asshole. I'm not a bed. I don't care if you choke in your own vomit."

The tall guy with the pistol said, "Play nice, boys."

Salez looked at him and said, "That ain't a Texas accent. Where you from?"

The man hesitated, and said, "Shut up, asshole." He raised the pistol like he was going to strike Salez.

Salez knew he wouldn't. That was another thing in his favor. This guy was an idiot.

Caren Larson stood up from the couch and walked around the trailer's living room to stretch her legs. It seemed much wider than Maria's trailer. She moved closer to the two prisoners leaning against the back wall with Tom Colgan hovering in front of them. She had a purpose in her casual trek around the trailer but didn't want to seem too obvious. She looked out the bay window at Duarte as he hustled around in the wide-open front yard. He rolled out what looked like plastic tarp near the little bridge that crossed the canal, then wrestled with one of the big fifty-five-gallon drums. He had not filled her in on his plan, but she wasn't worried. Alex Duarte was the steadiest person she had ever met. If he felt they could get out of this safely, she believed him. Even if she did think he was a little paranoid about not calling for help. After all, Tom Colgan worked directly for Bob Morales, and he turned out to be trustworthy. Of course, he didn't believe any of the things Garretti had said about his boss, but he appeared to be doing his job well. She gave him a sideways glance. Something in the back of her mind popped up. Maybe she was paranoid too. She wondered if he could be pretending to be on their side to find out more information. Maybe he would lead them into a trap? He looked harmless enough.

But none of that had anything to do with why she had left the couch. There was really only one person she wanted to talk to. One person with the answers she needed right this minute.

She stopped and turned toward the prisoners, then squatted down so she could look Mike Garretti in the eye.

Garretti, ever cagey, said, "Yes, ma'am, what do you need to know?"

"Why do you think I need to know something?"

"Because you've been tentatively circling us for five minutes. You just leaned down to look at me like I'm about to testify. Who are you worried about? Morales or Duarte?"

"Why would I worry about Alex?"

Garretti smiled. "Because you want to know what I meant about his service in the army. What happened in Bosnia."

She silently assessed the intelligent bomber. "Okay, what about his service in Bosnia? What happened?"

"He killed a kid too."

44

AFTER DUARTE HAD FINISHED HIS INITIAL PREP WORK IN the field in front of the manager's trailer, he surveyed his efforts and nodded, satisfied. At least for now. He tromped through the mixture of grass and weeds that were just a little on the dry side. Perfect.

At the front door, Duarte wiped his feet on the mat out of habit, though he doubted his ma would be yelling at him to keep these floors clean. It was still the courteous thing to so. He made a quick assessment of the room as he entered, mainly ensuring that the prisoners were still secure. Both men still leaned against the back wall, and Tom Colgan stood over them with a pistol in his hand. Good.

Caren was talking with Garretti as he walked in, but she stopped and turned to him.

Duarte said, "We're in good shape." He passed Caren to speak directly to Garretti. "Any ideas on remote detonation of your C-4?"

Garretti thought about it, and smiled. "You're gonna blow the bridge?"

"You read my file. You know it's what I do."

"That'll show these guys. Good one. But how do you get them to come to us and cross the bridge?"

Duarte smiled. "That's the easy part. Now, what about the remote detonation?"

"A current to the blasting caps will work. Any extension cords?"

"The little shed is full of them, along with dozens of other things we can use for defense. The old manager apparently bought in bulk."

Garretti smiled and said, "Don't wanna use too much C-4 on the bridge."

Duarte glared at him.

"See, I really did see your entire file."

Now Caren stepped closer to Duarte. "Alex," she started softly, so only he could hear her clearly. "What happened in Bosnia? He keeps dropping hints. Is it anything we should be worried about?"

He looked at her and then spoke in a plain voice, not needing to conceal anything. "I worry about it every night, but, no, it has nothing to do with this. It's just a coincidence."

"What is?"

"Having to blow a bridge with bad guys coming after us."

She kept her confused expression and said, "I don't understand."

He looked over to Maria, who was now watching from the rear of the couch and paying attention. Garretti didn't look smug; in fact, he looked like he was sorry he had brought up the subject. Duarte didn't feel this was the right time to keep secrets. He owed them the truth. Especially Maria. He looked around the room and realized he had everyone's attention.

"Well," he started slowly, "I was attached to a unit in Bosnia on the border with Serbia, near the Drina River. We received intel that three Serb tanks were going to cross the Drina and attack a Croatian arms depot. Our orders were to keep them apart. No direct fighting between the two armies.

"My commanding officer had dealt with the Serbs, and figured that if he blew the bridge over the Drina River they'd just move on to the next one, or maybe start shelling a small village from across the river. We had no real air support because, at the time, our F-15s were told not to break a twenty-thousand-foot ceiling. They didn't want to risk a downing of an American warplane or collateral damage to any of the villages that dotted the area. The nearest U.S. Army Abrams tank was an hour away and we didn't have any time. The answer seemed obvious: blow the bridge with the tanks on it."

They all hung on his every word. Even Maria had left the couch to join the group. Duarte felt a little self-conscious, but he had started the story and didn't feel like stopping now. This was the first time he had spoken of it since leaving Bosnia.

Caren prompted him. "Go ahead, we're listening."

"Well, I set all the C-4 I could lay my hands on under the bridge. I laid in pounds of it, with a long cord to detonate from a good distance. So we lay in wait in a ditch almost a quarter mile up the road from the bridge. Sure enough, the tanks came rumbling out of the woods on the far side, then over the bridge without hesitation. When all three were on the bridge, I detonated the C-4."

"What happened?" asked Caren.

"Just what you'd think. The bridge went up in a big way with two of the tanks. The third one had backed onto the land and immediately retreated back into the woods."

"So you accomplished your mission?"

"We did. The tanks were neutralized, and there was no contact between the Serbs and Croats."

"What was the problem, then?"

"I had used so much C-4 that it blasted fragments of the bridge everywhere. One piece, about the size of a dime, flew down the riverbank and hit a twelve-year-old boy."

Maria gasped.

"In the neck."

Caren put her arm around Maria as she started to cry.

"When we walked down to survey the bridge, we could see the boy's father and a few locals gathered around the boy on the riverbank. I knew something was wrong and raced down to them. As soon as I saw the wound, with blood pumping out of his neck, I knew it was my fault. We did everything. Called in a medevac. I tried to stem the blood with direct pressure, but there was nothing we could do. He died at the U.S Army first-aid station a few miles away."

Now Maria was sobbing, obviously connecting the story to her own tragedy, and possibly now realizing why Duarte had been so diligent on the case. He looked up into Caren's eyes and saw she now understood as well.

From the back wall, Garretti said, "Let me help you out there. I won't try anything. I can splice an extension cord and be ready to roll in a few minutes."

Duarte looked at him, considering the help from a guy who had more recent experience setting bombs.

Garretti said, "C'mon, you can keep the pistol on the whole time, but I need some payback, and this way I'll be saving our asses too."

Before Duarte could answer, Salez said, "If you're done with your boohoo story, I gotta take a piss, and unless you let me out of these cuffs someone is going to have to hold my dick."

Duarte said, "Tom, he's all yours. I'll take Garretti. That way you just have to concentrate on him."

Colgan nodded.

"And Tom," he waited for Colgan to look at him. "Don't hesitate to shoot him if you need to."

Garretti helped Duarte push another fifty-five-gallon drum of fuel into his trap. Garretti could see this guy knew what he was doing. He didn't know if that was from training or actual combat. This looked like one hell of a trap, but the plan had holes. The biggest, as far as Garretti could see, was how to get the bad guys where they needed them to go.

Duarte had good focus. He reminded Garretti of a missile that was streaking toward a specific target. Once everything was in place, Garretti followed Duarte to the shed at the side of the property. He noticed that Duarte had a Glock on his hip, and he was always aware of Garretti's location. He was subtle, this ATF man. He never allowed Garretti to be on the same side as his gun. He'd shift or sidestep. Once, he even used his hand to guide Garretti to the side. Garretti could tell by the way this guy moved that he was quick, and confident that he could stop Garretti if he tried to escape. Garretti was confident he'd be stopped too. But he had no plan to escape. At least, not at the moment.

When Garretti got his first look inside the shed, all he could say was, "Holy Mother of God."

Duarte smirked and nodded.

It was a treasure trove of wires, tools, chemicals, containers with oil, mineral spirits, hydrochloric acid and just about anything else that could burn, blow up or maim.

Garretti said, "Wow." He ran his fingers over a few of the farm implements, then stopped on some coils of leatherlike rope. "This quick fuse isn't even legal anymore. This is old as shit. This whole place is a dream."

"More like a nightmare. I wonder if the old manager knew how lethal this shed was."

"Bet he had no clue."

Duarte said, "I left out some C-4 with a couple of your releases for some small surprises." He guided Garretti to the workbench, still keeping him away from his pistol. He held up a glass jar filled with clear liquid and a small thin patch of C-4 wrapped around it. "Hydrochloric acid." He held it up to show Garretti where he would place them in the shed. "A homemade release for the cord, and these will make hiding in here uncomfortable."

"You don't fool around."

"Time for games is over."

"You're awfully sure they'll show."

"They'll come."

"And how do you get them in here?"

"Guys like that are lemmings. Scare them and they all flee the same way."

"I may have started this, but you sure seem eager to finish it."

"All this pain. Maria's boy, the others—all for profit. It doesn't seem right."

Garretti nodded. "Hey, it's your man, Morales, keeping it all going."

"He's not my man."

"Whoever he is, someone needs to set his ass straight. If I make it through this, I hope it's me."

"You'll testify?"

"On TV, if that's what it takes," Garretti said.

Duarte nodded and grabbed a coiled electrical extension cord. "This should reach from the bridge to the trailer."

Garretti said, "How about the second trap? How're you gonna ignite it?"

He grabbed some quick fuse as they left the shed. "You'll see."

They trudged through the weeds and thick dry grass to the small bridge. Duarte pulled out his folding BenchMark knife and popped it open with a hard flick of his wrist. He laid the end of the extension cord across one of the wooden pilings next to the bridge and cut the end of the cord. He split the remaining cord, then peeled back the plastic to reveal the two separate copper wires.

Garretti said, "That'll work." He watched as Duarte leaned under the bridge and attached the wires to the first in a series of blasting caps. Garretti nodded his approval, then followed Duarte as he uncoiled the cord to the side of the bridge heading back to the trailer. As they came to the front door, there was still thirty feet of cord.

Pausing at the front door, Garretti said, "So how do you get them here now that you have this great defensive position?"

Duarte allowed himself one of the first real smiles Garretti had seen. He held up his small Nextel cell phone and scrolled through some contacts. As he held the phone to his ear, he actually winked at Garretti. Then he said, "Chuck, it's Alex." He waited, and said, "Just listen. I have two witnesses in the bombing case hidden in the manager's trailer near the labor camp. It's the road that breaks off from the camp to the right. We're about two or three miles down the road, the only trailer back here." He paused, letting the other person speak, and added: "We'll be here another hour or so. No one will ever find us out here. I'll call you when we know what we're going to do." He flipped the phone closed and looked up at Garretti. "They tapped my phone. They believed that whole conversation. They'll be here in less than an hour."

Garretti nodded his approval. "You're smooth." He turned and climbed the three steps, then turned toward the door when it opened on its own, swinging out slowly. Garretti saw the tall FBI agent standing there.

Duarte said, "We're all set, Tom."

The tall man tried to speak, then fell face forward onto the landing as Duarte leaped up and caught him before he tumbled down the short flight of stairs. It didn't really matter. A butcher knife was buried in the back of his neck, deep in his spine, at an angle. Blood had already stained his light blue shirt.

As Duarte and Garretti looked up, they saw Alberto Salez with Colgan's revolver pointing at them. "C'mon in, boys. You're letting out all the air-conditioning."

45

ALEX DUARTE ENTERED THE TRAILER SLOWLY, FIRST checking to make certain the women were safe, then assessing his options. Both Caren and Maria sat frozen on the couch. Maria had her faced buried on Caren's shoulder. Neither made a sound.

Salez had dropped back to the rear wall and kept the pistol aimed at both Duarte and Garretti.

Salez said, "Now, Agent Duarte. Slowly pull your pistol, using only two fingers, and slide it to me." He carefully aimed the pistol at Duarte and added, "If I miss you, I'll turn to shoot our lady friends."

Any plans Duarte had of trying to quick-draw and fire from the hip were ended with that threat. Besides, he was better with his hands and feet than he was with a pistol. It would be a tricky mess to draw on a guy holding a pistol on him. He pulled the Glock as he had been commanded, then stooped and shoved it hard enough to slide part way to Salez.

The fugitive said, "I'm not falling for that again. You're too fast for me. I should just shoot you."

Garretti cut it. "You do and you'll never make it past our booby traps out there."

Salez turned his attention from Duarte. "What traps?"

"You shoot us and you'll never find out."

"I can wait until you tell me. I got food and water."

Duarte chimed in, "Nope, you got about an hour at most."

"Whadya mean?"

"Those nice men who shot up Maria's trailer are on their way over here right now."

Maria gasped at that news.

Salez said, "How do you know that?"

"Trust me, I do. Why do you think we've been laying those traps?" He looked at the wavering Salez and added, "Those guys are after you specifically. They're not gonna care what you have to say when they get here."

Salez waved the gun. "Both of you get over on the couch with the women." When no one moved, he shouted: "Now."

Duarte calmly moved around to the front of the couch, careful not to betray his growing anxiety that he needed to be watching for the arrival of the gunmen. Garretti had already sat down next to Maria, who seemed to be recovering from the sight of Tom Colgan being impaled with the long, thick knife. Duarte had reverted to his military training, and knew he'd be upset by the FBI agent's death when this was all over. Until then, he had to focus on how he would get himself and the others out of this situation in one piece.

As he sat at the far end of the couch, he watched Salez make a long circle around the couch so he could face them. "You're saying that I have a small window of time and I have to go. And I can't take the Taurus because you guys laid traps in the front yard." He seemed in a remarkably good mood for someone trapped with the rest of them. "I can cut through the back. I know the way. My Caddy is still at the camp."

Duarte said, "Then go ahead and take off, because I need to get ready for the visitors."

Salez considered the comment.

Duarte added, "Look, it's in your interest that I take those guys out."

"I'll say this: you're determined and logical. I won't deny it." Salez looked at the younger ATF agent and said, "Okay, you sold me. But I have one piece of unfinished business."

"What's that? You already have the file." He had seen the photos crammed in Salez's back pocket.

"But I owe that asshole." He pointed the pistol at Garretti, who gave no hint of what he was thinking.

Salez stepped closer and raised the pistol.

Maria flung her arms around Garretti and covered him with her body. "No, no. There's been enough killing."

Salez snickered and lowered the gun. "Maria, you know who you're protecting?"

She didn't move or show interest in what he was talking about.

Before he could answer, Salez snapped his head up to the side window. "Son of a bitch."

Duarte turned and saw the same thing. The SUV was coming down the dirt road that led to the bridge.

Salez didn't hesitate. He turned and darted out the back door. Not even looking back at his captives.

It was showtime.

Alberto Salez was not a runner, but fear fueled him as he cut through the thick woods and brush in an arc that he thought would take him back to the labor camp. He would've liked to shoot that asshole, Garretti, but he might need all his ammo. He had two guns with him. The FBI agent's little revolver and Duarte's Glock. He didn't know where Garretti's Browning was. He thought it might be in the Taurus.

His hand ached from his missing pinky, but the rest of him was charged with adrenaline as he waited to hear the sound of gunfire. The more people killed at the trailer, the better, as far as he was concerned. If they all killed each other, he might make a clean getaway.

He slowed to catch his breath. Man, had he been lucky today. If that FBI man had been more worried about him, and not so intent on looking out the window to make sure Duarte was all right, he never would've seen his chance coming out of the bathroom. He didn't hesitate to walk through and pick up the knife sitting on the counter. He drove that thing home as hard as any hit or punch he had ever delivered. It cut through the tall man's skin and muscle, bouncing off bone and vertebrae like a pinball. He couldn't believe the guy stayed standing for so long, and even made it to the door to warn Duarte. It had worked out perfectly.

Once he was a good distance from the trailer, after maybe six minutes of running, he slowed to a walk, still expecting gunfire. What he heard instead was an explosion. A big one.

Duarte watched the fugitive flee out the back door and fought the instinct to give chase. But Mr. Alberto Salez would not be forgotten; he'd just have to wait his turn.

He raced to the front door and sprang out to grab the extension cord at the foot of the steps. He dragged it back inside and slammed the flimsy door on the cord. Garretti joined him at the window for a better view, and since Duarte had lost his gun he didn't care where he stood. He didn't believe Garretti was a threat right now. At least, that was how he had read him, and he was starting to trust his ability to read people.

Caren came closer and said, "What're you doing?"

Garretti turned and said, "He has a good plan. Watch as these assholes come across the bridge."

Duarte kept his eyes on the window, the hand holding the plug of the cord poised next to the outlet. He saw the SUV come down the front road and slow to a crawl as they approached the bridge.

"Keep coming," murmured Duarte.

The SUV turned slowly and then eased, a foot at a time, over the bridge.

Garretti shouted: "Now! Now! Blow that fucking thing."

Duarte held firm with the extension cord plug still away from the wall.

Garretti reached over and put his hand on Duarte's, holding the plug. Duarte turned and said through clenched teeth: "Not yet."

They watched as the big Excursion pulled into the main field and almost came to a stop.

Garretti was outraged. "You let what happened in Bosnia get to you. Now they're here."

Duarte wasn't upset. From Garretti's point of view, this was a screwup, but he had other plans.

The man with the MP-5 climbed out of the Excursion and surveyed the field and trailer. If he had been dressed in fatigues instead of a green polo shirt, he would've looked like an army commander deciding how to storm a position. He finally yelled to them across the hood of the SUV: "We know you're in there. C'mon out and save the ladies' skin."

Garretti said, "You're not going to listen, are you? We still got booby traps."

"Would you calm down?" Duarte said, still not making a move.

From the Excursion, the man yelled: "Don't worry, Garretti. We got a trip to Seattle planned. We'll take care of your boy for you."

Garretti sat back. "Son of a bitch. How did he know about Tammy?"

Duarte said, "Doesn't matter."

"Why?"

"Because they're not going anywhere." Duarte shoved the plug into the outlet and instantly the bridge disintegrated in a cloud of dust, dirt and smoke. A second later, Duarte heard the light patter of the wooden fragments falling onto the roof of the trailer.

In the field, the men ducked low behind the big SUV, but at least one caught some shredded wood in his leg. He limped and wobbled to the front of the vehicle.

Duarte didn't hesitate. He stepped to the side door in the kitchen, with Garretti on his heels. In the small carport, he picked up the grill lighter he had pre-positioned at the gutter with a long strip of quick fuse he had laid. The fuse ran down the hill toward the field.

Duarte turned to Garretti and said, "Here's a new way to look at the phrase 'field of fire.'" He squeezed the lighter's trigger, igniting the fuse that led to the pool of gasoline and kerosene he had used to soak the tarps and puddle all over the field with the sheets of plastic. The fuse sparked, and sputtered down the slight hill. Duarte held his breath as he wondered if the old commercial fuse was still any good. He could hear Garretti willing the fuse to continue, muttering, "C'mon, make it, make it." Suddenly, it looked like the sparks and smoke stopped coming from the fuse. Duarte felt his breath escape as he stared at the quiet field. Then, after resparking, it continued its trip toward the broad field. After one final flash, it hit the large pools of gas from the fifty-five-gallon drums, causing the field to shoot up in geysers of flame.

The flash of the fuel mixture igniting hurt Duarte's eyes as it cut in front of the SUV.

The three men abandoned the vehicle en masse and started toward the shed, firing a few rounds in the general direction of the trailer as they did. The one man with the wounded leg lagged behind, ignored by his friends. But they all headed for the shed.

Duarte looked at Garretti and said, "Like I said: lemmings."

Caren Larson instinctively ducked when the bridge blew, but she could see Alex Duarte had waited until the truck was clear.

Had he really been afraid to blow up the SUV on the bridge because of what had happened in Bosnia? He seemed in control, but this was all happening so fast she didn't know what to think.

Then Duarte and Garretti raced out the side door, and a few seconds later she saw what he had in mind. The blown bridge was to keep them from escaping, not to kill them. He had set up a series of tarps with flammable fuels and liquids, which were now igniting like bombs. She saw the men jump from the SUV and race to the small shed in the corner of the property. Then she heard two smaller pops, followed by a man screaming. A second later, she saw him run out of the shed holding his face and dive into the muddy, nasty canal at the front of the property.

Duarte came back into the trailer with Garretti. He knelt next to Caren at the window to survey the mayhem he had caused. He looked excited, even happy, at his efforts.

He said, "Wow, look at that burn."

"You had this planned all along."

"Of course, why else would I bring us all out here?" His eyes widened as more of the tarp burned, giving off a thick black smoke.

He said, "I saw the acid bomb took out one guy. That leaves two more."

"Acid bomb. How did you . . ." She stopped, knowing that he had found a way and was doing it to protect her. It was just that an acid bomb sounded so cruel—like vengeance.

Garretti had gone to Maria on the couch and tried to comfort her, with his arm around her shoulder. She was shaking at the sounds of the explosions and sporadic gunfire.

Then Garretti asked Duarte, "What now? The fire will burn out in a minute, and we still have two armed men in the shed."

Duarte turned and said, "Salez blew part of my plan by taking the two guns. All we have is your Browning, but it's locked in my car." He looked past Caren and said, "I have that pack with an IED of C-4 and enough nails and screws to shred anything in fifty feet."

Garretti said, "We could run."

"No good. We need to attack. I'll get the pistol and advance on the shed while they're still confused."

"How long is the fuse on your knapsack bomb?"

"Three seconds. Why?"

Garretti sprang up from the couch and darted across the

room, snatching up the knapsack as he did. He paused at the front door, motioning for Duarte to stay there. "Let me. I owe you guys this much." He looked at Maria on the couch and added, "Especially her."

Caren stared as he turned and raced out the door. They watched his progress as he sprinted across the smoky field, the fires already dying out. His lean frame moved quickly and smoothly as he closed the distance on the shed in a matter of seconds. As he approached the small wooden structure, he didn't hesitate as he threw himself into the door of the shed. A few seconds later, the window in the shed blew out, then the rear wall collapsed, followed by the roof, as a fire spread in the ruins. Fueled by the stored chemicals, it quickly engulfed that entire corner of the property.

Caren sat back hard on the trailer's floor, trying to catch her breath. Duarte slowly stood, watching the fire outside.

46

ALEX DUARTE COULDN'T REMEMBER THE LAST TIME HE felt so totally exhausted. As soon as Garretti set off the bomb in the shed, he had called the sheriff's office for help. He had Caren and Maria stay inside the manager's trailer, on the couch, and they knew not to talk to anyone yet. Caren knew why.

Now he sat on the steps to the trailer, listening to Palm Beach County Sheriff's Captain Annette Cutter as she asked him first the obvious questions, and now she'd started inching around the more subtle ones. There was no one else nearby, as the bomb techs checked the remains of the deadly little shed Mike Garretti had blown to bits. Personnel from the medical examiner's office continued to recover the remains in and around the shed.

Captain Cutter leaned her large frame against the trailer. "So these men came to get the fugitive Salez and this other fella, Garretti, blew them up? That's what you're saying?"

He knew better than to shrug off an experienced cop like the captain. He knew what she wanted to hear, and was smart enough to know there was a lot more to the story, but he hoped she trusted him to tell her later. After he had settled a few things. Finally Duarte said, "Pretty much, it was all Garretti."

"And you expect me to believe that?"

"That's my hope."

"And the fugitive is in the wind."

"I'll get after him."

"The FBI has men on the way out here. About their agent." Her head bowed, like any cop's would, mentioning someone killed in the line of duty.

Duarte frowned. He had not forgotten the efforts of Tom

Colgan. "He saved all of us. It was Salez who stabbed him. That's why I know I'll catch him."

Captain Cutter nodded her head and cut her eyes to Duarte. "You gonna set things right?"

"I guarantee it."

"I'll wait a few days until we start writing everything up."

He nodded, too tired to answer, as one of the medical examiner investigators walked up.

The middle-aged man in the white biohazard suit said, "We got two bodies in the shed. Both blown to shit, with nails and everything else stuck in 'em. There's a third body in the canal, with burns on his face, a severe leg wound and bruises around his neck, like he was choked. We'll wait for the autopsy to say for sure."

Captain Cutter turned to Duarte. "That everyone? Or is there another?"

Duarte stood and said, "Let me have a look at the bodies." He started to walk toward the shed, where the three bodies were now laid out on a tarp. He didn't want to answer just yet. Once they were standing over the tarp, he looked down and could hardly tell the two bodies from the shed were human. He recognized the guy with the MP-5 from the remnants of the green polo shirt he was wearing, but his face was a red, pockmarked mask of torn flesh and exposed bone. He didn't know if it was his acid bomb or the improvised explosive device that Garretti had detonated that had caused the damage. The third body was the driver. Duarte could easily recognize him, despite the burns around his eyes and cheeks. He had the wood from the bridge in his leg. These were the men from the Excursion.

Duarte looked at Captain Cutter and said, "I think that's everyone. The Excursion had two or three men in it, but I'm not sure. I can't ID those two. But one must be Garretti."

The captain said, "I have many more questions about how you got here and why these men were after you, but I know I don't want to hear it now."

Duarte smiled slightly and said, "Captain, you're a very smart woman. But you have my promise everything will be worked out shortly."

"This is a federal problem, as far as I'm concerned."

* * *

Caren Larson sat in her hotel room in an uncomfortable chair across from Alex Duarte, who was seated in a similar chair. With Salez on the loose, they had set Maria up in the room next door until it was safe. She was no doubt sound asleep by now. She had experienced more excitement in one day than most people did in three lifetimes.

Caren was tired too, but was more interested in talking with Duarte right now. He had somehow slipped away from the scene without having to give a full account of what happened. Now she wanted to know what their plan was. She had come to believe everything Mike Garretti had told them. She worked for a monster, and it had to end.

She looked into Duarte's eyes. "You always seem to know what to do next. What's our plan?"

He wiped his face with his hand and sighed.

She wasn't sure if he was just tired or if it was something more. She had not seen him look so down before this.

She said, "We could go to the news media."

He shook his head slowly and remained deep in concentration. Finally he said, "We're not Deep Throat. We don't have an ax to grind. I refuse to think the whole system is corrupt because one pinhead tried to use it to his advantage."

"Then where do we go?"

"I'd start with us documenting what we have and talking directly to the U.S. Attorney for the Southern District of Florida. God knows enough crimes took place here to give him jurisdiction."

"But Morales would hear about it."

"Doesn't matter now. The cat's out of the bag. Besides, the U.S. Attorney is appointed by the president. He has some juice. I don't think any of them would want to be seen as helping a creep like Morales."

"What should we document? I mean, a lot happened, but what proof do we have?"

"I'll find Salez. He'll talk. It may be the only reason he lives. That guy was the worst of the bunch and I was worried about him being killed. I've learned a lot."

"You had no way to know."

He shrugged. She knew he was hard on himself.

Caren said, "How bad did Garretti look?"

Duarte hesitated. He swallowed hard and said, "All the bodies looked bad."

She searched his face for something else. The stress of the past two days was etched in his sagging eyes and shoulders.

He stretched and said, "I gotta get going."

She reached across and put her hand on his. "You could stay, Kojak." She winked.

He looked at her and said, "I better go home."

She could tell—any woman could—that he was still unsure of her because she had kept so much of the case secret from him. She didn't blame him. A guy like that expected honesty even if it wasn't what he wanted to hear. She hoped that time might change things.

After he left, she started to cry about everything, from her bad career move and ethical lapse to little Hector Tannza, whose mother slept in the very next room. She cried until exhaustion overtook her and she drifted off and dreamed about everything from her bad career choices and ethical lapse to little Hector Tannza. Only, this time, he was alive and smiling.

Alberto Salez had crouched in the same spot behind some bushes as he had since he watched his borrowed Caddy get towed. He had thought about confronting the tow truck driver with his pistols, but there were two tow truck operators and a Palm Beach County Sheriff's cruiser parked down the street. It took forever for all of them to clear out. He was stiff and tired, and his hand had continued to bleed steadily. He was a little light-headed, and the Percocets he had taken earlier had definitely worn off. The pain seemed to radiate with every heartbeat. On top of everything else, he was now dog tired and hungry. Really hungry.

He considered walking to the highway and tying to hitch a ride, but, considering his current condition and his fugitive status, he rejected that course of action. He would've broken into Maria's trailer but was afraid the gunmen might return, or, if they somehow escaped, Maria and that fucking ATF agent might show up. That might be ugly. He knew that if he saw that prick again, he'd shoot first and worry about how fast the guy was later.

He eyes wandered down the road to the single workers' bunkhouse. It was just a big trailer, but he had spent several nights with his posse there over the past months. He stood, feeling his joints creak and muscles stretch. He slowly started to limp along behind the hedge toward the trailer. He could see there were still a few lights on in the bunkhouse. It wasn't too late. He'd say hello, grab a bite to eat and then sleep off some of this pain. In the morning, he'd find a way out of this shithole.

He paused, and knocked on the front door.

After a few seconds, the door opened, and the youngest of his old posse, Iggy, said over his shoulder to the others, in Spanish, "I can't believe it. Berto came back to roost."

Salez stepped into the trailer but was surprised by the apathy that met him. No one seemed concerned that he had been kidnapped right in front of them at the pawnshop. As he looked around, there were more bandages than usual. Raul, his main pal, had his right arm in a cast and sling, and his nose was still flat like a pancake on his broad face. The ATF man, Duarte, had really worked these guys over but good.

Salez said, "So, you guys okay?"

The glares and grunts he got in return seemed to indicate he'd better be happy with any hospitality at all.

47

ALEX DUARTE FELT THE WEARINESS SEEP RIGHT OUT OF his bones once he lay down in his own bed. It was near dawn now, and he had survived the most dangerous day of his life—and that included his time in combat in Bosnia. He had no regrets about keeping his mouth shut about Garretti—something he might not have done a few weeks ago. He had read the guy well through his words as well as his actions. He hadn't needed to risk his life to save Duarte, Colgan and Frank when the gunmen had them cornered. He hadn't needed to charge the shed either, though that had also been a chance to escape. Maybe Garretti knew Duarte would remain silent about his missing corpse. Duarte wondered what the bomber had in mind to do now. He didn't seem like someone you'd want to cross.

As he shut his eyes and, for a change, felt sleep rushing in upon him, he heard a noise that brought him back to consciousness. It seemed faint and faraway at first, but then he realized what it was and sat up wide awake. He jumped out of his bed and followed the noise to his closet, where he dug through the pockets of his jeans and opened the cover to his cell phone.

"Duarte," was all he said as he answered the small phone.

He heard a spate of Spanish and paused.

Duarte then said, "Can you speak English?"

In a clear but accented voice, a man said, "This is Ralph Garcia."

"Who?"

"From the pawnshop. I came with Alberto Salez the other day. You gave us your number, if we ever saw him again."

"Oh yeah, I remember you. You better have seen him recently to be calling me at this time of night."

"He's asleep in our bunkhouse right now."

"At the camp?"

"Yeah. Down the road from Maria Tannza's home."

"I'll be there soon. It's more than an hour's drive."

"I don't think he's leaving anytime soon."

"You're a good man, Ralph."

"Don't tell anyone I called."

Alberto Salez woke up as the sun was just rising. He felt like he had been drinking tequila all night, then he remembered exactly why he felt like shit. Although his stomach rumbled, and the dingy sheets covering the cot he had slept on were covered with the blood still seeping from his severed finger, he knew he had to get out of here as quickly as possible. The only question was how.

He crawled off the cot and stood, stretching his back. He had hidden the ATF agent's Glock in his bed; he found it and slipped it into his belt. He had the other pistol—the one that belonged to the tall man he had stabbed—stashed in the bushes near Maria's trailer, in case he'd had to flee and leave the Glock. That's how he got ahead in life: planning and action.

There was no smell of breakfast foods in this trailer. These men all ate at the small cafeteria run by the camp. The only thing Salez smelled now was the old clothes piled near each bed and sweat from the previous day's work. Four of the six men who lived there were already awake and getting dressed for their long day of labor. Salez thought of them as a bunch of losers, spending their days working and never getting ahead. That's why he had been able to lead them around for so long. They had no drive. No ambition.

He looked over at Raul, with his flattened nose, and said, "Can you give me a ride?"

"Where?"

"Just to find a car?"

"Where?"

"I dunno, close by. I just need to get away."

"Where?"

"Raul, what the fuck is wrong with you? Give me a ride."

"I gotta get to work. Not many of us here, this time of year. We got a lot to do."

"Raul, don't give me any shit. I need a ride. Now."

The biggest of the men, Ralph, heard the last comment and crossed the long trailer to be closer to Salez. "What's your rush? Come eat and then we'll take you."

Salez nodded, then looked at the big man who had so willingly helped him try to capture the ATF agent. "That's all right. I can skip breakfast."

"But we can't." Ralph motioned to the others to leave the trailer.

Salez sensed there was a serious problem but couldn't put his finger on it. He pulled Duarte's Glock from his belt. He didn't point it at anyone. He didn't need to. "Hang on, fellas." This time, he spoke in English. "Somebody better tell me what you ditchdiggers have in mind because I'm in no mood to play games."

No one spoke or moved.

"Don't make me show you what kind of mood I'm in." He raised the pistol and pointed it randomly at the first man he saw, the youngest of the group—the kid named Iggy, who had not been involved in either fight with Duarte.

When still no one spoke, Salez fired a round through Iggy's left leg, dropping the young man to the messy floor with a scream.

Ralph and Raul jumped at the sound of the shot, then Ralph said, "We're not helping you because we know what you did."

"What I did. Tell me, Ralph, what did I do that offended you so much?"

"You did something with Elenia from the sports club. She left with you and no one has seen her since."

"I don't know what you're talking about. I dropped her off at her house." He left out that then he fucked her, twisted her neck and dumped her in a canal.

"And some of the locals saw you hold a knife to Maria Tannza's throat yesterday."

"That was just to scare the cops, so I could get away."

Ralph stepped forward, bold now. "No, Berto, we were wrong. The cop is tough, but he's not a bad guy. You are. He let us go from the pawnshop, even though you had us start the shit. He treated us okay."

"Okay? Are you kidding me? Look at Raul's nose and arm. He hit the man with a hammer."

"And didn't lie to us."

"That's enough." He pointed the pistol at Ralph's head. "Give me the keys to your Bronco. I'm leaving."

Ralph said, "What if I said I don't know where they are?"

Salez squeezed the unique trigger of the fancy automatic and felt the large frame pistol jump in his hand. The blast of the gunshot was brutal inside the trailer. Ralph fell back as a stream of blood shot out of his neck. The blood sprayed the wall and bathroom door like a sprinkler, as the big man fumbled around on the floor clutching at his neck. Salez stepped past him to Raul and said, calmly, "Where are the keys?"

Raul immediately pointed to the table, away from the beds. "Over there, on the table. It's the silver key."

Salez turned and stomped over to the table, barely registering Ralph's gasping as he tried to stem the blood pouring from his neck. "You guys better not tell anyone I'm in your Bronco or I'll be back. And you don't want that, do you?" He raised the gun again.

All the men shook their heads frantically.

Salez turned and opened the door a crack and said, "Thanks for the hospitality, boys."

Then he felt the door burst toward him, slamming into his face and arm at the same time. Something hit his wrist and sent the pistol flying across the room into the big, quiet form of Ralph. Salez turned toward the source of the blows and briefly saw the face of the ATF man, Duarte, then a foot hit him square in the chin and he fell backward as a few of his teeth soared out across the room.

As Duarte pulled up to the trailer that housed the male workers, he heard a gunshot from inside. He was out of his Taurus and had his backup Beretta 9mm in his hand instantly. He knew that Alberto Salez fired that shot, and he wasn't letting that asshole slip by him no matter what happened.

He tried to get a glimpse inside, but no window was clean enough to see the interior of the large trailer. He could hear shouts inside, then another gunshot. Now he rushed toward the door near the back of the trailer and waited outside it with his pistol raised. He preferred to use his fists but realized that when the opponent is well armed you better be too. There was more shouting from inside, and the vibration of people moving. He climbed the stairs and stopped on the landing in front of the door. He paused, considering the value of bursting inside. It wasn't just his safety at stake but that of the other people inside. He put his left hand on the door, keeping his pistol up with his right.

Just as he was about to turn the handle and rush inside, someone on the other side of the door opened it a crack. Duarte could see his pistol and the edge of Salez's face through the opening. He threw his whole body against the door, slamming into the fugitive. Then he saw the pistol extended in Salez's hand, and he delivered a hard, snapping front kick to Salez's arm. He felt the forearm break and saw the pistol fly out across the room, landing next to a man on the floor. Then, without conscious effort, he delivered a devastating front kick to Salez's chin, sending him crashing back into the wall, then the floor. Blood poured from the fugitive's nose, lips and even a cut on his chin. Duarte had to keep himself from kicking the man again even though the fight was over.

He holstered his Beretta, took a breath and then turned to retrieve the Glock. Duarte froze when he saw that the man on the floor held the gun in shaky hands. Blood still seeped out of a wound in his neck. His complexion was pale and his eyes snapped open and shut like he was about to pass out.

Ralph pointed the gun at Salez as the fugitive started to open his own eyes. He shook his head and looked up at Duarte. "Motherfucker. Don't you ever quit?"

From across the room, Ralph said, "Está diablo."

Duarte said, "I understand that. You're right. He *is* the devil."

Now Salez was fully conscious, and his eyes snapped wide open. "Don't let that beaner shoot me."

Duarte looked at him. "Why not?" He backed out of the way so Ralph had a clear shot.

Salez said, "That's not right. You have to protect me."

"Will you testify?"

"Yes, yes, you know I will."

Duarte looked at the panicked man and remembered his pledge to testify before he killed Tom Colgan. "Bullshit."

The argument didn't matter either way as Ralph started to jerk the trigger, popping off five shots before he fainted and dropped the pistol. Only two hit Salez. But that was enough. One entered his torn left ear and kept going into his brain, and the other into his side, shattering ribs and ending up in his heart.

Duarte immediately darted to Ralph, securing the gun and trying to render first aid to the big man, but it was too late. His last act was killing Salez.

This was going to take some explaining too.

48

MIKE GARRETTI SAT IN A TOYOTA HE HAD RENTED FROM A
Hertz office in Alexandria, Virginia, under one of his aliases:
Michael Barson. A good, nonoffensive name that couldn't be associated with any one region of the country. He had walked a
mile to the Hertz office after a trucker dropped him off. The
beefy driver, hauling a load of fruit baskets, had given him a ride
all the way from Daytona Beach. The bandage on Garretti's
shoulder itched, but it was better than having an exposed burn
rubbing against his polyester pullover. In the two days since he
had run past the shed on the farm in Florida and chucked in the
knapsack bomb Duarte had made, Garretti had been on the road
nonstop. He had one mission now. He knew his life as an army
sergeant at Fort Hood was over, and he'd have to be careful
about everything from now on—even how he approached his
mom. The ATF man, Duarte, was smart. He probably knew that
Garretti had managed to escape. The question was, how much
did he want to have him captured?

Garretti took a sip of the Coke he'd bought from a vending
machine. It seemed like no matter what he ate or drank, he still
had the taste of that nasty canal water in his mouth. He had intended to just sort of skip through the canal and then keep going,
but then he ran into the gunman who had jumped in the canal. At
first, the guy just clung to him like he needed help, then, when he
realized it was Garretti, he turned nasty. Garretti may not have
been a combat veteran, but he was fit and the guy was mostly
blind. He tried a sleeper, but it was easier to just close off his
windpipe and choke him.

He had a lot to atone for. He knew it. There were a pile of

bodies that were his fault, but mainly there was little Hector Tannza. Now he intended to set things right. Or, at least, a little more right. The adult deaths were bad, but he knew the best things about kids were that they were too young and innocent to know how shitty the world really is. Hector did not deserve what happened to him.

Garretti had gotten less and less sleep since that bombing and now he found himself just lying awake most nights. He'd see Hector's face and Maria crying. He hoped she never realized what he had done. Now he understood Duarte's drive to complete his investigation.

He drove slowly down the narrow street lined with BMWs and a few Mercedeses. The town houses all lined up and looked very similar. In Texas, these would be nice student housing. Here, they were nine hundred thousand dollars. He came to a set on a hill, with two stories on top of a garage built into the hill. Ten units, and the second-to-last one had the numbers 3207 on it. Bingo!

He parked as close as he could. He didn't have his usual tools of the trade, but he had a few. This was a good plan that wouldn't compromise his current status as "missing, presumed dead." He had a buck knife and screwdriver and hoped that would be enough to break into the small access door on the side of the garage without leaving obvious marks. The streetlight nearest the town house illuminated the front and side yards. How convenient for burglars; he could clearly see the door.

It was still dark, but he wasn't worried about waiting. He settled in and watched. He knew there was no way this jerk-off drove the simple Dodge in front. A few minutes after seven, his guess was validated when a well-dressed woman in her early fifties came out the front door, slipped into the small brown car and took off right past Garretti.

"Have a nice day, Mrs. Morales," he said as the car rushed past. He knew they had no kids, and Mrs. Morales had a mid-level job at the Treasury Department. Deputy attorneys general had a more self-determined schedule.

Garretti gathered his stuff, walked up to the sidewalk near the house and was ready to make his move when another car pulled up. Whoever it was had a garage door opener and drove a little Kia. He slowed his walk, but clearly saw a young woman—real young, like an intern—slip out of the car, walk to the inner house door and slap the garage door button—all without ever looking back. The garage door started its slow trek down, and Garretti knew this was his chance. He raced forward and dove into the garage, careful not to trip the safety beam near the floor. He ended up near the Kia, well out of sight.

He stood, felt his way around the dark garage and boldly flipped on the light. The bimbo wouldn't remember turning it off. He took a few seconds to survey the garage. No yard equipment or tools. That was about what he expected from a man like Morales. Just a few boxes on shelves in an otherwise clean garage. He wondered what bullshit Morales told his wife to keep her car outside. It was obvious the bimbo needed to see the coast was clear. The only other car inside was a new black Lincoln Continental.

He couldn't help looking in the Kia. Inside the glove compartment, he found the registration in the name of Judy Matulis. So that was the name of the tall, hot-looking piece of ass that slipped in the house.

He tried the big Lincoln Continental's driver's-side door and, as he would expect from a car kept inside, the door was unlocked. This just got better and better. He went to work.

Twenty minutes later, he slipped out of the car, retrieved the length of tubing he had salvaged from a Dumpster in Alexandria and fitted it over the exhaust pipe. He entered the car again through the rear door and lay down flat in the Lincoln's rear seat. He'd hear anyone coming in the garage. This was exactly what he wanted.

Almost two hours after he had darted into the garage, the inner door opened. He heard the beep of the unset alarm. He saw the young woman as she buttoned her blouse and checked her hair in the reflection from the window. Garretti thought, Forget the pussy, how does he get to the office at ten o'clock? He must dish some bullshit about briefing the president.

Garretti crouched down as he heard the Kia's light door open and close and then the sound of the garage door opening. She was careful that her car wasn't visible very long. Smart girl. He heard the garage door close again. Not only had she not noticed the light being on; she didn't even bother to turn it off when she left.

Ten minutes later, the door opened again. Garretti heard the alarm activating, then the door to the Lincoln opened. He waited for the right moment. The engine rumbled to life, and he knew it was time.

He popped up from the rear seat and said, "Hiya, Bob."

Morales nearly screamed: "Jesus Christ."

"Not a very Christian reaction there, Bob. But I guessed you would be surprised to see me."

"I was told you were killed."

"More like, my life ended. This is a new life, Bob."

"What do you want?"

"First, I need money and food from your house."

Morales remained silent.

"That a problem, Bob?"

"No, I just want you to leave."

"Your first priority should be that I don't kill you."

That caught the deputy attorney general's attention.

Garretti pointed toward the radio. "You see that new display on your dash?"

Morales took a moment to look at the flashing red numbers on the new instrument added to the big car's dashboard. Finally, after swallowing hard, Morales said, "Is that what I think?"

"If you think you just armed a bomb by turning on the car, you're right."

Morales froze.

"You can move around, you dumbass, just not off the front seat. I have you boxed in, but if you listen to me carefully everything will work out in the universe. Understand?"

"Not exactly."

"Okay, let me explain it so a shithead like you will understand. First, I have C-4 under the dashboard and under your seat. If you take pressure off the seat, it will detonate. If you shut off the ignition, it will detonate. If you put the car in gear, it will detonate."

"What do you want out of this?"

"First, I'm going into your house for money and some food."

"And then?"

"We'll talk about leaving me alone, and why that's to your benefit as well as mine. Sound good to you?"

"Listen, Garretti, I didn't want things to get this far."

"Save it. You sit tight and relax." Garretti leaned up over the seat and added, "Oh yeah, give me your cell phone."

Morales dug into his pocket and handed him a small flip phone.

Garretti said, "If you try any funny business, I let everyone know about Miss Judy Matulis. And I might blow a hole in your head."

"And if I stay still and let you take the money and food?"

"We'll reach an agreement, and you'll never have to deal with me again." He eased out the back passenger's-side door and left it open so the hose he had set up off the exhaust could point into the car's interior. "Keep your eyes forward and just relax. I'll be back in a little while." He left the door open and shuffled around the front of the big car's black hood. He took a last look at Morales behind the wheel, not moving, with his hands comfortably at his side. Perfect.

He really did make a ham sandwich and drank two cans of diet Coke from the fridge. He took a few minutes in the bathroom on the first floor. It was nice, with a padded seat on the toilet and plenty of *Coastal Living* and *Men's Health* magazines.

After a good forty minutes of exploring the beautiful town house, he popped his head out the door to the garage and took a peek at the deputy attorney general. Morales was dozing now, his head lolled to the side. Garretti knew he would've already felt a headache coming on before the drowsiness, but he would have attributed it to stress. After the picture Garretti painted of working everything out, he knew Morales wouldn't risk blowing himself up or having his affair with the lovely Miss Matulis exposed. Garretti smiled at his ingenuity.

Ten minutes later, after finishing a couple of deviled eggs and another diet Coke, he popped back into the garage and retrieved his bag. Then he removed the hose from the exhaust pipe and shut the rear door. He opened the front passenger's-side door and crawled in the still-running car. Morales was completely unconscious.

Garretti removed the digital tachometer he had bought at a discount auto parts store and spliced into the car's electrical system. An instrument not hooked to anything. Not even imaginary explosives. He reached across Morales's still form and lifted Morales's left hand to mash his index finger on the window button, lowering the driver's window. He checked his pulse. Weak, and it would get worse very soon.

Garretti opened the side door to the garage—the one he had intended to break in through—and casually strolled to his waiting rental car.

This was the first time he had managed to make a death look natural, and, just like he told Morales, now all was right with the universe.

49

IN THE THREE WEEKS SINCE CAREN LARSON HAD QUIT HER job with the Department of Justice, her mother had not once asked why. She just seemed glad to have her little girl back home. Caren had kept the *Washington Post* front page with the headline and subtitle that said DEPUTY ATTORNEY GENERAL COMMITS SUICIDE: Not Since Vince Foster Has a Death Inside the Beltway Raised More Questions.

Caren figured Bob Morales realized he had been found out and took the easy way around his problems. She was just as glad she didn't get tangled up in any of that mess. She was glad it didn't hurt Alex Duarte either.

Although she didn't know what she wanted to do, she had sent out a résumé to a law firm in downtown Cincinnati. She had other reasons for not rushing away from her mom's comfortable home.

She retained the same cell phone number, and had waited for Alex Duarte to call from Florida. He had once, right after she had flown back to Washington, just to make sure she was safe. He was always gallant. But now she wondered if he could ever be interested in her. She had decided that she had waited long enough. She wasn't a lovesick teenager. She would miss her Kojak.

Now she smiled as she hesitated by her mother's home phone. She dialed a number on the sheet of paper where she had written it. She hung up before the first ring. Then she dialed again and let it ring three times. When a receptionist picked up, she took a breath and then asked to speak to Barry. A guy she had not spoken to since law school. A guy she only had good memories of.

Her heart started to beat faster as she sat on hold.

Finally Barry came on the line.

She almost giggled and said, "It's Caren Larson. Remember me?"

She heard the warmth in his voice. "Remember you? I think about you every day."

"You were always so nice."

"I'm serious. Are you at your mom's or Washington?"

"You knew I worked for DoJ?"

"I kept track of you."

"You free for dinner?"

"I hope you mean tonight."

Her smile stretched so far across her face it hurt.

Alex Duarte sat at his kitchen table on a Thursday at around five in the afternoon, the earliest he'd been home in a while. He had no mail of consequence, and, the bright side of living where he did, had no bills either. He moved on to his bedroom, where he deposited his pistol and credentials on the top shelf of his closet. He sat on the edge of his neatly made bed and pulled off his Dockers to change into more comfortable gym shorts. His nightstand was down to just two books. An alternative history, and one titled *Start to Speak Spanish*. He didn't need quite so many books ready for the long hours of the night. He had found, for some reason, he had been sleeping in increasingly long periods over the past few weeks.

He glanced at the phone on his nightstand and the three scraps of paper next to it. Each piece of paper had different feminine handwriting on it. He picked up the first scrap, with Caren Larson's bold handwriting. He had wanted to call her. At times, he was surprised by how much he had wanted to talk to the beautiful attorney. He had waited because he wasn't sure how she would feel about him. He was afraid she'd associate him with her bad experience in the Department of Justice. He also knew she was still at her mom's since leaving her job. This might be a call he made later.

The second scrap was pink, and had the elegant script of Maria Tannza. He wanted to make sure she was doing well at the camp, where she continued to teach. He knew she was still re-covering from the loss of her son—if someone ever recovered from something like that. Somehow, he almost felt guilty that his work on Hector's death investigation had helped him come to terms with his own demons. He decided to call her in the next week to see how she was doing.

He picked up the third piece of paper. Alice Brainard's name was printed on it, with a smiley face over the *i* in her last name. He had kept such a low profile since the incident at the trailer in Belle Glade that she might think he had forgotten about her, but he had not. He picked up the phone and dialed the cell number. After three rings, he heard her light, Southern accent say, "Hello."

A smile crept over his face. "This is Alex Duarte."

"Hey, how are you? I wondered if you'd fallen off the face of the earth."

"Had a busy few weeks."

"I heard. Everybody heard. I checked with some of our guys, who said everything had worked out for you."

"Yeah, it's quiet now." He cleared his throat and hesitated. "I was calling to, um . . ."

"Yes?"

"I wondered if you might like to . . ." He swallowed and blurted out: "Can you meet me for that drink sometime?"

"You bet."

He felt relief sweep over him, and a smile. Maybe this dating thing wasn't so bad after all.

Turn the page for a preview of
the next book from James O. Born

burn zone

Coming soon from G. P. Putnam's Sons!

"YOU EVER THINK WE SHOULD WRITE SOME OF THIS BULL-shit down and put it in a book?"

Alex Duarte didn't even cut his eyes to his partner. Chuck had stupid ideas like that all the time. It was better not to encourage him.

The parking lot of the Publix shopping center was too crowded for things to go right. Duarte could see that as soon as they set up surveillance. The drug enforcement guys were used to these kinds of deals, so he figured they knew what they were doing, but he didn't like the bystanders. He made a quick check of the Glock on his right hip under the loose, unbuttoned shirt.

Chuck Stoddard, his partner, slumped in the driver's seat of the immense Ford Expedition, munching on Cheetos and breathing through his mouth. Duarte thought about lecturing him about his health again, but the gigantic man would only nod in agreement and continue to eat anything that had once been an animal, mineral or vegetable. The Glock on his hip looked like a popgun in comparison to his gut.

Duarte kept the radio on low to discourage conversation. He also liked the comfort of the radio show he listened to most mornings, the conversation between the hosts and their producer. He had to admit reluctantly that he knew more about them than about most people.

During a commercial, Chuck said, "You know the DEA invited us along just so we could lay paper on the suspect."

Duarte mumbled, "Uh-hum."

"Doesn't that ever bother you? They get all the fun and all we get to do is write up additional charges for the guns the dealers have on them."

"You know, Chuck, we *do* work for the ATF. Last I checked, guns were our main jurisdiction."

"I know, but I'm just saying, why can't they come on *our* deals sometimes?"

"Because if a guy is selling illegal guns, he doesn't have any cocaine or pot. If he did, he'd be selling the drugs instead. Much greater profit margin."

"DEA has got a lot more guys than us, too. Ever notice how they bring out ten guys on a deal like this?"

Duarte shrugged, keeping his eye on the lot. He had heard enough of Chuck's whining for the day. Now he just wanted to be involved in some police work. He liked being out of the office on a simple case: if the guy showed up and sold dope to the DEA undercover agent, then he'd be arrested; if he didn't, then he probably wasn't a serious dope dealer in the first place. Simple. After his last case he didn't need anything complex.

The parking lot was alive with activity: people pushing shopping carts, kids tagging along, couples talking. Most people never noticed, but on surveillance, when you were pulled out of the daily rat race and had a chance to watch, it could be pretty interesting to observe a place as simple as this. Like it was another universe but not quite parallel to the outside world.

Duarte was glad his friend at the U.S. Drug Enforcement Administration, Félix Baez, had called him in on this deal. The target was a local shlub named B. L. Gastlin, who was believed to be hooked into some Panamanian named Ortíz who traded guns illegally and imported marijuana by the truckload. That was why Duarte had jumped on the case so quickly: the possibility of working the investigation up the ladder to someone really important. He felt satisfaction when an insignificant dope dealer got an extra five years because of one of his "Armed Trafficking" charges, but to really make an impact he wanted to nail a big importer or exporter. That would also help him get a promotion. He'd passed up an opportunity for one a few months earlier, but now he wanted to try again.

Duarte checked the lot. He could see the various DEA cars, all Chevys and Fords parked near the entrances and exits. He knew that once the target drove in, they would contain him. No federal agency wanted to get involved in any kind of car chase; it was against policy and bad for the vehicles. At the end of the lot he noticed a Florida Power & Light truck with an extendable bucket parked next to a pole, a man standing in the bucket. That'd be a great surveillance ploy, he thought. No one would notice you, and you'd have a great view of the area. He still looked at situations like this from a military perspective, searching for optimum terrain and hazards once the action started. Unlike his time in Bosnia, though, there wasn't a lot of action in these kinds of deals. . . .

A blue Jaguar convertible cruised east on Southern Boulevard, and by the way the driver slowed and looked carefully toward the lot, Duarte believed this might be their man. At almost the same time, he heard someone on the radio say, "The target is in a blue Jaguar and just drove past on Southern. Stand by."

Félix, who was leaning on his car, a nice Corvette they had seized from a cocaine smuggler last year, straightened up, gave a quick nod to the two DEA cars closest to him and adjusted his shirt. Duarte was pretty sure he was checking the gun in his waistband.

Duarte had done very little undercover work and appreciated Félix's ability to remain calm and cheerful doing something so unnatural, but that was just his personality. Félix liked to talk to people—one of the differences between him and Duarte.

The radio crackled, "The target is in the east end of the lot, slowly weaving in and out. He's checking for us."

This was the hard part. Making sure you didn't look too much like a cop when a suspect conducted countersurveillance. The cars were spread out, though, and the DEA guys were smart enough to look like they belonged. The other thing in their favor was that suspects always thought they were smarter than the cops. He had never met a drug or gun dealer who didn't think he could outwit them all, bless their hearts. Arrogance was their downfall.

The Jaguar slowed to a stop near Félix and his Corvette. Although he couldn't hear anything, he knew that Félix had a transmitter somewhere on his body and that someone was listening to a receiver. His trouble signal was, "This don't look good."

Chuck wheezed and said, "Looks like it's showtime."

The man from the Jaguar, Gastlin, stepped out of the low car, his eyes still scanning the parking lot. Dressed in shorts and a loud, untucked shirt with a photo of Jimmy Buffet covering his wide stomach, he looked like a bowling pin compared to Félix's lean body. He leaned casually against the Jag, chatting.

The two men were about four rows away and ten spots back. When the arrest signal came, Duarte and Chuck would close the distance in the yacht-sized Expedition, then spring out with five or six DEA agents to secure the target and make sure Félix was safe.

Chuck said, "I know the DEA wants that Jag. You watch, they'll treat that car like a crystal egg. No matter what happens they won't hurt that car."

Duarte nodded, concentrating. Once Félix gave the arrest signal, Duarte knew he expected to have the cavalry rush in right that minute. Cops always claim the slowest time in the world is between when you give the arrest signal and when your buddies rush in. Your heart pounds, and adrenaline courses through your body.

The visual arrest signal was when Félix opened his trunk. That was the sign that he had seen the pot.

The DEA supervisor came over the radio and said, "Looks like it's going smooth. Don't move until I call it over the radio. And don't ding the Jaguar."

Chuck perked up. "See, I told you. I told you."

Duarte nodded silently, involuntarily checking his pistol. He preferred to use his hands or feet in a fight, but only an idiot tried to punch someone with a gun. He watched as the two men continued to talk, then walk to the side of the Jaguar. The target leaned in and motioned for Félix to look, too.

Then Duarte saw Félix jump. It looked like a whole body twitch, then the DEA man jumped away from the car and shouted at Gastlin. The pot dealer looked like he was trying to explain something when Félix shoved him.

Duarte sat up in the Expedition. "Chuck, something's up. Get ready."

The radio crackled on. "Let's move in. I can't tell what happened. Go, go, go."

All at once, four cars started to move.

Duarte felt his pulse increase; this was the stuff he loved about his job. Keeping his right hand on his hip, he reached across to the door handle with his left. What had happened to cause the arrest to go early? He saw Gastlin look up and notice the vehicles as they closed on him, notice, too, that, like any good undercover agent, Félix had stepped away so the arrest team had free access.

Duarte saw the target reach into the Jaguar and thought he might be going for a gun, but before the big Expedition could come to a stop, the target sprinted away across the lot with a satchel in his hand. He had grabbed the pot sample. For a chubby guy, he could really move.

The man had timed his run perfectly as the front vehicles stopped and the drivers were getting out of the cars. They also blocked the other approaching cars. The man darted toward Southern Boulevard just as Duarte jumped from the ATF Expedition and started sprinting after him. He knew big, lumbering Chuck would be behind him somewhere.

The pot dealer was obviously panicked, his head swiveling, looking for an escape, and then he saw the Florida Power & Light bucket truck in front of him and bounded up to the cab.

Duarte yelled, "Stop, police," and drawing his Glock, he raised it in the direction of the fleeing man, the DEA agents closing in from the other side.

The truck had had the engine running to provide power to the bucket, and now it lurched forward as the dealer tried to drive it away, the supports for the extended bucket scraping on the asphalt as the truck started to move. The man in the bucket shouted something, then hung on as the truck picked up speed, passing the DEA agents.

Duarte heard a car horn and turned to see Chuck in the Expedition right next to him. This was a pleasant surprise. Duarte yanked the door open and leaped into the seat. Chuck hit the gas, and they were in the chase. Alone for the moment.

The FPL truck sped up as the dope dealer apparently figured out how to raise the supports, while the man in the bucket worked the controls to lower the extended workstation as quickly as possible. The truck tilted to one side, then the other, as the pot dealer tried to negotiate the parking lot, and then suddenly the man in the bucket leaped into the low branches of a black olive tree planted in the swale.

Chuck said, "Did you see that?"

Duarte looked out over his shoulder and saw the man clinging to the tree branches. "Now he can speed up. Catch him, catch him."

The truck turned onto the side street heading south and

continued to accelerate as a DEA vehicle fell in with Duarte and Chuck's Expedition. The street was empty of traffic in both directions. Thank God, thought Duarte.

Chuck brought the big Ford SUV up behind the lumbering bucket truck in a matter of blocks, then said, "Know what?"

"What?" asked Duarte, still watching the truck.

"If I got next to this thing, you could jump into the back."

Duarte had to look to see if his partner was kidding. He looked serious. "Let's see what happens in the next few minutes."

"If you say so." Chuck didn't have any plan except to follow the big truck.

Two DEA surveillance cars screamed up next to them, obviously in the same dilemma. The truck took a hard left, causing the lowered bucket to swing wide to the right side. At the next corner, the pot dealer tried to take a sharp right, and as he turned, the arm to the bucket, which was sticking out from the truck since the last turn, caught a telephone pole and swung the truck violently in a tight arc until the arm was free from the pole. The truck kept running, only now it was pointed directly at a house's yard. The heavy FPL truck thumped over bushes, glanced off a tree, and then struck the side of the one-story, dark green, old Florida house, the sound of the impact shocking. It reminded him of the explosions he had caused in Bosnia. The effect on the house wasn't all that different from that of his C-4 concoctions. The wall to the house collapsed around the cab of the truck, and the destruction continued in a domino effect because the exterior roof began to sink until the entire peak of the roof dropped into the center.

Duarte sprang from the Expedition before Chuck had even brought it to a complete stop and raced to the front door, thinking about what might have happened to the residents of the house. The front door was unlocked, causing Duarte to fear that the residents were home. He shot through the wrecked house, noticing debris scattered across the furniture, a TV lying smashed by a falling beam, bright sunshine streaming through the wide swath now exposed to the elements.

"Hello, police!" shouted Duarte. "Where are you?" He no longer cared about the arrest, fearing only for the safety of the people who might be in the house.

He heard a voice and froze: "In here." It was faint and female. He followed the sound and pushed at the only closed door, on the east side of the house where the truck would've struck. He turned the doorknob and tried to open it, but it was hopelessly jammed by something low. He shoved and felt little give. The upper half of the door bent slightly inward.

He yelled, "Stand clear of the door!" Then he stepped back and launched the hardest, highest sidekick of his fifteen-year martial arts career. The door cracked at the site of his foot's impact. He repeated this twice more until the door split in half and he could scurry over the broken lower section. The truck's cab had come all the way inside the wrecked room, but he stole a glance and the cab was empty. A DEA agent was crawling over the wreckage into the house.

Duarte twisted his head, searching for the source of the cry.

He yelled, "Where are you?"

"In here," came the voice, and he noticed one more closed door, which had been blocked by a chunk of wall thrown by the truck.

He leaped over some wreckage, content to let the DEA guys and Chuck find the missing pot dealer. He bent down and lifted the piece of wall which had tipped down and didn't weigh that much. When he pulled the door open, an attractive woman in her early sixties stood in the middle of a large closet, wearing panties and a bra that covered very little of her breasts.

Duarte froze for a moment, staring at her. She didn't seem at all self-conscious. Finally she said, "Are you done?"

Despite his Latin coloring and dark hair, he felt himself blush. "Sorry," he said, looking down. "Are you all right?"

She mumbled something.

"Excuse me?"

She mumbled and then said, "Look at me again."

He slowly raised his eyes, but the woman was still unclothed. Now he noticed her eyes kept shifting to the shelf next to her. Then she cocked her head that way and he realized what she was trying to say. He pushed her out of the closet, then knocked out the shelf's support beam in a smooth motion, heard a yell and saw the tubby shape of B. L. Gastlin, former drug dealer, plop hard onto the ground.

Duarte dropped to his knee and threw a quick elbow into the dealer's face to incapacitate him for a second, then quickly patted him down for weapons. As he was about to call for help, the woman appeared again in the closet doorway.

Still nearly naked, she said, "Look what this asshole did to my house," and delivered a vicious stomp to the dazed man's face. If Duarte hadn't stopped her, she would've done it again.

She stepped back and said, "He shoved me in the closet and then balanced that roof beam so he could come in and let it hit the door behind him. He didn't think you'd check a room that was already blocked in from the outside."

Duarte nodded and pulled the now bloody man to a sitting position.

The woman threw in another kick to the man's ribs.

"Ma'am," Duarte said in a clear loud voice. "You'll have to stop that." He looked up at her and added, "Please tell the others where I am."

She disappeared, and a few seconds later Chuck and a DEA guy appeared at the closet.

Chuck looked down and said, "Man, Rocket, you really fucked that guy up." He looked at the DEA agent next to him and added. "Did you hear what the problem at the deal was?"

Duarte shook his head.

Chuck smiled. "He tried to play with Félix's dick."

Duarte could tell by the way the prisoner moaned it was true.

Chuck laughed and said, "Félix is old-school Cuban. It didn't go over too well."

Duarte shook his head. Some people were too stupid to live.

The DEA guy smiled. "He tell you anything?"

Duarte helped the stunned man to his feet. "Yeah. He said the Jaguar is a rental."

James O. Born is a special agent with the Florida Department of Law Enforcement, where he is involved with a wide variety of criminal investigations, from public corruption and economic crimes to drug cartels, antiterrorism, and homicide. He is also a former member of the FDLE Special Operations Team, which has handled unusual situations such as hurricanes and the Miami riots. Before joining the FDLE, he was a deputy marshal with the U.S. Marshals Service and an agent with the DEA. He also served as the technical consultant for the television series *Karen Sisco*. Born lives in Lake Worth, Florida, where he is working on his next novel.